# BOUND BY PASSION

"Carina, you should not have come here. You think me a good man, but I'm not."

Jared's hoarse, emotion-filled voice gave Carina another message, sweeping away confusion. "I had nowhere else to go. And as for what I think of you, I think you are a man much like any other. I don't think in terms of good and evil. There are people I like and people I don't like. You are one of the first group."

He felt the appeal of her warm voice and soft expression. He tried to tell himself that he'd warned her, given her the chance to flee, but he knew he hadn't. A bargain was a bargain. He had met her need; now she would meet his. "I wish I could let you go."

Carina shook her head slightly. More composed than he, she waited.

"I will not make you my wife, nor will I keep you long. What will you do then?"

Not answering him, Carina put her hand in his, and when he drew her to her feet, she followed, ready to give him all he wanted. . . .

# HEARTFIRE ROMANCES

**SWEET TEXAS NIGHTS**                                    (2610, $3.75)
by Vivian Vaughan

Meg Britton grew up on the railroads, working proudly at her father's side. Nothing was going to stop them from setting the rails clear to Silver Creek, Texas—certainly not some crazy prospector. As Meg set out to confront the old coot, she planned her strategy with cool precision. But soon she was speechless with shock. For instead of a harmless geezer, she found a boldly handsome stranger whose determination matched her own.

**CAPTIVE DESIRE**                                       (2612, $3.75)
by Jane Archer

Victoria Malone fancied herself a great adventuress, but being kidnapped was too much excitement for even Victoria! Especially when her arrogant kidnapper thought she was part of Red Duke's outlaw gang. Trying to convince the overbearing, handsome stranger that she had been an innocent bystander when the stagecoach was robbed, proved futile. But when he thought he could maker her confess by crushing her to his warm, broad chest, by caressing her with his strong, capable hands, Victoria was willing to admit to anything. . . .

**LAWLESS ECSTASY**                                      (2613, $3.75)
by Susan Sackett

Abra Beaumont could spot a thief a mile away. After all, her father was once one of the best. But he'd been on the right side of the law for years now, and she wasn't about to let a man like Dash Thorne lead him astray with some wild plan for stealing the Tear of Allah, the world's most fabulous ruby. Dash was just the sort of man she most distrusted—sophisticated, handsome, and altogether too sure of his considerable charm. Abra shivered at the devilish gleam in his blue eyes and swore he would need more than smooth kisses and skilled caresses to rob her of her virtue ·. . . and much more than sweet promises to steal her heart!

*Available wherever paperbacks are sold, or order direct from the Publisher. Send cover price plus 50¢ per copy for mailing and handling to Zebra Books, Dept. 2855, 475 Park Avenue South, New York, N.Y. 10016. Residents of New York, New Jersey and Pennsylvania must include sales tax. DO NOT SEND CASH.*

# EMERALD EMBRACE

## MARJORIE PRICE

**ZEBRA BOOKS**
**KENSINGTON PUBLISHING CORP.**

ZEBRA BOOKS

are published by

Kensington Publishing Corp.
475 Park Avenue South
New York, NY 10016

First printing: December, 1989

Printed in the United States of America

## Chapter 1

She stood in shadow, her face averted, waiting. It wasn't cold, yet she shivered as her tensed muscles rebelled at the unnatural stillness. After twelve hours of working in the mill, her back, legs, and feet were numb, but her mind raced like the locomotive that tore up the tracks from Boston to Lowell, spewing ashes and soot back over its thundering length.

She held her breath at the sound of footsteps. Were these imagined or real? The clamor of her heartbeat threatened to overpower her hearing. She could not fail. Her father's life and her brother's future were in her hands.

The agent's house stood before her, square and stark. Like the fort it resembled, it guarded the broad entrance to the mill. Three men stopped before the gate. Carina waited, praying they would not all enter together. She wanted no witnesses to her shame. She willed the tall man to send his companions away.

It was not to be. He stood back to let the two hatted men precede him up the brick-faced walk. Even bare-headed, he stood a head taller than the others, although they were both broad of chest and fit. Carina assumed that these were the two who had wrestled Patrick to the ground for Mr. Wentworth. He never went far without his bodyguards, but surely they didn't live with him. Or did they?

Without giving herself time to think, she stepped away from the wall. If she didn't seize this moment she would be lost. She would never have the courage to knock on that door once he was inside.

"Mr. Wentworth!" she called out. "I would speak with you."

Her voice seemed to echo from every brick and stone, unnaturally loud in the still night air, and yet she wondered, had she spoken at all? The men seemed not to hear her.

Then they did. Mr. Wentworth turned slowly to face the street, his hair pale as a torch. Instantly, the men were at his flanks, held back only by his restraining gesture. Carina did not need to be able to see his face to know that his eyes searched out the shadows around her. Once he realized that she was alone, he moved toward her almost eagerly.

"It's Miss O'Rourke, is it not?" He shook off one of the men who tried to hold him back. Turning on them, he dismissed them impatiently.

"It may be a trap," Grimes warned him.

Strother chimed in to add, "Her brother was the one—"

Enoch Wentworth's temper exploded. "Damn it, I *know* who her brother is—and her father! Now leave me!"

Strother persisted. "She could have a weapon."

Enoch took out coins and pressed them on the men. Even the darkness could not hide the close fit of Carina O'Rourke's sober-colored dress. He almost laughed as he asked, only partly in jest, "And where do you fools think she could hide a weapon?"

"Under her skirts, sir."

At that, Enoch did laugh. "Then I'll have to be sure to check under her skirts." He added to their payment. "Get your own wenches tonight. This one is mine."

Of their whispered conference, only Mr. Wentworth's

6

laugh came clearly to Carina. The sound of it chilled her, but she gathered strength from the fact that he was dismissing his men. That made them more even and reassured her. She didn't watch the men depart, only felt their eventual absence. But still she didn't speak. All her rehearsed words fled her mind, leaving a residue of terror. If her father found out . . .

That thought made her want to laugh. Almost. If she were successful, her father would certainly find out. That was to be expected. What Conn O'Rourke believed about her didn't matter. He would think as he chose—as he always did. What mattered was getting Patrick back. If her father had Patrick again, he would be able to cope with everything else.

"Suddenly shy, Miss O'Rourke?"

Carina shook her head sharply and smiled. Enoch Wentworth was a man like any other. That was what Welcome Purvis said. For now, Carina blocked from her mind what the girls in the spinning room said about Welcome. Carina had chosen to emulate her. Second thoughts would not do. She would flatter Mr. Wentworth, using the smile she generally reserved for playful moments with Margaret and little Kevin.

She cautiously stepped closer. "I'd like to talk to you about—"

"Of course, my dear, but not out here in the street." His teeth flashed briefly in a feral smile as he gestured for her to enter the gate.

Carina stopped just beyond his reach. "I don't wish to intrude, sir. Only a moment of your—"

"What a child you are!" he exclaimed petulantly. "I do not discuss my business in the street. If you cannot behave like a civilized person, be off with you!"

Knowing she was losing his attention and piqued that he would call her uncivilized, Carina strode past him onto the walkway. She wouldn't go inside, just stand here within the gate. It was private enough to suit Mr. Wentworth and public enough for her.

"I've come to ask you to withdraw your charges against my brother," she began bravely.

"Miss O'Rourke, are you simple? I've said you must come inside."

"Oh, sir, that wouldn't be proper."

"How old are you?"

The blunt demand confused Carina. "I'll soon be twenty-two, sir."

"How long have you worked at the Shattuck Mill?"

"Two years and seven—"

"And in all that time have I ever molested you?"

"No, sir," Carina answered truthfully. She didn't add that her father, her brother, and their many friends had conspired all that time to keep her insulated from his attention. To remind him of that would not be helpful to her cause. She had to keep that in mind.

"I'll have my housekeeper join us, if you wish."

"No, sir, I don't want to trouble you. . . ."

Enoch swore softly to himself. He was at the end of his limited patience. He couldn't believe she was twenty-two. That meant she wouldn't be a virgin, not among the Irish. They bred like flies. From keen disappointment, he moved quickly to excitement. If she wasn't a virgin, she would know things. . . .

"You came to me," he reminded her.

"To beg you to have my brother released. He's a good boy—"

"A good boy! He attacked me! I'd be dead now if it weren't for my men."

"Oh no, sir. He would never harm you. He was distraught because my father is lung-sick. If he goes back into the picking room, he'll die. He's been so much better out in the fresh air."

Enoch had given Conn O'Rourke a taste of what he wanted, yard work, to soften him up. The old bastard knew what he had to do to keep his soft job, but he'd refused. Well, a lot of good it had done him. His daughter was here anyway, begging prettily for her brother, the

8

one who had earlier begged for his father. What a sorry lot they all were. Except for this one.

Carina O'Rourke was special—beautiful. Her hair was blue-black, her eyes the blue of the hottest part of a fire. Under that dreary rag of a dress, her skin would glow like warm marble, smooth and soft to the touch. Without listening, Enoch watched her mouth move, picturing the things he would have her do with those pretty lips.

"Oh, please, sir," she said, breaking into his consciousness at last, "please reconsider and withdraw your charges. I'd be ever so grateful."

"Then come inside, my dear, and we'll discuss your gratitude."

Suddenly, Carina was drowning in revulsion. Some of the mill girls thought Mr. Wentworth was handsome. He was tall and fair, with regular features that just missed fineness. He was rich and powerful. But his eyes were cold and greedy, and his mouth had a cruel set. She tried to think of Patrick. He was in jail. Jail! For days she had been obsessed by Patrick's plight. How frightened he must be!

But now Patrick's fear was inside her. It was hers; she felt it for herself. Enoch Wentworth was not a man like any other. Welcome Purvis was wrong. Carina knew that with blinding accuracy.

She gave a startled cry as Enoch grasped her arm. She tried to pull free, but he countered her move and began to drag her toward the door.

"No, no. Please, Mr. Wentworth!"

Instinct alone made Carina struggle. Her mind told her she should not. She had known the cost of trying to win Patrick's freedom; she had even believed herself ready to pay it. Why else had she come? To fight him like this would only bring down his rage upon them all—perhaps even on Margaret and Kevin. They, too, worked in the mill, as doffers, carrying bobbins for the spinners. Mr. Wentworth could sentence them all to perdition with a casual wave of his hand. In trying to make things better,

9

at least for Patrick and her father, she was magnifying all of their problems. She would lose her virtue and *still* do no good.

But she could not give in. He frightened her. She fought every move he made. She dug her feet into the rough brick walkway. She even put her free arm around his knee and tried to pull him down. When she felt the worn fabric of her sleeve give way under his hand she gave a scream of pure rage that made him shake her off.

For a stunned moment she didn't recognize that she was free, and when she tried to scramble up from her knees it was too late. He caught her by the knot of hair at the back of her head. The back of his hand swept down, slashing across the side of her face. The force of the blow snapped her head around and cut off her ragged cry. She put her hand to her cheek, too dazed to notice the blood on her fingers. Closing her eyes to shut out the sight of Mr. Wentworth towering over her, Carina steeled herself for the next blow.

It never came.

"I see you're having your usual success courting a fair maiden, dear cousin."

The voice cutting into their violent tableau was too harsh and angry for true irony, although that fine point was lost on the two who heard it. To Carina it was the voice of deliverance; to Enoch, the voice of interference.

"Get out of here, Jared. This doesn't concern you."

"I'm making it my concern."

"She came to me!" Enoch shouted, facing off above Carina.

The man paced closer, stalking his cousin until he, too, loomed over her. "It looks to me as though she changed her mind, cousin."

"Stop calling me that!"

Incredibly, the man laughed. Carina couldn't see either of them, but she knew from Enoch Wentworth's voice that his eyes glittered wildly. She felt hostility flash between the two men, potent as lightning bolts. All she wanted from this exchange was the chance to escape. But before she could do that, the man called Jared bent down to help her up.

"Why don't we ask the lady her preference, *Cousin* Enoch?"

Knowing herself to be no more than the bone between two dogs, Carina took in everything she could about her savior while the men's attention was fixed on each other. She could see no family resemblence. Perhaps that was why Mr. Wentworth resented this Jared calling him cousin. He was dark almost to the point of swarthiness, and his black clothes, like those of Mr. Wentworth's men, emphasized the burly breadth of his chest and shoulders. Had she not seen those fellows dismissed, Carina would have supposed Jared to be one of them, returned to support his master.

He held her arm—but gently, taking care that his fingers held and supported without restraining her freedom. There was violence in the man, yet none of it was directed at her. As soon as she could stand on her own, he released her, giving her only the most cursory glance.

Carina broke away and ran for the nearest cover, the thick hedge flanking the gate. Like a hunted animal, she knew the open street held no safety for her. If the men gave her another thought they would assume that she had broken through the hedge to the street beyond, eager to put miles between herself and her molester. But Carina stopped as soon as she was well hidden. She had made an enemy tonight, but she had learned something as well. Her enemy also had an enemy. She wanted to know about him.

"You made a big mistake interfering tonight, *Cousin* Jared." Enoch Wentworth's voice rose agitatedly, becoming shrill. "I suppose you want the Irish whore for yourself. But even a begging whore won't have anything

11

to do with a devil like you!"

"Perhaps she mistook you for me," came the amused answer.

"I tell you, *she* came to me!" Enoch shrieked.

"To beg for her job? Is this the only way you can get a woman? Your father would be interested to learn how you treat the poor sods who work for you."

"From you?" Enoch's laugh sounded hysterical. "From the Wentworth wastrel? Why would he believe you? No one ever has!"

Carina heard a deep-chested growl and the sound of a blow. Seconds later, she started as the impact sent Enoch Wentworth to the ground.

"Let this be your warning, my dear cousin. While you're busy harassing your peons, you might want to keep an eye out behind you—particularly at night."

Scarcely breathing, Carina listened to Jared Wentworth's footsteps ring against the pavement. Then he was gone.

But Enoch Wentowrth was still there, prone before his own house. She heard his whimpers as he dragged himself to his feet. He had taken one blow, not the many he'd ordered for Patrick, yet it had unmanned him. Could Jared Wentworth be so strong? Or was it only that Enoch was weak?

Either way, Carina didn't dare move until long after Enoch Wentworth had gone inside. Her resistance was offense enough; he would exact greater revenge if he knew she had witnessed his disgrace at his cousin's hands.

After a long time, Carina shifted her weight, relieving the cramped muscles in her legs preparatory to leaving her hiding place. Then other footsteps froze her in place again. If she had parted the bushes to emerge onto the street, she would have landed at the feet of the approaching men.

"What do you care what Jared Wentworth was doing here? The master sent us away."

12

"I don't *care;* I just want to know the lay of the land."

"It's another kinda lay I'm looking for."

"Then go. I'll do the checking."

"And have you get all the credit? Oh, no. If there's any heroics, I'm in on it, too."

"Then shut up so I can listen."

They did their listening, just five feet from Carina. She held her breath and heard only the throb of her own blood.

"Listen to what?" the first man asked irritably. "To the tree frogs? I tell you, he's got that wench upstairs and he's banging her cross-eyed."

"But I heard something—a scream or something."

"Well, of course you did. That's the way he likes it. Jesus, but you're thick! Were you going to rescue the bitch? *She* came to him!"

Carina heard a short laugh. "So she did. Ah, what the hell. All it takes is money, right?"

"And I've got some burning a hole in my pocket."

Their steps resumed, no longer careful.

"That's not all that's burning a hole in your pants either, I'll wager."

After a brief, noisy scuffle that ended in backslaps, the men trotted off, back toward town again. Carina did not wait long after that to leave the hedge and make her way from shadow to shadow along the street. Her feet, nearly bare in worn slippers, made no noise as she ran for the wooded cover that lay between the broad streets of industrial Lowell and the section of town where she lived.

Years ago, it had been a matter of pride to Conn O'Rourke that his family didn't live in the Acre. That was the miserable, overcrowded patch of ground across the Western Canal from the cotton mills, where the early Irish immigrants who'd come to Lowell had been forced to live. Coming years later, and with some small savings in hand, the O'Rourkes had settled in Chapel Hill, across town from the Acre.

In time, Chapel Hill had threatened to become another

Acre, this one tucked into a bend of the Concord River just before that river joined the mighty Merrimack. From the time it was built in 1842, St. Peter's Church attracted the Irish workers who filled the tenements that sat around it like chicks around a brooding hen. Now, in 1853, even Conn O'Rourke had stopped fighting the reality of where he lived.

Although Yankees were generally reluctant to travel through an Irish neighborhood for fear of the wild-running gangs of boys, some of them only seven or eight years old, Carina had no fear for her own safety at any time of day or night. Neighbors might laugh at her father behind his back, but they respected him all the same. He had fled Ireland long before the potato famines of the forties, driven out by a different kind of hunger and bitterness. The son of a poor tenant farmer, he had aspired to the priesthood. When he'd found that his paltry education was insufficient to the task, he'd turned violently from Church and homeland.

Carina had heard several versions of his rejection. Sometimes he said that *he* had rejected a corrupt variation of the True Church, that it was bleeding his innocent homeland. At others, he alluded to a problem, beyond a lack of Latin, that had caused him to be dismissed. She suspected that his innate stubbornness and inability to see any point of view but his own was the true cause of his estrangement.

Now that he was sick, it was only a matter of time before he was reconciled to his faith. More than anything else, his quarrel with the Church was a lover's quarrel. At night, when he thought her soundly asleep, she often heard him moving the rosary beads that belonged to his mother, his only keepsake of her and of Ireland.

Carina slipped soundlessly up the steep staircase to their single room at the back of the three-story house. She hoped, without much expectation of success, to find her father still sleeping on his narrow cot. But he woke often, in the grip of a coughing spell, and then sought

14

comfort in a chair until the spasm passed. Sometimes she roused herself to ask if she could help, but he always waved away her concern. He had little patience with her in this as in everything else.

After repeated rejection, Carina had learned to ignore him, at least overtly. It wasn't hard to lie quietly in bed because her days were long and hard. Still, she couldn't help but hear him. For his sake, though, she feigned continued sleep. Her reward for sparing his feelings was knowing that he found comfort elsewhere, for it was at such times that she heard the discreet slide and click of his beads.

At times Carina envied her father his quarrel with Gód. Because of it, she had not been brought up as anything. Her mother, a Congregationalist from New Hampshire, had tried to instill a simple faith in God in her children, but her religion was forbidden them as was Conn's. Although Conn had loved her mother, he was as suspicious of Protestants as he was hostile to priests.

She and Patrick had been educated at home, taught to read and cipher by their mother, who, being a Yankee, could do both. Margaret and Kevin now attended the town school for the three months required by the mills, although every other child they knew went to parochial school. Being Irish in that all-Yankee environment was hard on them, but the situation wasn't new to any of them. They were O'Rourkes, and that meant being perpetual misfits.

Her father sat by the window, moonlight falling on his full head of white hair. For a wild instant, Carina was reminded of Enoch Wentworth, and she braced herself in the doorway, hoping against hope that Conn had nodded off in his chair. But his head was erect, and when she heard the faint sound of his beads, she gave up the notion of slipping into bed without facing him.

Knowing that his anger would be the worse if he suspected she had seen him at his prayers, Carina backed outside. She let the door bang and gave him time to hide his rosary before she entered. Although he was clever at disguising his deafness, the years of working on heavy mill machinery had taken a toll on his hearing.

"So you've come back from your prowling," he said, turning to look at her. The fall of light emphasized the deep vertical lines in his face and made his eyes glow like coals. In such moments he looked to Carina like one of the prophets in her mother's Bible—and he engendered the same kind of awed fear within her breast.

Since it was useless to protest the unfairness of his implication that she spent every night thusly, she didn't defend herself. Instead, she asked, "Is your cough worse tonight?"

"Why wouldn't it be?" he countered. "My daughter sneaks out of her bed in the dead of night to consort with some young buck millhand, and my one decent child lies in jail for trying to defend her dubious chastity!"

"Papa!" she protested, unwilling to take so much blame. "Patrick was trying to protect you, not me!"

"Aye, and what do you suppose I was doing?"

"You?"

"Don't be simple, lass. Don't you believe I could have me pick of the best jobs at the mill if I wanted?"

Carina shook her head. She was too tired for this. Twice in one night she'd been called simple. Perhaps she was. If all this struggle wasn't to benefit Papa's failing health, what was it about? "I don't understand," she whispered. "Don't you want a better job?"

"I did, and now that I see how useless it is to sacrifice myself for you, perhaps I'll take it back."

"For me?" She stared at Conn O'Rourke uncomprehendingly.

"Aye, 'tis a father's sorry lot—for all the good it does." His eyes rested on her torn sleeve, and his mouth turned up in a grim sneer. "Got rough, did he?"

"Papa, it wasn't my choice, you have to believe me. I only wanted to talk to him—"

"Talk!" he thundered. "Don't lie to me, girl!"

16

Carina cast a quick glance at the bed she shared with Margaret. In Patrick's absence Kevin had taken to sleeping there, too. The youngsters stirred briefly at the sound of their father's voice, but it took more than an argument to wake them. Arguments were Conn O'Rourke's entertainment. His children were used to hearing his voice raised in anger.

"I'm not lying, Papa. I went to Mr. Wentworth's house to wait for him." At his look, she hurried on. "I only asked him to let Patrick go free. I *begged* him! He tried to make me go inside with him, but I refused. He tore my dress, pulling on me. Then a man came and stopped him. His cousin, he said. I got away while they were fighting."

She would have given anything to have her father put his arms around her in comfort, even though she knew it would never happen. It didn't. O'Rourke caught her trembling chin with his hand and tipped her cheek to the moonlight as if to confirm that she'd gotten what she deserved. "You'll be the death of me yet, girl."

Carina lowered her lashes to hide her tears. She hadn't cried in years, and she didn't want to start again tonight. But if what he said was true, her going to beg Enoch Wentworth for mercy had been even rasher than she had known. Could it be true that her virtue was the price he would exact for everything?

Suddenly, it seemed too much to bear. Since her mother's death, she had tried to be everything to everybody—all the while knowing she could never replace the gentle woman whose memory was the heart and soul of them all. Her only guide had been the best answer she could find to the question: what would Mama do? But she had failed, totally.

Her father mistook her sorrow for guilt and, dropping her chin, muttered, more to himself than to her, "Aye, you're a sin and a shame. Like as not, you went off with the master's ill-gotten cousin as well!"

Too curious about Jared Wentworth to defend herself

17

against this new slur on her character, Carina asked, "Why do you call him ill gotten? He saved me."

"He rides with the devil, child."

Her father's figure of speech recalled Enoch Wentworth's charge—one Jared himself had accepted. "Mr. Wentworth called him a devil, too. What did he mean?"

"You've no business hearing such things!"

Carina would not be put off. She clutched her father's arm. "Answer me, Papa. I tell you, he was kind to me when he didn't have to be. How could he be bad?"

"The devil puts out his lure for the weak."

Carina had no patience with his rantings. She took her hand away and said daringly, "Perhaps he can help us with Patrick. He may have—"

"No! You'll not go near that black devil!"

"Tell me why."

He shifted in the chair, goaded by her directness. It was a quality he despised in women. "He consorts with men who go about at night, spiriting away people from their homes and robbing the unlucky. It's a wicked business they do. The work of the devil. It's a miracle you got away from him this once. If you did," he added darkly.

Carina regarded her father. What he'd said didn't fit with what she sensed about Jared Wentworth. Her instincts told her he was no kidnapper, no robber. "I don't know, Papa. He was very angry with Mr. Wentworth for hurting me. That doesn't square with what you say. *He* said Mr. Wentworth's father would not like it. Could that be so?"

They all knew that Enoch Wentworth's father owned the Shattuck Mill. That gave him more power than Enoch, who only managed it. Perhaps this senior Mr. Wentworth would be kind. Perhaps she could ask *him*. . . .

"His father!" O'Rourke scoffed. "As if old man Nathan doesn't know everything that goes on at the Shattuck! He has his spies."

18

"Who are they?" Carina demanded. Her notion of a second appeal was fading fast under her father's skepticism. "Perhaps they'll tell him and—"

"Do not blather so, girl. None of these Wentworths will lift a finger to help us. We have no recourse. Nor do you. The best you can do now is to marry Dennis and be quick about it before he finds out about your disgraceful wanderings in the night. He's waited for you to grow up, and it's time you stopped hiding behind your brothers and sister and relying on me to protect you. He'll take you on as he promised and we'll be quit of you."

"He's certainly done nothing so far to help Patrick—or you!" she said rashly, for Dennis Boynton was her father's creature. She had been promised to Dennis since she was sixteen, by her father's word, not hers.

Conn O'Rourke rose to his considerable height then. Carina saw it as a move he made when he was desperate for a way to control her, as if he would dominate her by sheer size when he could manage the task no other way. Again she had vexed him sorely, dismissing his logic and ignoring his parental authority.

"Do not deceive yourself, girl. You've let the devil turn your head, looking for rescue. 'Tis all your fault, this need for rescue! You'll not shame me further with your wicked ways. Tomorrow you'll wed Dennis Boynton if I have to drag you to him! Do you hear me, girl?"

"Marrying me to Dennis will not get Patrick back," she reminded him. "Our only hope for that is Jared Wentworth, I'm thinking."

"Thinking!" Her father lashed out with his hand to strike her cheek. "I'll have no more of your thinking! It's done, I say. You'll make no bargain with the devil!"

His slap reopened the cut high on her cheekbone, but Carina didn't cry out or turn away. She stared back at him, defiantly waiting until his eyes fell from hers before she moved away.

She got into bed beside Margaret, finding her comfort there next to her sister's burrowing warmth. Without

Carina to fight with, Conn would soon sleep, and better than he had earlier. It was his way. He found conflict bracing, Carina thought wearily, trying to accept what she couldn't understand.

Carina knew her father. He would, indeed, drag her to Dennis and insist that they marry. Years ago, perhaps, she would have obeyed, but not now. She was older now. She had seen girls her age and younger marry their sweethearts or the men picked out for them. She had seen them change from merry girls into drudges.

That was not what she wanted, not more of the same. And certainly not for the pleasure of Dennis Boynton. Dennis was a good man, comely enough and a good worker. According to Conn, he had prospects, but she did not want those prospects.

Lying in the dark, quiet and tense, Carina saw another man's face. Jared Wentworth's. Of all men, he was the only one to touch her gently, with regard for her well-being.

Tonight's failure could not be the end. Jared Wentworth had helped her tonight; he would help her again. It was up to her to try to gain his aid. She had to try or give up, allowing herself to be passed, like a dumb beast, from one man's dominion to another's.

Her father left her no choice. She would have to leave.

It was well into the Sabbath morn before her father's breathing eased into sleep and Carina dared to stir from bed. With no Mass to attend and no bells to summon them to the mill, they would all sleep as late as their early rising habits would allow. Moving soundlessly, Carina stripped off her own sorry garments, trading them for Patrick's.

She had never worn his clothes before, but she knew they would do. For all that he was younger and broader, they were of a size, and where he was now he had no need of them. The extra fullness of cloth would go far to disguise her feminine shape. With her hair stuck up into Patrick's cap, her costume was complete.

She knelt quickly beside Kevin and brushed his brow with her lips. He didn't move, but Margaret, who was eleven, tried to squirm into her embrace again. Gently, Carina disengaged her arms and whispered, "I'm sorry, my pet." She knew—and regretted—that most of her work would now fall onto Margaret's small shoulders. It could not be helped. At least Carina had the comfort of knowing that Conn O'Rourke would not find fault with Margaret as he did with her.

As the birds outside began their first sleepy twittering, she looked back from the open door and studied her father's sleeping form. In spite of the animosity between them, she longed to kiss him farewell and rest her head on his shoulder one last time. He looked old and careworn, yet peaceful at the same time. She smiled sadly to think that only in sleep could he look like the man she remembered from her youth. He would hate her for leaving, but not, perhaps, if her leaving restored Patrick to his side.

She raised her fingers in a small, fluttering salute and whispered, perhaps to them all, perhaps only to Papa, "I'm sorry."

Then she closed the door.

# Chapter 2

Conn O'Rourke had not always despaired of his eldest child. At first she had seemed a magical creature, at once symbolic of his new life in America and the embodiment of the love he bore her mother. Like Olivia, she was perfect. She had Olivia's starburst blue eyes and his black curls. Even her feisty spirit enchanted him. After all, without strength, he would never have dared to leave Ireland and Olivia would never have dared to marry him, an Irishman.

Rumors of work for the Irish had percolated from Lowell, Massachusetts, through upper New England to Canada. It took Conn two months to get there on foot. Sometimes he traveled with others, sometimes he went alone, finding work at farms and villages along the way. He met Olivia Howard in New Hampshire and carried her image in his heart from that moment.

In Lowell, building the canals that would carry the waters of the Merrimack to the textile looms, he felt invincible. Olivia's smile protected him from danger in the deep, narrow channels. No blast of explosive powder could char him. No tower of granite blocks could collapse atop him.

He was thirty-six before he had saved enough to return and claim Olivia. By then her parents had died and her unmarried brother worked the stony land in their stead.

Ansel Howard was wise enough to recognize that he had much to gain by opening his home to Conn O'Rourke. If he did not do so, Olivia would leave and he would have to marry to gain the services of another woman. Then too, Conn was a hard worker with capital to invest in stock Ansel wanted for the farm.

Neither Conn nor Olivia objected to buying sheep to raise on hillsides too rocky to support anything else. Nor did they mind paying for improvements to the little house. After all, their children were filling the rooms, and it was their home, too.

Except that it wasn't. It was Ansel's house and Ansel's farm.

One day in 1844, shortly after the spring lambing was over, Ansel announced that he was marrying the widow Hapgood, whose land ran with his on the west side. Although Olivia was surprised, even stunned—Ansel's courtship had been nothing if not circumspect—she was too warm hearted and too happy in her own marriage not to wish her brother joy.

He hardly cared for her good wishes; he had more pressing concerns. It seemed that Iris Hapgood wanted to live in his house, which was—thanks to Conn's improvements—the finer dwelling. Further, she wanted her daughter, who was also about to marry, to live in her present home.

Olivia gulped, swallowing her apprehensions. It would not be easy to share their living space with Iris Hapgood, but what else could they do? Smiling gamely, she assured Ansel that Iris was welcome.

There was more.

Iris was "nervous" around children. They would have to leave. Ansel produced his careful list of Conn's actual outlay of funds, both for materials and stock, and repaid the total amount. Because he was a generous man, he also added a meager sum he called "interest on the loan," adding that he "forgave them the just amount of rent he could have charged for all those years of free living."

Alternately cursing his own stupidity and Ansel's cupidity, Conn O'Rourke took his family to Lowell. It would be different and perhaps difficult, but at least the mill owners would pay him for his labor. Work for the Irish had begun to move into the mills from the canals.

Conn's first job was constructing a small addition to the Shattuck Mill. To live in, he rented one floor of a new three-story building on Central Street. Like that building, the area was new and a bit raw, but Conn was proud to be able to settle his family outside the Acre, the usual Irish district.

Then, before Kevin was born, Conn fell from a scaffolding. He was lucky only to break his leg. They took in boarders to pay the rent while he couldn't work. By the time he could go back, the building was complete. A few fortunate men got full-time positions in the yard, maintaining or guarding the physical plant, but Conn was not one of them. He still had blinding headaches, although he said little about them in order not to be considered troublesome and thus unemployable, and he was often sick. With their meager savings now gone, Conn took the best-paying job available to him.

While it was true that the Irish had never been welcome in Lowell, except as day laborers in the dirty, dangerous work of canal construction, things were changing. The famed "Lowell girls," who had originally left their New England farm communities to operate spindle and loom, were now leaving the mills, to take up their old lives or go on to other experiences. Mill work was no longer so desirable either. There was pay, yes; but as the mills churned out miles of fabric, the bountiful supply depressed the price. Mill owners began to require more cloth from each worker to offset the falling profit, and the Lowell girls, who had come to earn money and gain their independence, now exercised that independence. They went back home, and their tales of discontent did much to discourage their younger sisters from making the same trip.

So the mills needed workers, and who better to fill the need—particularly now that it was no longer desirable work—than the Irish? Not only were they already on hand, more kept coming every day, as the terrible potato famine drove them from their homeland in hordes.

Available jobs had always been categorized by sex, but now they were further segregated by "race." Yankee workers, known for their reliability and intelligence, were given the best and most profitable jobs. Conn, with his reputation for difficulty—he had, after all, gotten hurt, could only work in the picking room. There the huge bags of raw cotton were torn open and cleaned, preparatory to being carded. The work was hard and dangerous.

By the time the Shattuck Mill had been built, owners knew better than to attach the picking rooms to the main mill. Small, tightly contained rooms filled with loose, flying cotton fibers and heated by the activity of heavy machinery made for a combustible mix. The room where Conn worked was carefully separated from the rest of the mill by a firewall, and he and his fellow pickers were segregated from the Yankee work force.

Conn's dear Olivia never recovered fully from Kevin's birth. First came childbed fever, which left her sadly weakened and in no condition to fight off a second, virulent infection. She was not the only casualty of what was termed a "minor" outbreak of cholera that year in Lowell, but she was the only one who mattered to Conn. No one blamed him for grieving, for he had truly loved his wife, but there were those, like the Sweeneys, who did blame him for turning away from his children in the process.

For that reason, Mary Sweeney waited for him by the stairs one night, determined to speak her mind. A large, raw-boned woman with the persistence of a woodpecker, Mary could force even Conn O'Rourke to hear her out. "Bad enough that those little ones have lost their dear mother," she scolded, "but you've gone and made it worse! The way you're acting, it's like they've lost their father, too."

With Mary between him and escape, Conn tried to defend himself. "They've got Carina," he said brusquely.

"Little more than a child herself," Mary fired at his back, for he had maneuvered around her anyway. She could talk, even make him listen, but she couldn't change his heart.

"Hardly!" he shouted back.

Carina was fourteen—a blooming fourteen. And that blooming had become the stumbling block between Conn and his family. He couldn't bear the resemblance between his lost Olivia and this budding woman who had taken her place. The very things that had once pleased him about Carina—her determination, her intelligence and, most of all, her starry blue eyes with rays of light sparkling from their pupils—were now like stabs of a knife to his soft underside.

Worse, she would not behave modestly. Either she played like a child with her brothers and sister, or she assumed an inappropriate, adult role—as if she were equal to himself and truly their other parent.

Even her name set her apart from everyone else in her father's eyes. He conveniently forgot that she had not chosen her name. Olivia had. He had picked Bridget for a girl child, but Olivia had been adamant. She herself had longed to be called Carina just for the pure loveliness of the sound it made on her tongue. No other name would do for her child.

With Olivia gone, Conn made an attempt to get his obstinate eldest to accept being called by her middle name. She did not yield. Carina would not answer to Bridget, and no one else would use it. Another lost cause, it remained in Conn's memory to rankle still.

Carina—his problem, his curse. His secret pride?

No, never. He refused to believe that Carina could in any way, beyond the likeness of her beautiful eyes, be like his Olivia. *She* had been gentle and sweet, in all ways an ideal woman. He had long since discredited Ansel's stories of Olivia's hoydenish youth, when she'd chased after her brother and climbed trees to shake down the sweetest apples from the top. To Conn, Ansel's forcing them from the farm invalidated anything he'd ever said. No, Carina was the spawn of the devil and not his child at all.

Thus, as O'Rourke woke to find Carina's bed empty yet again, he convinced himself that he and his remaining children, including the absent but still-loved Patrick, were better off without her.

He put her balled-up and torn dress, the black faded to a threadbare green, into the ragbag and sent Margaret to fetch water. She didn't argue as Carina would do, only stopped at the door to ask, "But where *is* she, Papa?"

"Gone."

Still she waited, sensing that there was more.

"She will never be back," he said.

"Is she in jail? Like Patrick?"

"No. She's dead."


The long, low rays of the afternoon sun turned windows on the upper story of the house into unblinking golden eyes. There were five, in a row; wide, tall, and blank. The sight should have intimidated Carina, but instead she was enchanted.

It had taken her all day to find Jared Wentworth's house, so she was glad not to be disappointed. Although long, the search itself had not been without compensation. In the eight years she had lived in Lowell she had seldom been outside the Chapel Hill section except to go to the mill and work. Consequently, she thought of Lowell as crowded and noisy, not like the glorious countryside she had discovered today.

Her first thought had been regret that she could not share her ramble with the younger children, particularly with Patrick. Unlike the others, he at least remembered a life that was freer and more wholesome than the one they'd known in recent years. Thoughts of Patrick served to spur her on, however, for it was his freedom, not her own, that she sought.

Upon leaving the house on Central Street, Carina had first craved escape from Chapel Hill, where someone might recognize her, even in her ill-fitting disguise. From all she knew of folks like the Wentworths, she was sure Jared lived across the Concord River in Belvidere. Getting there did not take so long, but finding Jared's house proved impossible. Now she was glad for the difficulty. In Belvidere, she had seen *Nathan* Wentworth's house and so had that image to compare with this dwelling at Falls Village.

Belvidere was like the aptly named Concord River. Its surfaces were broad and smooth. Well-tended lawns sloped gently down to the complacent curl of the flat river below. Each house, including Nathan Wentworth's, sat like a gem in its placid, green setting, looking dauntingly perfect to Carina.

Believing the Wentworth house in question to be Jared's, Carina had approached it warily, only to be run off for asking to speak to him. No one there would tell her where Jared Wentworth lived, only that he was no more welcome at the house in Belvidere than she was. Although she had counted on Jared's influence with Enoch's father as a way to exert pressure on Patrick's accuser, she was relieved that the man she sought wasn't part of this too-tidy world.

To find where Jared did live, she had to retreat across the Concord River and skirt around Chapel Hill to the main part of town. Most of her inquiries came to naught, but eventually a man of about her own age directed her to Falls Village. While obtaining more specific directions, Carina learned to stand as far from people as possible, to deepen her voice, and to be on guard against the slightest trace of Irish cadence in her speech. It was a lot to think about, but slowly she adjusted, gaining confidence from each success.

Patrick's clothes helped. Just wearing pants freed her from the usual restraints imposed on her sex, and imitating a masculine gait was wonderfully liberating. As she strode along she tried to anticipate difficulties before they arose. She picked out a name to use, one that was plain and unremarkable. After settling on John Howard, she decided on one further safeguard. She went into some thick bushes and sacrificed the comfort of wearing Patrick's undershirt normally in order to bind her breasts flat. After that she felt indomitable.

That feeling was still with her now that she had found Jared Wentworth—or at least his house. She liked everything about it, just as she had liked his disinterested kindness to her. That her father disapproved of him only added to his appeal. Because she had seen so little of the man, she wondered if she would be able to recognize him. Except for his voice. That deep, rumbling sound, so like the river coursing below this property, would be with her forever.

Carina studied the house for clues to the life within. Its face was not unlike those of the long, narrow houses common to downtown Lowell. The sharply pitched roof ran from one end chimney to the other, like a heavy, dark lid set upon the house. Its line was unbroken by dormers, and it and the plain, blank windows seemed to shut her out rather than beckon her forward. Bushes and trees obscured the center front entrance and the four lower windows, while the path to the main door looked little used. She couldn't decide whether the house was old and overgrown or new and never groomed. Either way, it seemed an appropriate setting for Jared Wentworth.

She knocked boldly on the heavy door and finally, after she had repeated the exercise twice more, it swung open. The man who peered at her from within was as old as her father, but smaller and totally bald. His hairlessness surprised her as much as her presence startled him.

29

"I'd like to speak to Mr. Jared Wentworth." She sounded more timid than she'd intended. Eschewing a brogue was easier than remembering to sound masculine.

"Who are you?" the little man demanded. "And what are you doing here?"

"John Howard, sir, and I've business with Mr. Wentworth."

He shut the door in her face, saying, "Never heard of you."

Carina stepped back instinctively as the door banged shut; then she raised her fist to beat on it again. It opened immediately, catching her off guard. After an awkward moment in which both parties stared rudely at each other, Carina said, "Please, sir, it's very important that I speak to Mr. Wentworth."

"Important to him or to you?"

"To me," she admitted after a reluctant pause, adding hopefully, "but I don't believe he'll mind."

The man shut the door again on a disdainful snort. It took Carina a moment to realize he'd said, "Round to the back" just before the door slammed.

Feeling that she'd won a major victory, she scampered along the path to do his bidding. The "back" consisted of a large quadrangle, at one side of which was an extended ell attached to the far end of the house. Opposite the ell stood a stable with room for perhaps a half-dozen horses. Across from the back of the main house was a long, open shed in which a blacksmith worked a bellows at his forge. No one gave her a second glance so she was able to look around and satisfy her curiosity. Everyone was busy, but there was no tension. Carina had seen enough of workplaces to judge instantly whether or not a place was good.

This one was.

Carina watched the house, no longer anxious, waiting to see which of the many doors would open to her. It took longer than she'd expected, but finally the little man called out to her. When she was close enough to hear him, he said, "My master knows no John Howard and has no business with one." With that, he spun a coin through the air and shut the door.

Carina fell on the coin, then on the door, pounding again.

It opened to reveal an indignant face, but hers was more so. "I do not come begging, sir. If you have a job for me until Mr. Wentworth can talk to me, I'll do it, but I'll not take your coin."

Pressed to take the money back, the servant eyed her narrowly. In full light, Carina could see that he lacked even eyebrows and lashes. "We've no need for workers. Where do you come from?"

"From Lowell."

"Then go back there. The mills will take you on."

"I'll not go back."

"You've worked there?"

"At the Shattuck, sir."

He harrumphed to hide the fact that he had visibly softened to her. She judged herself right to mention Enoch and Nathan Wentworth's mill.

"If you've trouble there, there's naught Mr. Jared can do for you. He's of no influence there."

"I would but speak to him, sir."

Her persistence clearly puzzled him. Curiosity and irritation waged an inconclusive war for control of his features. Carina couldn't tell which had won, even when he snapped out, "Look here, son, to get to Mr. Jared, you'll *have* to tell me your business. There's no if about it!"

She had counted on speaking to Mr. Wentworth herself, and in private. She looked around. Everyone she saw was purposeful and at some distance, paying them no mind. He gave her no choice but to say something. "Mr. Wentworth took my part in a dispute between me and Mr. Enoch Wentworth. I want to thank him."

"Is that all?" He laughed, and the change of expression took away the egglike look of his face. "Then consider it done. I dare say Mr. Jared got as much good of it as you. There's little he likes as well as opposing Mr. Enoch."

Carina pressed what she saw as her advantage. "Then he'll like the rest of my message even better," she said, heartened now.

"No, no. He'll take on no more causes, I tell you. If he helped you once, you're lucky. It wasn't intentional. He did it for his own reasons and with no more consideration than a man sneezes."

With every protestation, the man only hardened Carina's resolve that she had done right to come here. "I understand, sir," she said.

He nodded and started back inside.

"I'll wait," she assured him.

His smooth, pink head bobbed in surprise and he muttered, "It's on your head then."

After standing by the door for a while, Carina strode to the barn, where a stout man groomed a glossy red horse. "I'm to wait for the master," she said by way of greeting. "Perhaps you have a chore I could do?"

Without missing a stroke with the currycomb, he looked her over. "How old are ye, lad?"

It was another question she'd prepared herself for during her walk. "Most thirteen, sir, and I'm stronger than I look."

"Save yer sirs for the house, boy. M'name's Ned."

Curiosity drew Carina along the row of stalls until she came to one special horse. She stopped walking, even stopped breathing, while she stared at the great black stallion. She didn't need to be told that this was Jared Wentworth's mount.

They eyed each other, the horse wary and imperious, Carina patient. She had just started forward when Ned yelled, "Hey! Stay back from that beast. He'll have ye fer supper."

Carina put up her hand to stop Ned from rushing her. The horse was indeed showing white around his eyes, but she wasn't afraid. "I have an understanding with horses, Ned. Don't worry."

Ned didn't go back, but at least he came no closer. "The master'll have m'head if he starts kickin' the slats outta his box."

"He won't. What's his name?"

"Infidel."

Carina laughed. "I expected Satan or Lucifer." She walked closer and, except for Infidel's brief response to a convulsive move by Ned, the horse did not shy. "I wish I had a carrot for you, Infidel. Will you accept my empty hand instead?"

She offered it out, palm up, for his inspection. He laid his ears back and put his face down to her hand, drawing his lips back as he sniffed, then blew on her palm. Moving slowly and smoothly, she brought up her other hand so she could rub his ear. He pulled back in surprise, then put his head close and butted her hand until she obliged with more scratches.

"Well, I'll be!"

Carina had forgotten Ned until he spoke. Now she looked back and asked, "Perhaps I can help with this horse?"

She could.

The rest of the day passed in a happy daze. She tried to make herself indispensable to Ned, mindful of only one drawback—the need to keep her face averted as much as possible. Ned was not stupid, and her masculine identity would not hold up to scrutiny if he saw her soft countenance in strong light. She kept Patrick's cap pulled low, and only thoughts of him in jail and of Margaret and Kevin having to take up the slack caused by her absence at home kept her from wallowing in joy.

She bedded down in straw in the corner of the stable that night and slept dreamlessly, happy to get up and do it all over again the next day. Everyone treated her well, sharing food and giving her a hand with heavy buckets. No one asked her business with the master—including the master.

That was the rub. She examined her plan again and found no flaws. Jared Wentworth couldn't leave without her notice as long as she stayed close to Infidel. The carriage was being repaired and a gentleman would hardly walk to town.

She finished laying new straw in Infidel's stall and went to fetch him from the crosstie. His coat shone like a mirror in the noontime sun. Busy unfastening the horse, Carina didn't hear footsteps behind her until it was too late.

"So this is the lad who's tamed my Infidel."

Carina rose and whirled around, her unmasculine cry part shock and part dismay. Although she bumped the horse, Infidel was with his two favorite people and thus imperturbable.

"John Howard, I presume?" Wentworth said, tilting his head to look at her with dancing eyes. Before Carina could make sure her cap was still aright, he swept it from her head. Her black hair tumbled down around her neck and shoulders in curling disarray. He watched it, a sardonic grin on his face. She forced herself to endure that, and her gaze was steady when his glance returned to her face.

"The deceit was not for you, sir. I only meant to protect myself."

He lifted her chin, much as her father had, to inspect her face. She knew it was smudged, but he only looked at the cut on her cheekbone. "His ring will leave a scar," he said absently; then he stepped back and folded his arms across his massive chest. "Don't you think you need protection from me?"

Carina smiled at the thought. He *looked* dangerous, but she was unafraid. "You protected me once; why should you not again?"

"Once it was my pleasure. Again it may not be."

"Then I will bear your displeasure." She shrugged, truly indifferent to such an unlikely prospect.

"What's your name?"

"Carina O'Rourke."

"You work for my cousin?"

"I did."

"You lost your job?"

"I have now."

"And your home?"

She nodded. His questions were easy and his manner gentle, leaving her mind free to absorb impressions of him on this almost-equal footing. He was as dark as she remembered, but his features were finer. His skin was sun-darkened, not swarthy, and his forehead, as noble as her father's, was set off by thick black eyebrows. She decided that it was his overall hairiness that made him look forbidding; that and the set of his mouth. Stubborn. Strong.

"Why did you go to my cousin?"

"For the same reason I come to you. He had my brother arrested for attacking him."

"*Did* he attack him?"

"He committed a desperate act. My brother is young. He doesn't bear frustration well."

"And you do?"

"I've had more experience with it, but in fact I did little better than Patrick. As you saw, Patrick asked mercy for my father, and I was asking for him. Who knows where it might have gone if you hadn't interfered."

"There are others?"

"Margaret and Kevin, but they are only eleven and seven. They should be safe for a time."

"You think I can help you?"

"I do. Patrick is a good boy. He only defended himself when Mr. Wentworth's men were hurting him. I know people who saw it all, but their word counts for nothing with the constable against Mr. Wentworth's. Your word would matter more."

"But I wasn't there."

"Nor did Patrick attack Mr. Wentworth. The truth is of little use sometimes."

Jared turned away from her angrily. "So young to be so cynical."

"Not so young, sir. I'll be twenty-two come harvest."

"A country girl besides," he murmured. One side of his mouth tilted up in a smile that changed his whole face. "I suppose that's where you learned to tame horses."

Carina gave him her widest smile. "Not tame them, sir. Never that. You'll find your horse unchanged. He has only decided to like me."

Carina wished that in this matter he and his horse would be of one mind. Instead, Jared drew his brows together in a fierce frown. "And what about your father? Did he send you here? Or did he perhaps send you to Enoch, gift-wrapped?"

She frowned back. "The problem began because of me, but I didn't know it until I went home with my torn dress. Now I want to be the one who ends it for the rest of the family. My father needs healthier work than the picking room or he'll die. Your cousin's price for that was my virtue. Patrick went to plead for Papa, and you know how that ended. But if you can return Patrick to him, then all will be well. Papa will not miss me."

Jared raised his eyebrows at her certainty. "You know that?"

She shrugged as she had before. "I've always been a care to him."

"I'll have no irate father coming after me," he warned.

"He doesn't know where I am."

"And if he learns? And he will. The world is small."

"I was to be gone from him anyway. He was going to have me marry yesterday in order to be quit of me."

"Great God! To whom?"

"I've been promised since I was sixteen, by my father's word."

"Why didn't your intended help you?"

"It was never his concern. He doesn't work the mills."

Jared took Infidel's lead from her, then nodded toward the house. "Go tell Bagley to take you to Agnes. Tell *her* to fix you up."

"Who is Bagley, sir? The little hairless man?"

Jared's head flew back, and he began to roar with laughter. By the time he stopped Carina felt quite shamefaced.

"I'm sorry. I didn't mean to be unkind."

"I hope not. He's my oldest friend, and I wouldn't want to see him hurt."

"No, sir."

He wasn't laughing anymore, but his lips had lost their harsh line. "He wasn't always like that, you know. He had a fever that left him afflicted."

"At least it left him," she said quietly.

"Yes, at least it did." He studied the ready sympathy on her face as if it interested him, then gave a puckish grin and said, "I wish I could see his face when he sees your hair like this."

"I could put it up." She began to gather the stuff into a coil.

He stopped her, and their hands tangled together in the silky web of it. "No!" As if her hair were afire, he pulled his hand back, putting it behind him. "You're never to put your hair up again. Tell that to Agnes, too!"

With that, he strode away, leading Infidel. Carina didn't move until he mounted up and rode away.

# Chapter 3

When Jared Wentworth left Carina he didn't have far to go to reach his destination. Which was just as well. He was sorely distracted, having left the better part of his functioning mind behind with her.

She intrigued him. How much of her story was true? It was so poignant. The cynic in him tried to laugh off his sympathy. He asked himself, would he be so moved if she were ugly?

But she wasn't, and he had witnessed the fury of her struggle to get away from Enoch. Another point in her favor was the honest way she'd admitted having gone to Enoch in the first place. He told himself that a liar often gives the partial truth to lend veracity to a larger, more important lie, but he didn't believe it. Every instinct told him she had spoken true. Besides, he knew his cousin. Enoch was entirely capable of using his position as agent for the mill to procure bedmates, willing or not.

The crucial question was, what was he going to do about her? To champion Carina and her family would mean upsetting the delicate balance between himself and Uncle Nathan. He couldn't do that lightly, it was too hard won. But if he did nothing, wouldn't that mean he was no better than Enoch?

The Stone House Hotel at Falls Village had been built before the mills of Lowell, and Jared liked to believe it would outlast them. It looked like two large, identical stone houses side by side, connected by an ell. Small porticos graced the center entrances of each building, but the true glory of the hotel was at the back.

There, from one of several balconies, one could dine in privacy and watch the waters of the Merrimack plunge over the falls. When the river was at full spate, a strong wind would carry moisture from the plume and deposit it like a fine mist over everything. At such times, Jared liked to imagine that the balcony was the prow of a ship and he its captain.

He indulged in no such fantasy today. The river's thunder was muted, and the sun was too bright as he made his way to where Silas Meade already waited for him. Silas was the nearest thing to a father Jared had. His own father had perished, along with his mother and sister, in the fire that destroyed their Cambridge home when Jared was twelve years old.

Although no one could replace what Jared had lost, Silas and his wife, Indigo, tried to make him believe he was one of their family. Between the Meades and the Coles of Philadelphia, his maternal grandparents, Jared knew he had fared better than most. Better than Carina O'Rourke, for instance, who—God help her—felt driven to appeal to him in her need.

He shook off that thought and extended his hand to Silas, who jumped up to greet him. As always, their handshake became an unashamed embrace, for Silas was a warm and affectionate man.

After Silas finished pounding the dust from the back of Jared's coat, he pulled back to inspect him. "It's been too long, son. Both Indigo and Susan gave me orders to bring you home with me, or not bother to return myself!"

Jared laughed and gestured Silas back to his seat. "I trust they are both well?" If Silas noted that Jared gave no promise, at least he didn't comment on it. They both knew he had broken Susan's heart once, when he had married. Now she was waiting for him to give up his grief and notice that she loved him.

"Well and busy," Silas reported with a wry shake of his head. "Susan recently enlisted Indigo's help with her younger classes so she could have more time." He paused before adding in a scathing tone, "For her causes."

Jared raised an eyebrow. "Causes? She's branched out?" Susan was already such a fervent abolitionist Jared wondered how she could take on more.

"Perhaps I misspoke. Her cause remains the same. She's only taken on additional projects to that end."

"You don't approve?"

Silas shifted in his chair and glanced around.

"We're quite alone, as you can see. But if it makes you uncomfortable, you needn't answer me. Surely you know that, Silas."

The older man let out his breath in a sigh of exasperation. "Damn it, she makes *me* uncomfortable, not you! And I've got to talk to someone about it or explode."

Jared touched his arm reassuringly. "Let's order first. Then, when you've unburdened yourself, you'll have something to fill the empty spaces. I can heartily recommend the glazed ham." At Silas's distracted nod, Jared summoned the waiter and ordered.

By the time they each had a small glass of whiskey before them, Silas was composed enough to speak. "You know how I feel, Jared, and you know I support her aims, but I hate to see her becoming so *involved.*"

Jared sipped his drink, listening to the unspoken message behind the words. It was nothing less than a father's pain that his child's choices were taking her further and further from the mainstream of life. He wanted her to have a home and family of her own and leave the tending of the world to others.

"This business is taking over her life, what with the Female Anti-Slavery Society and the Boston Vigilance Committee. I thought starting up that school was bad enough, but now this!" He lined up the silverware in front of him and began moving pieces forward as if cautiously pressing soldiers into battle.

Jared waited and finally Silas got it out. "She's taken up *writing!*"

Careful not to laugh, Jared repeated, "Writing? Do you mean letters or tracts?" He allowed himself a small smile. "Or has she decided to give Mrs. Stowe some competition?"

Published two years earlier, *Uncle Tom's Cabin* was a continuing sensation, both as a novel and in the stage production, at least in the North.

Silas didn't smile. "I don't doubt that Mrs. Stowe is her inspiration, but no. Susan is too literal minded for fiction. She's begun to interview former slaves in order to write up their stories."

"For publication?"

"She doesn't say that, although there's no assurance to the contrary. You know as well as I that someone will suggest publication eventually."

"Has she begun?"

"Oh, yes. She even has a title, *Voices of Bondage: Being True Accounts in Their Own Words of Lives in Slavery.*"

Jared had no idea how to respond. Tossing back the rest of his whiskey, he finally asked, "By the way, how are things in Boston these days?"

It wasn't as much of a non sequitur as it sounded, and Silas answered promptly. "Quiet." Upon reflection, he amended his response. "On the surface, that is. Underneath, things are simmering and ready to boil at the least provocation."

"You're afraid Susan's writings might provide the provocation?"

"They might," Silas admitted, leaning forward in agitation. "Suppose someone traces a former slave through her accounts. It could occur. After what happened to Sims, we can't be sure anymore that we can stop the slave chasers."

41

Thomas Sims was the first fugitive slave publicly returned to bondage from Boston under the hated Fugitive Slave Act of 1850. Although fugitive slave laws had existed for years, the Congressional Compromise Bill of 1850 had finally spelled out the penalties in reprehensible detail. They were severe. An individual who sheltered an alleged runaway slave or who aided in an escape was to pay a fine of one thousand dollars and to serve a prison sentence of six months.

In Boston and in certain other areas of New England, the act had been perceived as unenforceable. But that was before Sims was marched through the streets of Boston to be extradited to Savannah, Georgia, as recovered chattel. It had taken federal marshals and three companies of militia to accomplish the task, but it had been done. Over two years later, abolitionists were still absorbing the shock of their failure.

"You think it could happen again?" Jared asked.

"I know it could. Just think how devastated Susan would be if she were the cause of another such incident! I've tried to dissuade her from pursuing this project, but you know how little influence I have with her."

Jared did, and he smiled grimly.

Like many single-minded people, Susan wasn't subtle. If you were not for her cause unequivocally, you were as bad as the enemy. She was vocal about her beliefs, and she could not allow for disagreement. Nor could she imagine that her father worked as hard as she did for the same goals, but in secret. Though Susan loved her father too much to be openly disrespectful, Jared knew she would be thrilled to know he shared her convictions.

"You should tell her the truth," Jared said, not for the first time. "It would make your life easier."

Silas grimaced. "Only until she told the world about my special 'cargo.' No, thank you. I'll keep things the way they are."

Jared didn't deny that Susan might be indiscreet, but

he suspected Silas kept his silence for another reason. It was Susan's belief that an evil such as slavery could not exist if good people would condemn it openly. In this, as in so many things, Jared believed she was somewhat right yet enormously naïve.

So he grinned at Silas and said mockingly, "You're just afraid she'd call you a hypocrite."

Silas saluted him with his glass. "How well you know my daughter."

With the service of their first course, they turned their attention to the soup and fell silent except for occasional pleasantries. Meanwhile Jared pondered the problem of Carina O'Rourke.

"You seem to have something weighty on your mind, son. Do you have second thoughts about tomorrow night?" Although they had not spoken of it yet, their reason for meeting was to arrange the transfer of three escaped slaves.

"No, no, of course not." Jared's rush to reassure Silas didn't succeed entirely.

When Jared's brow remained grooved, Silas said, "If you can use a good worker, one of the people coming tomorrow has experience as a miller. He might be willing to stay here and work for you."

"Is he wanted?"

"He doesn't expect to be pursued, and if I could get him papers it might work. He's intelligent and industrious, but you can judge for yourself."

"Who are the other two? They're not related?"

"The other two are a mother and daughter."

"Perhaps a family in the making?"

"I don't know. The daughter is light skinned."

Jared's mouth tightened. "A story of Susan's tract, perhaps?"

"Indigo told me in confidence that Susan approached the woman, but she looked right through her and wouldn't say a word." Silas's sigh was loud. "Her heart is good, God knows, but Susan just doesn't understand that sometimes her zeal can be as harsh as an overseer's whip."

Because Jared agreed, he tactfully changed the subject. "There's a printer in Lowell who's reputed to be sympathetic. Perhaps I could get papers right here for your man. Has he any distinguishing features?"

"None that are obvious. You can discuss it with him. It may take two days before Ashland is ready to receive them." Ashland lived in New Hampshire and provided a stopping point along the underground railroad route to Canade.

Jared's frown deepened. Two days. His people, those who were aware of the visitors he entertained now and then, would not betray him. But what of Carina O'Rourke? What would she do with such information? Give it to the constable in exchange for her brother's freedom?

He dismissed the thought as unworthy—or tried to. But it wouldn't leave him. He couldn't begin to measure the desperation and courage Carina had displayed, not just once but repeatedly—going to Enoch, fighting him off, then leaving her home to appeal to Jared himself. Yet he was profoundly uncomfortable with the thought that she had deposited her burden on his doorstep. He didn't want it. He was not the hero she needed. And since he wasn't, his failure to help her could hurt others, innocent others.

"Shall I make other arrangements, Jared? Please be frank."

The unaccustomed sharpness in Silas's voice brought Jared back to the present with a start. He didn't offer a quick smile. That would have felt spurious. "What can you tell me about Nathan . . . and Enoch?"

Obviously unsure of Jared's turn of thought, Silas took his time answering. He was a handsome man in his mid-fifties with the honest strength of an oak tree, and although time had plowed twin furrows next to his mouth, his jaw was square and still firm. "Little that you don't know, I'm sure. They're your neighbors, not mine."

"Most of the time," Jared agreed. "But I rarely see them."

"Or want to, I presume."

"Except that I may need to approach my uncle about a matter. Do you think he'll be conciliatory?"

"It would depend upon the matter. . . ."

"And what of his it touches upon?"

"I was never much for riddles, you know," Silas said in mild reprimand.

Noting his tone, Jared thought how happy Tyler would be to receive so much patience from his father. It made him feel guilty—again. He shook off the feeling and forced his mind back to the issue he himself had raised. "I don't mean to be coy. It's just so hard for me to talk about him that I'm not sure I can manage to talk *to* him."

"Must you? Is it something I can handle for you?"

Jared shook his head dolefully. "I don't yet know what I'm going to say, or *if* I'm going through with it."

"It's not like you to be so cryptic, Jared. You know I'll do anything I can for you, but I can't help you blindly."

"Then tell me how you've managed to do business with Nathan all these years—talking contracts and deals, passing the time of day—without wanting to wrap your hands around his neck and choke the breath out of him? Can you tell me how you keep from wanting to do that?"

Silas went white, then red in the face, as if every inch of it had just been smartly slapped—as in a way it had. He raised his cigar to his mouth, then let it fall untouched, poking the air with it in agitation. "Is that what all this is about? My business dealings with Nathan?" he asked incredulously.

Jared was instantly contrite—for his crude phrasing, if not for the question itself. "No, Silas. I'm sorry." Resting his elbows on the table, he put both hands over his face, and brought himself back under control before he looked at Silas again. "That was an abominable thing to say, and I'm more sorry than I can tell you. I meant the question, but not the implicit accusation. Can you understand that?" Nudging his plate aside, he made room for his forearms on the table. "My question is this: I'm so full of hatred, how can I hope to control myself in his presence?"

Placated now that he understood, Silas relaxed. When he spoke, his voice was calm. "Perhaps you can't. Perhaps you shouldn't even try."

Unbidden, Carina's image filled Jared's mind, not the smiling one he would have chosen to see again but the gravely courageous face she'd put forth when he'd first confronted her. He saw again the rich tumble of dark curls around her face and the proud lift of her pointed chin.

"I must try."

It was that simple. Simple . . . but not easy, he thought distractedly. He had to try, but not out of fear that she would learn about the runaways he hid and betray them all. He had to do it because no one as daring as Carina O'Rourke should go unchampioned.

"Then I'll tell you how I control myself," Silas said. "Although you may not like what I say." He waited for that remark to sink in before he went on. "I tell myself that it happened a long time ago and that nothing will ever bring back your family."

When he didn't go on, Jared was curiously disappointed. "That's it?" he asked. He had told himself that a thousand times without noticeable effect.

"No, that's not all," Silas admitted. "I also tell myself that Nathan is as innocent as he says. That he didn't—"

"But he did!" Jared's explosion lost none of its effect because he didn't shout. "He was there. I heard him. My mother heard him—"

"He doesn't deny being there, Jared. He only denies causing the fire and the deaths."

"Murders, Silas! Nathan murdered them all."

Silas waited out the storm; then he shrugged. "You asked me."

Jared sank back into the chair, his rage spent. "So I did." He passed a hand over his face and tried to smile. "Forgive me. I—"

Silas cut him off with an impatient wave of his cigar. "I understand. I'm even glad you brought this up, although I don't understand the timing. Whatever it is that's making you reconsider, it's long overdue. Frankly, I thought perhaps you'd managed to deal with the past when you married Melissa." His expression clouded with the realization that he'd blundered into a second sensitive area by mentioning her.

But this time Jared didn't react. "No, not really. Not unless putting it out of my mind counts. I made a decision then to be happy. I didn't forget, and I certainly didn't forgive. I just refused to brood about it anymore. At least for a while."

Silas didn't respond, but neither did he withdraw. He remained open in case Jared had more to say.

In time he did. "Does it really help you to believe that Nathan is innocent?"

Silas took the question on. "Yes, it does. I didn't come by the belief easily, and it didn't come upon me suddenly either. It's made up of small pieces of the story. The way Nathan's driver, Wickham, never wavered about the time he waited outside your house for Nathan. The way the men at the 'Change were so solid about their testimony. But most of all, the way Nathan conducted himself. To my eyes, he remains a man without guilt."

In his mind, Jared argued every point.

Wickham was dependent on Nathan for a living. Naturally, he would say anything he was told and never waver. The men of the Exchange were Nathan's cronies. Their testimony was similarly suspect. And as for Nathan showing his guilt, that was pap out of sentimental fiction—even supposing Silas could recognize guilt when he saw it.

47

It was, as Silas said, a story made up of small pieces. As Silas had chosen to emphasize certain pieces, so had Jared. But his pieces were different. He had been there with his mother in the next room. He remembered the voices: his father and his uncle, Philip and Nathan, arguing; his mother, Felicity, sending him away, her voice anxious and urgent.

So while Wickham supposedly waited with his uncle's carriage to drive Nathan to the Exchange in Boston, Jared had obeyed his mother. He'd taken his young sister, Philippa, and hurried off in search of Silas Meade, the best friend of his father and the father of Jared's best friend.

But Jared failed in his task. He didn't find Silas in time, and he didn't keep his sister safe.

"Your father and Nathan *were* brothers," Silas reminded him.

"Quarreling brothers."

"Nathan didn't deny that either. But I could never imagine Nathan raising his hand to Felicity. Never."

It was the single concession Jared willingly made to Silas. Even as a boy he had known that Uncle Nathan adored his mother. Neither of his parents talked within Jared's hearing about their romance, and yet he knew they had met through Nathan. The story went that Nathan loved her first. If so, and Jared never doubted it, Felicity's preference for Philip certainly caused the initial problem between the brothers.

Jared refused to grant Silas even that point now, however. "Then how do you explain the fact that *both* of them had been hit on the head and left to die in the fire?" he asked.

It was a scene he had played out in all its grisly detail in his own mind too many times. His father struck down first. His mother rushing to Philip's side, only to meet the same fate. Sometimes he imagined the order reversed, but that made less sense to him. Nathan's quarrel was with Philip. The blow to Felicity would have

48

been dictated by "necessity" after that first strike at his father, a cover-up of his uncle's original intent.

Silas shook his head sadly. "Jared, listen to yourself. They died in an inferno, with beams falling all around them. Who can say what caused a particular blow? Or the order of their deaths? Be reasonable."

"I am. My father would have found a way out if treachery hadn't been involved. I know it."

"He would have tried, Jared. I grant you that," the older man said softly. "The truth is, though, we'll never know—and I for one find that I can live with that fact. I just wish you could." He ended on a bleak, oddly wistful note.

"I do, too, Silas. The fact is, I don't think I can. Not as long as I failed them all so badly."

"You did all you could, and you were only a child. Don't you think I bear guilt, too? If I'd been home, I might have helped. But I wasn't. All my life since I've tried to make up for that failure."

Jared wasn't surprised to hear that, just weary—overwhelmingly, totally weary—as exhausted as if he had walked miles and miles after days without sleep. He wanted to absolve Silas, but he knew it was futile. He had come to believe that absolution from guilt came from within. It came from the self, not from anyone else. No one's assurances had lifted an ounce of his burden—and he'd received many. Why should it be different for Silas?

Warily, they regarded each other across the remnants of their meal, like fighters still standing after a grueling brawl. Jared was the first to recover. He offered Silas a smile of chagrin and a hand up from his chair.

"We do have a way of passing the time, don't we?"

Silas took the cue and responded in kind. The exercise didn't entirely restore accord between them—they'd slashed too deeply for that—but it preserved the illusion each needed in order to pretend that all was well now. By the time Jared saw Silas into his carriage, he could press his hand warmly and promise, "Everything will be fine tomorrow night. Don't worry."

"I'm sure it will be." But when Jared stood back to let him drive away, Silas showed that he had more on his mind than fugitive slaves. He held Jared's eyes with his. "I meant to ask about Tyler. Will you tell him I asked about him? He won't care—"

"Your son cares very much." The words brought Silas's faltering gaze back to his. "He's fine, I promise you, and I'll convey your message."

"It's from his mother, you know."

Jared smiled broadly. "I do know. But that's a topic for another day, don't you think?"

Silas snapped the reins over his prancing bay, but not in time to hide his quick, answering smile from Jared.

Rachel Farmington was bored.

Uncle Nathan had seemed her savior three months ago when he'd appeared in Charleston to bring her home with him. Now he was her jailer. He had horses he wouldn't let her ride and a carriage he wouldn't let her take to town so she could shop. In all her seventeen and three quarters years, she had never been so bored. What good was it to have money if she couldn't spend it? She'd been poor in Charleston, but she hadn't been bored.

She barely knew Uncle Nathan, but from the little she'd seen of him she understood now why her mother had never petitioned him for aid during her lifetime. Even their helter-skelter existence on the fringes of gentility was better than this total dependency upon the whims of a man, merely because he held the purse strings.

Mary Rose, her mother, had sewed dresses for her elite clientele until she was cross-eyed with fatigue, but she'd also had her moments of stolen pleasure. She'd tried to hide her callers from Rachel, and because her mother's attempts at deception were so laughable, Rachel had pretended not to know. But she did know. After her mother's death, she'd even considered going to those men, one by one, and suggesting that they pay for her discretion. Each of the three gentlemen had a plump, well-fed wife and children who lacked nothing.

Looking around at the neat beds of roses, towered over by spires of delphinium, Rachel regretted that Mr. Dalrymple, her mother's solicitor, had been so prompt to summon Uncle Nathan. It might have been fun to see what the men would have done. Unlike her sweet mother, Rachel had a bent for deception and intrigue that was wasted here amid the drone of bees and the chirp of birds.

She had come to the garden in the hope that the gardener's helper was about. She had spied him at work yesterday under the supervision of crotchety old Harold, whose work today, she happened to know, had taken him to the cutting garden.

From the open window of the music room she'd heard a promising exchange of insults between the two. Harold had addressed the young man as Mick, a name he took exception to. Rachel had immediately dubbed him Michael, a more elegant name that sounded tantalizingly foreign. She'd never known a man named Michael. He would be her first.

What she'd like most about her Michael was his seething anger at Harold. It made him look dangerous. Danger attracted her, particularly the kind that came with flashing dark eyes and muscular shoulders.

Rachel had had little experience with men. She didn't remember her father, and except for her mother's callers, men didn't come to dress shops, especially one as tiny as her mother's. She'd had a fantasy that a rich man would come there to outfit his mistress and he'd fallen in love with her. Naturally, after that he'd dismiss his mistress. Rachel had no idea what a mistress did, but she was determined to learn. She intended to make a brilliant marriage and didn't want that union threatened by mistresses.

It never occurred to Rachel that her mother had been a

mistress and that, having lived with her, she had the closest possible knowledge of what a mistress was. Except as a possible source of financial support in the desperate days following Mary Rose's death, Rachel didn't think of those callers as anything but her mother's only recreation in an otherwise dreary life.

Spreading the skirt of her rose dimity dress over the bench in what she hoped made an enticing picture, Rachel swung her feet as she searched in every direction for the gardener's helper. Michael was nowhere to be seen and she was getting tired of posing. Perhaps she would seek out her uncle and implore him to take her to Boston. There had to be more people there than here, even if it was summer. Uncle Nathan told her no one stayed in the city in the heat, but the weather, though humid, was nothing like South Carolina's. Surely there was *something* going on in Boston!

She thought the real reason they were here in godforsaken Lowell was that her uncle was keeping an eye on his son's management of the Shattuck Mill. She knew all about the mill—much more than she wanted to know—because it was Uncle Nathan's chief topic of conversation.

All the way from Charleston he had bent her ear about cotton and the wonders of Yankee ingenuity that had harnessed the power of water and converted it to energy to drive the looms that made cloth. Every dress she wore inspired Uncle Nathan to discourse about the manufacture of that particular type of cloth.

In spite of the rosy picture he first painted for her, she had since learned that the wonderful mills also had serious problems, the Shattuck along with the others. The workers wanted a ten-hour day, particularly the Yankee workers. Uncle Nathan said his son was replacing those people with Irish workers as fast as possible.

The Irish were rather like slaves, she presumed; people so dumb and animal-like that long hours and hard work were nothing to them. But Uncle Nathan had said that, like the slaves, the Irish had their outlets and consolations. Theirs were religion and drink. Not so different perhaps from the pleasures slaves found in religion and music or whatever. Rachel had little personal knowledge of slaves. She had been too poor. She did wonder how anyone could work ten hours at anything, let alone twelve and thirteen. She certainly couldn't.

Once she met her cousin Enoch she understood why Uncle Nathan worried about his management of the mill. She didn't like Enoch. Hearing about him at first, she'd been disappointed to think he was her first cousin and thus not a man she could marry. It had seemed a shame she would have to waste all that opportunity, because, as Nathan's only son, rich Enoch would be easily accessible to her.

Now she was relieved to be safe from him. Enoch was as handsome as Nathan had promised. In fact, Rachel thought he looked rather like a masculine version of herself. Her hair was fairer, partially because of the lemon juice she used to rinse it, but they were both slender and tall. And he looked, as she did, like what her mother called a Farmington.

Rachel was no longer sure that was a compliment. Enoch had a way of looking at her that made her stomach uneasy. That look told her he didn't care that they were first cousins. It scared her, although she was careful not to let him see. Fortunately, he had his own house and was rarely in Belvidere.

Which brought Rachel back to her basic problem: the fact that *no one* was much in Belvidere—including the much-sought Michael. Rachel had now circled the entire estate without seeing anything more interesting than a waddling hedgehog. She would have to give up her pursuit for today.

She collapsed her ruffled parasol and tried one of the French doors opening out from the library, a little-used room near Uncle Nathan's study. After several attempts, the door suddenly yielded, proving that it was not locked but only jammed by the humidity. Rachel stepped inside, thinking how her mother would call this whole place, so near the water, unhealthful. In the South, one did not summer near fresh water, even if it was moving water.

Inside, Rachel felt cooler at first, being out of the sun, but the room was stuffy, with a closed-in smell. While she waited to let her eyes adjust to the dim interior light, she heard voices in the hall outside. They came as distant masculine rumbles, the words indistinct. No longer concerned about seeing clearly, Rachel ran to the door to listen. She recognized George, Nathan's manservant, but the other voice was deeper and more resonant. She tried to picture the man who would possess such a voice, but for once her imagination failed her. She had to see him for herself.

Pressed against the dark-paneled door, she waited for George to pass by on his way to announce Uncle Nathan's visitor, then she slipped soundlessly into the hall. She ran the dark corridor at a furious sprint, intending to stroll from there into the anteroom just around the corner where she expected the man to be. Instead, she barreled into him at full tilt just as he paced, in impatient haste, to the corner to peer after George.

The man's quick reflexes kept them both on their feet. Strong hands clasped her arms, holding her against a chest as hard as a wall. When she was steady on her feet, he set her away from him and smiled down at her. Amusement made small creases at the corners of his eyes.

With the light from the large front windows falling full on his face, his eyes looked black and wonderfully dangerous. Rachel immediately sensed that this man's potential was much greater than Michael's. Michael was little more than a boy, while *this* was a man.

Rachel lowered her thick lashes, one of her best features, and put a hand on her chest, her fingers spread in apparent consternation. She meant to draw his attention to the pert thrust of her heaving young bosom. "Oh, my!" she gasped. "I didn't see you!"

54

Jared had no reason to doubt her, but some of his amusement evaporated when her lashes lifted with practiced artistry to reveal eyes that were amber instead of blue. With her cheeks pinked by exertion, Rachel reminded him of a blushing rose so fully developed that the center was revealed in all its golden glory. Her actions, however—including her awkward attempt at seduction—proved to him that she was still in the bud of womanhood.

He bowed to her gallantly. "I hope I didn't hurt you. It was my fault for pacing about so. Please forgive me."

She dropped into a quick curtsy and smiled, showing the dimple in her left cheek to advantage. "Of course, sir. It was really all my fault, but you see, I *still* don't know my way about here yet."

Before Jared could respond, George announced pompously from the corner, "Mr. Wentworth will see you now."

"You came to see my uncle?" The question was inane, but Rachel could think of no other way to wring an introduction from this man. George, who should have obliged her, stolidly ignored her signals.

"Your uncle? Ah, then you must be Miss Farmington." Jared bowed again and murmured, "A pleasure to meet you, Miss Farmington."

This time Rachel's surprise was genuine. "You know my family, Mr. . . . ?" Her raised brow invited him to supply his name.

"I *am* your family—or rather, a distant part of it. My name is also Wentworth, Jared Wentworth."

Rachel could barely control her glee. Suddenly, Lowell was not such a dull place to be. She had heard enough of the family history to know that Jared Wentworth held himself carefully apart from Nathan and Enoch. There had been a quarrel, about money she supposed. Weren't all quarrels about money?

Her quick assessment of his appearance could not supply perfect assurance that his situation was not

55

financially desperate. His clothes were well cut, but also well worn and not particularly stylish. Perhaps he had come to petition Uncle Nathan for money. If so, and if Uncle Nathan were generous—which she had reason to believe he could be—perhaps then Jared would be welcomed back into the family.

A lot of ifs, she realized, calculating rapidly, but all of them possible and enormously desirable from her perspective. Unlike Enoch, Jared was the one Wentworth who was, as he himself said, a *distant* relative.

As Rachel swept into a deep, graceful curtsy that gave him a nearly unlimited view of her décolletage, she decided then and there that she would marry this man and be the instrument that reunited the broken Wentworth family. Jared extended his hand to help her rise, but just before he touched her, George cleared his throat loudly.

"If you would excuse us, Miss Rachel," he said pointedly, "Mr. Wentworth is waiting."

Rachel stood up, shooting him a look of loathing, which he ignored, and Jared turned politely away from her to follow George down the hall. She glared petulantly into the dim corridor for a few seconds, considering her chances of reaching the library again undetected. She decided that George would expect it of her and decided not to oblige him. Instead, she whirled away down the opposite corridor to the dining room. Another set of French doors opened onto a brick-faced area set about with tables and chairs for outdoor dining.

She moved like a minnow, darting around obstructions to reach the lawn along the back of the house. She made no attempt to conceal her passage from anyone looking outside. Despite her pretense of confusion to Jared, she knew every inch of the place, inside and out. And knew there was no one of importance inside except Uncle Nathan.

She had almost reached her goal when a tall figure rose suddenly in front of her. She skidded to a halt and choked back a cry of surprise. It was Michael. Had she been less single-minded about reaching the study window she would have seen him sooner.

The large pruning shears he held fell to his side as he turned to rake her with his eyes. "So you found me," he said complacently. "I thought you would."

He was laughing at her, Rachel discovered, suddenly as angry at his effrontery as she was at the fact that he was keeping her from her listening post. She drew herself up in an indignant huff that drew his eyes to her bodice. She ignored the insult for the sake of her mission. "Stand aside," she ordered, "or I shall scream."

"Will you be doing that now?" he asked softly, obviously unconvinced. He answered his own question with a shake of his dark head. "I don't think so. Not when you've been going to so much trouble to follow me out here."

"I didn't follow you, you blockhead!"

In her fury, she completely forgot that he had every right to believe what he said. She *had* followed him, but before she had met Jared Wentworth and come face to face with real excitement and real masculine challenge. Now she had a new definition of dark hair and dark eyes. This young man only towered over her because she stood in a small declivity. He was not as tall as Jared, not as deeply muscled and strong. And now that she was close to him she could see that his complexion was sallow and his teeth irregularly spaced.

Her insult and tone of voice made him less cocky, so Rachel pressed her advantage. "If you don't step aside," she said, making her voice as haughty as George's, "I shall report you to Harold—*Mick.*"

Her use of Harold's name for him took her as much by surprise as it did him. She used it almost innocently as a child tosses a knife, knowing that the blade will wound but not how severely.

She saw pain replace the rowdy arrogance in his eyes and, like the child who has inadvertently drawn blood,

57

she was appalled. The only thing she knew to do was flee. She turned and ran.

She had gone only a few steps when Harold appeared. "Is something wrong, miss?" he called out. Looking past her to his young helper, he demanded, "Did he bother you?"

Rachel burst into tears of humiliation and frustration. He had kept her from listening to her uncle and Jared and—worse—he had seen her stalking him all day. And he had laughed! "Yes!" she cried. "He . . . jumped out at me . . . and . . ."

Ashamed of her tears and ashamed of *herself*, she ran for the house before old Harold could ask more of her.

She hated them both!

## Chapter 4

As soon as Jared Wentworth rode out of Carina's sight she looked around to see if anyone had observed their exchange. Seeing no one, she still didn't relax her guard, but quickly bundled up her hair and pulled the disguising cap back into place over her forehead. In the process of returning the grooming aids to their proper places, she inspected each enclosed area for the presence of anyone who might have overheard Mr. Wentworth's orders. There was no one.

Assured of that, Carina considered what to do. She didn't want to give up her masculine identity, not yet anyway. She trusted Jared Wentworth and no other with her secret. If she went to Bagley with his master's message, what would he do? He seemed kind enough, but perhaps he was kind only when he was supervised. Of the Agnes he was to take her to, she knew nothing. She already had a secure place in the stable, doing useful work among people who treated her well. What more could she hope for?

On the other hand, it would not do to disobey Mr. Wentworth's specific orders. Perhaps it was a test of her worthiness. She didn't want to fail Patrick at this point. She had come so far and seemed close to gaining Jared's support against Enoch.

If only she knew how long it would take . . . She had

59

presented her case but won no promise of any kind. Men like the Wentworths didn't like to be pushed; still, surely he could understand that Patrick's need was urgent.

Normally decisive to the point of being impulsive, Carina found herself strangely unable to make a decision. Not to do so became her choice soon enough, and, of course, the hours of the morning were quickly spent. She worked hard though, keeping her distance from all but Ned.

After years of doing housework for her family and working at the mill, it was joy to be outdoors and with animals. At Uncle Ansel's farm she had been in charge of the small stock as soon as she could be trusted to carry out the hen's eggs without dropping them, and she had barely been allowed to care for the horses when they'd been forced away to Lowell. She picked up the ryhthms of barn, stable, and pen as seamlessly as if she'd never left New Hampshire.

As the sun began to edge toward the western horizon Carina dared not postpone going to the house as Jared had instructed. This time a trim maid opened the door. She snickered at Carina's request, stepping back ostentatiously from the barnyard smell of her. "It's *Mr.* Bagley he wants." She giggled behind her hand as she ducked away.

"Oh, it's you."

"Yes, sir," Carina said, speaking in her deepest voice. "Mr. Wentworth said I was to come to you."

Bagley peered around her as if expecting to see Wentworth.

"Before he left, Mr. Bagley."

The little man chuckled at that. "Just Bagley," he corrected, "although the 'sir' is not amiss." He looked her over and gave a resigned sigh, as if he'd expected no better. "I don't have to ask where you've been since then."

Carina smiled. "No, sir. He also said Agnes was to fix me up."

That surprised him into giving her another look, this one sharp.

"I believe he meant her to find work for me," she explained, hurrying to put her own interpretation on the suggestion.

He beckoned her in and shut the door, muttering to himself. Carina made out the occasional phrase, such as "find work for the whole country" and "be the death of me," as she followed his scurrying steps. She had no chance to look into the rooms they passed on the way to the kitchen, where four women were busy fixing dinner.

Assailed by the wonderful cooking smells, Carina overlooked the odors she brought with her, but the women did not. One got up from the table, squawking like the fowl she was preparing.

"Bagley," cried an angular woman, confronting them. "What do you mean, bringing him in here?"

"Mr. Jared said you were to find work for him, so I fetched him here."

Carina realized she was being rude to keep her cap on inside in the presence of ladies. But for her pungent smell, she was certain Agnes would have chastised her, ending her disguise. Instead, the women only wanted her gone, Agnes included. "Oh, for pity's sake," she sputtered, "what am I to do with him?"

"That's for you to figure out, I warrant," Bagley said.

Carina sensed that she had landed in the midst of an ongoing power struggle and that neither would yield, even to common sense, in following their master's directives.

"Perhaps I could go back to the stable—"

Both of them turned on her at once, saying "No!" in unison.

"Just get him out of my kitchen!" the cook yelled, flapping her apron.

The maid, who'd answered Carina's knock, solved the problem by thrusting a bucket of scraps at her. "Take this to the pigs," she said, pointing to the back door.

Carina grabbed her chance to escape, knowing that so many sharp-eyed women would not long overlook her thin disguise. When she brought the bucket back someone had another chore for her, even more onerous. That led to another and another, until she found herself on her hands and knees, scrubbing the rough floorboards of the storeroom next to the kitchen. Carina didn't mind. She had scrubbed floors before and would again.

Once they discovered what a willing worker she was, the women were pleasant to her, and from her place, near but not underfoot, she could listen to the servants talk and learn about the household.

Being useful and beginning to repay her debt to Jared Wentworth, she was content.


Jared's brief exchange with Rachel Farmington in the anteroom had put him in the best possible frame of mind for his interview with Nathan Wentworth. He could almost feel sorry for his uncle, knowing that the minx would lead him a merry chase. By appearance, she was Farmington through and through, but Jared saw a spirit in her that Nathan's wife, Lucy, had never had. Either that, or the years of living with Nathan had caused it to fade.

Nathan's appearance added to Jared's pleasure. He had not seen him in six years, and then only in passing. Face to face like this, he could see that the years had not been kind to Uncle Nathan. His father had carried the Wentworth stamp, as Jared did, while Nathan had never been as tall or as comely. With age, and perhaps ill health, he had shrunk and grown stooped, both conditions emphasizing the equine shape of his jaw and forehead.

He stood to greet Jared from behind the protective bulk of a massive mahogany desk, his hand extended before him in a cautious gesture of welcome. When Jared did not move to take it, Nathan motioned him to a chair and prepared to reseat himself.

"I prefer to stand."

Jared's curt refusal told Nathan his uncle that this was no attempt of reconciliation. He sat back down, heavily, the squeak of his chair nearly drowning out his faint, sighed response. "As you wish."

"Although we live in the same community," Jared began, "I try very hard not to notice that fact."

He had no idea where his words were coming from—or where they were going. He had not planned his approach, had not prepared for this encounter. Already, he was afraid his coming was a terrible mistake. What he'd said wasn't even true. He paid much attention to what went on at the Shattuck Mill and to everything the Wentworths did, although Nathan could not know that.

"So do I," his uncle said, lying just as glibly.

Jared didn't notice that Nathan had spoken; he was busy framing his next statement. "In spite of that, I find I can't overlook a situation that's come to my attention."

Now that he had Nathan's rapt attention, he knew what to say. It was just crazy enough to work, he realized, because it played on his adversary's deepest fear—and on his ignorance.

"You know about the unrest among the mill workers, of course, but it's worse than you believe. Much worse."

Nathan's eyes narrowed to slits. "What are you hinting at?"

Jared shook his head. "Not hinting, saying outright. Strike, Nathan. That's the word I'm using."

His uncle laughed uneasily. "Then you're the only one using it. Of all the problems we *do* have, you've just come up empty, Jared. The ten-hour movement is dead. We have plenty of new workers to replace those who are unhappy with their hours."

"Irish workers?"

"Of course they're Irish workers," Nathan snapped. "So what?"

Jared gave him a slow, superior smile. "But it's the

Irish who are talking strike now."

"Impossible!"

"Is it? How deep are your roots in the Irish community, Nathan?"

"What are you getting at?"

"The truth, my dear uncle. You rely on Enoch to keep you informed—"

"I do not. I have other sources that are completely independent of Enoch."

Nathan had just confirmed what Jared suspected, that his uncle distrusted his son as much as he did. The fact that only Nathan, of all the mill owners, chose to live in Lowell, close to the mill, proved that he felt the need to remain at hand. He might pretend to the world that it was Enoch he wanted to be near, but Jared knew it was the mill he protected, and his financial stake there.

"How many of those sources are Irish?" he asked, sure he knew the answer.

"Your point, please?" Nathan demanded, his refusal to answer providing all the answer Jared needed.

"You have an old man named O'Rourke working for you," Jared said. "He's becoming a rallying point for the Irish."

"Conn O'Rourke?" In his surprise, Nathan supplied the name Jared didn't know.

"He needs to work outside or he'll die."

"If he's that bad, he'll die anyway," Nathan countered.

"Do you really think it doesn't matter to a man how soon he dies? Or to his family?" Jared followed his advantage as his uncle seemed to shrink visibly in his chair. "Last year mill owners in Amesbury and Salisbury used Irish immigrants as strike breakers. If the Irish pull together and oppose you, who are you going to get to work your shifts? And how will the other mill owners feel about you if trouble starts at Shattuck?"

"*If!*" Nathan shouted, suddenly roused from the stupor Jared had lulled him into. "You come in here with all these ifs, to . . . what? Threaten me? Scare me?"

"Warn you. Conn O'Rourke has been treated badly and all the Irish workers know it. He's a man of considerable stature in their community. He was given yard work, then it was yanked back because he wouldn't turn his daughter over to Enoch. The man's son, a young lad named Patrick, approached Enoch to plead for his father. Your son's guards beat him up and had him arrested."

"He attacked Enoch—"

"Who said so? Enoch? His bodyguards? What did the other witnesses say?"

Nathan's mouth opened and closed soundlessly.

Jared was sure of these facts because, after leaving Silas, he had checked out Carina's story. "Did Enoch tell you he's pressing Constable Meggers to have the boy sent to the workhouse?"

"And I suppose you're telling me all this out of the goodness of your heart," Nathan sneered.

"You could say that."

"I won't, and I don't buy your story."

Here was the resistance Jared had expected. He kept his level gaze on Nathan. "Fine," he said. "I thought as much." He turned abruptly toward the door.

"Wait!"

Nathan was on his feet, the cry wrung from his soul. As his nephew turned to look at him inquiringly, he forced himself to remain calm. Jared had come to him for the first time ever, and no matter what had moved him to do so, Nathan would do anything to keep their dialogue going.

Seeing Jared had been a shock; others had followed during their conversation. Jared looked like Philip brought to life again. Though he was younger than Philip had been at his death, his own tragedies had marked him, erasing some of the differences. He lived on the edge of respectability, but somehow his carousing and gambling at that den of iniquity on the Tyngsborough road had not tainted the decency at his core. In spite of everything he had done, in spite of the accusations he had leveled, Jared was still the sum of the two people Nathan had loved the most, his brother and Felicity.

If Jared had come to rail at him, so be it. But he had come. Nathan would take what he could get.

"How do you know all this?" he asked. "And why bring it to me?"

Jared watched his uncle sit precipitously, noting the quaver in his voice. "Because you're the only one who can control Enoch."

"But why do you care? I can't believe you'd grieve to see the Shattuck fail."

Since altruism was foreign to Nathan, Jared found an answer he could accept. "I believe you told Silas you put aside the fair valuation of half the business you shared with my father for me. Perhaps I'm protecting my own interests."

"But you've never touched that money."

"Is it still there?"

"Of course it is, producing interest every year, I might add."

Jared shrugged. "Then you can understand my motive."

Nathan should have been disappointed to learn that Jared wasn't indifferent to the fortune accumulating in his name. In fact, it made his nephew human. Nathan didn't believe in saints and wouldn't have wanted one near him.

"What do you want from me in exchange for this information?" he asked with barely suppressed excitement.

"I want the boy released, with all the charges against him dropped, and I want the old man given safe, healthy work—with no reprisals against anyone."

"And the girl?"

Jarred by the question, Jared realized he had underestimated Nathan—and made a mistake in mentioning

66

Carina. "She's safe already. Tell Enoch to confine himself to whores from now on."

"That's it?"

Needing to light on another request, Jared smiled, adding, "And I'd like your permission to call on your lovely niece. Rachel? Isn't that her name? Your man was a bit reluctant to introduce us. It's fortunate for me that the lady herself was not so backward."

He couldn't immediately gauge the effect his reference to Rachel Farmington had on his uncle, noted only that Nathan wasn't indifferent to his niece or unaware of her boldness. While his uncle considered his answer, Jared gave him more to think about. "I give you my solemn word, Uncle, that I'll hold young Rachel's honor with as much care as Enoch displays toward those innocents within his grasp."

With that, Jared took his leave, pleased with himself on two counts. He had accomplished his goals: had set his uncle as watchdog on Enoch and had, in effect, taken Rachel Farmington as hostage to guarantee Enoch's good behavior. He could scarcely ask for better results.

He strode down the hall to the door, looking neither to left nor right, his momentary satisfaction diminishing with every step he took. Now that he was quit of Nathan, a primitive need to lash out rose within him like a noxious flood of bile. Silas would have been proud of his self-control, but Jared was not.

To him, it was one more stain on his conscience. He had again been within reach of Nathan, and he had again failed to take his uncle's life. He had won only a small skirmish, not the war. That battle was what he ached for, and he feared he might never get to fight it.

Although he was filled with self-loathing, Jared didn't take out his anger on the stable lad who tried to hold Infidel for him. Picking up on his master's unsettled feelings, the horse was more difficult than usual, so Jared waved the boy away, wondering if even the sprite who waited for him at home would be able to work her magic on Infidel in this mood. The great beast's temper suited him, however, and he let the stallion take the road at a gallop.

They had not gone far when Infidel let him know that all was not well by tossing his head and prancing sideways at the fork of the road to the bridge across the Concord River. Jared reined him in sharply and discovered the cause. In spite of his earlier fury, he found himself laughing as Rachel struggled to keep her seat on a skittish mare by the side of the road.

"Your horse displays far more sense than you do, Miss Farmington," he said, taking the reins from her grip. Although his move brought Infidel close, the mare quieted. "Are you in the habit of waiting by the road for strange men?"

"You're not strange," she answered pertly. "You said yourself that you're family. I thought it only proper that we should meet again."

"Your sense of propriety leaves me breathless, my dear. Shall I help you down so we can get on with our acquaintance?"

"Certainly not," Rachel snapped. She had changed into riding clothes in order to maintain the pose that she only happened to be riding this way. That she hadn't carried out the pretense added piquancy to the moment. Still, her temper flared at his audacity, and her hand itched to strike him with her crop.

As if he read her mind, Jared glanced pointedly at her whip. "Don't even think of it," he warned in a tone so frosty it could not possibly have caused the heat that flashed through her tense body. Rachel decided it was another manifestation of her temper.

The day had not gone well for her on the whole, what with the young gardener at first unavailable and then, when she no longer wanted to see him, popping up from behind a bush. And the day wasn't over yet. She knew her uncle would hear about this ride and restrict her more sharply in the future as punishment.

68

Meeting Jared Wentworth was the first bright spot in her life since she had come North. He was certainly an outcast of some kind, but in a place where society barely existed, could that be so terrible? She would plead ignorance of his status and deny that she'd ever heard of him before.

She *had* heard, of course, but what she'd heard hadn't prepared her for Jared's reality. Enoch painted him as a skulking, dark monster and Uncle Nathan called him dissolute. She understood why. Enoch was jealous, Uncle Nathan disappointed.

But today he had come. Perhaps this was a signal that something was changing in the family. More than anything, Rachel regretted being prevented from overhearing their conversation. For that, if not for his boldness, Michael—or whatever his name was—deserved to lose his job.

"Then control your horse," she said, matching his icy tone.

To her dismay, he laughed again. Handing back her reins, he maneuvered the stallion behind her nervous mare. "I can do better than that, you impudent child. I can control you."

So saying, he slapped her mount and set her off, unwilling on the road back to Belvidere. Her hat nearly fell from its rakish perch as she lurched to keep her seat. Holding hat and reins for dear life, she looked back to see him grinning. He bowed, then rode away without a backward glance to see that she didn't fall off and hurt herself.

Laying the crop to the confused mare, Rachel vented her frustration in a ragged run back to the stables. There, she slid to the ground unaided and threw the reins to the boy who came running to serve her. When she turned on him, crop in her raised hand, he ground to a stop. The winded mare was going nowhere. He let her pass, certain she didn't even see him. He felt lucky.

Propelled by her temper, Rachel didn't stop until she

reached her room. There she met her image in the cheval glass and broke into a laugh as hearty and lusty as Jared Wentworth's.

She looked wild—and beautiful. Her golden hair spilled over the shoulders of her robin's-egg blue riding jacket and every inch of her face glowed. She had finally met a man worthy of her fire and passion. Winning him would not be easy, but oh, the chase they would have!

Turning in an exultant circle, Rachel spun her hat across the room to the bed, then followed to fall on it, still laughing.

# Chapter 5

Jared's second encounter with Rachel Farmington left him with a bad taste in his mouth. Her blatant pursuit gave him the excuse he needed to justify using her as a pawn in his game with Nathan, but he liked her little better than he liked himself.

Her loveliness was too . . . obvious. She was both young and foolish, as only the indulged can be. And she played at a woman's game that would never touch her heart. He found himself pitying the man who chose to take her on.

He knew it would not be himself. He was too impatient to get home and see how Carina O'Rourke had fared in his absence. After a dose of Nathan and Rachel, he needed to look upon the sweet gravity in Carina's face and do something, say something—anything—to make her smile as she had this morning.

He squeezed his legs around Infidel's sides, urging him forward, teased by the image of Carina waiting for him. He didn't think of her clothing, but of her hair, that dark cloud of silk around her face. Perhaps she would sup with him. He wasn't hungry, but he could serve her and watch her dainty mouth . . .

So clear was his picture that he was torn between anger and puzzlement when he strode into his home and did not see Carina. He shot an accusing look at Bagley and demanded, "Well? Where is she?"

"Where is who, sir?" Bagley did not always address his master with deference, since he alone remained of Jared's childhood household, but in the company of others he was appropriately formal. The choice was his own, not Jared's.

"The girl," Jared barked. "From the stable." He watched Bagley's eyes slip away from his and followed his glance to Agnes. She looked utterly blank. "I sent her to you. Do you mean to tell me . . ."

Then he thought of her independence and strode to the door. "Perhaps she never came . . ." She liked the stable; perhaps he had missed seeing her there.

"Mr. Jared," Bagley called out, stopping him. "You mean the lad from the stables?"

"The *lad* is a girl, Bagley. I sent her here."

Agnes and Bagley seemed to shrink within their skins as his glare raked over them. The nervous dart of their eyes toward the kitchen told him the story. Without a word to them he started forward, pulling them behind him by the force of his momentum. His progress into the kitchen scattered maids and cooks, who quickly fell silent at his unheard-of appearance there.

When Jared still didn't find Carina he turned on Bagley. The little man rushed forward to put himself between his master and the storeroom door. Giving him no chance to speak, Jared motioned him aside.

Carina was nearly done with the floor. A good job it was too, she thought, surveying it with pride. She had moved the stores around to get at each section and then replace them as the wood dried sufficiently.

When she saw Jared, followed by Bagley and Agnes, she stood up to face them but spoke only to Jared. "This is no one's fault but mine. I wanted to work and repay you for your kindness."

"You seek to repay my kindness by disobeying my explicit request?"

The only answer she could give—that it seemed best—

she would not say to him before his household, so she said nothing. She didn't, however, lower her eyes with false meekness.

After a telling silence passed, Jared said, "Agnes, please see to my guest's comfort. I suggest some water for bathing and some decent clothing."

Agnes bustled past him and took the scrub brush from Carina's hand. She didn't touch the girl, merely herded her before her skirts. On the way past the maids, who, curious, had poked their heads into the doorway, she gave the scrub brush to one of them. The woman's mouth moved to protest, but she made no sound.

Jared's voice stopped the determined woman just inside the kitchen. "Oh, Agnes . . ."

"Yes, sir?"

"I want that cap burned."


"Mr. Wentworth said I was not to put my hair up again."

It was the first time Carina had spoken during the long and sometimes humiliating process she had been subjected to at Jared's request. She was not overly modest, but there was a difference between living under crowded conditions with one's family and being bathed and dressed by disapproving strangers.

Carina got through the ordeal by concentrating on the unbelievable luxury of bath water just for her. She remembered baths at Uncle Ansel's, when she and Patrick, jammed together in the tin tub, had played with wood-shaving "boats" until the water was cold and their fingers and toes were shriveled. Margaret had been a baby then. She remembered few baths since coming to Lowell, for there it was hard enough to carry essential water up to the third floor.

Agnes, assisted first by plump, arthritic Nellie, then by Trudy, who was little older than Carina, saw that Patrick's old clothes were carried away and feminine

73

apparel found. Alone with Agnes and Trudy, Carina wished the soft-eyed Nellie would return, but when she did, it was only to drop off a dress. Agnes sighed over the garment and announced that it would have to do.

It was a clear blue, like summer's sky, and Carina couldn't be sure she hadn't stopped them from putting up her newly-washed hair just so she could wear the dress sooner. Trudy stopped brushing her hair abruptly and turned to Agnes. "Mum?"

Carina looked from one to the other and smiled. "Of course," she said, surprised she hadn't seen the resemblance at once. "You're mother and daughter. How wonderful!"

They exchanged identical looks of disbelief, and then Agnes said, "Better you took his advice earlier, before you made trouble for us all."

Since she'd already taken the blame upon herself, Carina fell silent, wishing she had never spoken at all. But no amount of disapproval could make her dislike the dress. She couldn't keep her fingers from running over the still-crisp cloth. She knew the products of the mills well enough to know it was inexpensive material. The wonder of the garment, for her, was that it was still new, not faded and limp from use.

She looked up from the skirt to find Trudy assessing her with a wry smile. "Gwen won't like the way she looks in it," she said to her mother.

Hurt in spite of herself, Carina looked down quickly, wondering what was amiss. It didn't seem possible anything so lovely would not enhance her appearance.

Although Agnes laughed, her eyes seemed to approve of what she saw. "No, but then it's not Gwen who needs to like it, is it?" She tugged at the bodice in a futile attempt to discover another half-inch to give to the tightly stretched cloth there.

Suddenly, Carina understood their meaning and flushed. Since she had developed her woman's shape, her generous breasts had been a source of embarrassment.

74

Her father was always hissing at her to "cover" herself, and men were always staring at her there. Delight in the pretty dress had made her forget to hold herself modestly.

"Even bound as she was," Trudy said, "it's hard to believe no one noticed."

"Ah, but *someone* did," Agnes reminded her.

Neither of them saw that Carina wanted to melt into the floor, especially when they continued congratulating themselves on a job well done. "He'll be pleased, I warrant."

"Well then, come along, miss," Agnes said, addressing Carina directly at last. "He'll be waiting."

Following Trudy and Agnes down the steep back stairs was harder than going to Enoch Wentworth's house. Carina thought her borrowed shoes were elegant, even with the toes stuffed to fill them out, but after years of pattens and cloth slippers, she had to concentrate on placing each foot carefully on the step. Then too, the gown was long and had to be held up so she didn't trip over it. Without so many physical difficulties, however, Carina might have bolted for the door, so great was her dread of seeing Jared Wentworth again.

Bagley met them at the bottom of the stairs and took her over. Once again she was torn. The women hadn't been warm, but they were at least women and she was loath to lose their dubious protection.

She needn't have worried. Bagley led her to a small sitting room, where a table had been set for one. The youngest maid served her the most wonderful meal she'd had in years: garden peas, small roasted potatoes, and lamb—not mutton. Her joy in the food was diminished by two things, a stomach too full of butterflies to hold much food and the poisonous looks she got from the maid at every turn.

When Carina had done her best, Bagley returned to ask, "Do you not care for the food, miss?"

After she assured him that it was excellent, only too

generous, he stepped to the door and said, "Gwen, you may clear now."

Carina's sympathy was immediate. She touched Gwen's hand as she reached out to take her plate, "I'm sorry you had to give up your lovely dress," she said. "I'll take very good care of it for you, I promise."

Startled at being touched, Gwen snatched back her hand, knocking over a glass. The spill was slight, but when Carina tried to help clean it up, Gwen gave a strangled cry and ran from the room.

Carina didn't know what to do. She had never been waited on before. Mr. Wentworth called her a guest, but surely no guest was put into a room all alone and left there. Although her family had been poor, occasionally they had had guests who always ate with them. Dennis Boynton, for example, was not only given the best of their food when he came to spend the evening with her father, he was also—quite literally—company for them, someone to talk to.

But Jared had not come to eat with her. Did that mean she wasn't really a guest? Should she perhaps pack up the remains of her meal and take it to the kitchen? Or did rich people treat their guests differently?

She wanted to help Gwen, but she was afraid to do something else wrong. Jared had been angry that she hadn't followed his instructions. Another mistake and he might decide not to help Patrick.

She compromised. She stacked the dishes into a neat pile that would be easy for Gwen to carry, but didn't leave the room. In time, when no one came, she left the table for a more comfortable chair. The light grew dim as darkness fell, and it was a struggle to remain awake. Her day had been long and wearing. She tried to sit the way her mother had taught her, amusing herself as long as the light lasted by cataloguing the contents of the room. Someday she would tell Margaret about the candle sconces and the framed miniatures on the wall.

In the meantime, her head grew heavy upon her

shoulders and keeping her dress smooth lost its urgency. She slid down in the chair and rested her head against the high back. Just for a moment, she promised herself.

She woke gradually, aware of discomfort, strange surroundings, and something else. The eerie feeling of being watched.

Jared Wentworth stood just inside the door, peering at her through the gloom. "So this is where they put you."

Carina's thoughts skittered like the cotton lint that danced around the feet of every mill worker. Her mouth was dry. Had she been sleeping with it open? Although the evening was mild, Wentworth wore black, filling the doorway with his bulk.

Her father's words came to her, a command she had disobeyed. "You'll make no bargain with the devil." But she had, and from the look of him he had come to collect.

"They fed you well?"

She nodded, unable to work her tongue. He brought a sense of the night to the room, along with the scent of horse and leather. Carina realized that he had been out riding. Concern for him moved in her breast. "Have you eaten?"

"What I wanted." Jared didn't tell her his meal had been mostly liquid. He wasn't drunk, but he had taken liberal draughts from his flask of whiskey. Even now he felt the heat of it stirring his blood.

She was so calm, sitting there as though she had no more emotion than the footstool, while he, the one supposedly in control, had needed liquid courage even to approach the door. But he knew her emotions were strong. Love for her brother had sent her here, and her resistance to Enoch had brought her to his attention. Would she scream at him and fight if he approached her? He didn't think so, and yet she had gone to Enoch first, then changed her mind. Didn't that mean she could change her mind again?

He felt such tenderness for her, and still he was afraid. Afraid for her and for himself. Tenderness alone wasn't

77

enough. He had felt that in abundance, along with love, for Melissa. Some men would say Melissa had failed him, but he took the blame upon himself. He had not been able to give her the pleasure she deserved, not ever. Since then he had taken Tyler's light-hearted advice: stay away from virgins. But all women started as virgins, so surely their differing paths were more a matter of personal tendencies than merely experience.

Jared wished he could laugh at himself. He had not answered the unanswerable in his evening ramble on Infidel. He had told himself repeatedly to leave Carina O'Rourke in peace. She did not deserve the injustice he would do her.

He moved closer and lit a lamp to brighten the room. "You must be tired," he said, taking the chair opposite hers. He had placed the lamp to show her to himself, never thinking that he was also exposing his face.

Seeing the lines of weariness etched into it, Carina instantly became sympathetic. "No more than you, sir, and I have been dozing."

"Jared," he said. "I would have you call me Jared."

Carina smiled and quickly looked down at her hands. He couldn't know that he had been more Jared than sir in her mind, but even with his permission she didn't dare say it out loud.

"Carina."

She looked up.

"It's a lovely name."

"I think so. It was my mother's choice. She had the name long before she had me, she said. It's the name of a constellation." Embarrassed, Carina ducked her head and murmured, "But you probably know all that."

"I don't. What constellation?"

"It's in the south. My father told me its name means keel in Latin. When I was small I picked out a star I thought was in it, but it wasn't. I was wrong."

"How does your father know Latin? From the Mass?"

"Mostly, but he doesn't know enough. When he was a

78

young man in Ireland, he aspired to be a priest. When the church refused him, he came here."

"With your mother?"

"My mother lived in New Hampshire. He met her on his way to find work in Lowell the first time." At his questioning look, she explained about her family's move.

"So that's why you don't sound Irish. You take after your mother."

Carina was pleased, not because she scorned her Irish heritage but because she cherished her mother's memory. "I try to."

"And your mother?" Jared asked, trying to understand everything that had sent her to him. "Is she no more anxious about your whereabouts than your father?"

"She's been dead since Kevin's birth. Seven years."

He felt a shift in the pain that never left him. "Ah, yes," he sighed. "A perilous business, that."

"She died of the fever, cholera; not from childbirth. It came hard upon the heels of her confinement," Carina said.

It was a strange conversation they were having, she thought. She had not told anyone so much about herself in years. In Chapel Hill everyone knew the O'Rourkes and their story. Some understood and some did not. With Jared she couldn't tell what he thought. He seemed to be a man of feelings rather than intellect. It made him very different from the only men she knew, her father and Dennis Boynton.

Her father's only emotion was bitter disappointment. Beyond that, he was all theory and ideas. He and Dennis could talk for hours, analyzing the nature of evil and the influence of the devil. They mentioned God, goodness and love only in passing. Carina was sure they considered those forces not only weak but also boring. The devil and hell interested them—no, *fascinated* them.

She had found their talk tiresome, as much for its repetitiveness as for the subject matter. Evil, to her, was the lack of love and goodness—nothing more, nothing less. Once, in order to make herself attractive to her future husband, she had offered her opinion to them. They had been sharply divided on some matter at that point, yet as soon as she'd spoken they had closed ranks against her. Dennis had been particularly scathing in his remarks, and later her father had told her she had shamed him. For a while after that, Conn had worried that Dennis would break off the agreement to marry Carina. No man, he told her, wanted a brazen woman.

Except that her father cared so much for Dennis, Carina would have felt relieved to be free of that promise. Dennis never spoke to her, and he watched her only when she was about her endless chores. She was sure he wanted her only as a beast of burden, mute and docile, but that was not what she wanted. Her mother had not been like that. She had sung at her chores and made up riddles and games to play with her children. Papa had forgotten her in his bitter loneliness since her death, but Carina had not. Loneliness made her cling to every shred of memory that reminded her of being loved.

"You were far away from here," Jared said, cutting into her thoughts.

Carina caught a look in his eyes that pleased her, and she smiled. "Not so far away, sir."

He shook his head. "Not so far away, *Jared*," he prompted.

She laughed and said his name.

He thought he had never heard sweeter sounds. Her laugh was low and musical, his name a whisper of breath. Because he liked it so well, he got to his feet abruptly and paced away.

Confused by his withdrawal when she had only done what he asked, Carina looked down at her tightly clasped hands. Undoubtedly, her father was right about everything. She was too forward. Just because Jared was kind and interested enough in her to draw her out in conversation, that didn't mean she could please him.

She knew what he wanted of her, and it was no less than what his cousin had wanted. Unlike Enoch, Jared would be gentle and pleasing to her, but knowing that he found her inadequate would cut her more deeply than physical ill-use.

Helpless even to control her own eyes, she followed every move he made. If Papa was right about Jared, if he was the devil, she was as bad as Dennis and Conn, for he fascinated her. Even the room had taken on a measure of his appeal. The cabinet where he stood to pour a drink for himself was now *his*. Alone, she had hardly noticed it.

Jared drank until he felt the fiery liquid hit his stomach; then he paused. He was stoking fire with fire— or was he trying to make himself incapable? His need was too great for drink to stop him; not tonight. All it could do, he decided, was make him insensitive, and he didn't want that.

He put down the glass and turned to face her. "Carina, you should not have come here. You think me a good man, but I'm not."

His hoarse, emotion-clogged voice gave Carina another message. The way he looked at her, his rigid stance, and the harsh rasp of his speech worked on her like a tonic, sweeping away confusion.

"I had nowhere else to go. And as for what I think of you, I think you are a man much like any other. I don't think in terms of good and evil. There are people I like and people I don't like. You are one of the first group."

Her dignity and simplicity were worthy of a queen, but he responded only to the appeal of her warm voice and to her soft expression. He tried to tell himself he'd warned her and given her a chance to flee, but he knew he hadn't. To be fair, he would have to tell her he'd already arranged for her brother's release, yet even that might not free her. She would feel bound by gratitude.

A bargain was a bargain, even when the terms were not made explicit. She had asked; he had answered. He had met her need, now she would meet his.

"I wish I could let you go."

Carina shook her head slightly. More composed than he, she waited.

Still he didn't move. "I will not make you my wife, nor will I keep you long," he said, strangely compelled to keep on in this vein. "What will you do then?"

"I will . . . do the best I can."

He didn't think himself lovable, so he had no fear for her heart, only for her honor and chastity—both commodities that in his world carried a price. Although she was as lovely as young heiresses should be and seldom are, he knew he could well afford her cost to him. Telling himself he would be generous when the time came to pay up, he held out his hand to her.

After several seconds' pause, during which she seemed to measure him against some standard he couldn't imagine, Carina put her hand in his. It was small, cool, and firm. When he drew her up, she followed.

Jared Wentworth had no taste for human sacrifice, but not even her air of determination could diminish the fire of his need for her.

# *Chapter 6*

From the moment Carina felt the warm clasp of Jared's hand, she gave the whole of her being into his care. She could not have said why. She didn't hold herself cheap, nor was she overawed by his fine home. It simply happened and she accepted it.

He walked beside her up a broad staircase lit by a lamp that was set on a table in the niche where the stairs turned. Each wonder—the stairs, the roomlike turning, the lamps left to burn for no reason—registered upon Carina as if it were part of a dream. Only Jared Wentworth, his hand holding hers, was real.

He took her to a room smaller than her family's that was just for him. A chest, a small table, a straight-backed chair, and a bed completed the furnishings. Carina saw none of it. She kept her eyes on Jared's masklike countenance. From the time he had come to stand in front of her, his face had lost all expressiveness. Only his eyes were alive, like smoldering nuggets of coal burning in an empty grate.

Here again stood a glowing lamp, and this time Carina wanted to extinguish it, for it seemed to make the bed grow in size to fill the room as soon as he let go of her hand. As if he understood her need, he lowered the flame until, for Carina, the glow was better than darkness. In the dark she would have been afraid.

She stood where he left her, unsure what she should do. It occurred to her that once again her body was to be touched and tended by alien hands, yet this time she could not seem to distance herself from that fact. Her inner self, instead of withdrawing, had expanded and was pressing against her skin, making it sensitive. She could feel Jared, although he wasn't touching her anywhere.

"Your face is all eyes, little one." As before, he took her chin, framed it with thumb and forefinger to tip her face up to his. "You have such beautiful eyes."

His words, however true, rang hollow in his own ears. How must they sound to her? Did he really think soft phrases would lessen the violation? He didn't, but he couldn't stop. Not the words of praise. Not the violation.

Her hair was a night-curtain he wanted to draw tight around him. He filled his hands with its fragrant length, as clumsy and greedy now as a boy half his age. He meant to move slowly, but when her scent filled his head he went a little crazy. His arms slid around her shoulders, bringing her flush against his body, and he bent to put his face into her neck, where the scent of her lived, unwittingly arching her back. She didn't protest or respond, merely accommodated him the way a reed bends before the wind, bowing to his force in order not to be broken.

The sound of his own breathing was so loud and harsh that he pulled back in an effort to gain control. She was not without spirit, he reminded himself. She would scream . . . she *should* scream.

He took her shoulders and held her away from his importunate body. The feel of the stiff, poor cotton under his hands shamed him. She deserved better—and would have it, he vowed.

"Let me help you with the dress." To offset the rasp of his voice, he smiled and turned her gently. "I'm a poor lady's maid, I fear, but so is this a poor dress. That makes us a match."

Carina stood, passive as a child, while Jared undid the

84

dress and drew it from her shoulders. He didn't caress her, but even in her turmoil she felt the difference between his gentle uncertainty and the deft indifference of the women who had dressed her. It came to her as caring. He lifted her hands, one at a time, to free her sleeves, then let the dress fall.

She stood without a petticoat, in plain white underwear and stockings that were remarkably like the masculine attire she had worn as disguise. These clothes were lighter, flimsier, but he marveled that anyone had ever been fooled. Her breasts were round and high, her hips a sweet flare from the narrow span of her waist.

Rather than fall upon her again, he lifted her by her waist and set her on the edge of the bed. Her shoes fell off as soon as she left her feet. Surprised, he picked one up and found the stuffed toes. When he took her foot onto his thigh to rub her toes, he discovered a fold of stocking material wadded under them. It angered him, but he tried not to show her, aware that she wouldn't understand the true cause of his displeasure. He used the emotion to make short work of her stockings, then turned away to cast off his own clothing.

He heard the bed give behind him and, half-in and half-out of his shirt, spun about to see her gathering up the stockings and dress. He grabbed her arm, thinking she meant to escape. "No!"

She twisted away, and rather than hurt her, he let go to get between her and the door. But she only smoothed the clothes into a neat fold and put them on the chair. Before he could be unmanned by the relief that swept over him, he gathered her in his arms and carried her back to the bed, following her down, his head on her breast.

Her heart raced under the softness pillowing his cheek. He turned his face to nuzzle at her breast, and for the first time she lifted her hands to touch him.

"I thought you were running away."

"No."

Jared reared up to look at her, wanting desperately to

find more than simple denial in her expression. She didn't meet his gaze, but looked at what she was doing, helping him out of his shirt. The simple act didn't require the concentration he saw in her face and his old doubts and fears rose to assail him all over again. He was hairy, disgustingly so, Melissa had thought.

"Do you mind?"

Carina drew back her hands, her eyes wide with alarm. If she could have, she would have rolled away, but his weight held her in place.

"I'm sorry," she whispered. Once again she had been forward.

"No, no, Carina." With one hand he turned her face back to him. He shrugged the shirt from his arm, watching her expression. He saw curiosity and wonder, even—incredibly—shame, but no disgust. He took her hand and placed it on his forearm. "I am not so finely made as you. I thought you might mind."

She glanced to his face, assuring herself that she heard aright. "You are most . . . manly." She had not thought to touch him like this. Even she wasn't that bold. She'd been helping with his clothes, a service she thought appropriate. His arm had a coating of dark hair that felt silky to her fingertips. It made her want to investigate the intriguing pattern of hair at his chest.

Her hesitant touch and the direction of her gaze sent a fierce shaft of pleasure through Jared's body. He covered her mouth with his, tasting her surprise and hesitation. He kissed her over and over, gently increasing the pressure of his lips until he couldn't bear not to linger, then settled himself beside her and turned her into his arms so she could feel in control. Gradually he took that control back as her mouth softened and some of the tension in her limbs ebbed away.

Carina had not thought of this, of kissing, or of the feelings rising in her. Too wary to give in to them, she fought the melting sensations, the comfort of his arms around her. He would still mate with her and she had to be ready. But how?

Jared moved over her. With one hand he held her head, his fingers tangled in the web of her hair, his weight on that forearm so he could touch her body. He stroked from her shoulder to her hip, following the curved contours, learning her shape and softness under the thin cotton covering. He even separated the chemise at her waist and lifted it to skim over her ribs. At the same time he deepened his kiss with slow, penetrating movements of his tongue.

Shocked and soothed at the same time, Carina was helpless. Her breath came in gasps that he took into his mouth. Another sweep of his hand bared her breast and she stiffened in protest. The action lifted her breast so it fit into his hand. She made a small, broken sound at the feeling of heat, and something else, that burst over her.

She never got a chance to discover what it was. He pulled her up and took off her chemise, skimming down the drawers and his own trousers. It was happening faster and faster. Sensation piled on sensation at a dizzying pace. His mouth on her breast . . . was that right? She lashed her head, trying to get free. There would be pain, not this heat, not this strangling need to escape. But from what? The need was hers; it rose, choking her, holding her for his touch.

He wanted to look at her. She was lovely . . . lovely. Her flesh was soft and giving, sweetly scented and sensual. He felt her twist and knew her confusion. His own was nearly as great. With no art at all beyond her simple beauty, she had taken control of his mind.

Leaning up over her, he made a place for himself between her knees and bent to her breasts. He poured praise over her like honey, licking it up as he went. When he touched between her thighs to prepare her, she opened her eyes and cried out softly.

"Carina, Carina, it's all right."

His image swam before her, shadowed, his dark hair falling over her brow.

"See me, Carina. It's Jared." With her eyes glazed and unseeing, he pressed into her. He fought for control of his own body. She was hot and yielding. Overcome by need, he thrust into her deeply, bursting through her natural resistance into the overwhelming heat of her body.

Paralyzed, knowing that the slightest movement would trip him into completion, Jared held himself rigidly, utterly still. Carina didn't even breathe. She had no idea of the reason for this cessation beyond her own adjustment to his invasion. She had felt a hot tearing sensation, something like pain, but so briefly it barely impinged on her overloaded senses.

She couldn't assimilate half of what she felt. There was his weight against her—not his full weight, she knew from the tension of his arms; but weight nonetheless. She felt it as heat and pressure—tension that communicated itself nerve to nerve, awakening tensions in her. Tears slid from her eyes—tears she couldn't control or understand.

Then the poised moment shattered, splintering into motion, sensation and color. He moved, a scant stirring that called to life something deep inside her that was both herself and part of him. He surged against her once, then again.

Resistance was impossible, undesirable. Slowly, deeply, he moved and began taking on the rhythm of her need, of the blood pounding in her veins. She clutched at him, frightened and exhilarated. Her craving was as relentless as the machinery that drove the looms or the force that chased water over the falls. She gave herself up to it, letting it spin her around and drop her over the cataract.

And when she fell, she fell with Jared Wentworth holding her, his body joined to hers in devastating intimacy.


The sky was just pearling with the promise of dawn

when Jared eased from bed to dress. He found Carina's underwear alongside his rumpled clothing on the floor. Remembering her neatness, he folded her things and put them on the chair with the dress and stockings. He had other garments to put on, but she did not.

After a fitful, restless night, Carina finally slept in peace or exhaustion. He left her now so she could continue, knowing his presence, if not his actual demands, had disturbed her rest. If last night had been a first for her—as of a certainty it had been—it held elements of novelty for him as well. Regardless of her reason for lying with him, Carina was not a whore. Her innocence encompassed something much deeper than virginity, something of the spirit he couldn't name.

Whatever it was, it had kept him from forcing himself on her a second time while at the same time giving him no reprieve from his lust. The first he could claim as a virtue; he had not wanted to hurt her. But the second? If there was virtue in the way he still ached to possess her, he couldn't think what it was.

He made his way through the silent house to the kitchen, glad there were no servants about to remark upon his presence there. He helped himself to bread and cheese, wrapping it in a napkin to take outside, then stuck his head under the pump and drank thirstily. His thirst reminded him of his overindulgence, but he suffered no other symptoms. He shook the water from his hair, wondering at his luck. Perhaps his lust had burned away the usual ill-effects of drink—another first in his life.

Jared waved away a sleepy Ned who stumbled out to investigate when he led Infidel out of his stall. Years ago Jared had begun many days with an early morning ride. When had he stopped? And why? Seeing Ned's surprise reminded him that he had become too set into routine and habit. Starting today, he would change that and anything else that didn't please him. It was what? Tuesday? Today he would not go to the machine shop, for example, or do the expected.

With a start, he remembered something he couldn't change. Tonight he would have three guests to hide and keep until Ashland could take them. He didn't worry that Carina would interfere. She would not need to know, of course, but even if she did he was certain she would do no harm. Someone so gentle and sweet . . .

Jared pulled himself back from that line of thought. He'd spent the night that way; it was enough. This ride was meant to clear his head. He'd make decisions about Carina when he got home.

Infidel was a tireless beast but a slow starter. He walked to the road and headed, without prodding, for the river which invariably drew Jared to its banks. Waterpower fascinated him.

Like Francis Cabot Lowell, for whom the city was named, Jared had come to Lowell because of the Merrimack River, specifically because of the over thirty-foot drop of the Pawtucket Falls. From England, in his head, Mr. Lowell had brought the plans for building the first power looms in America, thanks to his photographic memory; but Jared had a different bent. He studied waterpower as a scientist, learning about its wonders. To that end, he tinkered with bits and pieces of machinery, making improvements in design. Most of what he did had no direct application to commerce, but he had no doubt that ultimately work such as his would change everyday life in America.

Unlike Lowell and his associates and followers, however, Jared had no desire to oversee the uses of waterpower that he or anyone else developed. That involved power of another kind, one that was anathema to Jared's disposition.

He was a loner. Despite the kindness of friends like the Meades and the love of his Pennsylvania grandparents, his view of himself and of the world had become fixed in one moment of horror and helplessness when he was twelve years old. His one attempt to live as others did, his marriage to Melissa, had ended in disaster. He would not do that again. Some people were not destined to enjoy the comforts of a family, surrounded by love.

Jared accepted his life and its circumstances. It was what it was—the bleak landscape he inhabited. Although he lacked certain things, he had others: friends and supporters, a fine home, useful and interesting work. And now, thanks to another accident of fate, he had Carina O'Rourke.

He could not love her or give her children, but he could have her for as long as it suited him. She had nowhere to go, now more than before. And why would she leave? He would shelter, feed, and clothe her, she would enjoy greater comfort than she'd ever known.

The gift of her body, bartered to him out of love for her brother, meant that she was ruined for an ordinary marriage, even for the loveless kind her father had arranged.

Jared turned the equation over in his mind, seeing it from all sides. He could find no flaws. It would be an arrangement, more honest than most marriages, that benefited them both. She would have protection and respect—at least in his household—and he would have her company.

He already knew she would find it acceptable. She was of a calm, rational mind or she would not have come to him, and that made her the kind of woman he could enjoy. And when he no longer enjoyed her—as he vowed would happen—he would settle her elsewhere with enough money to attract a good husband.

A lot of suppositions, he acknowledged ruefully, but wasn't he a scientist? And there was one certainty—Carina had nowhere else to go. No matter how he tried to feel ashamed, he couldn't manage it. Fate or God—some force—was finally smiling on him. He couldn't lose.

Carina woke to the sound of a choked gasp of surprise.

She reared up, as shocked to see Bagley as he was to see her. His entire head flamed with color, and in his confusion he backed noisily into the door before he managed his exit.

Just as embarrassed, Carina jumped from the covers and then back under them again. She was naked. She pulled the sheet up under her chin and stared about her. She remembered now. Everything.

Daylight flooded the austere bedroom. She had slept too long. Only panic could push aside her heavy feeling of unease. She didn't know what to do, what she was *supposed* to do. Just as her father always said, she had not thought out a sensible course of action.

Eyeing her clothes, which seemed a continent away, and the door, where she expected to see Bagley's head reappear at any moment, she pulled the sheet from the bed and wrapped herself in it. She dressed under its protective folds, all her pleasure in the fine clothing gone. She would have to give everything back, but what if Agnes had truly burned Patrick's cap? Would someone give her another when she could not promise to return it?

She was almost glad to have such a practical worry as she returned the sheet to the bed. There, for all the household to see, was the proof of her shame. Even if Bagley didn't talk about her, the laundress would. Such a stain would not go unremarked.

She consoled herself that she would not be here to know and remade the bed. She needed to find Agnes or Trudy. If only she had paid proper attention last night, she could do without their help now.

Carina was steeling herself to venture from the room when, after a peremptory knock, the door opened and Agnes strode in. By her brisk manner, Carina knew Bagley had summoned the woman. She looked around the room as if assuring herself that nothing was disturbed, then her glance settled on Carina.

"Where is Mr. Jared?"

Carina's face grew warm. "I don't know." Did the

woman think she was concealing him? She fought down the nervous need to laugh. "I was about to look for you, Mrs. . . ."

"Just Agnes will do."

"I would like my clothes back, please. Particularly my cap."

Agnes had the clothes, including the cap, tied into a bundle outside the door. It was dangerous to disobey Mr. Jared's instructions, but she had done so in order to save him from himself. He had an unduly generous nature. She could just imagine the story this one had concocted, thinking to make a place for herself here—what with that pretty face and fetching shape. This girl wasn't the first to try, and she wouldn't be the last.

There was something else about this one though—and about Mr. Jared's reaction. He hadn't acted normally. It worried Agnes. She didn't want to put a foot wrong. She wasn't like Bagley, who had been with Mr. Jared forever. She was as fiercely loyal, but her employer would not thank her for crossing his will.

"Mr. Jared said to burn it."

Carina's expression grew anxious. "I know he did, but if you haven't done that already, I'd be much obliged if you'd give it back to me."

"You *want* to leave?"

Carina stared. Suddenly she saw everything the other way. She *did* want to leave, but if Jared Wentworth wanted her to stay and she didn't, he wouldn't help Patrick. It was natural to want to escape her shame—as if she could—but it was also reprehensible. Until she knew she had attained Patrick's freedom, she would have to remain here, particularly if Jared ordered it.

Agnes watched Carina's face, aware that one thought chased another through her mind. The girl, she saw, hadn't the wit or, perhaps, the guile to hide what she was thinking from anyone with eyes to read her expressions. Agnes prided herself on judging books by their covers. For an unlettered women, it was the only way to learn.

93

This child, whatever her age, was obviously an innocent—as Agnes herself had once been. The woman was not unmoved by the girl's plight, but her loyalty remained with Mr. Jared.

Agnes saw Carina conclude that she would have to stay and read that to mean that the possibility existed—heretofore unconsidered—that she *could* remain. Agnes intended to quash that notion immediately.

But before she could do so, the girl answered her question, giving her something else to ponder.

"I will do whatever Mr. Wentworth wishes," Carina said.

Agnes was suspicious. Such professed humbleness didn't square with the girl's air of self-assurance. Agnes had seen too many quality folk not to recognize the way they held themselves. "What's your name?" she demanded, vexed at her own uncertainty.

"Carina O'Rourke."

"You may have your clothes—and your cap." A few steps to the door and Agnes was back, bearing the sorry bundle of rags. She thrust it at Carina.

Taking it, Carina caught the woman's arm. "I wish to leave here, Agnes. Please believe me. But what if Mr. Wentworth isn't . . . doesn't want me to." She could think of no way to say it. "It wasn't my choice to come here this way. I wanted to *work*. . . . I would have done anything," she added miserably.

Agnes didn't believe her any more than her father had. Besides, what Carina wanted didn't matter. It never had. She had proved herself willing to do "anything," but having done so, she wasn't leaving without some surety that it wasn't in vain.

"I must *know* that Mr. Wentworth wants me to leave," she said.

"He does," Agnes answered, her voice firm. Before she left, she added, "You may leave the clothes on the bed and come to the kitchen for some porridge on your way out. I'll tell cook to expect you."

Awash with shame as she was—again—Carina found it hard to speak up. "Agnes!" she called out, stopping her at the door. "Please, would you thank Gwen for the use of her lovely clothes? I tried to last night, but . . . well, and thank you and Trudy . . . and Bagley and Nellie for your kindness."

Agnes shut the door without answering. She had not been kind at all. She stood just outside the room, concerned all over again about what she'd done. If Mr. Jared . . .

No, she told herself firmly. The girl is Irish. Trash. She warmed Mr. Jared's bed, that's all. And she lied, saying it wasn't her choice coming here, when everyone knew she'd come days ago and hung around the yard, waiting to talk to Mr. Jared.

That she stood straight as a duchess and talked as nice as Miss Meade herself didn't matter. Even if Mr. Jared did find her pleasing, he wouldn't miss her. He had only one use for a girl like that. Why, he was probably off somewhere now, riding that black devil of a horse, waiting for the wench to be gone so he could show his face again. Fine folk like Mr. Jared, even the *good* ones, were all the same. They always wanted someone else to do their dirty work.

Well, she had done it. She was sure she was right . . . almost sure anyway.

She was less sure later when she went back to Mr. Jared's room. She found Gwen's "lovely" clothes meticulously folded on the bed, the shoes lined up precisely on the floor next to it. Although the bed was well made up, she took it apart—and found what she half expected, half feared to find.

Fear for herself threatened to choke off the unwilling sympathy for Carina O'Rourke rising within her. Mr. Jared's displeasure was a fearsome thing to bear. She'd rarely had its full brunt directed at herself and she didn't want to receive it for this . . . whatever it was. She had not listened properly to the voice of caution within, she knew that now.

Agnes gathered the linen into a hasty bundle, torn between running down to the kitchen after the girl and fetching fresh linen for the bed. Pride in her skills as a housekeeper won out. She put the laundry next to the back stairs and got out clean sheets. The girl was eating in the kitchen, safe enough for now, and it wouldn't do for her to go running down there so soon. She would think of a way to reverse her directions without seeming to. With a few minutes to think, she would come up with something.

She didn't get her few minutes.

Jared burst from the stairway into the upper hall, headed for his room. Before Agnes could waylay him, he opened the door and surveyed the emptiness within. He turned to her. "Well, where have you stashed her now? In the attic?"

The attic was one of the hiding places for fugitive slaves.

"I'll get her for you," Agnes promised, hurrying down the hall to the back stairs.

"Agnes," he shouted after her, "if you've put her to work again I'll feed your wretched bones to the pigs!"

"I did not, sir," she vowed, frantically wondering how she could explain the fact that the girl was back in her boy's clothing. "She's only breaking her fast, sir."

"In the kitchen?" he roared. "I told you last night she's my *guest!*"

Oh, Lord! Agnes nearly fell down the steep staircase in her haste, wondering how she could have been so wrong. She told herself that Mr. Jared's bark was worse than his bite, but she didn't believe it. If he ever found out what she'd done, she'd have to borrow the wretched boy's rags for herself and take up begging by the road.

No matter how she ran, it was not her day. Mr. Jared had *flown* down the front stairs and beat her to the kitchen. He wheeled around to say accusingly, "She's not here."

Her mind a total blank, Agnes stared at him witlessly.

Little, bent-over Nellie—bless her—finally spoke up. "I believe I saw the child walking toward the road a while ago."

"Of course!" Agnes sang out. "It's a lovely morning! She decided to take a walk." She headed for the door. "I'll see if I can find her for you."

"Toward the road?" Jared asked, pinning Nellie with his glistening black eyes. "I just rode up that way. Why didn't I see her?"

Nellie had no answer she dared to give, and Jared's eyes went from one to the other in the room before fixing on Agnes.

She had stopped walking, frozen in place like a falcon awaiting execution. He stepped up to her and took her arm, leading her out of the kitchen. "Thank you all," he said to the others. "Go back to work. Agnes and I will handle this."

When they were alone in the hallway, Agnes opened her mouth to explain, but Jared didn't let her speak. "I'm going after her, and you may be sure I'll find her. Then we'll get to the bottom of this, Agnes. I don't think I have to tell you that the way Miss O'Rourke is treated is important to me."

## Chapter 7

After she dressed in Patrick's old clothes and slipped out the back door of Jared's house, Carina began to consider all the things she should have thought through before. She didn't go to the kitchen to eat because she'd never be able to swallow in the presence of so many, especially when they knew where she had spent the night.

She wasn't sure that Agnes spoke for Jared, but it was possible she did. He could have told his housekeeper to send her away, although she rather doubted it. If so, why had the woman asked where he was? It didn't make sense.

She hadn't gone far along the road before she heard a horseman approach. Fearing that it might be Jared, she dove into the undergrowth to hide until the rider passed. Even disguised as a boy, that would be her response whenever she heard a horse or carriage from now on. Once she was certain the rider couldn't see her, she chanced a look and was rewarded with a glimpse of Jared's broad back and dark head. She had to agree with her father that he looked like the devil—or at least one of his fallen angels—but she could not say he frightened her.

Quite the opposite.

But she would not think of that now. She would have the rest of her life to think about her night in Jared

Wentworth's bed. This morning, the morning after, she had to be practical for once.

She could not go home. She hoped and prayed that Jared would fulfill his end of her bargain and see to Patrick's release from jail. Even if he didn't, she could do nothing more for her family. They were now, in Conn O'Rourke's words, quit of her. From here on, she had to make her own way.

It wouldn't be so bad. She could work in one of the mills, earn enough to keep herself decently and still put something aside in savings. She had seen others do it. Although the mills all over New England kept lists of troublesome workers, lists they shared among themselves, she doubted that her name was on one yet. Enoch Wentworth might have her barred from the Lowell mills, but she would not go there.

Thanks to Dennis Boynton's other interest besides religion, which he discussed almost as endlessly with her father, Carina knew about all the mills in the area. Dennis supported the labor movement the same way he practiced his faith—intellectually. But because of that, Carina knew where to go for work and what to do once she was there. She would go to Manchester, New Hampshire, and apply under a new, Yankee-sounding name. She would be Catherine Howard, taking her mother's middle and maiden names.

Loyalty to her Irish family and background was all well and good, but she was as much her mother's child as her father's—and for that she would not suffer. Without an Irish name, she would be able to work as a dresser or perhaps as a drawing-in girl. She was bright and nimble-fingered enough, and both jobs paid well beyond what she'd be able to earn in the spinning room where Irish workers were tolerated.

As Jared had noticed, she didn't sound Irish, so why should she penalize herself unnecessarily? Would Agnes have turned her away if she'd called herself Catherine Howard? Or even Carina Howard?

She would give up the name Carina only to make this break between her past and her future complete and clean. Her father would never follow to seek her out. What Dennis might do, on the other hand, she couldn't begin to guess. And there was always Enoch Wentworth's enmity to worry about.

She didn't think about Jared Wentworth or let herself wonder what he would do.

At the road, Carina chose to travel upriver. New Hampshire lay a day's walk beyond the far bank of the Merrimack. There might be a bridge downriver, but she wasn't sure, and to go in that direction would take her out of her way. With no thought that she was being pursued, she set a comfortable pace along the most direct route possible.

Likewise, when Jared came to the road he had no trouble deciding which way she had gone. He knew she had hidden earlier or he would have met her, therefore he kept a particularly sharp eye along the roadside. Where there was sparse cover, he rode smartly. Knowing she would hear the horse anyway, he made no pretense at stealth, pausing now and then to bellow her name, then listen.

With so much warning, Carina should have been safe, but she had seen a green-apple tree and it had tempted her. She wasn't hungry yet, just thirsty, and the apples looked plump and juicy. She left the road to forge a path through some knee-high grass and climbed the trunk to reach the best apples.

The sound of her name shouted on the morning breeze was startling. She went totally still as her heart began to pound. She heard the horse and decided she was as safe where she was as she could be anywhere. She would not move and he would go thundering by.

But Jared rode slowly. He was convinced that she was near. She hadn't had time to go much farther, and he intended to make a thorough search. The terrain was varied but quite open. He halted Infidel next to a crumbling stone wall and peered over it, then nudged his mount along slowly.

"Carina!" he called out. "I know you can hear me. I don't know why you left, but I'll do anything I can to make you happy *if* you come out now! Don't play games with me. I'm not a patient man."

His words came clearly to her. As their meaning penetrated she was suddenly as afraid of this man as she had been of his cousin. What did this pursuit mean?

Jared worked his way along the roadside until he spotted the swath of trampled grass and the apple tree. He dismounted and tossed the reins into the branches of a bush, then began to follow the path. Now that he knew where she was, he had no need to call out. He stalked to the base of the tree, every sense alive and singing. His anger simmered beneath the surface, overridden now by pleasure such as he'd not felt in years. Whatever else she was, Carina O'Rourke was not boring.

Obscured by the thick foliage, Carina couldn't see Jared's approach. She sensed his nearness, however, and knew that any movement of hers might betray her hiding place. She stayed as his voice had found her, perched on a branch, watching a pale green worm dance at the end of its thread. Even when she no longer heard the horse's slow footfalls, she didn't dare move. She was sure they'd not gone on past. The strain of trying to listen over the thud of her heartbeat wound her nerves into an explosive spring.

When Jared suddenly spoke from directly under her, she cried out and started, losing her grip on the branch above. She fell into his arms without harm to anything but her pride and Patrick's shirt, which caught on a branch.

"Now this is what I call an apple," he said as his arms tightened around her.

His black eyes sparkled with laughter and something else that Carina feared was barely tamped-down anger. She closed her eyes rather than see it reemerge to overshadow his amusement.

He didn't put her down but walked, carrying her like a child, back to the road. He set her onto Infidel and swept up behind her, holding the reins. Before he urged the horse forward, he studied her face briefly. Carina met his gaze stolidly, then wet her lips. "I can explain . . ."

"And you will. But not now."

He took off the cap from her head, grunting in satisfaction when her hair fell down in disarray. Then he threw the cap so that it sailed away into the grass. Carina watched it go, knowing the gesture was a declaration of intent on his part. What it meant, exactly, she didn't know. In spite of herself, she began to nourish a small spark of hope. She knew it was wrong and foolish, but she couldn't help herself.

Throughout the silent ride back, Jared fought down his warring feelings, mastering first one, then another that bubbled up from the stew inside him. He didn't question his anger at being defied. He understood that perfectly. Nor did he mind feeling possessive. She was his. He knew it, and she would come to know it soon enough if she didn't by now.

What bothered him—immensely—was the hurt welling up from some source he couldn't explain. He named it pride in order to tame the demon and dismiss it. She was an insignificant scrap of womanhood, no matter how lovely or innocent. Her running from him had *not* hurt him. It had only nicked his pride and angered him. He was bringing her back because it amused him. And he would keep her only until she no longer pleased or amused him. She wasn't unwilling, just willful, but that would cease when she understood her true situation.

He helped Carina down from the horse without fuss, noting her matter-of-fact demeanor with Ned. She neither smiled at him nor avoided his gaze, and Jared found that her poise came close to shattering his.

He didn't touch her, but he couldn't shake the need to keep his eyes on her, as though she would evaporate like dew if he looked away. Agnes and Bagley met them just inside the door, where the pair had waited in a proper state of anxiety for Jared's return. He found their palpable worry soothing after Carina's unconcern.

He ushered the unlikely-looking trio into his study and shut the door. "Now," he said, resting his eyes on Carina, "I would like that explanation."

If Carina felt the weight of Agnes's and Bagley's tension, she didn't let on. She spoke to him with her usual combination of forthrightness and diffidence. "It's all my fault," she began. "My leaving, that is. It was what I believed right."

When he didn't comment, Carina went on to address what she considered the most serious issue. "I know you told Agnes to burn my cap, but I begged it of her as long as she hadn't yet done that. She wasn't willing at first, but then, I believe, she took pity on me. Without it, I wouldn't have been able to go freely along the road."

Jared hardly noticed his servants' relief as he stepped from the door and waved them out. He would not have witnesses to the rest of his discussion. He shut the door carefully and turned back to her. "You gave me to understand that you had no home to return to."

Carina heard the implicit accusation. She wasn't surprised, only distracted by the look of him. Last night she had thought him compelling, if not handsome, but the contrast of his white shirt against his darkness now gave him an aura that took her breath away. She still couldn't make it real that he had pursued her. She was of no value to him except—perhaps—as a pinprick to his pride.

Yes, she decided, noting his imperious stance. That had to be it. He didn't *care*, she knew. How could he care when her own father, to whom she had given love, service, and all of her meager earnings from the mill, did not?

"That's true," she answered.

He lifted his eyebrows, glaring. "Yet you were going

103

back to Lowell. To beg your intended husband to take you back?"

Anger flared in Carina. She wanted to tell him she didn't beg favors of men, but she realized she had done exactly that—twice. That it had been for Patrick and not herself didn't matter. She had begged and then given herself in payment. She could no longer afford to be proud.

But she wasn't going to tell him her plans. Let him think whatever pleased him. Someday she might yet need to go on as she had intended today.

"I wasn't going to him, only to seek employment. I've worked the mills for over two years."

"Surely you know Enoch's had you blacklisted by now. No one will hire you."

His assertion reinforced her suspicion, and she looked down, momentarily overcome by the unfairness of it all. "There are other mills," she said softly, goaded into defending herself. "I would have found a place."

It bothered Jared that she was right. Workers were in demand. Someone would have taken her on, blacklist or not. And then how would he have found her?

"Why did you want to leave?"

Her quick glance snagged on his. "I thought you would want me to."

"Did I say that?"

"You didn't say you didn't."

No, he hadn't. "I wanted you to rest."

His gentle tone nearly undid Carina. She couldn't remember when anyone had expressed concern for her—not for years and years. Not since they had come to Lowell, and before that she had been a child.

She wanted to ask him what he wanted of her—and for how long—but she didn't trust her voice. She knew she should ask about Patrick, but she was afraid to press him. The anger in him had eased. For now that had to be enough. What he offered was scant perhaps, but it was more than anyone else was offering.

104

She swallowed a lump in her throat and waited for him to direct her.

Jared watched her face, seeing expressions he couldn't read move over her features. It was like watching shadows pass over a field, darkening it, as clouds moved across the sun. He wanted to question her, but he sensed that she was near the edge of collapse. More than answers, though, he wanted a sign from her that she was not unwilling to stay.

Seeing her head bent before him had leashed his need to prevail over her and had stemmed—temporarily—his lustful feelings, but it had raised other needs and feelings that were just as dangerous. Although he had won this skirmish, he had the notion that he couldn't afford many more such "victories."

"You will stay here," he said, not allowing his voice to rise in question.

She nodded, and he made his escape.

It wasn't hard to find Agnes. She was "dusting" in the next room. From her haunted expression, Jared knew she was merely waiting until she could talk to him. Regardless of what Carina had reported, he knew there was more to the story of her departure than she had intimated. Nevertheless, he trusted Agnes. That didn't mean he intended to listen to her.

"Mr. Jared—"

"I want you to obtain appropriate, *attractive* clothing for Miss O'Rourke," he said, cutting off her apology or whatever it was she planned to say. "That doesn't mean you should ransack the scrap bag, Agnes. It may mean sending for a seamstress to have dresses made. In fact, that's probably the best way to go. She has nothing to wear, and I would have her well dressed."

"She is to stay then?"

"She is."

"For how long, sir?"

It was a daring question, but Agnes didn't back down when he stared angry holes into her. "I need to know how

105

much clothing she'll need," she said, as stubborn as he.

"She'll need an ample supply, let's say."

"Is she to direct the household then?"

Jared ground his teeth. "She is to be my *guest*," he got out finally. "Have I not said so repeatedly?"

"And where will she be . . . staying?"

He wanted to hoot at the delicacy that made her back away from the work sleeping. "Give her a room—a decent room, Agnes; even a *fine* room. Do I make myself clear?"

"Perfectly." She looked like someone sucking a lemon, determined at all cost to drain the rind. "You say she is to be a guest, sir, but have you considered how she is to pass the time that takes you away from her company?"

He hadn't, and he didn't want to. "You'll have to find something she can do about the house. She's intelligent. She can learn. Work that out between yourselves."

"Yes, sir."

Jared heard resistance in her words and saw it in her face. She had managed his household as long as he'd had one. She was brisk and efficient, even with her own daughter. But that wasn't what he wanted for Carina. Already tired of the issue, he wanted to dismiss it—and Agnes—but he couldn't let it go as it stood.

He expelled a breath and tried another approach. "I would have her treated well, Agnes. I know your loyalty and appreciate it, but this goes beyond that." He met her gaze, seeing that she was genuinely troubled by what she was hearing. "Let's just say that I will count a kindness to Miss O'Rourke to be a kindness to me."

She absorbed his message without flinching, saying at last, "I believe I understand."

Jared wasn't convinced by her expression, which remained adamantine, touched by—if anything—a crafty light in her eyes. He decided not to challenge her further and turned away. She wasn't stupid.

106

"Will you be going to Lowell today as usual?" she asked.

His vow to shake up his life and do the unexpected flashed through his mind. Following that came the picture of Carina, who remained in his study for want of a room of her own and clothes to wear.

Deciding that he'd already done enough to shake up his life in the last twenty-four hours, he said, "Of course," as though he'd never considered doing anything else. In fact, the prospect of a few hours of mechanical experimentation had suddenly taken on great appeal.

But before Jared could complete his escape from the house, he had to endure one more encounter, with Bagley. Seeing his man bear down upon him, Jared longed to be able to laugh as he had once before at Carina's characterization of Bagley—the little hairless man.

At times it seemed that for every hair he'd lost, Bagley had grown a scruple in its place. And where Agnes forbore to criticize, Bagley's tongue was free to wag at will. At *his* will.

To the world Bagley was his servant; to Jared he was much more. He had been the one to pull Jared from a heedless rush into the deathtrap of his burning home. Bagley had the scars to show for his heroics, scars that Jared saw daily as testimony of the little man's love for him. He didn't presume too much most of the time, but occasionally Jared did not want to be held to Bagley's exalted standard.

This was such a time.

"If you wanted a whore, my boy, why did you not tell me?"

Jared sighed and tried a jest. "Is that your new sideline?"

Bagley fixed him with a baleful eye. He came to Jared's breastbone, and yet he had a way of peering from under half-closed lids as though he were feet taller, as he had

107

been when Jared was a lad. "Better mine than yours," he retorted. "But perhaps you mean to elevate the lass to wifehood?"

"What I intend is clear enough, I think."

"The more shame to you."

Jared edged to the door but didn't bolt. Instead, he waited for Bagley to get it all out of his system. "Is that it?" The waiting was tiresome. "Because if it isn't, I'd just as soon hear it all right now. I don't relish putting up with your piecemeal complaints."

"She's Irish," Bagley said, seemingly apropos of nothing. Jared knew better.

He laughed. "So you noticed. And I was worried that you might be slipping into your dotage. Did you figure that out before or after you found out she was female?"

His jibe slid off Bagley's smooth facade like rain running down window glass—or down the dome of his head. "And how do you think that will sit with the women here?"

"How should it sit?"

"The should of it won't matter," Bagley insisted. "It won't be pleasant for the lass."

Jared had considered how Carina would be treated as his mistress; her Irishness had never entered his mind. He tried to dismiss the notion. "I bring escaped slaves here and no one abuses them."

"They do not come to your bed. Or is that your next thought?"

Jared could only stare. He knew there was sentiment against the Irish, but was it that strong?

Seeing his disbelief, Bagley shook his head. "I know you meant to do well by the child—"

"She's a woman grown, Bagley. Twenty-two years old."

He plowed on, unhearing. "You meant well. I grant you that. You jumped in between the lass and Enoch, but this way . . . how are you better?"

Jared couldn't stand having his own gravest doubts

spoken aloud, not by Bagley. "There's nothing you can say that I haven't already said to myself, old man. If I don't hear myself, what makes you think I'll hear you?"

Bagley's expression conceded that the situation was worse than he had feared.

Tacitly, Jared agreed. He had not raped Carina, nor had he been other than gentle with her. Nevertheless, she had wept in his arms and tried to leave his dubious "protection." She'd be a very rich woman, indeed, were he to compensate her fairly for her travail at his hands. And it wasn't over yet—not if he had any say.

Sighing noisily, Bagley stood aside to let Jared go. He isn't a lad anymore, and there's only so much I can do for him, the old man thought. Perhaps over the years I've done too much smoothing—who can say?

This time, he decided, watching his master leave, he'd do his smoothing in other directions.

# Chapter 8

"He's besotted."

Bagley didn't turn from his contemplation of the door Jared Wentworth had just closed. He didn't argue with Agnes either.

"What Miss Meade will make of this, I can't imagine."

He turned then to stare at Agnes in amazement. "Haven't you given up that notion yet?"

Agnes flushed angrily. It irritated her that she was an outsider within what she regarded as "her" household. Not only did she not share Bagley's history with Mr. Jared, she was also excluded because she was female.

Agnes longed for a mistress who would wrest control of the household away from Bagley and give it to her. For that, she deemed Susan Meade to be perfect. The woman would soften the harsh, masculine edges of the establishment, and yet, because of her temperament and interests, she would not interfere with or alter the arrangements Agnes already had in place. She had known such a reign only briefly, during Mr. Jared's marriage to Melissa Hartwell. Melissa had relied on Agnes and excluded Bagley—which, Agnes was sure, was why he had never cared for the first Mrs. Wentworth.

"It's not a notion. Marriage is perfectly sensible. It's what Mr. Jared needs, and Miss Meade is perfectly suited to him. I can't think of a single drawback to it."

Bagley gave a silent chuckle. "I can think of one, and so can you if you try real hard."

"She isn't . . . she doesn't . . . count, Bagley."

"No?" He studied her and shook his head. "I've never known you to be stupid before. I told you to tread softly this morning, but did you? Don't you realize she could have crucified you for what you did?"

The gratitude and relief Agnes had felt earlier had already been replaced by annoyance. An Irish waif from the streets of Lowell threatened her security. She couldn't bring herself to be grateful for that fact. She pursed her lips, rejecting the expression of her thoughts. The truth was, now that the crisis was safely past, she had convinced herself that Carina O'Rourke's generous act had been motivated by cowardice and not courage.

Bagley knew Agnes wouldn't thank him for advice, but he offered it anyway. "If I were you, I'd make a friend of Miss O'Rourke."

Agnes watched him walk away, hating the sight of his bandy-legged shuffle. The instant he was gone, she set in motion the important part of her double plan. She would be kind to Mr. Jared's mistress—for his sake, not hers— but she would also do everything she could to make him see the error of his way. To that end, she set Trudy, Gwen, and Nellie to work. Then she went to the study.

She found Carina by Mr. Jared's bookshelves, holding a book as if she were reading it. The girl had the grace to look guilty, if only for an instant before she replaced it on the shelf and turned to Agnes inquiringly.

Taking a deep breath, Agnes did what she had to. She apologized. "Before we get started carrying out Mr. Jared's directives for you, I'd like to thank you for what you told him about your leavetaking. He would not have been pleased by what I did."

"I only told him the truth as I saw it," Carina said.

Agnes was careful not to show her displeasure at having her apology thrown back into her face; in her mind, thanking Carina was the same thing as apologizing for her own misdeed. After a moment of looking down at her hands, she said, "Mr. Jared told me that you will be staying. You're to have clothing, a room, and perhaps something to do to fill the hours when he is unavailable."

Carina was pleased by everything but that last expression. It touched too closely upon the reason Jared was keeping her. "That's very generous of him, but what I'd like to do is talk to him again."

"That's impossible. He's gone."

"Gone? For how long?"

"I really don't know," Agnes answered truthfully. "He's not expected for dinner tonight."

Carina's heart dropped disconsolately within her breast. She didn't trust Agnes any more than she knew how to fight her. If she asked to be assigned to help Ned with the horses, she was afraid Agnes would thwart her wishes anyway. But she didn't mind hard work. Pehaps, through it, she could win respect, if not affection, from this woman Jared trusted as she did not. "Then I'll just have to do my best," she said, shrugging off her disappointment.

Agnes gestured, and she followed her up the narrow back stairs to a large bedroom that was already a beehive of activity. Agnes stopped at the threshold for a brief survey, then rushed inside, scolding, "No, no, Gwen. Not like *that*."

Carina couldn't see the fault, but she saw the way Gwen glared at her. She wanted to help, but didn't dare to wade in as she would at home. The room was filled to overflowing with ornate furniture, rugs, pillows, and curtains. There were even curtains hanging around the bed. A fresh breeze lifted the draperies at two large open windows, already beginning to dispel the musty smell of stale, trapped air.

Nellie sent her a shy smile that encouraged Carina to forsake the doorway and help her move a small settee. When that was accomplished, Carina looked around for something else to do. The room was already clean and

112

neat—or it had been before the women had begun to move everything around.

Before she could ask for direction, Trudy came in. She went straight to the bed and dumped her armload there. This time Gwen squawked. Tossing her head at Carina, she said to Agnes, "Let *her* fix this. *I* have other chores."

Although Carina expected Agnes to reprimand Gwen, or at least call her back, she did neither and Carina was relieved to have her gone.

Agnes and her daughter unwrapped what looked to be sheets from the bundles on the bed. They threw those onto the floor and held up one garment after another for inspection.

"Oh, my!" Trudy cried. "Remember this?" She held a blue gown under her chin and whirled away into the middle of the bedroom. The dress rustled and fluttered around her ankles. Although she was an outsider, it was impossible for Carina not to get caught up in Trudy's excitement. Even Agnes was smiling with pleasure.

She held out a maroon gown of heavy velvet and satin. "And this one?" she asked. "Remember this?"

"For the Christmas Ball in Boston!"

Without Carina saying a thing, they both turned and looked at her. Unsure what she should say, Carina smiled. "You both must have looked wonderful," she offered hesitantly. "Those colors are most becoming."

To her mortification, the two women burst out laughing and couldn't stop. When one managed to control herself slightly, the other kept it going. Trudy was the first to recover enough to talk. Swiping at her eyes with the back of her hand, she put down the dress and said, "Oh dear, I'm sorry. That was rude, but it was just so *funny!*"

Which left Carina still without any way to respond until Agnes called Nellie over and asked. "Do you think these will fit Miss O'Rourke, Nellie? She's quite right about one thing—the colors are *very* becoming. Especially the blue."

Carina stepped back in alarm. "For me? Oh no. These are . . . ball gowns! They're most unsuitable. I can wear the clothes I had before." Then she remembered Gwen's anger. But surely a maid's feelings weren't so important that this finery was the only alternative.

"Mr. Jared said you were to be *well* dressed, miss," Agnes said. "Those are my orders."

"But I can't work in clothes like that."

Trudy interceded. "Carina . . . may I call you Carina?" At her distracted nod, Trudy went on. "You're not to work at anything strenuous. You're Mr. Jared's guest."

"But I want to earn my keep," Carina blurted out.

"And so you shall," Agnes put in, "but not scrubbing floors. Mr. Jared was definite about that. This is to be your room, and you must be well dressed."

Hearing that the room was hers put all thought of clothing from Carina's mind. "This? Is mine?" She stared around, unbelieving.

She barely noticed when Trudy ushered her mother out of the room and took over. She began to paw through the heap of clothing until she found a robe. "Take off those clothes now and let Nellie take your measurements. We'll find something that's not too fancy for a starter," she said soothingly.

As when she and her mother had bathed Carina, Trudy went about her chore deftly, sending Nellie to a dresser for underclothes. "I don't know why we didn't think of these things yesterday," she said when Nellie brought out soft shifts, drawers, camisoles, and petticoats of linen and cotton. She held one garment to the light and pronounced, "This will do nicely for now. The others need bleaching in the sun."

Soon Carina was dressed in elegant undergarments that were trimmed with handmade lace. Nellie measured her in every direction, using a tape she marked with pins placed according to a code that had meaning to her if not to Carina. Then Trudy brought out other dresses from

114

the welter on the bed. They probably were, in Trudy's term, not too fancy, but they were no less fine for their simplicity. Carina felt as though she were being fitted for heavenly robes.

The process was not easy. First she tried on three dresses, right side out; then they were reversed so Nellie could pin the excess cloth Trudy pulled out at the seams. Carina had to be extricated from each dress without disturbing the pins. By the time this was all over, she was as tired as if she had scrubbed floors after all.

Nellie hobbled away with the three dresses over her arm and Trudy began to straighten the remaining mound of clothes, wrapping them back up in the discarded sheets. She helped Carina into the robe, promising that she'd be right back.

"Let me help you," Carina offered.

If she'd thought the exercise they'd just been through had made a friend of Trudy, she saw now that that was an illusion. Trudy's face again became a blank mask as she refused, curtly, Carina's help.


It took Trudy three trips to return the clothes to the attic. But for the fact that the attic was outfitted with beds and chairs, she would have been glad for Carina's help. Unlike her mother, Trudy wasn't blind. She had seen Mr. Jared's face when he'd come to the kitchen searching for the girl. She intended to befriend Carina O'Rourke. The young woman would need a maid if she stayed any time at all, and being a personal maid to the master's mistress was easy work. It would also get Trudy out from under her mother's domination.

But she couldn't take the chance of exposing Mr. Jared's activities to outside scrutiny. If the girl stayed and if Mr. Jared confided in her, that would be different. It was his decision to make, not hers. After all, there were many others here who didn't know about the special visitors, because the honest fact was, the fewer there were who knew, the fewer there were who could tell on Mr. Jared.

Trudy checked provisions in the room on her way back. The doorway was cunningly concealed by boxes, but if the constable was searching for a slave—and for his reward—that wouldn't keep the room from being found. Mr. Jared didn't want it to look too secret, so he could claim that it was a servant's room. It was just about as nice, and private, too. Since she shared a room with her mother, Trudy appreciated that.

She didn't envy the fugitives though, not since she'd seen the whip marks on the back of one woman no older than she was now. Mr. Jared wouldn't let a horse be treated that way. People in Lowell thought he was a scoundrel. That always surprised Trudy when she went into town. He was supposed to be so wild. He *was* gone a lot at night, but other than that he was the quietest man. She felt sorry for him, especially since his wife died . . . and the baby. It made Trudy hope he would get some pleasure from this girl. He was way past due having something nice come into his life.

Just like me, Trudy thought with a laugh, skipping down the last steps. She understood how Gwen felt in a way. She'd had her dreams about Mr. Jared, too. Well, that's what they'd been, just dreams. There was nothing in her face, any more than in Gwen's, to draw Mr. Jared's eye. Still, it gave Trudy hope that a little nobody like Carina O'Rourke could attract Mr. Jared like that. If an extraordinary man like Mr. Jared could fall in love in a flash, perhaps an ordinary man like Ned would notice her, given enough time.


After being rebuffed by Trudy, Carina took herself firmly in hand. She made up the bed with the linens Gwen had left, marveling at the smooth texture of the sheets. She was too practical to be downcast for long, particularly when she'd fallen into such luxury. Just this

116

morning she'd started walking north, toward an uncertain future, hopeful that someone in Manchester would hire her as a mill girl. Such a future had not included fine sheets and a room like this.

Looking around, Carina began to wonder about the room. It was, or had been, a lady's chamber, for there wasn't anything masculine within sight. Compared to this place, Jared's bedroom was plain and empty. She wondered whose room it had been and where that person was now. A bureau drawer was filled with gloves and handkerchiefs with hand-rolled edges. Feeling guilty that she'd been prying, Carina closed the drawer and went back to perch on the settee.

A sudden thought made her feel almost sick. She was Jared's mistress now; that was why she'd been brought here to be outfitted in those lovely dresses. The woman whose room this had been must have been her predecessor.

Where is she now? Carina worried. Had she been ousted so abruptly that she'd had to leave all her belongings behind? Then Carina had another thought. The clothes and furnishings were here because they belonged to Jared Wentworth. He had bought and paid for all this. The woman—whoever she was—was gone, just as Carina would be someday. Jared had tired of her predecessor and he would tire of her. Then it would be her turn to leave. And all these things would stay here for the next woman he wanted to have in his bed.

Carina pressed her hands to her face. She was shocked and more than a little frightened. She'd done one heedless thing, for reasons that made sense to her, and suddenly she was in the most terrible mess. Papa was right. She didn't *think*, and even when she tried to, she didn't do it right.

She tried to think now. What were her options? She'd tried to leave once; she couldn't do that again, at least not right now. She no longer had Patrick's clothes, for one thing. And she still didn't know whether or not Jared had

117

seen to Patrick's release. As long as she was here, and comfortable, she should make sure that this time she'd succeeded in helping her brother before she left.

And if she left, she couldn't undo the past. She could live with that, she decided, just as she could live with these circumstances. On the road, she would have slept in the open or tried to bed down secretly in some farmer's barn. At least here she was safe, and as long as she understood that this was not permanent, that everything here—from the clothes on her back to the room she slept in—was on loan, she would be all right.

She would take it day by day. She would learn everything she could about this place and find a way to leave when the time was right. She would be able to replace Patrick's clothes with others. Then, one day when no one was paying attention to her, she would don those clothes and slip away—perhaps at night.

Having a plan, even a poor one, helped Carina repress her anxiety. She didn't dare investigate the room further, so when Trudy brought her noon meal, much delayed, Carina was still sitting primly in place. She didn't ask Trudy any of the questions bristling in her mind either. She was too cautious to trust Trudy again.

After the meal was gone, time crawled for Carina. She was used to working, and if she'd sometimes prayed for less to do, she'd never aspired to idleness. When Nellie came with the first dress, Carina greeted her with a joy that had nothing to do with clothes.

"Blue's your color, all right," Nellie said, surveying Carina in the dress.

It was the one she liked best, neither as fancy as the ball gown nor as stiff as Gwen's dress. The square neckline was cool and bare, too bare she feared. She put her hands over her exposed collarbones, wondering how she'd failed to notice earlier. "Perhaps I can find a scarf to fill it in," she murmured, turning away from Nellie.

Nellie took her hands down. "No scarf, miss," she said, her kind brown eyes taking the sting of reproof from her words.

"But it's immodest. My papa—"

"Mr. Jared's not your papa. He'll approve."

Carina looked at Nellie anxiously. "You're sure?" She had never worn a dress that didn't come up under her chin, and even then Papa made her wrap a scarf around her shoulders if the dress fit closely—as this one did. It felt so cool, so . . . daring.

"Fine ladies aren't 'specially modest, my dear."

"But I'm not a fine lady."

"In that dress you're better than a fine lady," Nellie assured her. "You take my word on it."

Carina wanted to. Oh, how she wanted to believe Nellie. She could hear Papa, warning her that voices like Nellie's were the work of the devil. She was being tempted, and she knew it. But why shouldn't she be? She was already a creature of great sin, just being here. If that was so, why shouldn't she also be cool?

She held out the skirt with one hand and turned slowly, the way she imagined that great ladies moved when dancing at a ball. "It's so beautiful, Nellie. I can't thank you enough for fixing it for me."

"'Twas my pleasure." For Nellie, the words were true. She had great hopes for this slip of a girl and Mr. Jared. She'd seen him with his wife, and she'd seen him after her death. This girl with her pure, sweet smiles and her sparkling eyes was just what Mr. Jared needed. She only hoped Mr. Jared was what this girl needed as well. She rather feared he was not, but that was another story and not her concern.

Carina stopped turning and regarded Nellie closely. "Could you teach me to sew like this, do you suppose?"

"To take in dresses, you mean? Why, there ain't nothing to that."

"You know how to make dresses from scratch, too, don't you? I can sew and I'm quick to learn. My hands are clever, I've been told. I'd like so much to learn dressmaking. Do you think you could teach me?"

119

The half-formed idea suddenly seemed brilliant to Carina. If she learned a skill while she lived here, then when she left she wouldn't have to go back to millwork. She could go anywhere and always find work. She'd seen dress shops in Lowell, just from outside of course, but sewing on beautiful dresses had to be pleasant work compared to the spinning room.

"Oh, do say yes, Nellie. I have to have something to do here, Agnes says, and that's what I'd like best."

It sounded like paradise to Nellie. Her knees ached so when she had to go up and down the narrow back stairs. Sitting with the girl, teaching her . . . She turned away before she betrayed herself by crying. "'Twould suit me fine," she said brusquely.

"Oh, thank you, Nellie." Carina took the woman's gnarled hands in hers. "Can we start today? Right now? I could help you with my dresses—if they are to be mine?"

"They are."

"Good. Then let me come with you. We can bring everything here and get started."

Nellie couldn't hold back a grin. Agnes wouldn't like that, but what could she do about it? "I 'spose we could, miss," she said.

"Carina. You have to call me Carina."

"Carina. Yes. I 'spose we could just do that right now."

No one kept them from carrying Nellie's workbasket and the clothes up to Carina's room, and no one interrupted them all afternoon. Nellie was a patient teacher who had little reason to call on her patience, for Carina was an apt pupil. She had not forgotten what her mother, a fairly skilled needlewoman, had taught her, and she was eager to learn more.

That night, dressed in a shift of the finest embroidered lawn, Carina's thoughts were mostly happy as she tried to fall asleep in the wide bed. There was only one exception to that circumstance. She'd not been able to get Nellie to tell her about the woman who had slept here before.

"That's not for me to tell," Nellie had answered.

And that's all she would say, no matter how Carina attempted to draw her out on that subject.

"Should I ask Agnes?"

"Shouldn't ask nobody," Nellie said firmly. "Better not."

Carina trusted Nellie's kindness, but her advice made for a wakeful night. Ironically, she longed for the comfort of Jared's arms—the very thing that had kept her from sleep the night before. Then she had wrestled with her conscience, trying to fight down the fierce and totally inexplicable joy rising within her. To be held like that, sheltered by one strong enough to deflect the buffeting blows of careless fate . . . Remembering it was another torment.

She turned over, seeking a cool spot on the bed. Tonight she missed Margaret. If she couldn't be comforted, she wanted to offer comfort as she had for years to her sister. She wasn't used to being alone. Here in this rose-colored room she had only disquieting company—the ghost of the room's previous occupant and her unanswered questions.

It wasn't completely silent, however. Instead of her father's snore and Kevin's occasional restless murmurs, certain country sounds came to Carina from the open window. She heard the patterned hoot of an owl and began to anticipate the sound with remarkable accuracy. The bird's call had two variations. She found she could predict just how long the silence between outbursts would last. Holding her breath in order not to miss the beginning, Carina strained to listen.

The owl didn't hoot and she expelled her breath noisily, both amused and irritated by her foolishness. Then she heard something else, the muffled sound of a horse, and knew why the owl hadn't called. It had been frightened away.

She turned over, determined to seek her rest, then sat

up, more awake than ever. It was late for horses to be about. Her father's words came back to her, rife with accusation. What had sounded preposterous then, when she'd been fresh from Jared's rescue, seemed plausible now.

Agnes had said Jared wasn't expected for dinner, but that, Carina assured herself, didn't mean he had been doing something wrong. Evil like that existed only in Conn O'Rourke's twisted mind. The man who had held her tenderly last night would not be kidnapping and plundering tonight, regardless of what Papa believed. She was sure of it.

Nevertheless, she crept from bed. She knew herself. If she didn't satisfy her curiosity she'd never get to sleep. Her imagination would paint scenes so vivid and convincing that only the sight of the deserted quadrangle below would vanquish them.

Her room, as she'd learned during her trips to the servant's quarters with Nellie, lay across the hall from Jared's at the upper, back corner of the main house. The window at the end of her bed faced east and looked down upon the overgrown entrance to the back of the house. Although the sound had come from that direction, all she would see there was the leafy top of the tree below.

She went to the back window instead, pleased and relieved to look down on nothing. The half moon rode high enough in the sky to illuminate every quiet foot of the yard. Carina lifted the curtain, lingering to let the cool night air refresh her. She leaned forward, kneeling to brace her arms against the sill, and filled her lungs. In that moment she saw something, a motion at the stable door. She dropped the curtain back into place and peered between the two fluttering lengths of material.

After a pause that was long enough to make her doubt her own senses, three figures stepped out into the moonlight. One was Jared Wentworth, and he was carrying something or someone in his arms. The other two—a man and a woman from their attitudes—followed

122

in his wake, the man either aiding the woman or forcing her along in front of him.

Shocked, Carina watched their stealthy entrance at the back door. Long after the quadrangle was empty she continued to stare down at the space, trying to make sense of what she had seen.

# Chapter 9

Barefoot, Jared stood in the middle of the floor, his black shirt pulled from his breeches, eyeing the bed with disfavor. Already well past cockcrow, it was all too easy for him to make out the expanse of white sheet awaiting him. Light seeped around the draperies Bagley had drawn for his comfort. But it wasn't the room's brightness he objected to; he was tired enough to sleep atop a picket fence.

The bed was empty.

Picturing Carina there as she had been, Jared would have given everything he owned to be able to lift the sheet from her lovely body and slide into place beside her. Just to hold her, to feel her breathing, warm and alive, beside him. She wouldn't wake, yet even though he made no demand upon her, she would turn to him and nestle closer, offering the soft comfort of her nearness.

So real were his imaginings that Jared was immobilized. It took effort and concentration just to raise his hands to fumble at the front of his shirt.

He let his arms fall again in disgust as he realized it was his own fault that he was alone now. He hadn't been prepared to understand or accept Carina's effect on him before she caught him off-guard and ran away. Then he'd let Agnes bully him with her old-lady objections, to the point that he threw up his hands and let her make decisions that were not hers to make. He'd brought Carina back, then failed to specify that he wanted her with him.

It sobered him to realize that he had no idea where Agnes had put her. That was unbelievable—and unacceptable. It was his house. He was in charge here, not Agnes. Was he supposed to go from room to room, searching for her?

He thought of waking Agnes and demanding to know where Carina was. Wouldn't that be something? As if his going to the kitchen twice in search of her hadn't caused enough gossip among the servants.

He took off his shirt and was tossing it aside when something tripped in his mind, like a cog in one of his machines, telling him where he would find Carina. If he hadn't been tired, he would have known instantly the significance of the fluttering curtain in Melissa's bedroom.

Anger coursed through him like water in a spillway, sweeping all before it, cleansing him of weariness. He snatched up the shirt, jabbing his arms into the sleeves. Unsecured, it flew open as he strode to the door and yanked on it, muttering, "Damn you, Agnes!"

He was halfway down the hall before he regained enough self-control to doubt his conclusion. He stopped and weighed the consequences of his impulsiveness. Before he beat on her door and berated her, he should be sure of his facts.

The room was cleaned regularly. Perhaps someone working there had raised the window and forgot to close it. Instinct told him the simple explanation didn't apply in this case, but he had to be sure.

For the first time since the night Melissa had died, Jared approached the door to her room. His steps were slow and soundless, cautious and reluctant. The door gave easily. It wasn't kept locked because he never wanted to give the room special significance. It wasn't preserved, just unused.

125

Jared didn't need to step inside to answer his question. He could see the drawn draperies and the curtains lifting and falling in a ghostly dance at the windows. Morning light, made rosy by the Turkey carpet on the floor, plainly showed the bed and Carina's sleeping form.

He gripped the doorknob, intending to back out and close the door. Then Carina sighed and turned over. Jared moved closer. He remembered those sighs while he was holding her and the troubled frown that puckered the space between her eyebrows.

Her arms were bare and one hand rested by her face. He studied her hand, finding it both delicate and capable looking. Her fingers were slim but strong; they curled, like the petals of an opening flower, around her narrow palm. As with a baby, he thought, they would fold around his finger, should he place it in her hand, in that beguiling combination of trust and need that took his heart and shook his soul.

Seeing her like this troubled him. She didn't deserve her fate. Such innocence and loveliness was wasted on him. He was too jaded, too maimed—inside where it counted—to give her what she needed.

He stepped back from the bed and let his eyes coast over the room and its furnishings. There were changes already; chairs that had been precisely arrayed were drawn intimately close, a sewing basket with materials spilling from it marred the pristine surface of the settee. Jared took it all in, his jaw clenching and unclenching with emotion. Moving stiffly, he walked out and closed the door behind him.

He stood just outside the door for a long while. He told himself he was too tired to be rational, but now that he had seen the room, and Carina, he knew he wouldn't be able to sleep. He wanted action. He wanted to bellow the house down. The first wasn't wise, the second impossible.

Unfortunately for her, Agnes chose that moment to

126

emerge from the back stairs. She became aware of him at the same time he saw her, and the color drained from her face. Her footsteps faltered, then speeded up as she attempted to scurry off on some early morning household errand.

"In my room, please, Agnes." Jared's tone was low, out of consideration for those still sleeping, but his voice carried down the hall to catch her, as stinging as the tip of a whip. He waited, without moving the few strides across the hall, until she was there to precede him into the room.

Her mouth tightened as she took in the untouched bed and drew her erroneous conclusions. She turned to face him with a level gaze, however, even when he braced himself, intimidatingly, in the doorway.

"Once I would have said you enjoyed your position here," he said.

"I do, sir."

He raised his eyebrows in mock surprise. "Is that why you seek to make me uncomfortable in my own home?"

"I don't—"

"Oh, but you do," he interrupted sharply. "I must be the judge of my own comfort. Perhaps what you mean is that you don't *seek* my discomfort?" He paused significantly, inviting her to respond.

"Yes, sir."

"Then let me make clear some things I object to. I don't like having you twist my words around to suit some purpose of your own. I don't like having my guests—"

"I beg your pardon, Mr. Jared, but you said she should have a *fine* room and I knew of no finer one."

Jared was thankful for the interruption because it saved him from foolishness. He knew Agnes wasn't innocent. She meant to remind him that Carina wasn't his wife. Nor was she—in Agnes's view—wife material. She had intentionally broken the tabu that had grown up around Melissa's room, a tabu she had created as much as he, in order to embarrass him.

127

But he couldn't say that.

"You tax my patience, woman. If you can't find a way to run my home as *I* wish it run, I'll find someone who can. Is that clear to you?"

Agnes sagged, her defiance melted away. "Yes, sir. I'll find another room for her this morning."

Jared came out of the doorway at a glide, energized by the battle he'd won. Pictures of the room where Carina slept flashed through his mind. Suddenly he wanted her to remain there.

"That won't be necessary," he said, then cast about for justification of his decision. "She would misunderstand the reason for her removal, and I won't have her disturbed. *That* is the point I'm trying to make you see."

From her shocked expression, Agnes did see—perhaps more than he wanted her to. Her eyes darted over his features, measuring, reading. "About the clothes, sir . . ." Her voice faded nervously, then cracked as she began again. "I took the liberty of getting down some clothes—"

"That was fine," Jared said, stopping her struggle. He remembered seeing clothing in the room. He wished Carina joy from it. It was just the room, the bed . . .

Agnes stood in the doorway now, poised for flight. At another time, under different circumstances, she would excuse herself from an interview with him, particularly when he fell silent, distracted by his thoughts. She didn't dare do that now, and he was cruel enough to make her wait for him to decide that he'd punished her enough. He was afraid he hadn't, but finally he waved her away.

She bowed in a show of respect and asked, "Would you like your breakfast served here this morning?"

He had to think about that. "No. I'll eat in the study before I go to town. Miss O'Rourke will have a tray in her room though, and make sure it's a hearty one. She needs fattening up."

\*   \*   \*

Across the hall, Carina fumbled for the blanket to wrap around herself. Her coldness wasn't entirely physical.

Something had awakened her, something in the room that was different, some quality that charged the air and urged her up. Although she woke, she didn't move until it was gone, and then she understood what it was—or rather, who. Jared.

As soon as he closed the door she sat up, free to move then. Hard on the heels of relief at being alone again came another feeling—fear—and this one wouldn't be so easily relieved. She knew he had come to the room because of the first woman who had slept in it, not because of herself.

Carina pulled the blanket tighter, feeling cheated. Jared had come to her bedside and stared at her—she knew she hadn't imagined the weight of his attention bearing down upon her. But he had been studying the impostor, not the person she was. And he had gone away.

She had known not to follow him as soon as she sat up, yet she felt robbed of something precious—of the possibility of pleasing him.

Then, before she could recover from that feeling, she heard him speak to Agnes. Now, she thought, I'll find out whose room this is.

But she didn't.

She found out that Agnes had put her here against Jared's wishes, but not why. Instead of solving the puzzle, her eavesdropping had only deepened it. Jared had regard for her, as Agnes did not. No surprise there perhaps, but there were elements of surprise around her.

She wanted to know about the people she'd seen with Jared last night. They were the reason she'd heard footsteps overhead after that, but again she didn't know who they were or why they were there.

Her father would say they were Jared's victims, but she didn't believe it. Papa was right about many things. She was impulsive and wrongheaded. She'd proved that again and again, just as she'd proved his adage that a listener never hears good about herself. But Jared Wentworth was no devil.

Carina slid down under the covers to wait for her breakfast. She would pretend to sleep and plan her day. She had two projects. One was to find out about, and perhaps meet, the people in the attic. Her sewing offered a perfect excuse for going there. That was the easy part. The other would be hard. She had to ask Jared about Patrick. To do that, she had to talk to him again, and he was already gone.

She closed her eyes, imagining a different result to his visit this morning. If only she had stirred as soon as she'd felt his presence. Would he have stayed? Would he ever come to see her again, or had he already decided to send her away?

The ride to Lowell cleared Jared's head nicely. Unfortunately though, the effect wore off within fifteen minutes of being enclosed in the shop. The ring of metal on metal was tiring on his best days, and this was not one of those.

He stared at the diagram before him. Billy Nichols lived and died by diagrams, while Jared preferred simply to tinker until he got something to work. Ordinarily, he appreciated the fact that Billy's way saved wasted effort and material, but this day wasn't an ordinary one.

"I reckon we should put a gauge right about in here," Billy said, stabbing the paper with a meaty forefinger. "What do you think?"

Jared closed his eyes and shook his head, hoping to clear his vision. He had seen two of Billy's fingers.

"No?" Billy snatched the drawing to examine it incredulously. "Why not?" he demanded. "I told you it didn't work the other way."

Putting up his hands in surrender, Jared said, "I know, I know. You're right."

But he had insulted Billy, and that wouldn't do. Big,

130

barrel-shaped Billy Nichols was sensitive. It had taken Jared months to get Billy to open up enough to offer his opinions, and even now he was quick to take offense at implied criticism.

Jared put an arm over Billy's shoulder and steered him to the open back door. Shutting it behind him, he leaned against it.

"You all right, boss?"

"Just tired." He squeezed his eyes tight and opened them. "I wasn't seeing things right in there, but this is better. There's only one of you now."

"You should go home. Go to sleep."

"You're right, but I wanted to talk to you."

"About the gauge?"

"No, that's fine. About someone to help out here. We need someone else, don't you think?"

"I've been saying so long enough."

"How would you feel about having a free black working in the shop?"

"You mean one of them slaves?"

"He's not a slave anymore. He has papers from his former master, freeing him."

"What's he like?" Billy asked.

Jared thought it was a fair question. "He's intelligent, clean, and wellspoken. He's worked two jobs that I think make him a natural for us."

"Not just picking cotton? I thought that's what they did."

"They do everything that gets done down South, as near as I can figure it," Jared said. "He's worked on a paddle-wheel steamer on the Mississippi, and he's helped run a flour mill. I'm sure he did the least desirable parts of both jobs, but then that's what he'd be doing here, too. Helping you do whatever you need done."

He studied Billy's face, watching for signs of resentment. Billy was the key to the entire shop. If he didn't accept Marcus, no one else would. There was also a chance no one else would even if Billy *did* accept the man. "Be honest with me, Billy. If the idea bothers you, I won't push it."

"You like the guy?"

"Yes, I do. I haven't seen much of him, and I certainly haven't discussed the job with him. He may have other plans. I wanted to talk to you before I ask him."

Billy liked that, being considered first. "What happens if he doesn't work out?"

"I guess it depends on why he doesn't work out—whose fault it is. I don't want him given special treatment either way, not better, not worse. If you don't think that's possible—and you know the shop better than I do—say so now. I don't want to get his hopes up for nothing."

"God knows we need the help," Billy said, more to himself than to Jared. "The Paddies won't squawk. They're glad for the work. The only one who might is Ira. Can I ask him?"

Jared flinched inwardly at his designation of the Irish workers as Paddies, but he only said, "Yes, but do me a favor and try it out as something that's pretty much set. I don't want Ira to think he runs the place."

Billy nodded. "I won't let him ruffle my feathers," he promised with a grin. "Is that it?"

Jared smiled. He was being dismissed; for his own good, but dismissed nevertheless. "That's it." He stepped aside to open the door. "Oh yes, I forgot. Can you tell me where I can find Dennis Boynton without going to the *Chronicle* office?"

"This time of day he's probably at Prescott's. The shoeshine boy's a friend of his."

"Mac?"

"They solve the world's problems there most every day," Billy said with a smirk.

"Ah, of course. I should have thought of that." He shot a quick look at Nichols's pudgy face. "You don't think much of Boynton, I take it. Is he unreliable?"

Jared saw that Billy understood what he was asking.

132

"He talks too much for my taste, but I've never heard that he was unreliable. Fact is," he added significantly, "he's known for *being* reliable in certain things."

It was grudging praise, but Jared appreciated the information all the more because it didn't come easily. "Thank you." His eyes followed Billy into the dimness inside. "I'll be back in a day or so."

"Make it two or three. We'll be right as rain."

As Jared walked down Merrimack Street to Prescott's Tobacco Shop, he thought, that was Billy. *He* was right as rain. If anyone would be a friend to Marcus, Billy would. He probably knew exactly what Jared wanted of Dennis Boynton, too, but no one could ever make him divulge a word of it.

Look for a tall redhead, Klaus Manley had said, describing Boynton. So Jared did. He bought cigars for Silas from the tobacconist. He pretended to consider buying a meerschaum pipe and take up smoking. He got his boots shined.

Then he got lucky. Boynton delivered a stack of *Chronicles* to the shop and took the chair next to Jared's under the awning in front of the store. Just as Billy had promised, Boynton settled in to talk to Mac, as Randolph MacPherson was called.

For his part, Mac was gracious enough to draw Jared into the conversation. Then, generously tipped by Jared for his work and his tact, Mac bowed out, saying, "I'll leave you two fine gentlemen now. *You* may be men of leisure, but I'm going to need a bowl of Annie's stew to stoke up the engines for the afternoon." Laughing, he patted a stomach big enough to hold several simple engines and ambled off.

The silence Mac left behind quickly became uncomfortable for Jared. He got no help from the man beside him, who, minutes before, had been full of affable banter. "Klaus Manley said you might be able to help me," he said finally.

Like a pebble dropped into a deep well, his words

produced a reaction that was all but swallowed up by the wary distance between them. Jared understood that. He was as chary as Boynton and stood to lose just as much from a mistake.

"Klaus is a friend of mine," Boynton admitted.

"So he said." Jared realized it was futile to wish that Dennis Boynton would make this exchange easy. As an Irishman, he had reason to mistrust Jared, who could be a Know Nothing, one of that formless group of political troublemakers who opposed every group they termed "non-native." As such, Jared could be out to trap Boynton and send him to jail. "He also said you could get papers printed," Jared added, pressing for a response of some kind.

Boynton's lips, almost buried in the curling red hair of his beard and mustache, turned up in parody of a smile. "That's my job. I print the *Chronicle*—and deliver it." He gestured to the shop behind him.

"So you do." Jared leaned hard left, maintaining eye contact and mirroring the man's stance as he strained away from him. A rope strung between them would be stretched tight, with the outcome of their tugging match very much in doubt.

"I had another kind of papers in mind," Jared said. "For a free black man. He was freed two years ago in Raleigh, North Carolina. By Cecil Hopkins. When he died, his daughter's husband decided that old Cecil hadn't been in his right mind when he'd let his slaves go."

Tired of pulling on the rope, and just plain *tired,* Jared passed a hand over his face and slumped back into the chair. "Look, if you can't help me, just say so. It's all right."

"What's the man's name?"

"Marcus. He took Hopkins for his last name. Before that, his owners called him Thomas Jefferson."

Boynton laughed. "Original."

"He's tall, probably in his thirties, dark. He has what my mother called good bearing."

"Distinguishing marks?"

"Old whip marks on his back, from childhood— before Cecil Hopkins. He used to stutter, he says."

Jared knew that asking questions was Boynton's way of accepting the job. He didn't mention the sum of money he would offer in payment. He was afraid of insulting Boynton before he had the papers for Marcus. Telling the man's story was like putting the lash to his own back. It fired him with determination to help Marcus.

When Boynton nodded his agreement, Jared felt relief and gratitude out of proportion to what was reasonable. As if Dennis Boynton had solved all his problems for him. He told himself he was just tired, but his feelings weren't diminished. From being his enemy, Boynton had suddenly changed, becoming a man he cherished.

"Thank you, thank you," he said—effusive for him. "You won't regret this."

Afraid he'd already disgraced himself, Jared got up to leave when he was seized by an impulse. Without stopping to think, he asked, "Do you know the O'Rourke family?"

"Conn O'Rourke?"

"Yes, yes, that's the name. I understand the old man and his son had some trouble with my cousin. Do you know how that came out? Is the boy—Patrick, isn't it?— is he out of jail?"

"I believe he is," Boynton said.

"Good, good! I'm glad." Jared stopped himself from saying *that* twice, but only just. This being tired was strange—tricky. Like being drunk. He seemed to be two people, one who disapproved and one who did things the other disapproved.

But at least now that he knew Uncle Nathan had kept his unstated promise, he could go home. He was glad he didn't have to seek out someone else to ask about Patrick

O'Rourke. Checking with Boynton had been a good idea, even if the man was back to acting stiff again. Perhaps he was sensitive about being Irish. People were, Jared knew, though he couldn't see why. Carina was Irish and she was perfect.

The thought of Carina was almost more than he could bear. He had to get back to her. He had news for her, news that would make her happy and grateful. Imagining the form her gratitude would take, he looked for Infidel along the rail. Finally he recalled walking from the shop and deduced that the horse was still back there. He waved good-bye to Dennis Boynton, remembering to thank him again, and, renewed by his eagerness for Carina, set out for home.

The man he left behind watched him go with narrowed eyes.

Dennis had not made a place for himself in Yankee Lowell by being a trusting fool. He knew Jared Wentworth's reputation and his relationship to Enoch and Nathan Wentworth. The latter was reputed to be a matter of mutual displeasure, but Dennis was suspicious. Blood was always thick, and Yankee blood especially so. Might not the apparent rift in the Wentworth family be more appearance than reality?

Given that, what did Jared Wentworth's request of papers mean? He was not abolitionist. According to Ira Wagenknecht, Jared ran a decent sort of shop even though he was too much the absentee owner. But he was a Wentworth.

Was the request a trap for Dennis? He'd more or less given his word to supply the papers, but he wouldn't slit his own throat for anyone, no matter how affecting the story given. And Jared's story had affected him. It sounded sincere. Odd, but sincere—perhaps even sincere *because* it was odd.

Dennis shook his head, exasperated with himself. He was thinking too much again. It was a failing of his. He had razor-sharp instincts that failed him only when he cluttered up his responses with thought.

He took off his left boot, put it onto the form Mac kept handy, and applied polish. As he worked, he stripped away his thoughts and recaptured his responses to Jared Wentworth's singular declarations. He considered each impression and let himself feel it all over again, starting with his resentment at Wentworth's simply assuming Dennis knew who he was. *Arrogant bastard,* he thought.

He put the brush to his boot, fueled by anger, using it to bring out the sheen of good leather. His boots were better than the ones his adversary wore, and that amused him. Buffing with a cloth, he restored his sense of humor along with a mirror-bright shine. He skipped over the issue of papers for Marcus Hopkins because he trusted his instincts there. That request was sincere and Dennis would honor it. Whatever else Jared Wentworth was, he wanted to help that particular escaped slave.

Sitting down, Dennis changed boots and took up the polish and his line of inquiry at the most troubling point. Wentworth knew about Conn's and Patrick's quarrel with Enoch and the Shattuck Mill. Try as he could, Dennis couldn't find a connection between the O'Rourkes and Jared. It had to be there, though. A man like Wentworth didn't take an interest in an Irish family for no reason.

Suddenly, the motion of his hand flagged. He knew the connection. Carina. It had to be. Conn had been trying to keep Carina out of sight of Enoch Wentworth— futilely, as it turned out. A lecher like Enoch was always on the lookout for a fresh face. The miracle was that Conn had kept her safe for so long—if he had.

Dennis grunted and threw down the brush to stuff his foot back into the half-shined boot. Something had happened—something involving Carina—to bring Jared Wentworth into the picture.

A ripple of fear moved through Dennis. Enoch Wentworth would never tempt Carina. If anything, he would drive Carina to his protection. He'd offered it

137

often enough, but she—or Conn—had resisted. Conn depended on her, Dennis knew, and out of regard for his friend, he'd allowed them to put him off. But if Jared Wentworth was a contender, Dennis would wait no longer. Carina was his promised bride.

He meant to collect on that promise.

## Chapter 10

Carina stood with arms akimbo, deeply involved in her imitation of Mary Sweeney scolding her father. "I tell you, Mr. Conn O'Rourke," she said in a brogue so rich the rolled *r*'s obliterated all other sounds, "your—"

She stopped the instant she lost Nellie's attention. Turning slowly, she saw why Nellie's eyes widened, then fell to her sewing in confusion. Jared stood just inside the opened door.

He didn't speak, just looked at her. Taking the hint, Nellie scurried past Carina as fast as her arthritic legs could carry her. She bobbed her head to Jared as she ducked past him.

Carina refused to be cowed. She endured his silent, and perhaps disapproving, inspection, all the while fighting down the urge to blurt out apologies. For what, she wasn't sure.

"You have a fine gift," he said at last.

Puzzled for a second, Carina frowned; then she looked around. "Oh yes," she said, putting out her hand to the clothes. "Nellie is helping me make them over—or rather, *I'm* helping her, and learning."

"Not the clothes. You," Jared replied. "Who were you mimicking?"

Embarrassed, she bent her head. "Just . . . a neighbor. Actually, it wasn't kind of me. She's always been good to me."

"You're too hard on yourself," he said without moving. "I saw no malice in it."

Thinking that Mary Sweeney might not concur, Carina started to disagree. But then she noticed the way he hung by the door, and instead, she remembered her manners. "Won't you come in?"

"No, thank you. I just came to ask—"

She never heard his request. "I'm sorry. I *know* this is your house, I just thought—"

"Carina! Will you stop this?"

His sharp tone brought her up short. Pride warred with humility in Carina. In the confusion she said nothing more, unwilling to apologize again.

"This is your room for as long as you're here, so you have every right to extend an invitation. As do I." His expression softened into a smile. "I came to ask you to join me in my room."

It was what Carina wanted. She hadn't been able to get beyond the attic door in her attempt to find out about the people up there. The door was locked and Nellie, the only person she'd seen so far this day, wouldn't talk about anything except sewing. She'd thought that part would be easy and talking to Jared difficult, but now he was here, asking for her company.

Or was that what he wanted? A picture of his sparsely furnished bedroom went through her mind, together with a welter of thoughts and fears. He wanted to mate with her again, she was sure. But as it was still daylight, surely he didn't mean that. If he did, however, she couldn't refuse him. It was why she was here, wasn't it?

But to accept . . . how could she?

The jumble of her thoughts made her hesitate long enough to see his smile falter. In that moment she noticed how drawn and tired he looked, and she stepped forward, her sudden concern for him making her decision easy.

"Of course," she said, offering her hand. She was not

one to do things by half measures.

Her response beat back some of the hurt in his eyes, but his smile now was askew on his mouth. "Someday," he said softly, "I'm going to be able to read the thoughts behind those expressions that flit over your face."

As he led her across the hall, Carina fervently hoped his understanding would be a long time coming. Although he treated her better than anyone ever had, other than her mother, she found it difficult enough to accept the fact that he had claim to her body. For him to have access to her mind, too, would make her life unbearable.

But then he blasted that hope to pieces.

Confronted with a table set for dinner with two chairs in his room, Carina couldn't hide her reaction in time to keep Jared from laughing. He leaned indolently against the door, watching her. "Perhaps I won't have to wait too long after all. I just saw relief, very large, and shame. But for what, I wonder?" He started toward her, then backed to the door again in mock fear. "And now I see anger."

Carina turned away quickly, only to be embarrassed by the sight of the bed.

Jared laughed, but differently this time. "I think I should feel flattered by your fears—or hopes, as it might be." He took her arm gently and his voice became low and sympathetic without losing the thread of amusement that laced his speech. "Poor little Carina. There's so much you don't know."

His knuckle grazed her cheek, turning her face so he could study it. Whatever he saw seemed to disappoint him, for he grew sad. "If only I could leave you alone," he said on a sigh of breath.

Knowing she had disappointed him somehow, Carina's pride was touched on a tender point. "I know I'm ignorant of many things, but I can learn. And I want to."

Instantly, she restored his humor. If his laughter was again pointed, at least it was laughter, and Carina felt

141

pleased. She went with him to be seated at the table. It seemed strange to her, this eating in a bedroom when there was a room elsewhere set aside just for dining, but at least this time she was not going to be left to eat alone.

Bagley brought a wheeled cart to the table but didn't stay to serve them. Jared did that himself. Carina tried to imagine her father serving her mother this way. She couldn't do it any more than she could hide her smile at the picture in her mind.

Jared caught her amusement and acted offended. She knew it was an act by the gleam in his eyes. They were the secret to reading his moods, she decided as they bantered throughout the meal. When it was over she couldn't remember a thing she had eaten. She only knew it had been wonderful.

She helped him clear the table of dishes, packing everything onto the cart, in order to allay her own awkwardness now that the meal was over. She would have been happy to trundle the cart away as well, and wash the dishes. Although she had tried to amuse him during dinner, she knew he did not want her for conversation. His look was too purposeful for that.

She waited uneasily, stuck halfway between the bed and the door. One look at her and he had no trouble reading her mind. He smiled, a little wryly, a little sadly, and held out his hand to her. Two unsteady steps took her to him. He raised her hand to his mouth and, sighing, placed a kiss on her knuckles.

The courtly gesture, no matter how wearily or regretfully performed, went straight to Carina's heart.

Instead of releasing her hand, Jared turned it over. Holding it before him, he began to speak, all the while staring at her palm as if he were addressing it and not herself. "I'm much too tired to deserve your maidenly fears, Carina. I've enjoyed your company so much that I've changed my mind about requiring you to sleep beside me now."

His eyes flicked from her hand to her astonished face,

but he didn't let her go. His thumb moved over her palm in a caressing, restless circle that mesmerized her. She held her breath and stared into his dark eyes, fixing his image in her soul.

"It's not yet dark and you may still feel well rested, but I do not. I must have sleep." His words came precisely, as though they might turn on him unless he were vigilant. "You should go now . . . to your own room."

Because he tugged on her hand even as he spoke of letting her go, it came as no surprise to Carina when he said, "More than anything I would like to have you beside me this night. Just to sleep . . ."

He cast her hand away then, as if to prove to himself he could do without it.

"It's your choice," he said, abruptly turning away. "I make no demand."

Carina fled the room.

Jared stiffened as the door closed. Disappointment dropped around him like an immense black shroud, suffocating the small flame of hope he'd nourished throughout their meal. She seemed so generous of spirit. He'd been . . . not sure, just so foolishly hopeful. He knew his mistake. He'd given her a choice. Not much of one, to be sure, but enough that she felt safe to refuse him.

He shucked his clothes, dropping them where they fell, and got into bed. Exhaustion had wrung him like a limp rag. He wanted to feel a surge of anger instead of this crushing sense of loss. Reason told him she had no cause to seek his company. He had forced himself on her, and no matter how good he planned to be to her, she had scant evidence so far of his great goodness. She was a simple girl, but not so stupid as to be won over by a few hand-me-down dresses and the dubious honor of being virtually imprisoned in a gaudily furnished bedroom.

Praying for the obliterating bliss of sleep, Jared threw

his forearm across his eyes to blot out the still-light room. He'd partially drawn the curtains before he fetched Carina, but decided not to make the room too dark. He hadn't wanted to scare her. Now he was too weary to get up and draw the draperies.

Next time, he vowed, he'd give her no choice.

When he heard the snick of the door unlatching Jared caught his breath and held it. Bagley, he told himself. Only Bagley, come to check on him like the meddlesome old fool that he was. Straining to listen, he lay perfectly still. Was the door open? Or was he imagining things?

Finally he could stand the suspense no longer. He turned over and caught Carina standing in the doorway, poised in indecision. She wore a white gown, a sleep shift of simple design, and an expression of dismay.

Jared sat up. He had to restrain himself from leaping out of bed and going to her. If he could tolerate wearing a nightshirt he could have done that, but he didn't want to frighten her with his nakedness. He held out his hand. She had come this far; he would help her come the rest of the way.

She didn't move. Her hands were attached to the door like hardware, one wrapped around the edge, one glued to the knob.

"Come, Carina, my brave girl. I won't hurt you, I promise. Just let me hold you."

The low throb of his voice reached out to her, extending a lifeline to the bed. She shut the door with great care and put one unsure foot before the other. She would have run if she'd been able to, just to have that perilous passage behind her.

His arms went around her, catching her up in a fierce embrace. It was almost painful, but she didn't protest. No one had ever wanted her presence before. She'd been so afraid; afraid she'd misunderstood his request, afraid she'd taken too long to dress for bed, afraid she'd disturbed his much-needed rest by coming at all.

144

She put her face into the hollow of his throat and took soul-satisfying drafts of his scent. It was a clean, wonderful smell, like air-dried laundry mixed with the ever-present odor of horses and leather. There was something else, too; something she called Jared for lack of another word for it.

He drew her under the sheet without letting her go. Assured of her welcome, Carina let herself relax as much as the strangeness of the situation permitted. She knew how little sleep he'd had the night before. She was nearly as tired, but her nerves were too tightly wound for sleep.

Instead, there were other compensations. His arm under her neck. The thud of his heart under her cheek. His fingers tangled in her hair. His lips against her brow. Most of all, Carina knew the joy of pleasing someone.

She couldn't remember the last time she had pleased someone. Never her father or Dennis, in spite of how hard she had tried. Not just by working either. She had molded herself this way and that, always against her natural tendencies, seeking to please.

She hadn't expected praise from them or even thanks. It would have been enough simply to know, as she knew now, here in Jared's arms, that Papa approved of what she was and of what she tried to do.

He could have smiled at her as he did at Patrick. He could have valued her. So could Dennis. What would it have cost him just to look at her as though he saw the person she was and liked her? She didn't mind being plain and drably dressed. That was the outside of her. It didn't matter. But she was more than a drudge. She had love to give and the human hunger to be loved in return.

Jared's arms went slack around her as he fell into sleep. Instead of moving away from her, he burrowed closer, pushing in on her until he could nestle against her breast. Like Margaret, he sought comfort and a human connection, even in sleep. He was no longer holding her but letting her hold him; yet there was nothing childish

145

about their embrace. His breath was moist and warm on her breast. Although different in character from his deliberate caress, it reminded her of that confusing time.

She needed to think about that time. He didn't love her. He'd made no vows—would make no promises, not even the one implicit in the bargain she'd made with him in her mind. She didn't know Patrick's fate. At dinner she hadn't dared ask. Now she couldn't until he woke, and she was honest enough to admit she might not dare ask then either.

None of that mattered. He wanted her. It was enough.


It took the sharp sound of thunder, still at some distance away, to pull Jared from the cottony clouds of sleep. He was so at rest, his sense of well-being so intense, that he responded slowly—and found Carina snuggled trustingly in his arms. They were arranged together as neatly as spoons in a drawer, her back to his front, her head nestled under his chin. Her hair smelled of lavender soap.

With the thunder came a rising wind to play with the curtains, setting them to dancing at the windows. Uncovered himself, he covered Carina by half-sprawling along her length, his arms pulling her almost under his body. She didn't seem to mind.

Chuckling silently, he acknowledged that he certainly didn't. He considered waking her and decided against it—for now. He wanted to relish the pleasure of holding her. It was everything he'd wanted last night, and more.

Best of all, she had come to him of her own—more or less—free will. He hadn't forced her or enticed her; and although he was aware that because of her position in his house she felt an obligation to him, that didn't seem to be the reason for her coming. He refused to analyze it anymore. He was grateful.

The thunder rumbled closer and Carina stirred. Her nightgown had twisted up to her waist, and when he slid his hand beneath to cup her breast she accommodated his possession without waking. Her naturalness intrigued him. He wanted her, no question about that, but he didn't want to alarm her. He had promised not to hurt her. He wouldn't this time anyway, although she probably didn't know that. The trick, he felt, was to bring her gently out of sleep into arousal.

Her body delighted him. She was sweetly made for a man's loving. Although the room was dark, he could see her in his mind. Each sensation his fingers discovered matched an erotic picture he had filed away. The textures of her skin and hair spoke directly to his senses.

And he spoke to hers, he discovered. Her breathing became sharp. Her heartbeat accelerated. He moved over her pliant length, laying soft kisses over her neck, and heard her gasp.

"It's all right, Carina. I won't hurt you."

"Ja . . . Jared?"

He laughed softly. "Who else?"

"What? Umm," she murmured, then stiffened.

"No, sweetheart, just relax."

"I don't think I can." Her hands came up awkwardly, perhaps to push him away.

"Are you afraid of thunder?" he asked.

"No." She put her hands on his shoulders as if for safe keeping.

The tentative touch made him shiver. "Do you like me to touch you? Like this?"

Her assent was a moan he took to be delight.

"I like to be touched, too." He took her hand from his shoulder and put it between them on his chest. He moved it for her and made a sound much like hers. "Yes, like that. Umm, that feels good."

The idea of participating in this game he played was obviously new to Carina, but he didn't have to pretend at pleasure for long. He felt the difference the moment she became embarrassed by her boldness, perhaps because she was more fully awake now. He let her withdraw without protesting, knowing he had already won an immense victory.

A sharp crack of thunder announced the beginning of rain. The flash accompanying it showed him a glimpse of Carina's face as her eyes flew open. Jared felt the connection between them course through his body, bringing the storm into their bed. The air around them pulsed to the rhythm of the wind-blown rain.

Carina's arms tightened around his shoulders. Delighted by her response, he surged against her. "Don't be afraid," he murmured.

A sharp intake of her breath and he was home. He kissed her wooingly, teasing her with his tongue, before he moved within her unresisting warmth. Soon she was more than unresisting. At each stage of her response she hesitated, more uncertain than unwilling. Winning her over had nothing to do with conquest. It was much more satisfying than that. She called out his gentleness, wedding it to his innate power, giving it back to him in fulfillment.

Exhilarated, Jared found himself taken over by the storm outside. It was part of him—the rain, the lightning, and the immense boom as thunder crashed around them. The sound covered Carina's cry and his shout of pleasure as he found his release.

Rolling to his side in order to relieve Carina of his collapsed weight, Jared took her with him by refusing to relinquish his hold on her. Nor did she release him. In time, his breathing slowed and he was filled with peace.

Carina, on the other hand, remained tense despite his attempts to soothe her with caresses. Hoping her lack of ease was because of the storm and not the result of his failure to please her, Jared said, "It's all right, little one. The storm is passing."

Her answer was to pull away.

Reluctantly, he eased his grip without letting her go completely. "What's wrong?"

"The rain," she whispered. "Please."

"Please what?"

"The curtains will be soaked."

It was such a non sequitur to Jared that he laughed in disbelief. She was disturbed by the thought of wet curtains? He let her go, but when she moved away, trying to straighten and pull down her nightgown, he stopped her. "I'll do it. You stay here." At the back of his mind was the fear that once she was out of his bed she would go back to her room.

He strode to the windows and lowered them. The floor beneath each was damp and the curtains were heavy with water. He didn't care. A distant glimmer of lightning showed him the way back to the bed and briefly illuminated his nakedness, but if Carina saw him she showed no fear.

Her nightgown back in place, she waited until he drew her back into his embrace before lying down. "You're cold," she said after touching her cheek to his shoulder.

He chuckled. "Impossible."

"No." Again she tried to free herself, and this time, finally trusting her not to leave, he let her go. She scrambled to the foot of the bed and brought up the sheet and a light blanket to tuck around him.

Tears sprang to his eyes at her tender concern. He blinked them away, thankful for the darkness that covered them now like another blanket. When he had her enfolded in his arms again, he breathed a soundless sigh of relief.

Carina heard the sigh and sensed Jared's subsequent drop into sleep, but she was unable to manage that feat. She wasn't unhappy, just afraid. It would be so easy to get used to being held like this. But if she did, what would happen to her when he grew tired of her?

She pleased him now—a little—but she was only here on his sufferance. Her room and her place at his side were hers "for as long as you're here," he'd said. He was a strong man and a man of strong needs. She burned with shame, as well as with remembered desire, at the thought of the way she had responded when he'd wakened her.

If he was the devil, with her wanton ways, she was his fitting mate. How little effort it took for him to make her writhe! Surely that was not proper, but no matter how she sought to hide her weakness from him he found her out.

Now that he slept, however, Carina allowed herself to feel the joy of his closeness. She found she could even touch him without disturbing his rest. His dark hair had a surprising silkiness as it slid through her fingers and his jaw already bristled with a new day's growth of beard. The slight rasp against her cheek seemed more proof of his astounding virility. She fell asleep eventually, lulled by his even breathing and the patter of rain on the window.

When he began again to caress her at some time deep in the night, she hardly opened her eyes. It was easy to pretend she was dreaming. Perhaps she was. The feelings he aroused in her belonged in some other world where cares were few. His touch was, if anything, gentler than before, like sweet rain falling in the aftermath of a storm. She kept her eyes closed, not to deny him, but to see him better with her mind's curious clarity.

Her only concern, how she would face him in the morning light, turned out not to be a problem. He was gone when she woke. Mindful of her embarrassing encounter with Bagley the time before, Carina hurried back to her room as soon as she saw that the hallway was deserted. Although she was wide awake, she got into bed for a while so it would not be obvious that she'd spent the night with Jared.

Her precaution was in vain. No one came to wake her or bring her food. Unsure of the time because the rain still fell, Carina finally rose to bathe from the basin and dress. She didn't make the bed, however, out of a need to deny the way she had passed the night. It was a small point, but foolishly important to her.

150

When it became obvious to her that it was up to her to get her own food, Carina ventured from her room, stealthily as a thief. She'd spent the morning sewing and now discovered that the sun was now drying the newly washed world. The house hummed with energy as maids and even a lad or two went purposefully about their mysterious chores. It amazed her that the keeping of one man could require the work of so many.

For all the activity elsewhere, Carina found the kitchen empty. She took two slices of bread, both heels that looked to be fated for pudding, and tucked them into her skirt. Knowing the bread would be dry, she looked for something to drink. There was milk and buttermilk, both favorites of hers, but she was afraid to take either. The cook might have plans for them. Then she remembered the pump in the yard. Water would be fine, she decided.

Going through the storeroom to the outer door, she spied a basket heaped with apples. She knew no one would miss just one apple and the sight was too tempting. Reminded of the apple tree from which Jared had plucked her, she chuckled at the thought that he owed her this one for depriving her that day, then set off on a walk.

Although the quadrangle was busy, no one paid her any mind. She spotted Ned across the way, but didn't hail him. She wondered if he knew the boy he'd aided was now his master's mistress. She hoped not.

Past the woodshed and woodpile the path narrowed enough to give Carina the sense that she was walking where few people went. Next to knowing Jared, living in the country was the best part of being here. She didn't miss Lowell at all.

She understood that for many Yankee mill girls the city with its exciting pace was as much the attraction of mill work as earning a wage. That told her how different life was for them in their boardinghouses. They worked as hard as her Irish friends and co-workers, but the rest of their day was their own. They did not go home to cook and wash and clean. When Dennis had told her about

151

their routine it had seemed the height of luxury, but she could not have conceived then of the way she lived now.

She was well beyond the sight of the house when the path diverged. Carina took the one promising to lead to a pleasant stand of trees. Entering the little grove, she looked around for a rock or stump to sit on. The one she found was already occupied by a man sitting so still that she decided she was imagining him.

Startled, she backed away just as he jumped to his feet. "I'm sorry," she said.

In the moment she spoke she saw that his darkness was extreme and that he was more surprised than she. In fact, he looked frightened. She realized that he was of the race her father called Negro. Conn and Dennis spoke of such people sometimes with a combination of pity and condescension, for they were slaves in the South. They were not much seen in Lowell, although Dennis warned that mill owners occasionally threatened to replace striking workers with slaves.

"I didn't mean to startle you," she said when he didn't move. "I was looking for a place to sit and eat." She drew out her bread and apple. "Perhaps you'd like to join me?" Tall and well formed, the man didn't look needy, but her heart warmed in sympathy for someone who'd lived in slavery.

"Thank you, but I'm well fed." His voice was deep and well modulated, his manner formal to the point of wariness.

"My name is Carina." She held out her hand, taking the necessary steps so he could shake it. He did so only after a long hesitation. She backed away and looked for another rock so he could sit down again. She broke off a piece of bread, saying, "I missed breakfast this morning."

The bread was very dry, so she alternated it with bites of the apple until that was gone. The rest of the bread she crumbled and scattered for the birds. Although he hadn't watched her eat, she was aware of his attention.

152

Sighing, she contemplated the crumbs of bread. "I can't get used to wasting anything like this," she said. She thought she saw a look of understanding in his eyes when she looked up. It made her smile.

She wanted to ask him the questions in her mind, but knew it would be rude to do so. He had such an air of dignity that she feared offending him. "I'm sorry I disturbed you," she said, "but it was nice to see another person. I live up at the house now. I'm new there, so I don't know anyone much yet."

"Is it a good place?"

Carina was pleased to have wrung the question from him. Her mother had often teasingly said that her chatter could force a stone to speak in self-defense. She was glad she hadn't changed completely. "I think it's good. Mr. Wentworth seems to be a fair man, a man of his word." She hoped he was anyway. "No one has been unkind to me. Do you live there, too?"

"For now."

She nodded, understanding perfectly that his welcome might be as temporary as hers. "Do you have any family?"

Again he hesitated. "Not anymore."

Carina looked away, knowing that the pain she saw on his face was the image of hers. She got to her feet and tossed away the apple core she still held. Smiling, she watched it go and said, "Green apples remind me of home. I used to eat so many I got a tummy ache—every year."

She brushed her skirt of stray crumbs. "I should go back now. Perhaps I'll see you again sometime." She didn't offer her hand again because that made him uncomfortable. "Thanks for your company . . . ?" She paused as if she couldn't remember his name.

"Marcus," he said, smiling in acknowledgment of her trick.

Carina considered his smile and manner as she retraced her steps. He had exactly the air that Bagley sought but couldn't attain because of his lack of stature. If Marcus had been a rich man's servant in the South, she wondered how and why he had left there. Then she remembered—he had been a slave.

Carina returned to the courtyard behind the main house just as an elegant carriage clattered to a halt. Ned and a stable lad ran to hold the matched pair of prancing palominos for the driver, who hopped down to open the door. When Carina saw the golden-haired lady emerge she knew the gold-colored horses were no accident. From head to toe, the lady looked as if she had been dipped into gold. Even her skin glowed. She was a fairy-tale princess come to life.

Agnes rushed past Carina to greet the woman, crying out, "Oh, Miss Meade! How wonderful to see you!" She tossed her apron aside without looking to see where it went. Carina caught it and watched the women. Trudy followed her mother at a more sedate pace.

"It's good to see you, Agnes," Miss Meade said, including Trudy with a regal nod.

Carina was torn between her desire to see everything the woman did and her need to run and hide away in her room until she was gone. Here, obviously, was someone of whom Agnes approved, someone elegant and beautiful enough to be Jared's lady and the mistress of his home.

Not knowing how to leave without drawing attention to herself, Carina stayed. Still holding Agnes's apron, she faded back as Agnes escorted Miss Meade to the door of the main house.

"I take it that Jared isn't here?"

"I'm sure he would be if he'd known you were coming," Agnes replied.

"Well, *I'm* not sure of any such thing," Miss Meade answered, giving a laugh that sounded like the chiming of a tiny golden bell. "He's such a naughty boy!"

Carina nearly guffawed in relief, delighted that she had stayed to hear such an unlikely description of Jared. She knew now that Miss Meade—no matter what her name—had to be related to Jared instead of a potential mate for him. No woman who had experienced his passion would ever term him a boy, naughty or otherwise.

Reassured, Carina trailed distantly behind Trudy, trying to work her way to the kitchen.

"Is my room available now?"

"Of course," Agnes said. "It's always ready and waiting."

"Oh, good. I'm ready to put my feet up and have a rest," Miss Meade said, stopping in the hall. "But first, I'd love a nice cup of tea."

Before Agnes could assign the task, Trudy spoke up. "I'll get it for you."

"Thank you, Trudy. You're a dear."

Carina stepped aside to let Trudy pass and drew the lady's eye. She bobbed her head respectfully, as Nellie or Gwen would do, and turned away.

"Wait!"

In front of her, Trudy stopped short and turned back, but Miss Meade was not talking to Trudy. Carina looked over her shoulder and found that the lady was slowly walking her way. "Stalking" was the word that came to Carina's mind. She waited politely.

"What is your name, girl?"

"Carina O'Rourke, ma'am."

Without taking her narrowed eyes from Carina's face, Miss Meade asked, "Agnes, why is this girl wearing Melissa's dress?"

Carina looked down at the dress. Melissa. Now she had a name for her predecessor. She was vaguely aware that Agnes was upset and that her answer came faintly. "It was Mr. Jared's wish."

"I see." The woman's eyes widened, revealing their color to Carina. They were cat's eyes, green and yellow. "Do you work here?"

"No, ma'am."

"She's a guest, Miss Meade," Agnes said in a solicitous

155

voice. At the same time, unseen by Miss Meade, she was gesturing for Carina to leave.

"Excuse me, please, ma'am," Carina said, bobbing another curtsy.

This time she was permitted to escape, but not before she heard Miss Meade say with an unamused laugh, "Well, at least he hasn't given her *my* room!"

# Chapter 11

It was three o'clock by the pocketwatch that was all Jared had on his person that was his own. He snapped it shut and held it in his palm. So late; almost morning. He looked up at the darkened house, a hulking shape against a lowering sky filled with streaky gray clouds. Somewhere behind those clouds the moon shone, and somewhere inside the house Carina slept.

The thought of her sweetness had sustained him during the past hours—twenty-three, to be exact, since he'd slipped from her side and gone to the attic to fetch down the woman and her child for the next leg of their flight to freedom.

Marcus came with him to carry the sleepy child, but he didn't leave with them. He had decided to stay in Lowell and work for Jared, even though he didn't yet have the papers Dennis Boynton was going to provide. The little girl protested as Marcus tried to extricate himself from her embrace. He stilled her with a whisper and a farewell kiss. She wasn't his child and they would probably never meet again, but they had formed a bond in their days together, one stronger than the bonds of oppression from which they fled.

Virginia, the child's mother, accepted Marcus's help in getting into the wagon with the aloof stoicism that characterized everything she did. Jared considered it a mask to cover her terror. She was moving another step closer to her destination in Canada, where a cousin awaited her, but she was losing someone she'd grown to know as dependable. Her courage in leaving and Marcus's in staying humbled Jared.

They would travel in a farm wagon pulled by powerful but slow-moving workhorses. The rain would make the long trip even longer and more miserable. It provided an excuse for Virginia and Lilla to hide in the back under an improvised shelter, but it soaked and chilled them all to the bone. Jared, dressed in the rough clothes of a farmer, changed into dry apparel that was no better for the return trip. He brought back a wagonload of cheeses and cordwood as his excuse for making the journey.

No one challenged them going north in the rain, and the loaded wagon with its mud-mired wheels was equally uncontested coming back in the dark. His good deed done, Jared should have felt pleased. He never did, however, and this morning his depression was deeper than usual.

He tried to ascribe his unease to the necessity of treating human beings like cargo, but that wasn't the real cause. He didn't like dealing with the Ashlands in New Hampshire—they epitomized the kind of fiery-eyed zealots who made him uncomfortable—but that, too, wasn't why he felt low this time. It was something more personal, a feeling of pursuit and danger, a sense that someone was breathing down the back of his neck, about to overtake him.

Jared shook off the feeling and stretched. He was just tired. He walked to the back door and took off his boots. In the storeroom he cast off his clothing, putting on the robe Bagley had left on a hook for him. Bagley's first act of the day would be to take away the soiled clothes and boots, erasing even this trace of Jared's escapade.

With Carina still very much on his mind, Jared filled a pan with tepid water in the kitchen and bathed away the mud and the smell of wet horses. Bagley had left bread

158

and cheese under a towel, but he wasn't hungry for food. He wanted Carina, her warmth and her softness.

She wasn't in his bedroom. He smiled at the thought that someday she might feel bold enough to surprise him there, for there was boldness in her. It had only to be directed toward him and released. He left his door open and went across the hall, opening her door soundlessly.

It was no longer full dark, and Jared's eyes were well adjusted to the available light. He saw immediately, without leaving the doorway, that Carina's bed was empty. The sheets were in disarray and even the pillow was out of place. It lay in the middle of the bed, folded over upon itself. The signs of her turmoil pleased him, instantly allaying the insidious fear that came too easily, the one that said she had run from him again.

Even before he spotted her sitting at the east window, staring out at the dawn, he knew she was thinking of him. Not wanting to startle her, he let the door's latch fall with an audible click.

She turned her head, and he went to her. "Did you miss me so much?"

"Have you been away?"

Jared frowned. "You know I have."

"I know nothing."

Her cold tone shocked him. This wasn't Carina. "Are you ill?"

"No."

He struggled to understand. She sat wrapped in a shawl, huddled against the damp night air. He knew how cold that could be. "You will be if you stay here in the damp like this. Come to bed and let me warm you."

"I'm fine right here."

Then it dawned on him. She was angry because he'd left her without telling her good-bye or saying when he'd be back. "I'm sorry I left that way, but I had no choice about going and I didn't want to disturb you. You looked tired still."

Her mouth tightened, straightening the full line of her

lips, but she didn't respond.

"Carina, please, I'm very tired and I'd like to go to bed."

She didn't speak. Her eyes, more daring than she, said a number of impertinent things. At another time, he'd be amused at the contrast she made with her clutched shawl and her flashing blue eyes. The lines radiating from her pupils sparked with resentment, but at the moment he couldn't imagine what he'd done to offend her.

Tamping down his own resentment and disappointment at the lack of a welcome, he tried to cajole her one more time. "Come, Carina, I won't hurt you, I promise. I just want to hold you while I sleep."

"That's what you said last night," she said bitterly, "and it was a lie."

"I didn't hurt you and you know it."

She stood up, facing him boldly. "But you didn't just hold me."

Jared gave her a superior smile. "No, I didn't, and you enjoyed it just as much as I did." He put his hand on her shoulder, but she slid away under his touch, leaving him the shawl.

She marched to her bed and turned to look at him as she sat down. "I'll sleep here tonight."

"The way you have been?" He waved his hand at the scrambled covers.

For answer, Carina began to straighten the bed. She plumped the pillow with unnecessary force, still glaring at him.

Jared was drowning in baffled rage. He felt betrayed; the gentle, sweet girl he'd held last night was gone. His pride demanded that he win over this changeling, this harridan who'd usurped Carina's place, but he was too tired to figure out how to do it. Leaving was out of the question now. It had been from the moment he'd been stupid enough to come in here to get her.

He had one option, but it was one he didn't want to use. Biting back the angry words on his tongue, he said carefully, "You are distraught. Whatever is bothering you, let's sort it out tomorrow." He held out his hand to her as he had once, willing her to respond as before. "Come with me now. Everything will look better tomorrow."

She folded her arms across her chest, tucking her hands out of sight for good measure. Only the fact that she seemed to need that extra margin of protection from his appeal kept Jared's temper from boiling over.

He withdrew the offer of his hand by pointing to the door. "This is your last chance to come with me under your own power," he said, exercising great self-control. "*Now.*"

"If you touch me I'll scream."

Jared made himself smile, refusing to let her guess how humiliating that would be for him. "Carina, I am master in this house. If you think anyone would rush to your rescue, think again. Of course, some might be curious. . . ." Shrugging indifferently, he let her picture a corridor filled with spectators.

Instead of rising docilely to come with him, she swung her feet up to lie down. "I shall stay here tonight, but you may join me if you please."

His temper snapped. Bending down, he scooped her from the bed and tossed her over his shoulder. In two long strides he was across the room, yanking the door open. He closed it behind them with a careless shove and dumped Carina onto the bed.

She bounced up from her impact with the mattress, ready to fight him physically, angry as a spitting cat and just as exciting. Her hair fell over her eyes and down her breasts. She came to him with nails and knees. The only thing she didn't do was scream.

Jared caught her hands and pinned them together above her head, using his weight and superior strength to hold her down on the bed. He flung one thigh across her thrashing legs, finally succeeding in subduing her—but not before she did damage to him with one lucky thrust of her knee. Fortunately for him, and for her, she missed a direct hit to his groin.

Their struggle had loosened his robe and displaced her nightgown, bringing their exertion-heated bodies intimately together. The consequences for Jared were entirely predictable. He was thoroughly energized and aroused; sleep was the last thing on his mind.

He had barely enough sanity left to know that in this mood he could easily hurt Carina, but he didn't want to let her go. Nor did he dare to, for her temper remained as high as his had been. And she seethed with frustration.

He made a single misguided attempt to caress her with his free hand and saw that he was compounding his offense. Instead of being soothed, her already taut muscles stretched tighter in her futile attempt to withdraw from him. He eased his hold on her as much as he could without letting her fly off. Her unrepentant fury touched him more than she could know.

She was so damned *brave*.

"Carina, please," he said, trying not to beg, "tell me what's wrong. Talk to me. Believe me, little one, you have my complete attention."

Her expression changed, becoming slightly less obdurate, although she still wouldn't look at him.

He tried again, amazed at his patience. "I didn't want to vanquish you like this, you know, and I won't force myself on you, no matter how you taunt my pride. I'd only hurt you and ruin something we have that's beautiful."

Having drawn her eyes to his, he found it easy to go on talking. Her tension didn't exactly ease, but he felt that it would at any second. That hope was a spur to his thoughts. "Perhaps you don't know that it's beautiful. You probably can't see that, but I can and I won't spoil it if I can help it." Shaking his head, he gave her a lopsided smile. "One thing I know, I have to stop coming to you when I'm dead on my feet. I need my wits around you."

To his utter amazement, her face suddenly crumpled

and the fight went out of her. She began to cry. He gathered her into his arms and rolled onto his back to pillow her on his chest. Her cheek rested on the lapel of his robe, which absorbed her tears.

There were a lot of them, for all that she cried soundlessly. He stroked her hair and brow and back, occasionally rocking her in what he hoped was a soothing manner.

He crooned her name and patted her until she was comforted and he was lulled to sleep. Within minutes, Carina joined him.

An hour after Jared and Carina fell asleep in each other's arms, Susan Meade woke in the room at the opposite end of the house. Like Jared's chamber, it was spacious and airy, having two front-facing windows and a third that caught the dying rays of sun from the west. Although it was the quietest part of the house, something impelled Susan up from her accustomed habit of sleeping late. Something she'd heard in the night or sensed as a force in the house drove her early from bed.

She'd been able to get no satisfaction last night, no answers to her hints as to Jared's whereabouts, not even from the usually compliant Agnes. Worse, the woman had been embarrassed as well as secretive about Jared's so-called guest, Carina O'Rourke. Naturally, Susan had stopped short of asking out-and-out questions, but she didn't like anything about the situation.

She wrapped herself in an embroidered silk robe and went barefoot to the hall. After pausing to listen at the main stairwell, she walked lightly to the door of the bedroom next to hers. As she knew the house well, this seemed the most likely room for such a guest as Carina O'Rourke. Although it was next to Jared's room, it was modest and ill furnished. In summer, it was often uncomfortably warm, with only one window for ventilation. In winter, the lack of a fireplace made it cold.

163

Halting briefly at the door to listen for sounds of occupancy and hearing none, Susan eased it open. The stale air that greeted her told the story, but so strong was her conviction that this was the girl's room, she had to see for herself to believe otherwise.

After a moment's disappointment she was elated. "So," she whispered, turning away, "she doesn't even rate the poorest guest room." Then, abruptly, her triumph turned to dust. She saw the door to Melissa's room standing open. Her heart began to hammer and her palms grew damp.

Melissa's room. What did it mean? Agnes had explained away the clothing, saying the girl was a waif who had nothing at all to wear. But Melissa's room? The place where Jared's wife and baby died?

Dear God, this was serious!

Susan crept forward, afraid of everything—of what she'd see, afraid of being caught snooping, and, most of all, of what all this meant. She didn't have to go inside to see that the room was used now. The furniture was different, one chair pulled to the window and another moved close to the settee Melissa had prized.

But it was the bed that drew Susan's eye. It had been roughly used and partially made—or the other way around. And a shawl of Melissa's lay abandoned on the floor.

Susan stared at everything, trying to read the signs like tea leaves in the bottom of a cup. It was not good news, especially because the girl wasn't in her bed. She looked over her shoulder at Jared's tightly closed door and shook her head. She couldn't look there. She didn't want to believe it was possible.

She returned to her room like a sleepwalker and shut the door. Leaning back against it for support, she found her knees were shaking. All her joy in the beautiful room she'd decorated years ago to her own exquisite taste was gone. The gold draperies framing lace curtains embroidered with gold thread as delicate as fairy tracings, the white on white sheets of Egyptian cotton, the Queen Anne chairs flanking the fireplace—all meant nothing if Jared never turned to her for comfort.

She had waited so long for him. It wasn't fair that he turned to someone else. Dear God, not again!

Once, years before, she had just begun to make him see her as a woman and not a kid sister, only to lose him to Melissa Hartwell. Unlike Melissa, Susan had been too young then to fight for Jared. She hadn't known how. But she was twenty-four years old now, and she knew a few tricks. She wouldn't be caught napping again.

She was already considered a spinster in her social group, and her zeal for the cause of abolition was well on the way to making her unmarriageable by ordinary standards. Her family's wealth and position excused a lot, but if she lost Jared again she would get no other chance at an acceptable marriage.

And she did want one. Badly. The abolishment of slavery was a noble cause, but she had only pursued it so strongly because she knew Jared wasn't put off by it. Not really, anyway.

Of course he wasn't helpful to the cause, but she knew she could change him once she had his commitment to her. He wasn't a strong man, any more than her father, Silas, was. Men like that were all surface bluster. They could be managed. Her mother did it with smiles and gentle suggestions. Melissa had done it by guile. She would find her own way, given the chance.

But would she get the chance?

Suddenly cold and more afraid than she'd been in the three years since Melissa's death, Susan wrapped her arms around herself. Flinging off her robe, she drew the covers up around her neck.

She would prevail this time. She had courage. After all, wasn't she the woman who had braved the United States Militia to march behind a coffin draped in black, singing dirges and chanting "Shame!" when the fugitive slave Thomas Sims was taken from Boston?

What was winning a man compared to that?

For the first time in their strange relationship, Carina woke before Jared. She didn't move for the longest time, paralyzed by a sense of unreality. She was afraid of waking him, unwilling to face him again. Had she really acted that way?

She bit back a moan of pure anguish and turned her head to look at the man beside her. How could she have provoked him so? Her hand went reflexively to the small scar on her cheekbone; Enoch Wentworth and her father had put it there. Neither of those men would have been the least bit forbearing in his place. But Jared had spoken of something beautiful between them. He had shamed her with his kind words.

In sleep, his face lost its sharp liveliness without actually becoming soft. It was too strong for that, with prominent bones like the flinty rocks lying just beneath the soil of New England, shaping and strengthening. A proud face, dressed out with a jutting nose and forceful chin. But he was not all harshness. There was his mouth, too. Mobile. Expressive. He smiled and snarled with equal ease. And kissed.

Carina smiled ruefully. He hadn't kissed her this morning, and she didn't blame him. Her only excuse was a poor one. She was ill prepared to understand and accept what she had become, especially when she was confronted with the image of the lady she could never be.

Susan Meade was beautiful, wealthy and lucky. According to Gwen, who'd been all too pleased to say so last night when she'd brought Carina's dinner tray, Susan was going to marry Jared. She was a lady. She knew everything about managing a great house such as this. She had perfect taste and lived in Boston, except for the times she came to visit Jared, and they had, it seemed, grown up together. Her family had also been his from the time he was twelve, when he'd lost his folks in a terrible fire.

Hearing that, Carina's heart had ached for Jared. Her mother's death, horrible as it had been, didn't compare to such a loss. She looked at him wonderingly. How had he borne it? Yet knowing his pain, had she sympathized? Comforted him?

No. She'd been selfishly wrapped in her own misery, wanting, but not daring, to tell him to go to Susan Meade if he wanted to hold someone as he slept. But that was only spite. She didn't want him to go to Susan—ever.

How had she come to this? Gentle as he was, Jared degraded her each time he came to her. Didn't he? What she did was wrong; so how could she be enraged at the thought of him with any other woman? She should feel relieved, happy.

Carina was hopelessly confused. She hadn't even been happy that he hadn't gone to Susan, that was how lost she was.

In time, unable to stand her thoughts, Carina got up. She had to pry herself out from under Jared's arm to do so. At some time in his sleep, he had shrugged out of his robe, so she tied it around her and walked to the window. Because of the cloud cover, it was difficult to tell the time, but it was certainly edging toward noon. Now that she was up, she became aware of household noises around them and decided to go to her room.

Or was it still Melissa's room? Whoever Melissa was. Gwen would have told her, had Carina asked, but she'd not wanted to give Gwen the satisfaction of showing her curiosity. It was all Carina could handle just to maintain a blank look of indifference in the face of Gwen's maliciousness. Someday, if she stayed for long, Gwen would tell her about Melissa, she was sure. But did she want to stay? And more importantly, could she bear to stay?

The hall was mercifully empty when Carina looked out the door. She scooted to her room and ducked inside without noticing that the door, which Jared had left open, was now closed. Inside she found out why.

Susan Meade sat on the settee.

Carina was too startled to do more than stare. All she could think was how impossibly beautiful this woman was. Her dress was a golden brown like dark honey, a color no other woman could wear without looking drab. Creamy lace inserts cascaded down the bodice from a ladylike collar, and cuffs of the same color set off her pale, perfect hands. They were idle, folded patiently in her lap. Her demeanor reminded Carina of a nun. Though secular in dress and appearance, her very existence seemed designed to torment real people by holding out a perfect self as an unattainable example.

Carina had never done well with nuns, not even religious, kind ones. They had come to her, expecting to be welcomed as they chided her for her father's failings. They asked the impossible, making her feel inadequate and responsible for things she couldn't alter.

Having just come from Jared's bed, she was already at a severe disadvantage with Susan Meade. Unfed and unwashed, she was in no mood to be hospitable.

But Susan was. She smiled, as welcomingly as if the room were hers. "Ah, Miss O'Rourke," she said. "You're back."

"As you see," Carina answered. Jared's robe hung to her ankles, her hair to her shoulders, but she imagined herself regally gowned, with her hair held up by jewels big as hen's eggs. She would not be intimidated. "Are you in the habit of entering other people's rooms uninvited?"

"Not usually," Susan allowed, "but in this case I find it hard to think of this as someone else's room. Jared and I are so close, you see, that whatever he has is more or less mine."

"In this case you shall have to change your thinking, Miss Meade. What I have is definitely not yours."

"But what do you have? Borrowed clothes?" She skimmed Carina's covering with a look of distaste and gestured to the room with one elegant hand. "A borrowed room?"

"Things that are nevertheless mine alone for as long as I'm here."

"And how long will that be? And where will you go then?"

"That's none of your concern."

"I disagree. Jared and I will marry sometime soon—"

"Miss Meade, your plans don't interest me. I'm here because Jared wants me here, and here I'll stay until such time as he wills otherwise. Or until *I* choose otherwise."

"Miss O'Rourke, I don't know how you managed to gain this place you're so proud of in Jared's household, but I *do* know it won't last. You admit that yourself. Whatever your problem is, I assure you it's the height of folly for you to depend upon Jared's kindness. You must take matters into your own hands and see to your own best interests before he simply puts you out onto the road."

Some of what Carina was hearing made perfect sense to her. She did need to plan her own future. She thought she had already, but it was possible she wasn't thinking straight. She didn't trust Susan, however, she would listen.

Sensing that she was making progress and determined to succeed, Susan went on. "You're a reasonably presentable young woman, Carina, and well enough spoken. I have many friends in Boston and I'm sure I could find you a fine, secure position in one of their households. You'd have everything you have here— food, shelter and clothing. *And* you'd have your self-respect," Susan added with an air of triumph.

"How very kind you are, Susan," Carina said, taking the liberty of using Susan's given name as Susan had presumed to do with her. It jolted Susan visibly, but she let it pass as if that were a small sacrifice to make for her larger goal.

Keeping her face carefully bland, Carina left her place by the door and took the chair next to the settee. "Do you suppose that these good friends of yours in Boston would still take me in service if I were carrying Jared's child?"

All the glowing color drained from Susan's lovely face. She pulled back from Carina angrily, dropping her mask of sisterly concern. "So *that's* your game," she spat out, rising onto unsteady feet. "You think you'll trap Jared into marrying you so you'll have a decent father for your brat. Well, it won't work!"

Carina's knees were shaking, too. She was thankful she'd taken her seat before she spoke. She couldn't manage the kind of crafty smile her role called for, but she kept her chin up and her eyes on Susan. "Neither will your plan work," she said evenly. "I won't be driven away."

Susan hovered over Carina. Clearly, she wanted to slap her and run away. After a moment's struggle, she did opt to run.

When she got to the door Carina called out to her in a clear voice. "And, Susan, you should understand one more thing about me before you try to arrange any more of my life. My self-respect is quite intact."

Hissing with rage, Susan scrabbled at the doorknob before she could wrench it open and leave. Having done so, she hurried out, slamming the door behind her, and ran blindly down the hall to her golden room.

In her haste Susan missed seeing Bagley at the top of the back stairs. He carried a breakfast tray set for two. He'd already been into Carina's room to make the bed, so he knew she was with Mr. Jared. Now he paused, considering what to do.

There was no question in his mind.

## Chapter 12

Twenty minutes later Jared knocked on Carina's door. He gave her a few seconds, then knocked again and called out a warning. "I'm coming in, Carina."

He found her dressed in a simple white frock that, except for the shapeliness of its design, reminded him of the shift she wore to bed. She was looking out the east window again. She watched him approach without smiling. "What is it out there that fascinates you so, I wonder?"

He put his hands on her shoulders and peered past her dark head. He could see nothing exceptional beyond her soft cascade of hair. He breathed in her scent and turned her to face him. "Bagley's brought us a meal, something between a breakfast and a nooning, I guess. Come and join me."

"What do you find distasteful about this room, Jared? Is it me?"

"If it were, would I ask you to come with me?"

"If I come this time, will you answer my questions?"

"That depends on the questions. There are things I don't want to talk about." Seeing that her determination remained unmoved, he sighed and said, "I'll try."

Carina gave him her hand and let him seat her at the little table set up for their meal. This time she found no amusement in his strange dining habits. She understood

171

them now. She was his mistress, so she did not eat in the dining room. That place of honor was reserved for ladies like Susan Meade.

Still, Carina was surprised to see that Bagley was there to serve them. As soon as she sat down, there he was, as if he'd been hiding under the bed. He was, she realized, Jared's insurance that she wouldn't interfere with his digestion by asking her pesky questions during the meal.

Bagley's presence didn't bother her; in fact, she found him rather comforting. Once or twice she looked at him quickly, hoping to catch him off guard and surprise him into showing his colors. He *seemed* to give out benign emanations, but her trust was badly shaken and she couldn't be sure.

Jared played the polite host and plied her with food; mounds of creamy eggs, plump sausages, fried potatoes, and something she'd never had, fried green tomato slices topped with cheese. She tasted, nibbled, and complimented everything, but with her stomach tied in knots, there was little room for food. Finally, Jared was satisfied and signaled Bagley to clear the table. "But leave the coffee," he ordered, sitting back.

Carina had learned not to help clear her place, so she, too, sat back. In doing so, she caught Bagley's gaze once again, this time when he was standing directly behind Jared. He gave her a huge and unmistakable wink, then bent to his work.

Heartened by this evidence of support from someone she'd first doubted, Carina's mind eased a bit. Jared noticed, and when Bagley was gone, he said, "There now, I knew you'd feel more like yourself once you had something to eat."

She couldn't help smiling at his satisfaction. "I'm always myself," she argued mildly. "I don't know how to be anyone else."

"But last night you were different—upset."

He was leading her where she didn't want to go. "You said you would answer my questions."

172

"Bagley told me you met Susan Meade. Was she unkind to you?"

Surprised by the source of his information, Carina refused to be drawn out. "Shouldn't you be spending this time with her?"

"I didn't ask her here," Jared answered, his voice as hard as the piercing light in his eyes. "*Was* she unkind?"

"Why would she be? She's a beautiful, well-bred lady."

Jared's mouth jerked into what might have been a smile. "God protect the world from beautiful, well-bred ladies," he said fervently.

"Is that why you tolerate my company, because I'm not beautiful or well bred?" It wasn't the question she meant to ask, but a cry of pain that came straight from her heart. Looking at him, she knew her expression was painfully revealing. She put her hands over her face and shook her head. "I'm sorry," she whispered.

Jared reached across the table and took her hands down. Holding them, he looked into her eyes. This time his smile was natural and very sweet. "Obviously you haven't looked in the mirror in your room, little one. I suggest you do that."

Carina had looked—and had seen excatly what Susan had, a "reasonably presentable young woman," one with tumbledown hair and big eyes in a pale, drawn face. Her features were even but unremarkable, her chin too pointed, her nose too short and her mouth too wide. And of course the girl in the mirror hadn't been smiling. What had she to smile about when confronted by such an ordinary image?

Then too, sometimes Carina tried to see another person in the mirror, the woman who'd lived there before. Melissa. It was fanciful to do so, and of course it never worked. Since last night the phantom Melissa had been supplanted by an all-too-real rival, Susan; but Carina couldn't talk to Jared about her. It wouldn't do to complain about someone so special to him, even if he did invite her confidence.

Instead, she said, "It isn't really my room, Jared. Will you tell me about Melissa?"

He dropped her hands and sat back, avoiding her eyes.

"Why did you send her away?"

He looked at her then, hard. "What have you been told? By whom?"

"Only her name. No one speaks of her."

He grunted with what might have been pleasure, displeasure, or even pain.

"You yourself have told me the most, by your attitude. I woke up when you came to the room that first morning. I felt your presence—and your disapproval."

"The disapproval wasn't for you."

"No. It was for Agnes."

"So you heard that."

For something to do with her hands, Carina poured more coffee for herself after checking to see that Jared needed none. The pot sat in a cunning rack above a squat candle that was keeping it warm. The device was an invention of Jared's, according to Nellie, who considered him to be a genius. Carina wondered if he was. She hoped not. After Conn and Dennis, she wanted nothing to do with brilliant men.

Jared watched broodingly as she added cream to her cup. Finally he said, "Melissa is one of the things I don't want to talk about. But I will, for you, this once. Otherwise, someone else will tell you another version of the story, one that won't be true. There are many such versions around, and I'll thank you not to listen to them."

Carina nodded and swallowed hard, her eyes on his face.

"Melissa was my wife," he said in a flat, emotionless voice. "She died over three years ago, giving birth to a male child—who did not survive."

Carina's eyes rounded with horror and sympathy. "Oh, Jared," she breathed out. "How much you've lost.

174

Your family . . . twice."

He gave her a grim smile. "Then you've heard that story."

"Only the outline, that it was a fire."

"That's enough. It happened a long time ago, Carina. I don't want your pity."

She almost smiled at his look of disdain. "You're not a man who inspires pity, Jared. You probably didn't even when you were a child." She didn't tell him the emotions he did inspire, knowing they were no more welcome to him than pity. But she felt them anyway. He could command a lot from her, but her emotions were beyond his control—and hers, too, it seemed.

He appeared to be surprised by her observation and looked away, as if he were uncomfortable.

"I understand, Jared." His eyes flew back to hers and widened into question. "About the room," she answered softly, leaning forward. "I have no desire to stay there anymore. It's much too fancy for me."

"You don't like it?"

Afraid she had offended him, Carina rushed to reassure him. "No. No, I don't dislike it. How could I? It's just much too lovely for me."

"I disagree—and I don't want you to move."

"But why not?"

"Carina, I never meant the room to become a museum. That was Agnes's doing, and even that was probably unintentional. It just hasn't been used. And it should be. It's only a room, not a memorial."

Carina didn't quite believe him and showed it.

Jared smiled at her expression. "I like having you near, and I like the changes you've made in the room. I hope you'll regard it as truly yours from now on. If you want to make further changes, have Bagley help you and ignore anything Agnes tells you about it."

She nodded, still not convinced but unwilling to continue arguing. She had other points to make. "About last night," she began, tackling the first and most

175

important issue between them now that she knew about Melissa. She looked down into her coffee as if the words she needed would appear there. "I'm sorry I was unpleasant."

When he didn't answer she had to look up to read his response. To her amazement, he was grinning broadly. "In retrospect it wasn't *all* so unpleasant," he said, letting her know by the gleam in his eyes which part had been pleasant. "Anyway, I figured it out this morning when I found that Susan had arrived. You were just jealous."

His complacent, even smug, expression revived Carina's anger, but before she could reply, they were interrupted.

"Mr. Jared," Bagley called over his own tapping from outside the closed door. "The carriage is ready to go to Lowell, sir."

"Thank you," Jared called back. "I'll be right there." He got up immediately, giving Carina an unrepentant smile. "Now I know why I've put up with him all these years. He has perfect timing."

Carina got to her feet at the same time, her feelings in turmoil. She knew he was teasing her and she didn't want to play the sourpuss again, but she was also outraged that he had read her emotions so easily. She wasn't that simple.

He dropped a careless kiss on her forehead, patted her shoulder and left, still wearing an irritatingly cocky smile. Carina followed him into the hall for the privilege of watching him stride after Bagley without a backward look. She went to her room, opening and closing the door with exaggerated care. She didn't want to give him the satisfaction of knowing how completely he had upset her.

She fed her outrage by pacing the room and replaying each aspect of his arrogant behavior. He'd taken her apology and thrown it into her face; then he'd walked off—undoubtedly as the result of some previous arrangement he'd made with Bagley to assure his rescue from her!

The room, once so glorious she couldn't imagine being permitted inside, became more a prison with each impatient stride she took. She'd felt sorry for him, when it was herself she should have been considering. He had his freedom to come and go at will. He could summon her here and there, drag her to his bed, and then stroll off wherever he wanted without giving her a thought or a backward glance.

Thoroughly riled, Carina stalked to the window that looked down into the quadrangle, the place she'd come to think of as the courtyard. She arrived in time to see Jared hand Susan up into the carriage—*her* carriage—and then bound inside after her. As soon as he shut the door, Susan's driver cracked his whip over the team of golden horses and they were off, leaving Carina to wallow in her impotent rage.

Not only had Jared left her, he'd left her to go off with Susan Meade. Long after they were gone, Carina remained at the window, her burning cheek pressed to the glass.

"Oh, Carina," she said mournfully, "you've been such a fool. And you thought you were so smart!" Papa had told her long ago she exhibited the wisdom of a fool. She'd run from an unsatisfactory match with Dennis, only to mire herself in a situation that was far worse. And for what? For Patrick, she told herself for the umpteenth time.

But this time that answer didn't satisfy her. If she'd traded her virtue for Patrick's welfare, why then, she asked herself, hadn't she found out how Patrick fared? Why hadn't she asked Jared about her brother?

Because the time or the situation or his mood, or whatever, was never right. This time she didn't believe that answer, and her anguish doubled. She knew what Papa would say about her bargain with the devil. She feared that he was right.

Patrick was her excuse. Jared had rescued her from Enoch Wentworth and won her heart then and there.

She'd come to him out of desire—for herself—and now she was the one captured and imprisoned. And she'd done it to herself.

Carina took her time at the window while she absorbed the reality of her situation and of her part in it. Once she understood it all, then she began to work out what she would do now. It wasn't like her to be a victim—even of herself.

Duty as well as love had tied her to her family, but Jared had no claim to either. She wasn't foolish enough to run away today, but from now on she would harden her heart against Jared's appeal and prepare to leave.

In the meantime, she would do what she could for herself. She had more to learn about dressmaking, for example, and then there was this room . . . Jared had said for her to make it her own.

She began at once. Pushing furniture around was a wonderful way to use her anger. Her activity soon drew attention. Agnes came first to scold, then, when she couldn't stop Carina, she fetched Bagley. Carina put him to work and together they succeeded in driving Agnes away. They eliminated several pieces of heavy furniture, which they put out into the hall.

"I like it, Miss Carina."

"So do I, Bagley, so do I." She'd kept a chair at the east window and flanked the fireplace with the settee and another chair. With one chest for clothing and the mirrored table and chair against the plain wall, Carina had achieved the spare look she preferred. She had taken down the heavy bed curtains. "I want the window draperies taken down, too," she said, eyeing the one still-discordant note in the room.

"I'll do it," Bagley offered.

"Thank you, and have the extra pieces put into storage, will you?"

"Certainly, ma'am."

Carina only just kept herself from explaining where she was going and why. She had to keep reminding herself that she was the authority in this case. Her authority was borrowed from Jared, but Bagley at least seemed to respect it. She decided to leave before she undermined it by doing something inappropriate like kissing Bagley's shining dome. Instead, she smiled and left him to finish for her.

She had other plans for herself.

During the ride to Lowell, Jared sat back in Susan's plush carriage, content to let her entertain him. For all her cheerful chatter, she was not pleased with him. Now and then she let a barbed remark pass her lips even as she smiled relentlessly.

But she was no real concern. He could handle Susan as well now as when he'd acted the older brother, the only role he wanted to play in her life. She might not understand that yet, but she would. He'd make sure.

Last night, in the face of Carina's changed disposition, he had begun to question once again his ability to understand women. But then he'd learned that Susan had arrived and everything had fallen into place.

He'd spent so many years baffled by Melissa and her moods. With her, hindsight was a wonderful thing, but at the time he had been in hell. No matter what he did to please her, it was never enough—or if it was enough, it was wrong in some other way.

Carina's simplicity attracted him. He could read her mind in her face. Oh, not all of it, but enough. And with her, he was in charge. He wasn't going to let that change.

Susan's voice cut sharply into his reverie. "Jared! You're not listening to me."

"Of course I am. You're chiding me about my many faults."

She shook her head reprovingly, but she smiled. "But *which* fault was I discussing?"

"My neglect of Indigo was the one that sticks in my mind."

179

"She does miss you, although why she should I can't imagine."

"She won't have to miss me much longer. I'll be moving back to Boston soon."

"Permanently?"

"Of course not." He watched her excitement fade and said gently. "Susan, you must face reality. This is my home. My life is here in Lowell and here it will stay. I *visit* Boston and your family—"

"Which is your family," Susan reminded him.

"Which is, indeed, my family—all I have and all I will have. You know how much I treasure all of you."

Susan didn't like the sound of that. "Jared, you have to put Melissa and your loss behind you."

"I've done that. You needn't concern yourself about my grief, Suzie. It's gone."

Warmed by the use of her old nickname, she smiled. "That's wonderful. Mother will be so glad to hear it." She knew she should stop at that, but she couldn't. She had to test the waters more. If giving up his grief meant taking up with a . . . with someone like Carina O'Rourke, it wasn't good news at all. "Mother wanted you to get married again, you know. She seems to have given up on Tyler, but she thinks you need to be married."

All Susan's pleasure in her careful phrasing, in her subtlety, evaporated when Jared threw back his head and laughed. She could feel her face getting warm, first with embarrassment, then annoyance as his mirth went on and on. By the time he had himself under control she was glaring at him.

He wiped at his eyes with the back of his hand and continued to smile idiotically. "Oh, Suze, what would I do without you?"

Susan knew it wasn't a compliment. "Perhaps you'll have to find out someday."

"I hope not," he said fondly. "I really do."

She felt as if he'd just reached out and ruffled her hair. She'd loved the gesture when she was nine or ten. Now it made her feel bleak inside. She wanted to scream at him: *See me! I'm not a child anymore. And I'm not your sister!*

"In case Indigo should ask about my marital intentions," Jared said, his mouth still twitching with the impulse to smile, "I hope you'll tell her for me that I'll never marry again."

"Why not?" Susan tried to ask the question lightly, then gave up the effort. It was a lost cause anyway. "Oh, Jared, you mustn't harbor such bitter feelings. Losing your wife and child was terrible, but you can find happiness again with another. I know you can."

Jared shook his head. "I don't want to, Susan. My mind is made up on that score. No one, not you or Silas or Indigo or all the angels in heaven can convince me that marriage is right for me. Not again. Not ever."

He sounded so final, so sure. She looked away quickly to hide her hurt. "You'll change your mind," she said just as firmly. It was what she believed, what she had to believe. In one horrible way, she took his liaison with Carina O'Rourke as a sign of his reawakened interest in life. If he could need a woman's . . . company like that again, then he *was* recovering from his grief. It was positive, a renewal, even if of the vulgar sort that she, like women through the ages, would have to overlook. At least for now.

Jared reached across the carriage and took her hand. Surprised, Susan looked into his eyes. She knew them well—and hated the sympathy she saw there. "Suzie honey, I love you. You know that. You can count on me to help you anytime. But don't count on me to change my mind about this."

Susan pulled her hand from his grasp. Looking out the window, she searched for something to say, and quickly. "Oh look," she cried out. "There's a man giving a speech there on the steps of that building. Do you suppose he's one of those agitators?"

"Probably," Jared said, glancing to the window without interest. "For all the good it'll do him—or anyone else."

Here was a subject upon which Susan could vent her passion legitimately. She turned to him. "You're so cynical. You and all the other men in this world! You have all the power, but do you do anything about it? Do you do anything at all to make the world better for people like that poor man? No, you do not!" she said, answering her own questions before he could say a word. "And you make me sick!"

Knowing that she was transparent, Susan clung to her temper to save her from the humiliating certainty that she was about to cry, especially when Jared said wearily, "For my part, Suze, you can have all the power you want. I just doubt you or anyone can make much difference in the long run."

"Someday women will be able to vote," she said. "Then the world will find out the difference!"

He was giving her that superior look she hated, so she went back to looking out the window. The carriage barely moved because of the crush of people in the street.

A tall man at the back of the crowd drew Susan's eye. His red hair and beard gave him a raffish look that reminded her of Tyler, although her brother was as blond as she and smooth-shaven. Watching the man, she decided it was his slender build and bearing that was like Tyler's. Whatever it was, she kept him in view as Maurice, her driver, inched them along the roadway.

All at once the carraige began to move forward, and just at that moment the tall man turned to look their way. Susan's breath caught as his gaze met hers. Feeling that she had somehow caused him to look her way, perhaps because she had been staring, she shrank back into her seat and tried to pull her eyes from his.

She couldn't do it. He held her, just with his eyes, the way a pin holds a butterfly to a display board. It was an insolent, assessing look that took in the showy splendor of her equipage as well as her appearance. She felt measured to her soul, then dismissed, cast away abruptly from the ranks of the worthy as if she had no more value than the butterfly he'd made her think of.

Shaken to the soles of her kid shoes, Susan looked at Jared, wondering if he had noticed the man. He was studying some notes taken from his pockets. Strangely relieved, she shifted on the seat. The man had been real, she knew, but she had only imagined that look. He could not have seen her, and even if he had, it made no difference to her what a perfect stranger thought of her.

But it did matter. Somehow, it mattered.

When Jared reached his machine shop he suggested that Maurice go with her on her rounds of the shops, but Susan refused to leave him, saying she had no interest in shopping.

Which was suddenly and inexplicably true.

Although the Lowell shops didn't compare to Boston's, shops of any kind generally interested her. However, that was no longer true. That man, whoever he was, had robbed her of her frivolous desire for another amusing scarf or trinket. She felt purged and challenged.

Jared, on the other hand, was exasperated with her. He snapped, "I thought you came to shop."

"I came for the ride and to keep you company."

"Shall you come to the tobacconists with me?"

"I didn't know you smoked."

"I don't." Hands on hips, Jared tried to stare her down, but when she held her ground he threw up his hands. "Oh, never mind. Come with me. See if I care."

"How can I refuse when you invite me so graciously," she teased, taking his arm before he could change his mind. "I won't be in your way, I promise."

Their route along Merrimack Street took them back the way they had just come in the carriage. The farther they went, the more people they met, until they were like fish struggling up a river. Susan clung to Jared's arm, ducking a bit behind him so he could clear her way. When he stopped abruptly, calling out, "Boynton! Over here, please," she bumped into his broad back, knocking her hat askew.

She lifted her head to set her hat right and looked straight into the same compelling eyes that had captured her attention on the street. The man was even taller than Jared. This time he didn't stare back at her. He was absorbed in conversation with Jared.

They stood amid the stream of people—mostly men, Susan noted—like three rocks breaking the surface of traffic, until Jared worked them to the shelter of a doorstep at the side of the street. Then she could catch most of what the men said.

"I don't want your money or your business, Wentworth," the man was saying.

"Fine. But I pay my debts."

"That's debatable, in my opinion."

Susan felt Jared's muscles bunch under her hand and, to avert trouble, she pushed forward so that she stood in front of Jared. "You haven't introduced me to your friend, Jared."

"That's because we're not friends," he answered curtly.

She ignored his rudeness and his attempt to remove her from his path. "I'm Susan Meade," she said, putting out a gloved hand.

The man was nearly as impolite as Jared, but finally he took her hand. "Dennis Boynton," he said.

"Mr. Boynton." She bowed slightly and searched her brain for an appropriate social comment. "Didn't I see you among the audience just now? What was the topic of discussion?"

His lips turned up into a sneering smile that ridiculed her civility. "The topic of discussion, Miss Meade, was the impossibility of earning a decent wage for an indecent amount of work—something you wouldn't know about!"

Before Susan could find a suitably scathing reply, Jared put her behind him again. And this time he held her there. "That's enough, Boynton." He stepped back, moving Susan with him. "All right. This time we'll do it

184

your way, but I don't like it."

"You don't have to like it. You've got what you want, and there'll be no next time."

The smile Jared gave him was a cousin to Boynton's sneer. "That's all right by me."

They backed away from each other, like opponents pacing off the distance for a duel, with Susan as Jared's bewildered second bumping along at his side.

Boynton nodded once, then he turned and loped away.

Susan had to be dragged away. She'd never seen a grown man move that way. He had practically *run,* and yet he hadn't acted afraid. Quite the opposite. He wanted to fight Jared and showed the same primitive blood lust that marred Jared's face.

"What a perfectly odious man," she said as soon as Jared slowed down and let her catch her breath.

"I quite agree."

They were packed away in the carriage, heading home, before Susan realized that she didn't understand what had taken place between the two men. One look at Jared's hard face and she decided not to ask.

# *Chapter Thirteen*

Rain had made Jared Wentworth's trip to New Hampshire a misery, and it had plagued his uncle on the way to Boston a few days before. For companionship, Nathan had his niece, Rachel Farmington, not the stoical escaped slave who shared Jared's wagon. Whereas Virginia sheltered her child from the rain with her own body and ate bread, cheese, and fruit without complaint, Nathan was not so fortunate. Rachel, who preferred train travel, protested aloud at each jarring lurch of the carriage.

There were many such lurches. Weeks of dry weather had the roads well coated with a fine powder of dust that instantly turned to gluey mud with the addition of water. The high-wheeled carriage made slow headway, finally failing completely outside of Cambridge when one of the thin wheels snapped under the strain.

Rachel wasn't grateful to be rescued by a pig farmer and said so—often.

The farmer sat through her tirades if he were deaf, but finally Nathan had had enough. "If you say one more word, I'll have this good man stop the wagon and put you out. You can walk the rest of the way—if you can figure out where to go."

Although Rachel resented his order, she didn't test his temper further and the rest of the journey was as quiet as it was wet. When they reached Mount Vernon Street, Nathan paid the man handsomely for his trouble, a fact that Rachel tucked away as ammunition in her campaign to provide herself with the finest of everything.

During her stay in Lowell Rachel had learned a lot. That Uncle Nathan was not a popular man. That Southerners were not well liked either. To offset the effects of these two impediments to her ambition, Rachel was sure she needed more than her own natural loveliness. She needed the appearance of great wealth.

For that, she had to have the ultimate wardrobe. Thanks to her mother, she knew exactly what to wear, and she had won Uncle Nathan's promise to equip her well. Just how well, he didn't know—yet. Rachel intended to break the news to him gradually, postponing as much bad news as possible for as long as possible.

Uncle Nathan's house disappointed her immediately—as did Boston, or at least the part she could see. It was dreary and dirty, even when she made allowance for the weather.

Still, it was Boston and a place to start.

For Nathan, coming to Boston meant starting over, or nearly so. He had to rally support for the Shattuck Mill among his investors. He was listed as the owner of the mill, but in fact the true ownership belonged to those who had loaned him money to finance the operation. Being the owner in name only meant that if he didn't provide his investors with the profits they anticipated, he would be ruined when they took their capital elsewhere.

He hadn't wanted to leave Lowell, and he had little stomach for the exercise he faced. Bringing Rachel meant he had to launch her properly into the marriage mart, at far greater cost than he could afford. His early hope for salvation by way of her making a brilliant match faded every time she opened her mouth.

He knew now he'd made yet another mistake in bringing her North to live with him. He'd misjudged her in much the same way he had Lucy years ago. All he could hope for now was that another fool would take her on, someone simple enough to be gulled by her pretty smile and fetching shape.

Rachel had caught him at a weak time. Disappointed once too often by Enoch, Nathan had looked upon her arrival as the promise of another chance when he felt that time was running out for him. She was young, lovely, and grateful. But that was then.

Now, only weeks into their relationship, she showed that she possessed an abundance of what Nathan called the Farmington Factor. Another name for it was greed. Given one dress, she wanted twenty more. She would get more than he wanted to give and far less than she wanted, but that was the way life was.

Nathan had wanted Felicity Cole and had settled for Lucy Farmington when Felicity had made it clear that he was the wrong Wentworth for her. Given his life to do over, Nathan would choose to remain single. Lucy had persuaded him that she loved him enough for both of them. Perhaps she had once, but the strain of living with someone who obviously preferred another, ultimately— perhaps inevitably—had eroded her love. Finally, it was no more than a thin veneer over bitterness at being considered second best.

He couldn't blame Lucy for feeling as she did. He, too, was second best, and although his relationship to his brother Philip wasn't as intimate as marriage, it had suffered in much the same way. He and Philip became estranged. They quarreled, and the rift between them widened to a gulf. Each quarrel made it worse, particularly because they could never fight about the real issue between them, Felicity. Insteady, they picked on each other's habits and business practices.

Before Felicity, they'd been close, their strengths and weaknesses balanced so that together each was better than he could be alone. But traits they had lovingly accepted in each other became thorns. Nathan the bookkeeper. Philip the big thinker. They hurled names

188

and even—though rarely—fists, in their futile attempt to work together.

Nathan knew he should have bought out Philip or sold out to him, one or the other. Philip knew the same thing. But it became one more bone of contention between them. Who would buy? Who sell? Both loved the business—then it was shipping—and neither wanted to give it up.

Finally Philip would have sold out to him, but Nathan had refused to buy. It had felt too much like the business was a consolation prize for losing Felicity. And anyway, he didn't want to run it alone. He needed Philip. Needed his vision, his breadth.

Then came the fire.

Nathan always thought of that watershed event in dramatic terms—now. There had been years and years when he couldn't think of it at all. Philip, Felicity, and little Pippa, their five year old daughter, all dead.

And Jared telling the world that *he*, Nathan, had killed them.

Nathan told himself he understood, but he didn't and he never would. Over and over he told his story. An accident. A terrible accident. It had to be that. He had loved them all, Jared included.

But Jared was his accuser. Still.

Nathan had accepted that much. He could never be Jared's uncle in fact as he was in his own mind. Jared would not permit it. So the enmity lived on. And the terrible stain on his reputation. The whispers that followed behind him like ripples after a ship. Living in virtual isolation in Lowell was only a partial solution. Now and then, as now, he had to come back to Boston and face society. Maybe having Rachel to launch would give the gossips something else to discuss whenever he appeared. It might be worth the cost of her wardrobe after all.

He changed his mind about that the instant he heard the first of her plans.

"No!" he thundered at her. "Damn it all, no and no and no and no!"

Rachel looked up from her samples, pouting prettily. "But Uncle Nathan, I want you to be proud of me. You're such an important man that I just know everyone will be looking at me. I want to reflect your prestige in everything I do."

"Then wear mirrors," he snorted. But she didn't crumble. "Look at me, girl. Do I look like a fool young puppy to be fed such nonsense?"

"Of course not, Uncle Nathan," she said, changing her tactics with the practiced ease of a politician. "And it's because you're a wise and experienced man that I can appeal to you this way. You know the value of the right appearance."

"Humph!" Nathan could feel the edge of his harshness slipping away. Damn, but the girl was clever. She had her tune, and she played it perfectly. "I'm a generous man, Rachel. More generous than you deserve. But I'll not sit still for any such business as you propose."

"But Uncle Nathan—"

"No! Cut it in half or have nothing!"

"Half!" she wailed. "But that's impossible! I'd as soon go naked as that!"

"Good," he barked, throwing himself heavily into a chair. "That way maybe we'll get some offers for your hand and someone else can have the privilege of dressing you up in silks and laces."

"I will get offers—wonderful, rich offers—*if* I look the part," she said, dancing closer to offer him a preview of how one especially lovely and outrageously expensive piece of cloth would look draped over her bosom.

He enjoyed the show, but he shook his head obstinately. "Young, unmarried girls do not dress that way here. This is *Boston*."

She sighed and gave up on that issue. She was wise enough to concede the point. Besides, she had seen the women of Boston in the past few days. They were definitely not like the women of Charleston. "All right, Uncle, I'll do my very best to keep down costs. Will that pledge help you feel better?"

Nathan was instantly suspicious. "What's the catch?"

She didn't pretend there wasn't one, but looked him straight in the eye. "I've met an interesting man."

He groaned. "Some worthless scoundrel with a pretty face, no doubt."

Rachel didn't flinch. "A scoundrel certainly, at least by reputation, but he's not worthless and not just a pretty face. He's a full-grown man, and I think he deserves me."

"God help him then. What's he done? Robbed the poor box at Saint Anne's?"

Rachel put the cloth aside and looked down at him. "Worse. He's robbed you of your good reputation. He's—"

Nathan jumped to his feet. "No, by God!"

"No? Why not?" She stood toe to toe with him, her nose nearly level with his.

"Just . . . no. That's all." He had to turn away to hide the hurt she'd uncovered. Was nothing in his life safe from this little shrew?

"I would think you'd welcome the chance to bring Jared Wentworth back into the family fold," she said, watching him with her knowing eyes. "After all, what better way could there be to silence the gossip that still follows you than to marry the two estranged branches of the family to each other?"

Nathan couldn't think of an answer. Her question bounced around in his brain, setting off alarms and other questions. It had its own insidious appeal as well.

Rachel fed the conflagration with a shrewd addition. "He has money, Uncle Nathan."

She made him feel stupid, slow, and old. "He would grind you into little pieces, girl. He's not a callow boy you could wind around your finger."

"I met him the day he came to see you, did you know that? And I think we'd deal well together," she said. "I

191

think he found me attractive."

"Of course he did, but he's not a fool."

Rachel's eyes narrowed as she watched him bluster. "How strange that you admire him so. One would think you'd resent the lies he tells about you. Unless they aren't lies?"

"If you heard as much of the story as you pretend, then you know that to him they aren't lies. And I've never denied being there or quarreling with my brother. I didn't harm him or his wife, however, and I didn't start the fire."

"But *someone* did and as long as Jared Wentworth accuses you, the world will go on accepting his word against yours."

"It was an *accident!*" Nathan roared. "I've said so for years."

"And I, for one, believe you," she said sweetly. "Perhaps I could persuade Jared to my point of view, don't you think?"

"No, I don't think."

"If he married me the *world* would believe it anyway. Beyond that, what do you care?"

Her reasoning was as seductive as it was fallacious. He cared far less—most of the time anyway—about the world than he cared about Jared. But she did have a point. Even if he couldn't change Jared's mind, an alliance with him would probably silence his accusations. Provided, of course, that he cared at all for his wife.

The thought brought Nathan up short. He was going crazy. Rachel was a pleasing little minx, but she had him building castles right along with her—and on the most unstable ground imaginable. One chance encounter with Jared, and Rachel thought she would win him to marriage.

What folly!

Then he remembered his own encounter with his nephew. Jared himself had brought Rachel into their discussion. Didn't that mean he was interested in her?

192

Not in the context of that ill-fated interview, he decided. Jared had brought up Rachel as a threat, intending to use her as a hostage to ensure that Enoch kept away from some Irish family. The O'Rourkes.

Nathan felt a touch of vertigo, recalling the incident. He'd seen to the release of the boy as he'd promised Jared, but then he'd forgotten the whole thing. That wasn't like him. Once he would have been on top of the situation—whatever it was. He'd meant to find out about Conn O'Rourke's daughter. Had Jared mentioned a daughter or had he imagined that?

Gripping his stomach, Nathan sat down. He wasn't sixty-five years old yet. He couldn't be losing his faculties so young. His father had been hale and strong-minded into his eighties. He'd had a lot on his mind recently, that was all. Financial troubles would put any man into the grave before his time.

"Are you all right?" Rachel asked. "You look pale."

Her concern touched him. Perhaps her idea had merit. She was comely enough to turn the most jaded head and shrewd enough to hide her sharp tongue until she had Jared well hooked on her charms. This Irish thing couldn't be anything except more of Jared's strange habit of championing the downtrodden. For a supposedly dissolute man, he did a lot of that.

"I'm thinking," he said. "That takes effort for an old man."

"You're not old, Uncle Nathan. You're a man in your prime."

He laughed. "And you're an incorrigible flatterer."

She grinned broadly. "Of course. Do we have a deal?"

"You'll keep your expenses down?"

"As only my mother's daughter could," she vowed. "Will you mind returning to Lowell?"

Nathan laughed again, feeling carefree as a boy. "It won't be necessary. Jared comes to Boston every winter to stay with the Meades. And that's where you'll meet your competition, I fear. Silas Meade has a daughter who's rumored to have the inside track. Jared and Susan grew up together."

Her smile never faltered. "I'll manage."

Just that quickly, Rachel's confidence made a believer of Nathan.


When Carina went to ride she took two apples from the storeroom, one for Infidel and the other for Marcus. He wasn't in the grove when she began her outing, so she was doubly happy to see him as she made the loop on the way back home. She jumped down and went to join him, tossing him the apple. His smile made her think of Kevin. Like her brother, he smiled with his whole body.

Glad as he was to see her, he said very little. Carina told him about Infidel, which led her to stories about New Hampshire and Uncle Ansel's farm. When he still didn't comment she asked, "Is that different from where you grew up?"

"Well, I've never seen snow. It must be . . . strange."

"Oh, it's beautiful. You just need lots of warm clothes to wear. Will you still be here in the winter?"

He lost his smile. "Perhaps."

"I hope so, Marcus. I'll teach you to make snow angels." She meant to cheer him, but he remained serious and that made her feel guilty. "Do you miss the South so much?"

"Sometimes."

"And your friends more. I hope you'll let me be your friend. I don't have any either."

"You?" In surprise, his eyes went to where Infidel cropped the tender new grass growing at the base of a rock.

Carina understood. Riding the master's horse was a sign of favor. "I just took the horse," she explained.

Marcus's eyes widened in fear for her, and he shuddered.

"You were a slave, weren't you, Marcus. Was it so bad?"

"It was bad and good, like everything."

"You're so wise."

"No, I've just lived different. I was bought by a good man when I was twelve. When he first got sick he freed me, gave me papers and all, but I stayed because he was sick. Then his daughter's husband took back my papers and burned them. He said Mr. Hopkins didn't know what he was doing. He was going to sell me again."

"What happened? Did you run away?"

"Not soon enough. I was going, but I had family. . . ."

"Oh, Marcus."

"My wife, Simmie—she died, but I had a boy. They called him Harris, but me and Simmie named him Tad. They took Tad off to Chattanooga. At least that's what they said. Then, when I was low, they sold me to the captain of a Mississippi River boat."

"But you got away," Carina said. He seemed so lost in the past she wanted to remind him that he was no longer there.

"I went to Chattanooga, but I couldn't find him."

Carina couldn't help herself. She had to touch his hand. She needed sympathy as much as he did. She wanted to tell him he'd see Tad again, but how could she? After a long silence she asked, "How did you find your way here?"

"I walked at night and hid in the woods during the day. In Virginia I met a man who took me with him to the coast. He said I should go to Boston, that there would be people there who'd get me papers again."

"Will you be safe then?"

"I reckon so, or I can go to Canada. But I think I'll stay here awhile. If I can."

"I hope you can."

Carina thought about Marcus on the way home. His story saddened her, but it also made her realize how fortunate she was. She wasn't really alone, and she knew where her family was and that they were safe—at least they were if Jared had kept his word. She determined then and there to waste no more time before asking him about Patrick. Jared had gone to Lowell; he would soon know whether or not he'd been able to secure Patrick's release.

With that settled, Carina considered how she would get the clothes she needed for her own escape to freedom. Like Marcus, she would walk north and hope to find a good place to live and work. Her path would be easier, but not without problems. She needed access to the stable lad's clothing, to take a few items over as long a period of time as possible.

It bothered her to steal, and from people who had so little, but she could think of no other way to manage. She consoled herself that Jared would replace whatever she took and not hold others responsible for her misdeeds.

As she directed Infidel past the woodpile and into the back courtyard Carina saw that her arrival could not have come at a worse time. Ned and Susan's driver were leading her golden horses from their harness, while Jared helped Susan alight from the carriage. Carina pulled sharply on the reins in reaction to the unwelcome sight, but only succeeded in drawing attention to herself as Infidel executed some dancing sidesteps in agitation.

Although she saw Susan's surprise, Carina was most aware of Jared's reaction. He dropped Susan's hand to take in every aspect of her appearance, his eyes sliding over her with insulting thoroughness. She was not well turned out. Her hat had slipped back on her head, and her riding suit was an unflattering shade of green.

She halted Infidel and waited for Jared to approach. "I see you took my advice to make yourself at home."

"This is all my fault," she said immediately. "I took Infidel when Ned was busy elsewhere, without asking him."

Jared took the reins and lifted her down, his expression

196

divided. His mouth was firmly set and unsmiling, but his eyes sparkled with hidden laughter. "How quick you are to take blame," he commented dryly, surveying her from his superior height.

Carina wished herself upon Infidel still. She felt caught between the horse's great bulk and Jared's looming disapproval. She wet her lips and said, "For good reason, I'm afraid."

Surprisingly, Jared laughed. "You afraid? I very much doubt it." Then he swept the hat from her head and gestured with it for her to precede him.

She did so gingerly, feeling that he would do something unexpected while her back was turned. After a few steps, she realized that he wasn't following her. He had taken Infidel to his stall instead.

Once she reached the door she ran pell-mell to her room, feeling fortunate to have escaped so easily. She hadn't even seen Susan close up.

She was not so lucky later.

Trudy knocked on the door and directed servants to bring in the bathtub and pails of water. Although Carina was pleased to be able to bathe, the idea that Jared had ordered a bath for her rankled. Even the fact that he'd requested her presence at dinner couldn't make up for the humiliation of having him order her cleaned up for the occasion. It made her feel like an errant child. Trudy's offer to dress her hair didn't improve her mood either. Rebelliously, she left it loose and chose a dress other than the one Trudy put out for her.

Agnes watched Carina's brazen entrance to the dining room with pursed lips. She had laid a splendid table, partly in honor of Miss Meade and partly in the hope of tripping Miss O'Rourke into displaying her undoubted lack of manners.

Whatever gaffe Agnes hoped for, the meal itself went smoothly, in spite of what she saw as Mr. Jared's unbelievable rudeness in having his mistress at the same table with his future wife. It shocked Agnes to the core and, of course, made for an evening of strained conversation.

Miss Meade was quiet and distracted, hardly looking at either Mr. Jared or his companion. Agnes deeply regretted her part in Miss Meade's obvious discomfort. By putting Miss O'Rourke in Melissa's room she had meant to jolt Mr. Jared to his senses. Instead, her plan had backfired and left Miss Meade embarrassed and unhappy. It was small compensation to Agnes that she kept the service flowing so well that the lack of conversation was not the problem it might have been during the meal.

Nevertheless, there were awkward moments, such as when Mr. Jared said, "You're quiet tonight, Susan. Did that mob in town upset you so much?"

Miss Meade barely heard him, but Miss O'Rourke was instantly interested. "What mob was that, Jared?"

"Someone making a speech on Merrimack Street."

"What about?"

He gave her a strange smile. "We couldn't tell from inside the carriage and Mr. Boynton wouldn't tell Susan."

Agnes noticed how Miss Meade came alive at that moment. Her eyes came up from her plate and she looked around almost as if she didn't know where she was. It was so strange that Agnes missed seeing Miss O'Rourke's reaction, but she had drawn Mr. Jared's attention by asking sharply, "Mr. *Dennis* Boynton?"

"Yes. Do you know him?"

She seemed to be having trouble keeping her eyes on Mr. Jared. They slipped away from him and fastened on Miss Meade's avid gaze. Then she looked down and said, mumbled really, "Everyone in Lowell knows Mr. Boynton."

"Oh? What do they know of him?" Miss Meade asked.

"He works for the *Chronicle*," Carina said, as though

198

that explained everything.

Miss Meade looked to Mr. Jared for an explanation. He smiled at her. "You'd like it, Suzie. It's the radical mouthpiece in Lowell, full of support for abolition, women's suffrage, and the labor movement, such as it is."

Miss Meade turned back to Miss O'Rourke. "Do you know Mr. Boynton personally?"

"He and my father are well acquainted."

"Is he always rude?"

She didn't quite smile. "Nearly always."

"I see."

Miss O'Rourke looked to Mr. Jared, apparently seeking help. Agnes was glad to see that he gave none. In the silence that ensued Agnes signaled to Gwen to clear the table for dessert. Cook had baked Miss Meade's favorite pie, huckleberry and cream, but when it was put before her she barely glanced at it. Agnes had never seen her so unresponsive. It was another grievance for her to lay at Miss O'Rourke's door.

Mr. Jared ate heartily for a while, then said, "Bagley tells me you've decided to leave in the morning. Is that true?"

"I must. I have a project I left unattended," Susan answered.

"Silas told me." He took up his coffee and watched her over the rim as he said, "Perhaps Mr. Boynton will persuade the owner of the *Chronicle* to publish your work." He was as surprised as Agnes when Miss Meade suddenly burst into tears and ran from the room.

He sat perfectly still for a few seconds; then he put down his napkin and cup to follow her. Although it wasn't the ending Agnes expected, she didn't mind. Miss O'Rourke hadn't disgraced herself, but at least she was left alone at the table.

# *Chapter Fourteen*

Until the next morning, Carina had never had much cause to sympathize with Gwen. She had only been awake a few minutes when she heard Susan shriek. Quickly upon that scream, which brought Carina to her feet, came the unmistakable sound of a slap, followed by a torrent of abuse.

"You miserable excuse for a maid," Susan screeched. "Look what you've done!"

Carina stopped at the door. She'd been about to go to Susan's rescue. Now she knew better. Neither combatant would forgive her if she went anywhere near them. Her safest course was to stay put and pretend to be deaf.

The rest of the household reacted differently. Carina heard hurrying footsteps in the hall, then Agnes added her voice to Susan's and Gwen was dismissed. Bagley and Trudy came to the hall, but were sent away as Agnes took on the chore of soothing Susan. She had not quite succeeded when Jared returned.

Listening to the commotion with emotions that bounced between amusement and irritation, Carina was particularly eager to learn what Jared would do. She couldn't believe that Susan's tantrum was the first in her life, nor could she imagine Jared indulging such behavior, and yet that was what he did.

"Agnes! What's the meaning of this?"

Carina reminded herself that Jared had missed the beginning of Susan's outburst. All he knew was that she was crying.

"It's not her fault," Susan wailed. "I'm just so miserable!" Her voice rose, breaking off abruptly into sniffles and muffled sobs that told Carina she was being comforted.

Carina couldn't condone Susan's treatment of Gwen, but she was too honest not to recognize that in Susan's place she might have been similarly tempted. Gwen could be provoking. And, like Susan, Carina had cried in Jared's arms and been comforted.

It was a sobering moment. Carina didn't like to see parallels between herself and Susan, nor did it please her to think that Gwen had stood as a scapegoat for herself. If Susan proclaimed herself miserable, Carina was the reason—not Gwen.

The incident strengthened Carina's determination to leave—and soon.

Toward that end, she took advantage of the disruption in the household routine that accompanied Susan's leavetaking. With Jared and Agnes seeing her off and the stable hands involved in readying her carriage and horses, Carina got a basket from the storehouse and slipped into the stables by the back way.

Careful to take nothing that was personal to any one lad, and nothing new or dear, Carina found a pair of breeches and two shirts. The breeches were torn but mendable, and the shirts were stained and dirty. She could wash and dry them surreptitiously, she was sure. They went into her basket.

Carina went from the stables to the garden. She needed a layer of cover over the clothing so no one who saw her return would suspect what she carried. She thought first of vegetables. She could pick beans or whatever was available and take the basket to the storeroom. With the clothes secreted there somehow, she could retrieve them later.

Then she spied the profusion of asters. With a layer of flowers in her basket she could go directly to her room with no one the wiser.

The stems were hard to break cleanly without scissors, and even when she had all she needed for a bouquet the clothes weren't completely covered. Carina looked for something else, something that would provide a dense layer, and decided on lilac leaves. She broke off many branches, knowing no one would mind her picking them when these bushes were so thick at the edge of the garden. Nevertheless, she felt strange as she worked.

The sun baked her shoulders as she moved around the lilac bush. She began to hurry, driven by the odd feeling that someone was watching her. She put down the basket and arched backward, putting her hand at the small of her back while she looked around.

There was no sign of anyone. She was just feeling guilty. Subterfuge wasn't natural to her—which was one more reason that she should leave. If she didn't, wouldn't she get used to dishonesty and never be able to live respectably again?

She snatched two more sprigs of leaves and jammed them into her basket. One last look around and she headed back to the house. Wanting to run, she forced herself to walk. If someone were watching, she should look innocent and natural. She thought of Marcus, but some sense told her it wasn't Marcus who watched.

It wasn't Jared either. He was just walking back up the drive after seeing Susan off. She waved to him and kept going, determined to reach the safety of her room. As soon as she did, she thrust the stolen clothes out of sight under her bed. Then she gathered the scattered leaves and flowers and sank down into a chair to rest.

If she hadn't felt so corrupt, she would have laughed at the thought of resting after picking flowers. She, who customarily worked in the spinning room for twelve or thirteen hours, then cooked and cleaned for her family, could not possibly be tired now. Her disgust was tempered by the realization that she had to make one more trip to the stables—for shoes. Without sturdy pattens she wouldn't last a mile on the road.

She spent the afternoon mending the stolen clothes, hiding each garment under a dress she kept handy for show. But no one came.

Now that she knew about Melissa and Susan, she felt easier about leaving Jared. From his history she was sure that his taking her in was an aberration in the life of an otherwise sensible man. He had been married once and would marry again, probably as soon as he was free of her. In making her his mistress, he'd been motivated more by kindness than by desire, she was sure.

In spite of her bravado before Susan, Carina had no reason to believe she was anyone special in Jared's life. He might gain a certain physical comfort from her presence, especially at night and when he was tired, but last evening he'd left her at the dining table to follow Susan when she'd been distressed and later, after the house was quiet, he had not come to fetch her to his bed.

Carina knew. She'd been awake, waiting in an agony of suspense. She'd heard Susan retire and still she'd waited. Somehow she was certain that Susan waited, too. Perhaps Jared knew that also. Perhaps that was why he went to his own room, alone. He wouldn't choose to insult the women he wanted to marry. She thought his steps had come near her door and even slowed there, but perhaps that was only her imagination. Although she was ashamed of herself, she wanted him to want her.

That—finally—was the most telling reason for her to leave.

Having eaten little all day, Carina was hungry well before the normal dinner hour and uncertain as to what to do about it. She didn't expect to be summoned to dine with Jared again soon, nor did she want to stay cooped up in her room any longer. The clothes were sewn and again replaced under her bed, so she decided to venture out in search of another apple.

At the foot of the back stairs she surprised a tall man clad in all black—or rather, he surprised her. But for the pale gold of his hair, she would have missed him standing in the shadowed hallway. She gave a guilty start, but he only smiled and bowed.

Something about him, perhaps the black hat he held under his arm or his playful bow, told Carina he was no ordinary visitor. If Jared made her think of a knight, this man resembled a courtier without the usual ruffles and plumes. She was sure he could wear them without embarrassment, however plain his present attire.

Carina gave a little bob and tried to hurry past the man, but he didn't permit. He stepped deftly into her path, forcing her to stop. "Excuse me," she said, barely looking up into his face. Although he was smiling, he smiled more from awareness of his own superiority than from genuine amusement. She'd seen the look on Jared's face once or twice and didn't much care for it.

"No, no, the fault is mine," he said, being deliberately dense about the expression she'd used. "Let me introduce myself. I'm Tyler Maxwell." He clicked his boots together for another mocking bow. "At your service."

Too conscious of her uncomfortable position in the household to give him the kind of smile Gwen might use, Carina simply held herself stiffly in place. When he didn't move, she turned to go back upstairs.

Before she could begin the climb, Trudy appeared in the hall and called out, "Oh good, Carina, I was just bringing you a tray. Would you mind taking it yourself?"

"Not at all." Another nod of the head to Mr. Maxwell and she made her escape.

That encounter, brief as it was, left her as shaken as the search for clothing in the stable. Whoever Tyler Maxwell was, Trudy knew him and did not find his presence unusual. It was more evidence that Carina was not suited to life as it was lived in a great house. Tonight, she vowed, she would find some clogs in the stable and ask Jared about Patrick. Then she would be free to leave. She might not even wait to wash and dry the clothes. Getting away from Jared and his complicated household was now paramount.

Jared pushed his account book to the side and rested his elbows on the desk. He felt tired and put upon. First it was Susan; now Tyler was here. At least their paths hadn't crossed, but that was the only blessing he could find so far in this day.

Of all the people who could have adopted him after his own family was wiped out, the Meades were surely the most unusual. Only Indigo was remotely normal. The others were all passionate reformers, each with a slightly different enthusiasm and no patience or sympathy with the others' causes or methods.

Jared loved them all, but they were, individually and collectively, driving him crazy. He was also increasingly afraid that they would cause his downfall; not intentionally of course, but a downfall was a downfall. He had all the enemy he needed in Uncle Nathan. If all of Tyler's foes came after him, he wouldn't stand a chance.

Tyler insisted he hadn't been observed coming here. But had he? He'd stirred things up in Lowell, then run to Jared to hide. He was like Susan, shortsighted and self-centered. It was a dangerous combination.

Sighing gustily, Jared dug his knuckles into the ache between his eyebrows.

"You've been holding out on me again, big brother."

Jared's hand dropped away, showing him Tyler lounging in the study doorway. He didn't smile at the old joke based upon his forty days of seniority. Today he felt a hundred years older than Tyler "Maxwell," as his friend called himself in the mill towns where he tried to organize disparate laborers into one "movement."

"Have I?" Jared parried, virtually uninterested in anything Tyler had to say.

205

"I've just seen your bluebird."

Jared stared, trying to make sense of the term.

"Oh, come on, Jared, don't be coy. It doesn't become you." Tyler moved gracefully inside and flung himself into the chair opposite his desk. "She has black hair and starry blue eyes? Wears a blue dress and a prim expression?"

Carina.

He hadn't said a word, yet Tyler gave a satisfied laugh. "Ah-ha. Then you have noticed her."

Jared's wit dried up, shrinking until it was reduced to one noisy pellet that rattled in his brain. He wanted to grab Tyler by the throat and warn him to stay away from Carina. But that would be a mistake. Just as bad would be pretending indifference. He had to find some neutral ground to claim—and fast.

"Of course I've noticed her. She's very attractive." When Tyler's amusement deepened, Jared knew he'd failed.

"Are you going to warn me off?"

"Of course not." Jared's attempt at a smile wouldn't have fooled a total stranger. "That would only challenge you."

Tyler acknowledged the hit. "What is she?"

"She's my guest." The answer was stiffly made.

"Guest," Tyler repeated, testing the word. "Then that explains why she gets her meals on a tray in her room."

With nothing sensible to say, Jared kept still.

"No, I haven't gone to her room—yet." Tyler's eyes sparkled with mischief. "When I saw her picking flowers this morning, I thought she was a new servant, not your mistress."

Challenged to claim Carina, Jared refused. Tyler already knew his feelings and, however much he was enjoying Jared's discomfort, he wouldn't actually poach.

"Did you have some purpose for coming in here and bothering me?" Jared asked, setting the account book back in place before him.

Tyler laughed and got up. "Just that—to bother you." He paused at the door and gave Jared a wink. "Don't worry, big brother. I won't steal your little bluebird."


Isolated in her room, Carina found it hard to judge the time. It was full dark and the waning moon rode high in the sky. She had been waiting for Jared to return before she went to the stable. She didn't expect him to come to her room, but she didn't want to have to explain her absence in case he did.

After agonizing for what seemed hours, Carina decided to chance going out. She could always say she couldn't sleep and took a walk. She had given no one a reason to suspect her—if anyone gave her a thought. She felt more forgotten than trusted, but one suited her purpose as well as the other.

She was dressed for bed, the better to back up her story, wearing a robe and soft slippers with her gown. Pausing at the door to listen before she committed herself to action, she decided to take a shawl as well. It would disguise her shape and cover the clogs she'd bring back with her.

Carina moved soundlessly down the back stairs toward the kitchen. The house and courtyard stood silent in the thin moonlight. She waited for a cloud to drift over the pale wedge of illumination, then slipped into the stable.

Once inside she realized she hadn't thought of everything. She had no candle to see by. She would have to prop the door open and sit in the dark until her eyes adjusted to the available light. At least she knew where to look once she could see. There always seemed to be a jumble of boots and footwear in the empty, rear stall.

Carina liked the sounds and smells of a barn. Even in near darkness there was a sense of life around her. Horses stamped and whickered, their tails tossing. The air was warm and fragrant, redolent of animal flesh and leather. She sank down to the straw and leaned her head back, resting.

She would stay right here at Jared's if she could work with Ned and not have to worry about being discovered as a fraudulent male. Jared had intended kindness when he'd installed her in his house and given her fine clothes, but she'd never been more happy than she'd been the night she'd spent here at the beginning of her adventure.

Chiding herself for being foolish, Carina got up and worked her way to the last stall. She could see as well as she'd ever be able to. It was time to get the shoes she needed.

While she was absorbed in groping around and trying on footwear, someone came to the stable door and pried it wide open. Carina heard the hinges protest and stifled her squeak of alarm.

She heard the low rumble of male speech outside, then another voice broke in all too clearly. "I don't give a damn. I've been cautious long enough. This is the time, I tell you!"

Carina couldn't identify the first voice, but the second undoubtedly belonged to Tyler Maxwell, the man in black who had waylaid her in the hall. He spoke rapidly, with none of his earlier flirtatiousness; his tone impatient and cold. The voice was the same, however.

Maxwell paused to give the man, or men, outside a say; then he went on as before, his voice loud enough to set up echoes in the barn. "I don't care. I'm going to get him and all the others—now! Lowell is a powder keg, and I'm going to light the fuse. If it blows up more people, well, that's too damn bad!"

Carina stood up and began to feel her way along the stall to the opening, afraid to hear more. There was a back door. Under cover of darkness, and while the men were involved in their argument, she'd be able to slip out the back way. She could hide—

"No, I can't guarantee that no one will die!" Maxwell roared.

After that, Carina couldn't hear the other voices over the pounding of blood in her ears. She reached the outer door just as Maxwell began to walk away from the entrance. His voice came directly to her, preceding him down the aisle of stalls. "No one saw me come here today, and no one will see me leave. Don't worry, I won't bring the law here."

Panic gripped Carina. She shoved on the door, terrified that Tyler Maxwell was coming straight for her. The door opened without a sound, and she slid through the gap. But when the heavy portal slipped from her nerveless fingers to fall into place, the sound was like a gunshot in her ears. She bolted away, forgetting her plan to hide and wait before going back to the house.

She couldn't cross the courtyard—that was where the men were—so she ran around the back of the stable, heading in a big loop for the kitchen door. Her footsteps were so loud she was sure she was pursued. Looking back over her shoulder as she ran, she tripped over a hummock of grass and fell full length. The grass was damp with dew and, jarred by the fall, she was slow to get up.

Having been forced to stop, Carina was calmer now. She pulled on the slipper that had been dislodged and straightened her loosened shawl. Then she walked to the corner of the stable, to the end most distant from the main doors, and rested there before going on.

In her newly composed state, she was twice as frightened as before to find herself suddenly face to face with a tall, darkly clad man. She opened her mouth to scream, then couldn't. Her lungs felt crushed.

"Carina? What are you doing here?"

She swayed on unsteady legs, ready to collapse from relief as well as fear and surprise. "Oh, Jared! Thank God it's you!"

"Who else were you expecting?"

"N-no one," she stammered, suddenly aware of how odd her behavior would look to him. She barely remembered why she was out, much less the story she'd concocted as explanation. "I have to talk to you. There's a man in—"

"Come with me," Jared said, taking her arm. He turned to lead her across the courtyard to the house.

Carina resisted. "Not that way. There are men out there by the stable."

He stopped and demanded, "What men?"

"I don't know them all, or even how many there are. I only heard one voice clearly. It was that man in black. He called himself Tyler Maxwell."

"What did you hear?"

"He said something about blowing up Lowell and not caring who gets killed. He sounded dangerous, Jared. I was so afraid for you."

"For me?"

"Well, don't you see? He's been here! People might think you were involved. He even said something about not worrying about bringing the law here."

"What else did you hear? *Who* else?"

"There was someone outside, but I couldn't make out the words he said. I could only hear Mr. Maxwell."

"Where were you?"

"I was inside . . . in the stable."

"Oh?" There was a wealth of suspicion couched in that expression—all of it justified.

Carina tugged her shawl closer. Her story about taking a walk wouldn't explain going inside the stable. "I remembered that I'd left my shawl there earlier today, so when I couldn't sleep I went to get it." She raised her hands, clutching the ends of the wrap, showing him that she'd been right. "I didn't want to lose it."

After giving her a hard stare, Jared seemed to accept her story. "All right," he said. "Come with me. It's not safe for you out here."

Carina grabbed his arm to protest, but he marched her along the side of the stable. He paused at the front corner, then hustled her across the vacant courtyard. Over her shoulder Carina saw that the stable door was closed.

Jared ushered her into the storeroom. "Will you be all right now?" he asked.

"*I'm* not the one in danger, Jared. Don't you see? If Maxwell brings the constable here in pursuit of him, *you* might be blamed. I couldn't tell you apart in the yard out there. He dresses just the way you do. What if it's deliberate?"

His grin was so out of place it angered Carina, and so did his words. "He's an old friend, Carina. He won't harm me."

"He's not a friend," she insisted. "Friends don't harm their friends. You may be *his* friend, but he said over and over that he doesn't care about consequences. He's . . . rash!"

"I'll be careful, Carina. I promise you." He put his hands on her shoulders comfortingly. "Now go to your room and wait for me. I won't be long."

She caught at his hand as he was moving away. "You're not going to confront him, are you?"

"I have to look into it, Carina. Thanks to you, though, I'm well armed against tricks." He gave her forehead a kiss and turned her toward the door. "Now scoot. I don't want him to get away."

Carina knew further protest would annoy him, but she left most unwillingly. Although she was concerned for Jared, she above all others knew his strength and trusted it. He was not a boy like Patrick to be led astray, nor was he an impractical zealot like Dennis Boynton to lead himself astray. He was a man, with a man's wisdom and courage. She had done her part, and now he would do his. She shuddered to think what might have happened if she hadn't been in the stable to overhear Mr. Maxwell.

\*     \*     \*

She sat on the edge of the bed, waiting tensely for Jared. She scarcely thought of the sturdy walking shoes she'd failed to get. It seemed especially traitorous for her to think of leaving just when she'd proven her value to Jared.

He had many friends and people in his employ, but who besides herself cared enough to put him first? She was only certain of Bagley, and he was old, perhaps too old to be effective.

Once or twice Carina looked at the window, but she didn't go to look *out* of it. She didn't want to know when Tyler Maxwell left. She knew Jared would send him away—what else could he do?—and she didn't want to see him go.

She had grown up on Papa's stories of explosives and their fearsome destruction. Maxwell had to be a madman to contemplate blowing up Lowell. Even knowledge *about* such a man could be dangerous.

When Jared finally came to her, she was hard pressed not to run to his arms. Given the right to take liberties with him, she would have run her hands over him and thus assured herself that he was whole. Instead, although she rose, she made do with looking at him.

He chuckled at her expression. "I should be glad to have such problems every night if I knew it would cause you to look at me like this."

"Is he gone?"

"Didn't you see him?"

Carina shook her head. "I didn't want to."

"He frightens you so much?" Jared stood just inside the door, looking relaxed and pleased.

"Mostly for you, but also for the innocent people he spoke of so indifferently. I don't understand people like that."

He nodded with understanding. "You wouldn't. You feel things so intensely."

"What he talked about isn't just . . . an idea, Jared. It does real hurt to real people."

"You're right. More people should have your perspective," he said, moving toward her. "But you may have misunderstood his intent, Carina. He doesn't mean to blow things up physically. He talks to people and gets them stirred up."

"Why? For what cause?"

"Labor reform," Jared told her. "With your background you should be pleased that people like Tyler are working to better conditions in the mills and shops."

"You mean he's an *agitator?*" she asked.

Jared's laugh had an uncomfortable edge as he watched her sharply. "Susan asked the same question in exactly the same breathless fashion. Am I missing out on something here? Are agitators so attractive to women?"

Carina found the question unintelligible. All that made sense was the reference to Susan. "Does Susan also know Mr. Maxwell?"

"She asked about Dennis Boynton, not Tyler," he said, not really addressing her question.

Suddenly Carina put the two men together in her mind. Tyler Maxwell and Dennis Boynton. Her eyes widened with fear. "You mean that Mr. Maxwell is involved with Dennis?"

Jared focused narrowly on her face. "That's the second time you've reacted to the name of Dennis Boynton. What is he to you?"

"He's my father's friend. I told you."

"You also told me your father had you promised in marriage to some man. It was Boynton, wasn't it?"

Carina was furious to find her face heating with a guilty flush. "It was, but as I also told you, he was nothing to me, only a friend to my father."

"Does he know you're here?"

"I don't know. I've not left this house since I came. How could I know?"

Jared seemed not to hear her. "So that's what he had against me," he said, speaking to himself. "I wondered at his hostility."

213

"I don't understand."

"Don't you?" Jared rocked on his heels, his hands clasped behind his back as he studied her face. "You came to me instead of going to your intended. Naturally he resents me."

"I don't believe that, Jared. If Dennis resents you, it's likely for your wealth and your station in life. Dennis never said two kind words to me—not even two *personal* words. When he agreed to marry me, it was as a favor to my father. He didn't want me."

Jared laughed without much humor. "Men marry for many reasons, Carina, but rarely to please a friend."

"No, truly. Like Papa, Dennis knew I was unmarriageable. Papa lived in fear that he would renege on his promise, especially when I persisted in speaking up."

"About what?"

Carina walked restlessly away from the bed. She didn't like telling Jared her faults. "Papa and Dennis loved discourse. They would talk all night long. About God and the devil. About the nature of evil. I wasn't supposed to take part; perhaps I wasn't even supposed to listen. But how could I close my ears? I'm not deaf, and I have ideas and thoughts, too. When I got tired of hearing theirs, sometimes I said something."

"Like what?" Jared asked abruptly.

It was a challenge Carina couldn't resist. He'd *asked* her opinion. Well, he'd get it. She drew breath and said, "I said I thought they spent too much time analyzing evil and not enough time appreciating the good things in life.

"Even in the ugliest mills there are good moments. One of the other girls will tend your bobbins for you so you can rest and get a drink of water. Once an old cat gave birth to three beautiful little kittens in the corner. And there are children like Margaret and Kevin who carry the bobbins for us. They are so sweet and good. They play games in the corners—cat's cradle, maybe—even when they're tired. And when you come out of the mills at night the air smells fresh and clean. It makes you feel good."

"Your father and Dennis," Jared prodded, "didn't they like what you said?"

"Papa was embarrassed for me. He said it proved how ignorant I am." She looked down at her hands. She was still wearing the robe over her gown. All she could think was how Papa would find fault with her now, dressed for bed before a man who was not her husband.

"What did Dennis say?"

"He never spoke to me directly, but I did discover that if I spoke up, that would tend to end the evening for them. I must admit, I did it sometimes just to drive him home so I could go to bed."

Jared chuckled at that, finding it surprisingly amusing. "Perhaps he was shy of you," he suggested.

Carina didn't think so, but she didn't care either. Talk of her family had brought Patrick to her mind. Now that Jared seemed pleased about something, she decided to ask about her brother. "You've never told me about Patrick, Jared."

"He's at home, little one—free and unharmed."

"The charges?"

"Were dropped. Your father's original job was also restored."

She opened her arms and rushed to embrace him. "Oh, thank you, *thank you!* I knew you could do it."

Without a thought for effect, Carina expressed her gratitude in the most natural way she knew. She hugged Jared exuberantly, peppering his face with kisses. It was not her intention to reward him physically, but his embrace, his warmth, his response to her, produced an answering response in her. He bound her close within his strong arms. His hand at her nape stopped her giddy kisses and held her still before him.

His dark eyes, already heavy lidded, moved over her upturned features in a caress as tangible as fingertips gliding over her skin. He didn't demand, he invited. Gently, reverently, he touched his lips to hers, a cat

215

delicately sampling cream. Though it was no more than a feather's brush, it was flint set to the tinder of her volatile emotions. Her anxiety, doubt, and ambivalence were transformed by that touch into passion.

Their mouths became hot and insistent, open and seeking. Carina pressed against Jared, as eager for him as he was for her. He bore her to the bed and followed her down.

For Carina, there was no strangeness in their coming together this time. It felt natural and right for her to urge him out of his clothes and assist him in the shedding of her own few garments. She had to touch him, to assure herself of his welfare. More, she had to give him the comfort of her body. Insofar as she was capable of thought, "comfort" was the word that came to her.

But there was no comfort for her in their joining. In fact, for the longest, most agonizing time, there was no joining. Jared didn't permit it. He held, caressed and stroked her to distraction, teasing her soft flesh with promising touches that never came to completion. When she sobbed in need, he laughed tenderly and redoubled his attentions. She had never known such misery, such joy.

"Oh, Carina, you are a wonder," he murmured, moving over her at last.

He held her hands to the bed at either side of her tousled hair as he bent to trail kisses over her face and neck. Her heated skin was sensitive to each separate aspect of his caress. His firm lips. The hot wetness of his tongue. The slight bristle of his emerging beard.

She tried to free her hands, but he didn't allow it. All his attention was focused on her body beneath his mouth. Without releasing her, his lips glided down to her breast where he circled the rising slope with his tongue. The trail of moisture cooled as he approached the crest, causing Carina to arch her back, lifting to offer him suckle.

Finally, he took the nipple into his mouth, drawing on

it deeply, as if for sustenance. He released her hands to lift her closer, and she was able at last to clasp him tightly. Her fingers plowed into his hair to press against his skull. Her breath caught in her throat as he shaped her breast to his design, tugging, biting softly, tonguing her responsive core.

Then, while she was stunned and lost, he surged into her, taking over her being in a complete rush of pleasure. It was the answer to her earlier pleading taken to an extreme she had never imagined. Feelings swirled within her, gathering in a storm that finally, *finally* broke and flung her, spent and limp, onto a distant, peaceful shore.

With all of her tumult, Carina was a long time recovering her equilibrium. When it came, it brought an unwelcome sense of shame. She had been so abandoned. Over Jared's deep, even breathing she could hear the echoes of her own cries, her *demands*.

What would he think of her?

She didn't want to know.

# Chapter Fifteen

Jared woke with the first call of a bird to its mate in the tree below the window. He was immediately aware of the sleepy burden he held.

Carina. How she pleased him.

She lay curled to his side, her head pillowed on his shoulder and her arm draped over his chest. He didn't remember covering her, but he must have. She had scarcely moved all night.

He lifted his hand, intending to touch her bare shoulder, then thought better of it. He didn't want to wake her. He knew her well enough now to anticipate her reaction to what had transpired. She would be embarrassed that he had fired the hidden passion he'd long sensed glowing within her.

He stroked her hair instead, content to sift the silky strands through his fingers.

Looking down, he could see the curve of her cheek, her dark lashes, and the tip of her nose. From them he could compose a composite of her. The picture it made was deeply satisfying.

She had such loyalty—and how he needed that.

Last night, her concern for him had made him forget himself completely. And here he was in this bed that was no longer Melissa's—thanks to Carina. All his anger and fear was gone, exorcised by this dark-haired sprite of a girl.

He felt reborn—strengthened and renewed. Stirred by the feeling, he shifted on the bed and felt Carina's reaction. She moved closer, throwing her leg over his as if she would keep him with her. His response was instantaneous, unwelcome, and amusing, all in one. Selfishly, he wanted her, but he resisted.

She need her rest; he needed to be about his business. Between them, Tyler and Susan had set him back more than he cared to think, especially in view of his impending trip to Boston. He had to settle Marcus in at the shop and find a horse he could ride back and forth—if he knew how to ride. Carina certainly did, and he wanted her provided for as well.

Moving carefully, he unwound Carina's limbs and settled her against a pillow, amused and touched that she wrapped it in her arms. He kissed her temple and dressed quickly before he could change his mind about leaving her in peace.

His work went so well that it took only an hour or so to accomplish what had been impossible the day before. He decided to reward himself with a ride before he spoke to Ned about the horses. But Ned was already at work.

He gave Jared a relieved look and said, "I'm glad ye came, sir. There's been a message. Fer tonight." His heavy brows beetled with concern.

"Tonight? You're sure?"

"'Twas the same man who always comes, an he apologized. Said 'twas special circumstances. yer to go to the farmhouse after dark."

"Damnation! This is getting old." Then Jared recalled himself. It wasn't Ned's fault, nor anyone's, likely. He clapped Ned's shoulder in thanks, then asked about the horses for Marcus and Carina.

Marcus's name drew a frown from Ned, but he was plainly delighted to consider a mount for Carina. "That one can handle anything!" he said, beaming with approval.

219

"She seems to think so." Jared's decision to keep her off Infidel was based on concern for her well-being, not jealousy or possessiveness. He didn't believe she had the physical strength to control such a large and powerful stallion, and he wanted Carina safe.

"She likes Merrylegs," Ned commented. "She's a pretty thing, too."

Jared frowned. "Wasn't it Merrylegs that gave Miss Meade so much trouble?"

"Well, yes, but *she's* got no touch a-tall. Got the hands of a plowman, that one!"

He didn't let himself smile at Ned's characterization of Susan because it was true. Instead, he asked, "She's not too moody?"

Ned looked pained, then his face brightened as he realized that he hadn't been asked to speculate on Miss Meade's disposition. "Oh, ye mean Merrylegs? Naw, she's a good girl. 'Course, she's a *mare*, but Miss Carina'll do her good."

That settled, Jared decided to go at once to Lowell and attend to his business there before nightfall. He tried to resurrect the charitable feelings for fugitive slaves that had put him at the center of this inconvenient business, but all he felt was annoyance. He wanted to spend the entire night with Carina.

His departure for Boston loomed, and she didn't know about it yet. He had to tell her his plans and settle her in properly before he could leave. Now that she knew her brother was safe, he was afraid his hold on her was weakened. Somehow, he had to make her want to stay on.

What would it take to hold her? More than Merrylegs, he knew. But what?

Carina struggled with her conscience all day without finding a solution to her problem. She had to leave, and yet how could she go when Jared was so kind?

As if it wasn't bad enough to know how truly she had

220

played the whore for him, he'd compounded her guilt by *giving* her a horse! Her face flaming, she had refused—adamantly. Jared had been firm. The beautiful bay mare was hers. He'd even brought a new saddle from Lowell that was to be her own.

For Carina, the afternoon ride on Merrylegs, at Jared's side, was an experience she would never forget. He'd taken her to the river and along his favorite paths. No one had ever treated her so well. No one had ever made her so happy—or so miserable.

After their ride they'd eaten dinner together. Because Jared had to go out for the evening, he'd said good night to her then, treating her much as she imagined he would a wife. He offered no explanation of his plans, nor did she ask. Nevertheless, her heart ached to think that his affectionate peck on her forehead would be the last kiss she would have from him. She'd had to bite her tongue to keep from calling him back or running into his arms for one more embrace, one more soul-shaking kiss.

As an extra measure of protection against his discovery of her plan to leave, she pretended to be tired and said, "I think I'll go to bed early tonight. The ride and the fresh air seem to have made me sleepy." Then she gave him a guilty look and said, "That is, if you don't mind."

It had been easy to blush and stammer as he expected her to do when making such a blatant statement, and of course he laughed, delighted with her discomfort. It bothered her that lying and pretending came to her so easily now. It was another sign that she would soon be utterly corrupt if she stayed.

True to the promise he gave her then, Jared had not "bothered" her upon his return home. But she had not slept, nor would she now. A soft rain fell outside, but that was not why she lingered. She was afraid to move, afraid of betraying herself.

And she didn't want to go.

Dressed in the clothing she'd taken, she dallied over

leaving, trying desperately to think of a reason to stay. But there was none. She'd even had the luck to find both pattens *and* a cap in the storeroom that night. She was just superstitious enough to take that coincidence for an omen. Some power, perhaps only her conscience, was telling her it was time to go. Now.

She gave the room a last, fond look and lifted her chin. She would not cry over a room or over a horse, and she had the rest of her life to cry over Jared. She eased the door open and peered out. Jared's door was tightly closed and the corridor was dark. Her stockinged feet were silent as she tiptoed outside and, with great care, shut the door behind her. Resting her cheek against the cool doorjamb, she took a deep breath.

She was not safe yet. She wasn't outside. . . .

"Carina?"

She gasped—quietly, a mere intake of breath. But inside she was screaming. Somehow she hung on to the heavy shoes and her sanity.

Jared stood in the shadows of the hall just beyond his own door.

Why *there?* Why *now?*

He moved to her, as quiet as she had been. With one hand on the wall next to her, he opened her door and herded her inside. As he closed the door behind him she could make out in the darkness his handsome silk robe, the sash carelessly knotted low on his hips. It was no comfort at all to know that he leaned against the door.

"Light the lamp."

"Jared, I—"

"Light the lamp!"

Her hands shook so badly it took several tries before she managed, and then she simply stood where she was. She had no desire to see his face.

After a long time, when the silence between them was stretched to the breaking point, he said, "I wasn't going to come near you. I . . . just couldn't sleep and—"

She turned to him then, to interrupt, and said softly,

"I'm sorry."

He didn't seem to hear her. "I was just about to go back to my room. You shouldn't have been in such a hurry. A few more minutes and you'd have been—"

"Jared! Don't." Her voice, like her heart, was breaking. "I didn't want to go."

He heard that. He came away from the door, stalking toward her. "Didn't you?" His eyes raked over her deliberately, moving from the cap on her head to the pattens she'd put down next to the lamp. "Perhaps you had a desire for a late-night ride on your new horse?"

"I wasn't going to take the horse!"

"Why not? Don't you like her?"

"You know I do!"

"No," he said, his hushed tone full of wonder. "I don't know anything about you, do I? I thought I did. I thought you were a simple, honest girl, but you're not. You're just like every other woman in the world. You get what you want any way you can, and you sneak and steal and lie. . . ."

Carina tried not to cry. It seemed to her that he would see crying as another ruse on her part. She didn't want that, but the tears came anyway.

Was that how he saw her? She wasn't like that. She *wasn't*.

But she was. She had lied to him—repeatedly. And she was wearing stolen clothes, caught in the act of sneaking away. She wanted to defend herself, but how could she?

"And you cry those big fat tears that are supposed to melt my anger."

His contempt flayed her. "No. I'm not trying to do anything to you, and I'm sorry." She drew a breath and tried again. "I *have* to go, and as long as you feel that way . . ." She shrugged disconsolately. "Let me leave and—"

"No!" He grabbed her shoulders with crushing fingers, his face a harsh mask of fury. He had looked no worse confronting his cousin. "Damn you, no. You will

223

not leave here until *I* say you can! You threw yourself on my mercy, and now, by God, you'll find out how little I have."

"You have a great deal." She spoke softly in spite of his fierce expression. "You've shown me nothing but kindness."

"And this is my reward?" He took one hand away to gesture to the door.

"No, it's what was . . . necessary."

"Why? What do you want?"

"I don't want anything. I just can't stay here."

"Because I've ruined you? You'll be just as ruined when you're gone," he said with hateful bluntness.

"Because I must go!" His baffled look frustrated her beyond bearing. "Oh, Jared," she wailed, hating everything about herself. "I have to go. It's just not *right!*"

"Right?" He sounded as if he'd never heard the word before. Dropping his hands away from her entirely, he stepped back and stared at her incredulously. "Do I have this right? You're leaving because it's *wrong* to live with me? Perhaps you think I should *marry* you?"

Carina's temper began to assert itself. Being in the wrong was one things. She would apologize, but she wouldn't let him ridicule her. Not like this. She glared up at him and opened her mouth to tell him so.

"I see." He gave a sudden and unpleasant laugh. "This is all a ruse, isn't it? You run away . . . but not very far— choosing the time to go when I'm right outside your door."

"No! I didn't know—"

"So I'll chase after you and bring you back," he snarled, his voice rising in anger until, finally, it climaxed in a weird kind of triumph. "So I'll *marry* you! Make an honest woman out of the poor little ruined whore!"

Carina flew at him then. Hissing with indignation, she lunged at him, desperate to do him damage. He sidestepped her attack, laughing like the demon her father called him. She squared off at him again, and this time he caught her in his arms, wrapping her in an incapacitating bear hug.

She fought him as hard as she'd fought Enoch Wentworth, bucking her body and flailing out with knees and feet. Without encumbering skirts she was more his equal, and in desperate energy she was superior. But he was stronger, much stronger. All he had to do was suffocate her attack and let her exhaust herself.

Which she was well on her way to doing when Bagley interrupted from the door. "Mr. Jared, sir!" he called over their nearly silent but intense scuffle.

It took Carina longer to come to her senses than it did Jared, so that when he released her suddenly, she got off one more kick—this one solid—to his shin before she too stopped and looked at Bagley. She was instantly embarrassed. They stood there like quarreling children before a disapproving school master.

The amused look Jared gave her told her he felt the same way. "What's the meaning of this?" he demanded of Bagley.

"Sir, Ned just returned from Lowell with news that the constable is on his way here to apprehend a fugitive slave in your protection."

"*What!*"

"He has several men with him," Bagley went on. "Including Mr. Enoch Wentworth. They mean to arrest you for sheltering a runaway slave."

"Ned saw them? How does he know their intent?"

"He heard them gathering men and came here to warn you. You must take the woman to the woods and hide—"

"It's not Marcus they're after?"

Carina's question, coming out of the blue, startled Jared into a forthright answer. "Marcus has papers now. They can't touch him, but I brought a woman here tonight. She's in the attic."

"Trudy's gone to wake her," Bagley said.

"And Marcus?" Carina asked.

225

"I doubt he could sleep through the ruckus they'll make searching the house," Jared said distractedly.

"How long do we have?" Carina asked Bagley.

"A few minutes yet, but to get away . . ." He turned to Jared with a look that implored haste.

Carina put her hand on Jared's arm. "Is it Constable Meggers?"

"Yes, but—"

"Can you keep Enoch from this room?"

Understanding of her fear gave Jared a gentle look. He patted her shoulder reassuringly. "My cousin will not come inside the house."

"Then leave everything to me, Jared. If you run, it's an admission of guilt and they still might find you. It's what they expect—or why so many men?"

"But what can you do?"

"Trust me." She turned to Bagley. "I want the woman here now and Marcus at the ready." To Jared she said, "But Enoch cannot see me. He knows me."

"Carina, have a care."

She pushed them into the hall. "You're both dressed just right. Play the wakened master and servant—and bring Meggers here."

Trudy came into the hall with a frightened young black woman in tow. She carried a bundle in her arms and looked ready to faint. Carina grabbed and pulled them into her room.

Snatching the woman's bundle from her, she thrust it at Trudy. At the same time as she spoke, she tore out of the clothes she was wearing and added them to Trudy's lot. "Take all these to the attic and spread them around to make it look lived in and natural. Then have Marcus come down with you when you're done. I'll need your help."

Trudy gave a quick nod and started out.

"My name is Annabel Larson," Carina called out, improvising quickly.

Trudy grinned and was gone.

Carina stripped and put on her night gown and robe, surveying the stunned woman before her. "What's your name?" she asked in as calm a voice as possible.

The woman's eyes grew rounder, showing white all around the dark pupils. She was hastily dressed and all but paralyzed.

"Never mind. I'm going to call you Mary, all right? I'm your mistress. Just try to do what I say. You won't have to say a word. You'll be safe, I promise."

Trying to convey a sense of safety to the woman with her soothing touch, Carina pulled her to the dressing table. She ignored the sounds of dissension that came from outside, then moved into the house itself. She recognized Jared's raised voice, and Bagley's. To the woman, who was little older than she, it must have sounded like madness.

Carina put a brush into "Mary's" stiff hands and squeezed her fingers into place around it. "That's it," she said. "It's all right to be frightened. I'm going to sit down and you will brush my hair." She sat and smiled up encouragingly. "I'm sorry, but I'm not going to be nice to you."

The door opened, letting in a lot of noise along with Trudy and Marcus. Carina addressed them. "I'm Miss Larson and this is Mary, my slave. Trudy, you'll be trying to placate me, and Marcus"—she met his gaze in the mirror—"just go along with me, please. Both of you."

Marcus was nearly as frightened as the woman, but he tried to give her courage by controlling his fear. Then there was no more time. The door burst open.

Carina jumped up from the chair to face the men who filled the doorway. One of the two middle-aged men in damp outerwear had to be Constable Meggers. She began to shriek before Bagley could say a word.

"What's the meaning of this?" Gasping, her hand going to her chest in outrage, she flew at the men. "How dare you burst into my boudoir like this?"

Giving them no chance to speak, she ran at her "slave"

227

and plucked the brush from her. "Mary! You are the most incompetent baggage I ever did see! If your mamma hadn't been my *mammy*, I just swear I'd have sold you downriver years ago!"

With the men all standing open-mouthed in the doorway, Trudy stepped into the breach. "Oh, Miss Larson, I'm so sorry about this." She put herself between Carina and the men. "Bagley, what's going on here?"

He pushed to the forefront and said, "I beg your pardon, ma'am. I did try to keep these men downstairs. This is Constable Meggers of Lowell, ma'am. He insists that he has a warrant for Miss Larson's maid."

Carina turned from "Mary" to the constable, squawking at first one, then the other. "Warrant? For Mary? Mary! What have you done? Why, we've hardly been here a day! What is the meaning of this?"

Constable Meggers consulted his papers, as if for assurance of his purpose. He cleared his throat noisily. "It says here that she's a fugitive slave and the property of one Mr. Clement Dodge of Winston-Salem, North Carolina."

Carina burst into an incredulous trill of laughter. "Mary? Why, sir, what kind of Yankee trick is this?"

"No trick at all, madam, I assure you. Her name is . . . Chantelle." He read the name, mispronouncing it in the process.

"Let me see that paper!" Carina held out her hand imperiously.

Meggers took a step back. "I can't do that. This is my authority."

"You have no authority over me at all, my good man. Why, I've never heard such outright nonsense! Mary was born to my family."

"She fits the description I have here," Meggers argued doggedly.

"Description!" She made a lunge for the paper, driving him back behind Bagley, to whom she appealed. "This man is crazy, Bagley. How dare he burst into Mr.

228

Wentworth's house like this? Why, back home in Virginia a gentleman would be shot for treating a lady like this. Where is Mr. Wentworth? Why isn't he here protecting me? I've never heard of such disgraceful conduct."

Without giving him a chance to respond, she flew at Meggers's accomplice. "My Aunt Tessie told me it wasn't safe to come up North, but she *never* imagined such an outrage! She said you awful Yankees would try to lure my slaves away by promising them freedom. But she didn't dream that y'all would just go right ahead and try to steal them!"

Meggers tried once more from the doorway. "Your maid fits the description I have here," he repeated stubbornly.

"What does that *wretched* piece of paper say then?" Carina demanded.

"It says that she's a slender girl of refined appearance and light skin, answering to the name of Chantelle." Again he said the name with the hard "ch" sound in cheese.

"Light skin?" Carina screamed in her terrible Southern accent. "Does that look like *light* skin to you?" she asked, pointing rudely. "It doesn't to me. And she doesn't answer to the name of Chantelle at all. Now you get out of my bedchamber, and you take your lying piece of paper with you!"

Carina burst into tears.

Trudy came to comfort her, and Bagley pulled the door closed, forcing the men outside. Even after the door was closed Carina continued to cry noisily and to fuss in a loud voice about the unfairness of it all. She kept her hands over her face because she was afraid the men would come back—perhaps with Enoch Wentworth, despite Jared's promise to exclude him.

As soon as the door closed behind the men Trudy went to stand beside it, her ear pressed to the panel. "They've gone downstairs," she reported in a hoarse whisper.

Carina took down her hands but remained at the ready. She wanted to dance a wild jig around the room. Instead, she went to the dressing table and sat down, her knees watery with relief. In the mirror she saw Marcus retrieve the hairbrush and give it to Chantelle, signaling to her to attend to Carina as if she were indeed the abused Mary.

The slim woman approached Carina timorously. Carina moved to the side of the bench and pulled her down beside her. Wrapping her arms around Chantelle, she leaned into her shaking form.

Trudy opened the door and stuck her head into the hall; then she came back and tiptoed to the window. Holding a finger to her lips, she whispered, "They're leaving. All of them. Mr. Jared's sending them away. Bagley, too. And Ned!"

Then she turned and opened her arms wide in exaltation. "You did it! Oh, Miss Carina, you did it!"

Carina could only think of the terrible things she had said. "Chantelle? Is that your name?"

The terrified woman lifted her head and nodded, looking at Carina with soulful brown eyes that were filled with tears.

"Forgive me for being so rude. I didn't know what—"

Marcus and Chantelle burst into laughter and Trudy joined in just as Jared came into the room.

"I see you all know," he said somewhat stiffly, looking from one to the other. "I understand that you make a formidable Southern lady."

"You should have seen her, sir," Bagley said, giving Carina a beaming smile. "I shouldn't wonder that you heard her downstairs."

"I was outside."

With his cousin, Carina remembered. She searched Jared's face anxiously, but it was closed to her, a cold and impersonal mask.

Trudy claimed her attention with a question. "How do you know the way they talk, Miss Carina? Have you ever been down South?"

"I'm sure real Southern ladies don't sound like I did. I just imitated someone I heard at the mill once." She was uncomfortable under their fixed attention. She would never admit to Jared that Susan was the model for her tantrum. "The lady was on a tour with Mr. Wentworth. Mr. *Enoch* Wentworth."

Jared nodded. "The wife or daughter of someone who supplies cotton to the mill. They are occasional visitors." He stepped back and said, "Thank you for your help, Trudy."

It was a signal for her to usher Chantelle and Marcus outside, and as she did so, Carina reached out a hand to each. Marcus squeezed her hand, and when Chantelle did the same Carina embraced her, making her cry. Carina kissed her then, her own tears rising again when Marcus guided Chantelle away.

Carina watched the door close, wishing she could go with them. Their lives were hard, but so was facing Jared. It was all she could do to meet his gaze.

He inclined his head to her. "I am in your debt."

"You know that's not true," she said softly, feeling miserable.

"I'm sure you helped out of feeling for Chantelle," he said in a frosty voice, "but I, too, would have suffered had she been taken. Enoch cares little enough for the reward he would gain, I think. However, he would dearly love to see me fined and imprisoned."

"Fined? Imprisoned?"

"There are penalties for harboring or aiding fugitives. One thousand dollars and six months in prison, to be exact."

Carina struggled with her gaping mouth. "Oh, Jared. I didn't know! I'm *glad* I didn't know or—"

"Or you wouldn't have helped?"

She shook her head in wonder. "You know better. I wouldn't have dared."

"You dare anything, I believe."

Shoulders slumping, Carina turned away from him.

He'd complained earlier that he didn't know her. Well, it was true. Tremors of fear still quivered along her nerves, yet he thought her a womanly version of himself, daring and strong, when she was only desperate.

Jared found it hard to keep his hands off her as she turned her back on him. Although he was still enraged to think that she had been leaving, he recognized fatigue when he saw it. Carina had plunged right from the midst of their quarrel into another taxing confrontation with Meggers. She had to be exhausted. He wanted to hold her close and comfort her. Brave as she was, he knew she had been frightened, if only of Enoch and the possibility that he might have discovered her ruse.

*As if I would have allowed it,* Jared thought angrily, remembering his moment of surprise when she'd voiced her alarm about Enoch. Then he had believed she was afraid for herself, not for Chantelle, but that was before he understood her plan. Even now he was awed by her quick thinking.

Gratitude—and the need for it—sat harshly on Jared. "You've had a tumultuous night, Carina. You must be very tired."

She nodded but didn't look at him.

"Then I'll leave you—with my deepest thanks for what you did."

She didn't unbend.

In spite of himself, he couldn't refrain from asking, "You will stay here tonight, won't you?"

Carina hunched her shoulders as though she were warding off a blow.

"Then I'll see you in the morning," he said, feeling small and miserable for saying so. Nevertheless, as soon as he left her, he went to find Trudy and Bagley.

He couldn't rest until he had recovered the male clothing she'd been wearing.

# Chapter Sixteen

Carina kept close to her room the next morning, plagued by every kind of uncertainty. She expected Jared's knock at any moment and dreaded the thought of facing him. She had promised to stay, and indeed, without the clothes she'd given over to Trudy, how could she leave? But she didn't know how she could stay either.

She dressed in her lightest clothing in deference to the weather. Last night's drizzle had done nothing to relieve prevailing drought conditions which, while not yet dangerous, had everyone feeling tense and strained. At this rate, Carina thought, August's already blighted foliage would become autumn's fallen leaves with no one able to mark the change of season.

Although it was strange that the air could continually hold such a concentration of moisture and let so little fall, Carina was used to humidity. Nature was only approximating conditions mill workers endured all year round in the unventilated, tightly closed spinning and weaving rooms. There the atmosphere was kept hot and damp for the benefit of the cotton fibers, which tended to snap and fray if allowed to dry. At least here the air was clean and fresh smelling.

Used to it or not, by the time Carina answered the knock at her door, her room was oppressively warm. She was almost ready to welcome Jared and his discussion.

But it was not Jared at the door. It was Agnes—and a smiling Agnes, at that. She carried a tray laden with fresh rolls, fruit, and coffee.

"Agnes, you shouldn't have. I could have come down, but I wasn't hungry."

"It's no trouble, Miss Carina. Cook did these rolls just for you. I'd have come sooner except we wanted you to rest."

"You're . . . very kind."

"Not at all." Agnes bustled around the room, setting up the place where Carina could best dine. She plumped a cushion on the settee and looked at Carina expectantly. "There."

Carina took the seat warily, wondering what was behind Agnes's performance. "Would you care to sit down?"

"Oh, no. Mr. Jared left a lot of instructions for me today. He took the woman to New Hampshire early this morning, and he'll expect me to make fair headway. But I thank you." She lingered at the door, exhibiting rare indecision, then announced, "Gwen will come for the tray later."

Carina stared after her in wonder. The "woman" in question was surely Chantelle. In helping her last night had Carina somehow found the key to winning over Jared's household? The fragrant rolls teased her stomach into growling in anticipation. She *had* once complimented cook on these rolls, but it was hard to believe the woman had made them especially for her.

Still, Agnes had brought them and had been extremely pleasant. Carina wouldn't argue with any of it, she decided, slathering butter on the delicious bread. She put down the knife and chuckled. Now if *Gwen* was pleasant, she would know her life here had changed.

Gwen was. Being Gwen, she couldn't change completely, but she smiled and didn't slam either the dishes or the tray on leaving.

It was enough to encourage Carina to leave the room,

especially now that she knew there was no need to worry about a chance encounter with Jared. She would talk to him on his return, but in the meantime she decided to learn what her true position was here. Until today, only Bagley and Nellie had made her welcome. If Agnes no longer resented her, perhaps she didn't have to leave after all. She would see.

The day was a revelation. She was greeted cheerfully and civilly everywhere. It was apparent that in helping Chantelle, and more importantly Jared, she had passed a test. She was now one of them. Agnes showed her how to arrange flowers for the tables and asked her preferences in food. Next, Trudy took her under her wing, giving her a tour of the best rooms in the house.

Carina especially noted Trudy's pride in two chairs, one delicately feminine with carved legs and arms, upholstered in rose damask; the other so sturdily crafted of smooth leather it might have been a saddle. These were, Trudy told Carina in an awed voice, Jared's only keepsakes of his parents. His mother's chair had come from Philadelphia, where Mr. Jared had lived for a time with her parents, his grandparents. The other chair was from the Boston office of Jared's father's shipping concern, the original Wentworth business.

Responding to some yearning she sensed in Trudy when she mentioned that she would go for a ride, Carina took Trudy with her to the barn. At first she thought perhaps Trudy liked horses, but once they were in the stable, Carina saw the true attraction for her new friend. It was Ned who drew her.

She couldn't be sure whether or not Ned returned Trudy's interest. He was an exceedingly shy man. Having seen him in action before, when he had believed her to be a boy, Carina could tell that he was woefully unaccustomed to the company of a woman. The best Carina could do for them was to ask him to show Trudy the horses.

Because Ned knew and loved horses, he lost some of

235

his bashfulness in pointing out the merits of each animal. Trudy was smart enough to ask questions and keep him going, and when Carina saw that everything between them was going smoothly, she slipped away for a ride on Merrylegs.

Upon returning to her room, she was quickly provided a bath, then Trudy came back to help her dress for dinner in the dining room, with the explanation, "Mum thought you might enjoy the flowers you arranged."

Indeed, Carina enjoyed everything except her nagging sense of unreality. Wasn't she the same person she had always been? Had they expected disloyalty of her?

But capping it all was a sense of her unworthiness. This was Jared's household, his stronghold, these were his people, and overall she had severely disappointed him last night. Not only could all this be taken from her at the snap of Jared's fingers, her attempt to leave him *ensured* that it would be. It was like getting a glimpse of paradise just as she was being told she didn't deserve to enter. Her "rescue" of Chantelle notwithstanding, she had tweaked the devil's tail by trying to run away. She would have to pay for that.

After dinner she went to Jared's study to retrieve the volume of poetry she had read in snatches while waiting for him once before. She told herself she wasn't waiting for him tonight, but she was. She knew the evening would be long, and sought entertainment. She could sew, but sewing only occupied her hands. She'd had too much time to think today.

She selected the poems of William Blake and a romantic tale by Sir Walter Scott, hoping that between the two volumes she would find diversion. In fact, both choices reminded her of Jared; she readily admitted this to herself as she left the room, a despairing smile on her face.

Carina stopped just outside, where Trudy and Agnes

stood talking in the hallway. Seeing their eyes fall on the books, she reddened with guilt and wondered if she would return them to the shelves. "I . . ."

Trudy spoke up quickly. "Mr. Jared is always pleased to share his books," she assured Carina. "We only stare in admiration and envy. Not many of us can read."

"My mother taught me. I don't know all the words, of course," she replied diffidently. Her mind began to whir with plans she longed to discuss with them, but in this, as in everything, she had to talk to Jared first. She needed his permission. Even more than that, she needed to clear the air between them.

With so much on her mind, it was no wonder the evening was so long. Nothing held her attention. She sewed and paced. She read and paced. Finally, she dressed for bed and paced. She was determined to be awake when Jared returned.

As it happened, she was asleep, but her senses were so attuned to his presence that she came instantly alert as soon as he entered the room. He made no sound, and she made no move until she felt him withdrawing.

"Jared?" She sat up.

He stopped but didn't turn around.

She held out her arms. "Please . . . I waited so long—" She broke off, disgusted with herself. She didn't want to sound self-pitying.

It was too dark for her to read his expression. He was looking at her, though. She got to her knees and scrambled to the edge of the bed. She wasn't doing well with words.

Carina flung herself at Jared with a muffled cry, something between his name and a plea. She didn't even know if he would catch her.

He did. His arms went around her like thick ropes. Although the night was still warm, he felt cool against her, fresh and alive and good. She pressed against him, raising her mouth to his. She turned her head to the side, increasing the contact between them, deepening the kiss.

He lifted her off her feet momentarily, and when she landed, she tripped as her feet tangled with his.

She plucked at his hand, tugging on him. "Come." Because of his earlier aversion to her room, she was urging him away, to his room.

Jared swept her back into his arms. Laughing, he moved back to her bed. "This is closer."


Teased to awareness by the smell of coffee and the soft chink of china, Jared discovered that he was alone in bed. Across the sun-flooded room, primly wrapped in a blue robe, Carina presided over a table set for two. He sat up and stretched, feeling decidedly disadvantaged by the contrast in their states.

"Good morning."

He frowned at the sunny lilt in her voice, making her laugh out loud.

"Come have coffee and you'll feel better." Her tone grew tender. "You must be very tired."

"Not anymore." He passed a hand over his bristled face and grimaced. "What did you do? Knock me over the head?"

"I didn't have to." Carina poured coffee and held out the cup as a lure.

Suspicious to the core, Jared nevertheless went for it as soon as he pulled on his robe. He would have preferred a full suit of armor at the moment, but the coffee helped. It was strong and dark and sweet, fixed exactly to his taste although she'd never served him before. For some reason, the fact that she knew his choice in so minor a matter cheered him.

Between sips, he regarded Carina over the rim of his cup. Something was different about her. She was as naturally and unaffectedly beautiful as ever, but underlying her composure ran a thread of excitement he'd never seen before.

"You're looking chipper this morning, or is it noon

by now?"

"Nearly." She sat forward to remove the domed cover from a plate, revealing thick slabs of bacon curled around perfectly fried eggs as yellow as daisies.

Nodding, he let her serve him, then began to eat. He noticed how little she ate and put down his fork as soon as the edge of his appetite was appeased. "Why don't you tell me now, Carina?"

She looked up, startled.

"You're going to explode any minute if you don't." He folded his hands and sat back. "Tell me."

"I want to make a bargain with you."

In spite of himself, Jared was surprised. "A bargain?"

"Not like the one we had before."

"We had a bargain before?"

"That's the way I thought of it." She looked away from him, raising her chin the way she did when she felt combative. "I asked for your help and . . ."

"Gave yourself in exchange," he said for her when she couldn't manage it.

She only nodded.

He had taken away her confidence and excitement already. And so easily. He wanted to be merciful and give them back, but not yet. Not before he knew whether or not he could afford to have her confident. He steepled his fingers under his chin. "So that's why you felt free to leave. You'd completed our bargain—or rather, you knew I had done my part."

Carina appeared to struggle with that, but then she nodded again, this time resolutely. "You could say that."

"What would you say?"

"It's not important now. What matters is the future."

Once again she surprised him, but this time he decided to keep quiet and let her get on with it—whatever *it* was. "Go on."

"You said last night that you didn't want me to leave. If that's so, I want to make the terms of our bargain clear."

239

"It's certainly so that I said that last night, but then I said quite a lot, as I recall." With all day to remember his words, he had much to regret.

She looked him straight in the eye, the silvery rays in her pupils particularly prominent. "Please don't be clever with me. This is hard enough as it is."

Jared could see that. Was that why he wanted to keep throwing up smoke screens? He didn't like to be cruel, but her posture antagonized him. All this talk of bargains . . . "I don't want you to leave, that's correct." He took up his coffee again and gave her a wintery smile. "Now, do we talk terms and demands?"

She didn't like that. "Yes, I suppose we do." She looked away, gathering herself together for what was obviously an effort. "I shouldn't have tried to sneak away as I did. It wasn't right. You did me a great kindness, and it was no way to repay you. I'm very sorry."

Kindness? Her soft words struck the pit of his stomach with the force of a sledge. Was she being sarcastic? She didn't look it, but . . .

There was more.

"I won't do that again. When I leave it will be done honestly, I promise you."

"*When* I leave . . . ?"

"Last night—well, really the night *before* last—changed everything for me here. Before then I didn't feel useful. I didn't know what to do with myself." She made a gesture to the room. "I hid in here. I had an idea to learn dressmaking," she confessed with a sheepish smile and a shake of her head. "But I think I can do better than that."

Jared was confused. Dressmaking? "What could be better than dressmaking?" he joked, trying to hide his bewilderment.

She leaned forward earnestly. "Helping other people. It came to me yesterday. Do you know that many of your servants don't know how to read?"

240

"You want to teach the servants to read?"

"Yes." The stars in her eyes glowed with her enthusiasm. "Oh, Jared, think of the good it would do. They'd be able to read a newspaper or a—"

"That's it? That's your bargain?"

Carina looked as if he'd struck her across the face. "You . . . mind?"

He fixed his gaze on her, narrowing his eyes. "What else do you want?"

"I don't understand."

"You spoke of a bargain," he reminded her coldly.

"Well, I needed your permission before I spoke to anyone, but I'm sure I could interest Trudy and Agnes . . . maybe Nellie. And Ned."

"Carina," he warned. She was getting swept away again.

She searched his face, evidently finding no help. Then her eyes brightened as she had a thought. "Oh, I understand. You're concerned that I'll take their time from work! I think I could arrange it so that I don't. Of course it would be better if you could release them from their work for an hour each day. That way no one would want to miss a lesson." Her smile invited him to agree.

"What do you want from me in return? I'd like to know now, before I agree."

"That's what I want, Jared. Your permission. There might be some small expenses, for slates and books, even pa—"

"Carina, forget the damn school!"

He had her attention at last. She fixed rounded eyes on his face as all the animation drained from hers.

"Now please, let's discuss the subject of us." He laughed at her shock. "Yes. Us. As in, you and me. You will stay here and I will— No. Someone told you that *I'm* leaving. That's it."

"Where do you go?" she asked equably.

Hoping to rattle her, he said, "To Boston. To stay with the Meades."

"I understand."

"What do you understand?"

"Why, that you would stay there. They are your family."

"I have no family."

"In a manner of speaking," she said softly. "But you will again."

*Ah-ha,* he thought. "What makes you think so?"

"You will marry Susan and have another family."

"Susan," he repeated. "Why not you? Isn't that what this is all about? You'll stay in the hope that I'll marry you."

The unclouded smile she gave him reminded him that she was a fine actress. "Oh, no. You must marry a great lady, someone who can keep your house perfectly and go with you to Boston."

"Someone like Susan?" At her nod he asked, "Why not someone like Annabel Larson?"

"I think you can do better," she laughed. "She's not worthy of you."

"But Susan is? I think perhaps she didn't treat you kindly."

"No one who wishes to be your wife could treat me kindly, Jared. It's asking too much."

He pushed to his feet angrily. "You play a subtle game, Carina."

"I play no game at all. I'm only . . . trying to make the best of my life."

"I won't marry you."

"I don't expect you to. I've told you so. Why don't you believe me?"

"Marriage to me would be a great advantage."

"But not for me."

"Especially for you. You have no other hope."

"I have *no* hope—nor do I want any. I would not yoke any man to me, least of all you."

"Least of all?"

"Most of all," she corrected, perhaps sensing his

growing annoyance because she was, apparently, rejecting him. "In marriage a team of equals should pull together. I could not pull as I should. I would hold you back, and you would grow weary of me."

"You seek to make me feel guilty," he said bleakly, seeing through her at last. "It's not you I avoid, but marriage itself."

Carina burst into peals of laughter at that. "Oh, Jared, I'm sorry," she said, seeing his offended expression. "I'm certainly aware that you're not avoiding me. I'm not avoiding you either—obviously." Her hilarity softened into a merry smile. "Like you, I have no wish for marriage, and *un*like you, I have no obligation to it either."

Jared wasn't as mollified by that as he should have been. He wasn't sure why not. Reassured to think that she wasn't expecting marriage of him, however, he tried to make light of her revelation. "As long as you seem to see the married state in terms of an ox-pulling contest, with great beasts yoked together in teams, I can see why you don't crave to be married."

Amusing as that comment was, Carina's smile lost its lightness. "My mother would not like to know that's how I picture the wedded state," she said on a pensive note. "She loved my father devotedly, and he her. But it's true. In spite of Patrick's predicament, and mine, it took Papa's threat to see me married immediately to drive me away. I could not think of it."

*Not to Dennis anyway,* Carina's innate honesty reminded her. She fought back against the part of her heart that hoped, and hoped hard despite all reason and good sense, for something more from Jared.

It didn't have to be marriage. Rationally, she knew it couldn't be. He was a Wentworth. His wife would have to be a great lady. But she knew he desired her already. Jared believed she was staying in order to make him want to marry her. He was wrong about that, but not entirely. She wanted his love, and wasn't that even more futile?

Carina's words also conjured conflicting images for Jared. He, too, saw Dennis Boynton, but not with Carina's detached distaste. Now that he had face and body to put with the man he'd heard of, first as someone who failed Carina in her need and next as someone intended to be her husband, he had a person to hate.

The depth and richness of his hatred surprised him. It didn't make sense. In one way he should be grateful to Boynton. Without him, Carina might never have come to Jared. Instead, Jared felt a primitive desire to punish Boynton. He had not made Carina feel desired, but Jared knew Boynton's thoughts anyway. The man *had* desired Carina and yet had failed her in every way. Jared couldn't forgive or forget such an offense.

But he didn't speak of Boynton to Carina. He pushed all that aside and thought on the way she'd spoken of her parents and their love. He knew exactly what she meant. A similar memory had led him to marry Melissa. His parent's love teased him still, promising possibilities. Yet the pursuit of them could only bring heartbreak.

"I know what you mean," he said quietly. "My parents loved each other the same way. They couldn't imagine anything happier than the married state, but it's not for everyone."

Giving him a determined if wistful nod, Carina smiled. "On that we agree. Do we also have an understanding?"

"A bargain?"

"Yes. I meant what I said. I want permission to teach reading, nothing else. For that, I'll stay until we decide otherwise. Will you agree?"

"Will you also teach the servants to hate their master? Teach them neglect of their duties and insurrection?"

"I don't believe I could. They're already loyal, and when you prove to be so kind as to provide for their education, it will only bind them more closely."

Enchanted by the grave thoughtfulness of her answer, Jared gave over trying to tease her. He knew better than she how the servants would respond to Carina, but how could he deny her wish?

"Then we have a bargain."

Jared had been gone over a week when Tyler Maxwell returned.

Carina had taken to eating at the dining table in Jared's absence. Sometimes Agnes served her, for it had been her idea that she do so—or at least Carina believed it was. In truth, the workings of the household were still a mystery to Carina. She didn't mind. She had her reading project to keep her busy and happy.

This night she found the table set for two. Her heart began to bang around in her chest at the thought that Jared had returned to surprise her, and she turned her happiest smile on the entrance, sure the steps she heard behind her were his.

"Now I can truly say that I've seen a face fall," Tyler said.

His amused smile made Carina feel unsafe and awkward. "You surprised me."

Bagley appeared immediately behind Maxwell, his presence all the assurance Carina needed for the moment. She knew Bagley's unswerving loyalty to Jared would not allow anyone to misuse his hospitality. She didn't like Tyler Maxwell, but she was no longer afraid of him. Jared called him an agitator, classing him with Dennis Boynton. She had eaten too many meals with Dennis as her guest to be fazed by the man.

As Tyler seated her, he noted her poise and wondered at it. She was the reason he was here, although the near collapse of his attempt to bring about a strike in Lowell provided all the excuse he needed. From the moment Jared sent him away because this woman had been frightened by words she'd overheard at the stable, he'd been determined to return and discover for himself what manner of woman she was.

He knew what Jared thought. He'd seen his friend's

infatuated look, heard the bemusement in his voice. It had made Tyler very, very suspicious. He knew Jared and feared that he was ripe for plucking by an opportunistic woman. From everything he'd seen and heard about Carina O'Rourke, she seemed exactly right for the job.

Beautiful. Innocent-looking. And greedy.

Better than anyone, Tyler knew that Jared was nowhere near as cynical as he needed to be. He'd been through hell with Melissa, but he was too idealistic ever to give up entirely on his search for true love. What made Jared particularly vulnerable, in Tyler's opinion, was the fact that he believed himself immune. Nothing was further from the truth.

On the other hand, Tyler had no illusions about the fair sex. He had never met a woman he couldn't charm out of or into anything he wanted. But with Carina O'Rourke, he knew he would have to be subtle. Already out of her natural element here in Jared's home, she was too wary to be easily unveiled. She had too much to lose, too much good standing established, to allow herself to be put in the wrong.

But Tyler had capital to invest in his unmasking project. He knew her background, he knew Lowell, and he knew Dennis Boynton. He would win over Carina O'Rourke and let her show herself up. He wouldn't have to do anything except set the stage. She would reveal herself.

He began slowly, apologizing for frightening her earlier, asking about her adventure with Constable Meggers. Her bland answers didn't please him, but he did touch her quick with one remark. "It must have been satisfying to pull the wool over Meggers's eyes after what he did to your brother."

"You know my brother?"

"Everyone knows the O'Rourkes in Lowell, Carina. May I call you Carina?" he asked belatedly.

"Of course," she answered without thinking, her mind

obviously on something else. "How is Patrick? Do you know?"

"He's well, working. No worse for the wear, I think it's fair to say." She barely began to look relieved when he added. "Dennis Boynton is keeping an eye on him, and on your father, of course."

"I see."

What Tyler saw was that mention of Dennis upset Carina. He wondered about that. Boynton was unscrupulous enough to have sent her to Jared as part of an elaborate scheme. But to do what?

Probing, he said, "Dennis has been busy lately, trying to take advantage of the shutdown of the mills."

"Shutdown?"

"You haven't forgotten that lack of waterpower shuts down the mills, have you?"

Absorbed in her own tiny world out here away from Lowell, Carina had forgotten that effect of the drought. Ashamed that it was so, she was especially unhappy to be reminded of it by Tyler Maxwell. "No, I haven't forgotten that. I only thought you meant there had been a strike."

"We hoped there would be, but it seems the workers aren't ready to risk it yet."

Anger flared in Carina. He was so smug, talking of risks he would never have to bear. "It's not easy to risk one's entire livelihood for a cause, Mr. Maxwell."

"Tyler, please," he reminded her gently. "But the owners can take the workers' livelihood away at any time. If everyone would risk a little, then there would be, in truth, no large risk at all for any one family or person."

"So we are told."

"We?" Tyler raised an aristocratic brow, amused and questioning.

Carina met his gaze squarely. He was the antithesis of Jared in appearance and manner, even in dress. The black clothes he affected, she supposed in imitation of Jared, were elgant and stylish, not the plain stuff of Jared's

247

apparel. But he had none of Jared's earthy strength. Instead, he seemed made for drawing rooms and elegant coaches. His golden handsomeness made him the personification of the ideal man for high society.

But not for Carina. Although his charm still frightened her, she was determined not to show it. Bagley trusted him—which meant that Jared did. She focused on that.

"I can see that you doubt my indentification with my family," she said carefully. "I can understand that. I haven't seen them for a while, but they are ever in my thoughts."

"I'm sure they are," Tyler said smoothly. "Tell me about your school here. It's all the servants can talk about."

Carina distrusted the question and tried to be offhand in her answer. She wasn't successful. The schooling was too dear to her heart. Pride in her students shone from her eyes as she told him much more than she'd intended, opening up under his skillful questioning. She tried to give Jared the credit and, when that failed, her mother. "My mother made learning into a game for us," she told him. "That's all I'm doing. It makes light work for the teacher when pupils are eager to learn."

Despite himself, Tyler was charmed. He was accustomed to enthusiasm for education, but Susan's was different from Carina's. Whereas Susan went on endlessly about methodology, Carina seemed honestly to believe she was blessed in her students.

Then there was the way Bagley beamed on her, looking like a well-polished egg. She had now been in residence for weeks, and no one was more loyal to Jared than Bagley. If she was doing anything at all underhanded, wouldn't Bagley know?

Tyler began to question himself. God knew Jared deserved a good woman. If only he had reason to believe there was such a thing somewhere in this world . . . Oh, there was his mother . . . and Susan. Susan was *good* enough, but she was a humorless thing and she didn't really love Jared. She only wanted to convert him.

The question Tyler wanted answered was: what did Carina O'Rourke want?

Toward that end, he asked, "When does Jared return from Boston?"

"I don't know."

"But you thought I was Jared."

"I only hoped," she said, blushing. "Seeing the table . . ."

"Will you go to Boston with him next time?"

"Oh, no. Never."

"Why never? That's a long time."

"It wouldn't be right."

"Right? What has right to do with it?"

Her blush deepened becomingly. "Mr. Maxwell, you're embarrassing me. You know why."

"My name is Tyler," he said, glad for something neutral to say. For all his probing, Carina O'Rourke was more puzzling now than before. She blushed like a maiden and seemed to pine for Jared. "If virginity were a requirement for entering society, Carina, it would be much more exclusive than it is."

"That's doubtless so. The truth is, society doesn't interest me."

To cover his disbelief, Tyler took her hand and said with mock fervor, "Ah, that only I had met you first, Miss O'Rourke. I didn't believe such a woman as you existed."

She took back her hand the very instant she could do so without giving offense. "And to be honest, you still don't believe it," she said simply.

Tyler laughed, but he was impressed. She was right. He didn't believe it—but he wanted to.

Oh, yes. He wanted to very much.

# *Chapter Seventeen*

Where else but in Boston could one find so many people who knew precisely what the world required for its improvement?

Jared shook his head in wonder as he surveyed the room full of expensively dressed people. Since coming to Boston, he had spent far too many hours in the company of these well-intentioned, deadly serious people. He respected them, even admired one or two of them, but he didn't much like them.

Except for the woman coming his way. Indigo.

When Susan matured she would look like her mother, regal and lovely. By fifty or so, Susan might also acquire Indigo's sociability and charm, but she could not *be* Indigo. Thus she was doomed to remain only a poor copy of the woman Jared most admired.

He watched Indigo work her way closer, her purpose firm while she dealt, graciously and easily, with each distraction that intervened. It was her way. Jared had seen it over and over. Garrulous old Mrs. Maplewood had no idea she was being smoothly set aside, and if she had known she wouldn't have minded. Indigo had smiled at her and asked about her cat. She had been honored.

When it was Jared's turn to be favored, he opened his arms and offered his cheek to her kiss. "I'm so glad you came after all, Jared. I wasn't sure you would."

"How could I resist?"

"All too easily, I'm afraid." She took his arm and led him away from the crowded sitting room, asking, "Have you had refreshments?"

It was a hostess's question, designed to win them privacy. She barely listened to his murmured response.

"You're going to Lawrence's from here, aren't you?"

Jared smiled. "Poor old Zach Taylor could have used your information system in the Mexican War. We'd have had a quicker victory."

She accepted his teasing with her own smile. "Of course we would have. Better than that, we'd have avoided the whole thing, but when have men paid any attention to a mere woman?"

"You have this man's complete attention right now," he offered.

As her hand fastened on his, she said without preamble, "Ask Tyler to see his father, will you?"

"You know I will, but—"

"But you can't guarantee anything. I know."

"He'd talk to you, Indigo."

Tears started in her eyes as she shook her head. "I . . . can't, Jared. I wish I could."

"Why not? If it would mend the rift? You know Tyler adores you, and so does Silas. If you talked to each of them?"

"No. It doesn't work that way." Her tears didn't fall, nor would they. She blinked them away and gave him a sad smile. "Have you ever wondered at the reason for the Beatitudes?"

The switch caught him short. "The Beatitudes? You mean—?"

"Blessed are the meek. Et cetera. Everyone knows why the meek can only inherit the earth in heaven—as if that were possible—but the peacemakers . . ." She sighed, shrugging her shoulders. "I think peacemakers have a rougher time on earth than the meek. It sounds so easy, but it's not."

251

"I take it that you've tried and lost?"

"It's been a while, but nothing has changed since then. I won't go behind Silas's back, Jared. He'd be hurt."

"I undertand." He squeezed her hand. "Perhaps I can do something. I usually feel that I'm just another obstruction. You know, if Silas didn't think of me as another son, he'd come to terms with Tyler."

"I know, but it's not you. It's the two of them. They're so alike."

"Stiff-necked and proud," Jared agreed.

"Does Tyler ever ask about us?"

"He doesn't have to. I can never outlast him, and I end up telling him everything. He plays me like a fiddle."

Indigo's eyes glowed with pride. "If only that ability could keep him safe. It's such a dangerous game he plays."

"He's master of it. No one here appreciates his cleverness. All they see is the silly surface he shows them."

"May they always," Indigo said fervently. She was about to turn away, her message delivered, when she saw Susan pass the doorway. Instead of leaving, she stopped. "Did something momentous happen in Lowell this time, Jared? I hate to say this, but since she came back, Susan has been particularly . . . I don't know . . . distracted. Did you see her just *drift* by the door? It's most un-Susanlike behavior."

"Have you asked her?"

That drew a sharp look from Indigo. "Something did happen."

"What did Susan say?"

"She looks right through me. It's as though she's not of this earth anymore. The only thing that interests her is her writing. I had to force her to come here today."

"I may have gotten through to her at last," Jared admitted reluctantly. Indigo was the most liberal-minded woman he knew, but he didn't want to tell even her about Carina. "I was quite blunt about my intention not to marry again. Perhaps I hurt her feelings."

"Oh, nonsense! That crush of hers lost wind ages ago," she said. "This is something else. It's new, different. I feel as if I'm seeing who she really is. Did she meet someone there?"

"Someone? A man, you mean?" Accustomed to the burden of Susan's hope of marriage to him, Jared was startled to hear himself dismissed so lightly. It amused him that he almost felt insulted.

"Of course, a man."

"No. She was only there a day."

Indigo patted his arm. "Never mind, dear. I'll manage Susan."

Jared never doubted it, but before he left the party, which was meant to introduce yet another abolitionist to those who were already converted to the cause, he made a point of finding Susan. As usual, Indigo's analysis was on the mark.

After first giving Jared a distantly polite smile, Susan focused on him only when he spoke directly to her. Then her smile warmed until it was about as fond as a well-loved older brother could expect. This time when Jared tested his emotions for insult he couldn't find any. Just relief. And gratitude to Carina, whose presence in his household had undoubtedly brought about the change.

"Indigo tells me you're hard at work on your writing project," he said, referring to her tract relating experiences of fugitive slaves. "That explains why I haven't seen you lately. It must be going well."

To his surprise, Susan's face clouded. "It's very difficult, Jared."

Because he was pleased to have her intensity directed elsewhere, he sounded a more enthusiastic note than he intended. "I'm sure you're doing magnificently."

As if she heard the emptiness of his praise, her frown deepened. "I don't know. I have the information, but I'm afraid of not doing justice to it. It's so important."

In spite of himself, Jared was impressed by the new

sense of responsibility he saw in her. It was enough to make him forget that he shared her father's misgivings about the project.

Before he could offer more of his ill-considered encouragement, Susan asked, "Perhaps I'll have to go back to Lowell and see if Mr. Boynton can help me. Do you suppose he would?"

"What sort of help do you require?"

Susan saw through his question. "Not what you think," she responded sharply. "I've kept a journal for years. The idea of telling the stories of the fugitives has been in my mind a long time. I'm sure my father made it sound impulsive, but it wasn't. The stories are all there in my records—nearly three years of them—but I need them organized and perhaps unified somehow. I've tried two different approaches and I'm unsure which is better."

"Perhaps someone here in Boston could be of more help," Jared said. "I'm afraid you saw Mr. Boynton at his best. Certainly he has no fondness for me, and although he works for the *Chronicle* I'm not sure where his sentiments lie." He suggested that she consult with members of the Boston Vigilance Committee instead.

The look she gave him for answer was every bit as distracted as Indigo had said. "I'll think about it," she said, with such obvious insincerity that he had to laugh as he left the party. Bemused, he realized that he had just been dismissed out of hand by someone who had heretofore cherished his every suggestion. Aside from the oddity of the experience, he felt liberated.

Once he reached the street outside, Jared stopped walking suddenly, assailed by an unwelcome thought. Indigo's question came back to him. Had Susan met a man in Lowell?

She had met Dennis Boynton. And remembered him.

He paused, considering the idea that Boynton interested Susan. It was as oppressive as the humidity steaming the air. Finally he dismissed the notion. Indigo was an unusually sensitive woman, but this time she was wrong. Susan was only being sensible for a change, recognizing that what he told her about himself was true. She could not have replaced him so quickly in her affections, and certainly not with Boynton. The man was a boor.

Relieved, Jared resumed walking, grinning to himself.


"You might at least try to look pleased to be here," Nathan said as he sidled up to his niece.

Her answer was a scathing look.

In two weeks of attending social functions—she could hardly call them balls—in Boston, Rachel Farmington still had not seen Jared Wentworth. Her uncle explained that Jared, through his association with the Meades, had entree into two levels of Boston society while he had only one. It stood to reason that since Jared lived with the Meades, he would socialize with them, but did that mean he never came to one of these gatherings?

Not that Rachel could blame him. As she surveyed the room with ill-concealed distaste, she wondered how the output of so much money could provide so little pleasure. At least for her.

At first she had been excited to be here. Uncle Nathan always told her the backgrounds of the people she would meet—and they were rich. One or two of the young men, Harvard graduates all, either lawyers or businessmen, might have interested her if she had not already met Jared Wentworth. Compared to him, even the handsomest and liveliest of the men looked pale and boring.

Instinctively, she knew she would be able to ride roughshod over young Henry Philbrook, for instance. His mother already had him well trained, and even the pleasure of defeating Mama Philbrook wouldn't compensate for having to put up with Henry's wet kisses. She had never kissed Jared, but she knew it would be an experience.

255

She let her eyes coast over the throng one more time, saying petulantly, "You promised Jared would be here."

"Patience, my dear," her uncle counseled. "It wouldn't hurt for him to find you in conversation with one of the eligible gentlemen when he arrives. After all, he shouldn't think you're waiting to pounce on him."

"But I don't see anyone remotely interesting," Rachel complained. Then she did. She spied a golden head towering over the host and hostess near the entrance. The man bent to listen to someone and turned, presenting his perfect profile. "Who is that?" she asked, clutching blindly at Nathan's sleeve.

"A penniless fool," he snapped. "Let's go talk to Amos."

Rachel resisted his tug, her gaze steady on her prey. "His name, Uncle Nathan."

"Tyler Meade."

Her eyes swung to Nathan's. "You said the Meades owned half the shipping out of Boston Harbor."

"They do, but Tyler is the black sheep. He's been cut off. Everything goes to Susan."

"Ah," breathed Rachel as she nurtured a small smile, "Another family spat. If you're not careful, dear uncle, you're going to have me believing all you Yankees ever do is squabble."

"This one goes deep, I hear. The Meades are people of strong social conscience. All Tyler does is spend money he doesn't have and chase skirts."

Rachel noted the besotted smile the tall, attractive man won from their sour hostess. "With great success, I can see." She knew without having to look around that Tyler Meade had drawn the eye of every woman in the room. She thought of her mother's favorite caller, a man she had characterized without rancor as an incorrigible ladies' man. Tyler Meade was another, she was certain. Even across the room she felt the pull of his appeal—and decided to resist it.

He would have to come to her.

"I'm feeling quite parched in this crush," Rachel said. "Do you suppose we could get a drink now?"

Relief put a spring in Nathan's step as he led his niece out of Meade's range. Black sheep or not, Tyler was the most dangerous man in the room, and Nathan could only rejoice that Rachel was too sensible—or too greedy—to risk her reputation for him. Being Southern, being his niece, she had handicaps aplenty to overcome. She could not, nor could he, afford the slightest whisper of compromise to be attached to her name. And Tyler Meade was compromise personified.

Once he had Rachel safely wedged between Henry Philbrook and his redoubtable mother, Nathan circulated amongst his cronies. They were a hardy lot. Disappointments of one kind or another dogged them, closely in many cases. One had an erring wife, another suffered ill health; but they put the best face possible on their miseries and did their jobs. They had loyalty, sometimes only to place and position, but more often to each other. He was proud to be one of them.

In that frame of mind, he welcomed seeing Jared Wentworth across the room. Nathan was not often in the same room with his nephew, and he intended to make the best of his chance. Without being obvious, he kept Jared within view, hoping to see him exhibit some interest in Rachel. He greatly feared it was not to be, but he knew Jared would not do anything to please him so he intended to disguise his hope.

His pleasure that Jared came to him barely outlasted his nephew's greeting.

"I thought I'd come say hello to you before the rumormongers begin to spread the word that I fear for my life around you," Jared said, spreading his arms wide. "Plainly, I don't."

Nathan felt his neck begin to burn. "Jared, for pity's sake—"

"Pity?" came the prompt response. "An interesting word to come from you. How much pity did you show my

257

family, I wonder?"

Nathan's only solace was that no one overheard them. Jared looked as affable as a snake-oil salesman the whole time he spoke. Except for his eyes. They glittered with suppressed rage that, by design, only Nathan could see. He looked away, drowning in frustration. "I wish I could make you understand—"

"So do I."

Nathan's gaze tangled with Jared's as something close to anguish passed between them. It wasn't understanding, but it was shared. For at least that moment everything else fell away. They were alone together in that room full of people.

Then, swiftly, it was gone.

But not entirely, for Jared said, "Silas tells me he believes your story."

"Story," Nathan echoed, unsure how to respond. "Why does that feel like one of those beating-your-wife questions?"

"Don't try to disarm me with wily answers, you old bastard," Jared said without heat. "I'm onto your game."

Again, Nathan wanted to hear a lack of animosity in Jared's voice, so he did. He told himself he wasn't deluding himself as long as he knew he was censoring what he picked up. "You're right about the old part anyway," he said.

Jared followed his gaze to Rachel and laughed. "That one would make any man feel old—or young again."

This was as much genuine sympathy as Nathan was likely to get, so he savored it. For that reason, he was unprepared for Jared's next hit.

Jared waited until Nathan was relaxed before he brought up his second unpleasant subject. He was still trying to figure out his uncle's relationship with Rachel. Nathan watched her no more than any other man in the room. Her dress was designed to snare a man's eyes, drawing them to sample, at least visually, her lush curves. Even with the most suspicious mind in the world,

Jared couldn't see anything worse than exasperated pride in Nathan's look.

But he didn't trust either one of them. He wanted to know what his enemy wanted.

"I understand that you're raising money for the Shattuck Mill," he said. "Why not use the money you've set aside for me? Is it such a bad investment as all that?"

He saw hope and suspicion battle each other in Nathan's expression. "It's a wonderful investment, but only if you choose to go into it. That's your money, not mine."

*Caution,* Jared thought, analyzing Nathan's response. He was angry at himself for being obvious. He wanted to believe the reserved money had been used by Nathan in some way, as collateral perhaps, but he knew it hadn't been. It—its inviolableness—was Nathan's only bulwark. As long as he held that trust fund sacred, he preserved his claim to innocence.

And Nathan was smart enough to know that the value of that claim rose dizzyingly even as his actual fortune sank. More and more, as Nathan's need for capital became increasingly acute, Jared's sympathy faded. He didn't care about sympathy, he told himself. He wanted justice for his family. They had received no sympathy, no *pity*—to use Nathan's word.

Nevertheless, Jared felt the same grudging admiration for the old man's stubborn insistence. Like Jared, Nathan never relented, never gave up his single-minded defense of his innocence. It would be so easy to accept the story . . . but he couldn't. He wouldn't.

"Such nobility," he said, his smile threatening to become a sneer. "Do you think I don't know what you're trying to do? Do you—"

"Why, Cousin Jared," Rachel said, slipping into place beside Nathan, "How wonderful to see you!"

He was ill prepared just then for sociability—as Rachel undoubtedly saw. He should have been grateful for the intervention; instead, he nearly broke the hand she presented. The feel of it, surprisingly strong despite its slender construction, brought him abruptly to his senses.

Easing his grip, Jared bowed and brought her hand to his lips. "Miss Farmington, I see you persuaded your uncle to bring you to Boston. I'm sure every man here is deeply grateful to him."

"As long as you are," she drawled, "the others don't matter."

Her voice recalled what Jared had heard of Carina's imitation of a Southern lady, and he smiled fondly. He saw Nathan note the change in him, and a piece of the puzzle that was his uncle slipped into place. He murmured a polite response as thoughts chased through his brain.

To Jared, Rachel's appearance at just this awkward moment signified a connection between Nathan's conscience money and Nathan's niece. Being aware of the connection gave him a step up on his uncle, for he realized that, with the lovely Rachel as bait, Nathan would not need to touch his unwanted trust fund. If Nathan married his niece to a man with more money than sense, he would have all the backing the Shattuck Mill could use.

Nathan went on to make the plot transparent by saying, "Rachel hasn't seen the sights of Boston yet, Jared. I've been meaning to take her around, but I'm sure she'd enjoy the company of a younger man as her guide."

At that moment Jared caught sight of Tyler bearing down upon them. He nearly laughed aloud at the way circumstances suddenly favored him.

Tyler's public persona was a carefully created, largely false construction meant to provide unassailable cover for his activism under another name and personality. But one part of it was true—his success with women.

Indeed, in this instance, reputation didn't begin to approach reality. Tyler's Byronic looks, combined with his social status as a fallen angel, made him irresistible to the ladies. From matron to ingenue, no woman was proof against Tyler's charm. Not one of them cared that his break with his family might be total and final.

The break was real enough, as Jared's discussion with Indigo proved, but it was not irreparable. A year or two, at most, and Tyler would be reconciled with Silas, Jared was certain. A few of the more astute ladies believed the same thing, of course, but that prospect in no way accounted for Tyler's amatory success.

Jared and Tyler were publicly known as arch rivals, another subterfuge. But of course, in Boston society even arch rivals were courteous, at least on the surface. So Jared had to introduce Tyler to Rachel, which he did with as little grace as he could manage.

For the sake of their rivalry, Tyler was quick to exert himself with Rachel, who clearly didn't mind having two men vie for her attention. If Rachel knew that her uncle was growing apoplectic under his thin veneer of indifference, she didn't let on that she saw his anguish.

Or she didn't care.

Either way, Jared saw his chance to make Nathan cringe. After skirmishing with Tyler for the sake of appearance, he said to his uncle, "It pains me that I won't be able to show Miss Farmington around Boston as you suggested. Unfortunately, I have to return to Lowell." He bowed to Rachel to ask with patently spurious hope, "Perhaps you'll still be here when I return?"

"I'm sure I will be, Mr. Wentworth."

"And in the meantime," Tyler put in smoothly, "it will be my pleasure to show your cousin the sights of Boston." He took Rachel's hand and put it through his arm, patting it in a proprietary manner sure to offend Nathan. "Why don't we begin by getting you some refreshments?"

For the sake of those watching—and there were many—Jared tried to look unhappy to have Tyler appropriate Rachel under his very nose. But he didn't disguise his real feelings from Nathan. Frowning mightily for show, he spoke triumphant words to his uncle. "They make a stunning couple, do they not?"

Both men heard Tyler dispose of formality, inviting Rachel to call him by his given name.

Jared's eyes were merry as he watched Nathan struggle to contain his wrath. He had baited his trap with Rachel's virginal loveliness in the clear expectation of having her capture a wealthy, well-connected suitor. Now he had to watch a most notorious womanizer steal the bait, leaving him with an empty trap.

## *Chapter Eighteen*

In spite of herself, Carina continued to mark time by the number of days since Jared had left. It bothered her that she did so, because his use of her shamed her. She knew it did. But here in the bosom of his household, tucked away from the world, she was protected—even from herself.

How could she feel properly disgraced when everyone here treated her like . . . ? Words failed her. Appropriate words, at least. What she felt like, living here, was a great lady. No one, not even Gwen, sneered at her anymore. Now that she had her school, she had friends, true friends, as well as something worthwhile to do.

Gwen was her greatest success story so far. Carina had long believed that education provided the key to a happy life. Because she had known—inside, where it counted—her own value as a person, even working as a virtual slave in the mill had not made her despair of her future. Now she was able to give that same hope to the people here. And Gwen was proof that it worked. She was a sponge who soaked up everything Carina could teach her.

The weather had changed since Jared had left, becoming cooler. The nights were crisp and clear, the days warm whenever it was not actually raining. And the rain, when it came, was welcome, although it came too late to save the fall crops.

Carina heard from Marcus that the mills had resumed

production on a limited scale. She wondered what that meant to her family. Patrick, at least, would probably have work even if there was none for the rest. They could get by on his pay alone, although it would be hard. She longed for a way to help them, telling herself that when Jared returned she would ask him for coin to send them. She knew she never would, though.

What she found hardest to overlook was the waste she saw around her. Jared's household, well managed as it was, was full of wonders that Margaret and little Kevin would relish. As she feasted her mind in Jared's study, Carina ached to give her father access to such bounty. And the kitchen help squandered more food than the whole Sweeney family saw in a week.

She tried not to think about it. Usually she succeeded.

Strangely, her anxiety about the future did not abate as her position in the household became more secure. The reason for that was obvious, but in this case knowledge and understanding were no comfort to her. The kinder the people around her were, the greater became her fear of having to leave and losing that kindness.

Liked or hated, she had no place that was truly hers. However loyal, however useful she had proved herself, nothing except Jared's continued desire for her would keep her place. She was his mistress, a role she was ill equipped to play. A man's mistress existed to please that man, something she'd failed to do with alarming frequency.

Daily, Carina reminded herself that she would have to go, but even that decision had been given over to Jared with her promise that she would not leave without his permission. She had bound herself by her word without receiving anything in return—no assurance, no pledge.

If anything, his last conversation with her had heightened her insecurity, for she knew she had riled him into reiterating that he wouldn't marry her. That he'd softened the sting by vowing to have no one else either was little comfort.

She had been honest in telling Jared she did not desire marriage. Early memories of her mother notwithstanding, she had seen few happy marriages. In Lowell and on the farms of New Hampshire, women were drudges who turned out baby after baby without missing more than a few steps along their wearying paths. In leaving her father's home, she had been running away from that reality as much as from Dennis himself.

But marriage to Jared would be altogether different. She let herself think of it rarely, knowing it was as much beyond her as the star that bore her name up in the heavens. Jared's wife would not labor as Carina's mother and Mary Sweeney had. Still, though her mother's work had been onerous, at least Carina knew how to do it. She did not know how to be wife to a man in Jared's position.

She tried to imagine what Boston was like—and failed. She could not imagine such splendor. She had seen Susan's carriage, Susan's clothes, and Susan's room. An entire city of people so equipped was frightening. To live there, Jared would need a wife like Susan, if not Susan herself.

Carina did not care much for Susan, truth to tell, and she worried more with each day Jared stayed away that he would bring her back with him, this time as his wife. Knowing how hollow were her own protestations about marriage, Carina judged that Jared's might be similarly insubstantial. Doubtless, he had his misgivings about the institution just as she did, but he had been married once. It stood to reason that he would marry again.

Early in the week Jared had sent word that he would return "in a day or so." That message, like others before it, had come to Bagley, not to her. She expected no personal word, but her feelings were terribly mixed about his return.

She longed for his company and—shamefully—for his closeness. She wanted to tell him about her pupils' successes because she knew he'd be proud of them. She had made a new dress, one of her own design, from entirely new cloth, and wanted to wear it for him.

Most of all, she wanted to see him. Just that. To know he was safe, well, and whole. And alone.

That most of all.

This day, as she had each day since Jared's message had been received, Carina dressed carefully, hoping—and fearing—he would come. She had taken to wearing her hair in a new style in his absence. It was a compromise between the comfort and neatness she craved and Jared's stated preference for unconfinement. She pulled the sides and front back smoothly and let the back cascade in free-falling curls.

Now she fingered the sides nervously as she worried about the word to use in a story she was writing for her students. She had begun to compose her own stories as a way to make the reading exercises more interesting for her adult learners. They responded so well to her some-times silly attempts that she continued trying to come up with at least a few sentences. They especially liked it when she used their names. This one featured Ned and some of the horses.

The problem was not with the story but with her concentration, or lack of it. She could not focus her mind on the task. Her eyes kept skidding off to the window, the way Patrick's had at home under their mother's tutelage. Like Patrick, she wished to be somewhere else, outside, preferably upon Merrylegs, riding through the yellowing woods.

"Excuse me, Miss Carina." Bagley appeared at the door, and her heart began to pound in alarm at the distress in his voice and manner.

"What is it, Bagley?" She sat up, clutching the much-revised paper to her chest. It was a poor defense against the calamity she knew he represented. Jared had returned and he was married. He had Susan with him and—

"Someone to see you," he said uncertainly. "A man."

266

"A man?"

Not Jared, Carina realized as relief, pleasure, and disappointment flooded through her in confusion. She frowned, then beamed. "Patrick!"

Bagley's face stiffened with offense. "He says his name is Dennis Boynton."

"Dennis . . . *Boynton!*" In the act of rising, she sat back down, hard.

"You know the . . . gentleman, then?"

"Yes, I do," she said in a faint voice, her mind whirling with questions. "He's a friend of my father's, Bagley. Oh . . . did he say what he wanted?"

"To speak to you, Miss Carina. Shall I send him away?"

"No!" Then less sharply, "No, I must see him. He may have news. My father . . . Oh, dear. What if he's ill?" She looked around the room wildly, trying to imagine Dennis here with her. He would think—

She brought herself up short. It didn't matter what Dennis thought. He didn't matter; only his reason for coming concerned her.

"Where is he?"

"In the hall, ma'am."

Carina scarcely noticed his term of respect, and it wasn't until later that she wondered whether he'd said it to remind her of her place or to show support. She stood and took a deep breath to steady herself. "Please, Bagley, show him in here."

"Would you like me to stay with you?"

She managed a smile. "No, thank you. It won't be necessary."

"I'll leave you then, but I'll be at hand, should you need me."

"Thank you." She understood what he was saying. Although he would not intrude or eavesdrop, he would be within the sound of her voice. It should have calmed her, but did not.

She had only a moment to prepare herself, then

267

Dennis was there behind Bagley, who bowed out, giving her a pointed, significant look that would have amused her at any other time.

Carina had studied Dennis enough over the years of their acquaintance to know his appearance well. He was tall and redheaded, with a piercing gaze she had once thought the mark of his superior intelligence. He and her father had made the room her family lived in seem inadequate to hold their voices, raised in thunderous discussion. Sure of his welcome there, he had filled the room with his confident bearing.

He seemed different here.

For one thing, he was overdressed. He wore a suit that was stiff and worn shiny with age. She had never seen him formally attired; but then, neither had he seen her in anything attractive—as his assessing glance quickly showed.

His awkwardness moved her to sympathy that made her greet him warmly. "How are you, Dennis?"

He carried a black hat that he had not given to Bagley. She wondered if he had been unwilling to part with it, for he turned it around and around in his hands. His eyes darted from Carina to her surroundings as he nodded and answered almost eagerly. "Fine, fine. And you?"

"Very well, thank you. I hope you don't bring me bad news from home?"

His fidgeting stopped. "No so bad, considering matters of late."

"The shutdowns? But surely that's passed with the recent rains. I . . . ah, heard that the mills were all operating again."

"So they are, although it'll be some time before most people are out of debt from it."

Carina nodded. She had not forgotten. "There was unrest, I heard."

Dennis smiled, and Carina saw a glimpse of his old arrogance in the flash of white teeth shining from the thicket of his beard and mustache. "You hear a bit out here," he commented.

"That's a train that runs both ways—or you would not be here," she said, giving in to the need she felt to defend herself. From what, she wasn't sure. His presence, perhaps?

"Did you think to lose yourself here?"

Her small rebellion had passed. "No," she admitted, but without adding any explanation. She didn't think he would be impressed by the thought processes that had brought her here, nor did she believe she owed him any explanation. Quickly, to forego the possibility of his pressing for one, she asked, "Is my father well?"

"Except for the worry, his time off from work was beneficial to him."

"But he is out of the picking room, isn't he?" In spite of herself, Carina couldn't keep her anxiety from Dennis.

She heard curiosity in his voice as he answered, "The news of his return to the yard came with Patrick at his return. Indeed, it came hard upon your departure."

Carina was so relieved to find Jared hadn't misled her that at first she overlooked the full implication of his statement—and the implicit question it contained. She wouldn't satisfy his curiosity about her part in Patrick's release, but it made her ask, and sharply, "Just *how* hard upon that time? Do you recall?"

"Of course I recall," he said. "You left on Sunday and Patrick returned on Monday."

"Monday! But—" She clamped her teeth together over the words that waited to spill out. It wasn't possible. She had not made her request to Jared until Monday. "Are you certain?"

"I was there when Meggers brought him. It was late, after full dark, and it caused a great commotion and an impromptu celebration. Conn was as happy as I've ever seen him, so I marked the day well."

Carina could not have predicted the pain she would feel at hearing the details. She was happy to know her sacrifice had not been in vain, but it hurt to know that no one marked her absence or felt her loss from their midst.

Along with verification of her father's disinterest in her—something which she had long been aware—came another blow to her self-esteem. This one was new. It hurt even more because it struck at her tenderest green growth as a woman.

Jared had taken her virginity under false pretenses. He had already arranged for Patrick's release from jail and for Conn's return to outdoor work at the mill, and *still* he had required her to mate with him.

She recalled his almost-reluctance that night with a rising sense of righteous indignation. While Conn and Patrick and Dennis had been celebrating back in Lowell, she had given herself up to be Jared's whore. She could have refused him. She could have left then without loss, with her family already secure.

But she hadn't known. Jared hadn't been gentleman enough to tell her the truth. Knowing that she felt under obligation to him, he had let her continue to believe that Patrick's fate depended upon her sacrifice.

A doubled sense of desolation fell over Carina like a shroud, blurring her judgment. Momentarily needing to justify what she had become—if only to herself—she forgot that it had been Jared's attractiveness that had drawn her to him. She had felt the obligation, yes; but it was Jared himself she had been unable to resist.

Carina's confusion and inner turmoil made it hard for her to think how to respond to Dennis. He watched her avidly. Did he know what role she had played for her family? What role she still played for Jared?

She knew he did.

Seeing him here had revived her shame in the direction her life had taken, shame that her isolation at Falls Village had deadened. Now that she knew Jared had played her false, the feeling was worse, more intense. A fine trembling threatened to overtake her, robbing her of control of her limbs. To offset it, she nourished outrage and anger. And pride.

That especially.

Carina lifted her chin in a defiant gesture Dennis probably knew well. She didn't care. She would not let him see her pain. She made her tone as offhand as she could manage. "That's wonderful news. By now the whole sorry incident must be over for everyone. It was so unfair. But then, that's Enoch Wentworth for you."

"He doesn't bother you here, does he?"

"Enoch? Oh, no. The cousins do not get along."

If Dennis wondered at the familiarity with which Carina spoke of her former employer, he didn't comment. It was Jared Wentworth that concerned him, not Enoch. "Carina, I didn't come here to chastise you, only to tell you I still believe that we're promised to each other."

Carina was shocked. "Oh no, Dennis. That's not . . . I could never . . . You couldn't—"

Unperturbed, Dennis stepped closer. "Carina . . ."

"No." She moved back, genuinely alarmed. "You don't understand."

"I think I do. You don't have to stay here." He raked the lovely room with a contemptuous glance, dismissing it. His eyes settled on her without losing their anger. "You should have come to me."

The accusation in his tone restored Carina's spirit. "What would you have done?"

"I wouldn't have disgraced you this way," he said through clenched jaws. "I would have married you. And I will."

"In spite of my disgrace?"

"It didn't exist then," he said tightly.

"But now it does," she reminded him.

"I consider the fault mine, Carina." His stance was a curious mix of his usual arrogance and a new uncertainty, perhaps caused by their surroundings. "I gave more thought to how Conn saw things than to how they appeared to you. I should have made my feelings clear."

Now that it was too late, Carina didn't want to hear

about what might have been. She shook her head. "It doesn't matter now. It's too late."

"Don't say that. You can leave here," Dennis insisted. "Come with me now."

"Where? Back to my family?"

Something moved over his face. Had he winced?

"I'd not be welcome, would I?" Seeing his reluctance, she pressed for an answer. "What does my father say about me?"

He paused, then said, "That you're dead."

She took in air sharply to offset the knifelike pain. "Is he . . . believed?"

Dennis shook his head, giving her a twisted smile. "Without a body? Everyone knows you went away. Most probably wonder why you didn't go years ago. Conn's known for a harsh man."

"Does this 'everyone' also know where I went?"

"No. I learned from Wentworth, when he asked about Patrick being released. I put the two things together. After that it wasn't hard to learn the truth."

Carina latched onto the one significant detail in his story like a drowning man to a log. Jared had asked about Patrick. "When?" she blurted out.

"When what?"

"When did Jared ask about Patrick?"

He had to consider a moment. "When he came to Lowell. It was after Patrick returned, a day or so perhaps. Why do you ask?"

She wouldn't tell him her real reason, although she cherished his answer. Days later. If he'd had to ask Dennis about Patrick, he hadn't *known* that he had been released.

Perhaps it didn't change anything between them and perhaps it did. She'd have to think about it when she was alone. Right now, with Dennis watching her and trying to figure out the meaning of her questions, she had to be careful. Dennis wasn't stupid. He had found her and learned why she was here. If he knew that all was not easy in her life now, he'd exert more pressure on her to return.

"I've no special reason for asking," she lied, "beyond wondering how long it will be before others know where I am. What about Patrick? And Margaret? What do they believe about me?"

"I don't know. Only that you're gone, probably. People speculate, but without basis."

"And you'd have me go back to that?"

"You'd be my wife. I'd protect you."

"You couldn't protect me from the gossip. It would follow me all my life."

"Then we could go somewhere else, where we're not known."

Carina smiled sadly at him, more touched than she wanted to be. Now that it was too late, Dennis would be her protector. "You're very kind, Dennis," she said. "Kind to come here. Kind to try to help me."

She couldn't tell him her plight was beyond him, but it was. Most of all, she couldn't tell him she didn't want to be rescued by him. Whatever motivated him now, whether he was moved by honor or a sense of guilt, she didn't believe it would last. She didn't want to be bound to him or to any man by gratitude. Her gratitude would turn to resentment just as quickly as his noble sentiments deteriorated.

She had seen too much of Dennis Boynton to believe that he wanted her for herself. Perhaps he had a score to settle with Conn or—more likely—with Jared. She was a means to an end for him. She knew it. And she wouldn't accept that role ever again. She might be whore to Jared, but he wanted her for herself, not for what she represented.

Even as she thought that, she realized it was wrong. To Jared also, she represented something—opposition to his cousin. He had championed her as a way to fight Enoch.

Her head was suddenly aching with contrary and confusing thoughts. Earlier, she had longed for Jared's return; now she was once again questioning the foundation of their relationship. The look she leveled at Dennis wasn't grateful anymore. She didn't appreciate being reminded of what she'd lost, no matter what he'd intended by coming.

He wasn't going to give up. "Carina, I don't have to stay in Lowell. I could go—"

Whatever he was about to say was lost to her. She heard sounds in the hall. Scurrying footsteps and Bagley's voice raised—in greeting or warning?

"Mr. Jared!"

If she could hear Bagley's false heartiness, certainly Jared could.

Dennis stopped talking and looked toward the door.

Carina took a step that way, then halted. She would not run to Jared with Dennis looking on. Nor would she try to hide him from Jared.

But before she could do anything, right or wrong, Bagley popped into the doorway, looking distraught. Behind him stood Jared.

"Would you care for tea, Miss Carina?"

She clung to her dignity by a thread. "No, thank you, Bagley," she said, dismissing him in order to deal with his master. "Welcome home, Jared." Indicating Dennis, she said, "I believe you know Mr. Boynton?"

Jared didn't leave the doorway to greet Dennis. He just nodded, his eyes narrowed with displeasure.

Dennis stood tall under Jared's hostile scrutiny. He had long ago tucked his hat under his arm, where it lodged, crushed but untipped in deference to another. She had not asked him to come, but she saw how difficult it was for him to stand on ground belonging to another and not wilt. She was perversely proud of him for it.

As Jared didn't make it easy for Dennis, Carina did nothing to ease the moment for him. She didn't ask about his trip, although she could have. Her father had called her bold, but she believed it would be foolish to try smoothing this social encounter.

Turning from Dennis, Jared glared at her before he turned away. "I will see you soon, I trust."

She gave him a stiff nod. Probably she should feel grateful he hadn't added the word *upstairs,* but she was hard pressed to feel any kindly emotion just then.

Alone with Dennis again, Carina felt more awkward than before. She wanted him gone, and yet she was unwilling to hustle him away with guilty haste. Jared would read ill into anything she did.

More than anything, she was uninterested in hearing Dennis again ask her to leave. To prevent that, she said, "I wish you would take word to Margaret, Patrick, and Kevin—that I think of them, that I'm well." It hurt not to add Papa's name to the list.

"I may find a way."

"I know you'll watch over Papa, but if the others need me, will you let me know?"

He pledged without words, his eyes full of other thoughts.

"As you can see," she said, smiling, "I *am* well—and happy. I'm well treated and not without friends. It is a good place."

Her expression dared him to contradict her, so he didn't. He bowed once and left her with another of his fierce stares. She knew Bagley waited to see him out, so she didn't follow. She couldn't have anyway; her knees were locked into position to keep her upright.

It was a long time before she could move back to the chair.


Carina found Jared in his room.

Although the door stood half-open in invitation, the look he wore was distinctly unwelcoming. Because she had tarried, trying to sort through her jangled spirits, he had already changed from his travel-worn clothing and made some inroads on the refreshments laid out for him. His shirt was unfastened and untucked.

Somehow that last, and the unsettling glimpse of chest it afforded, offended Carina anew. Everything did.

She wanted no more of Dennis now than when she had run from the prospect of marriage to him, but his coming reminded her of hurtful things. That Jared would summon her to his presence and then make no attempt to cover himself decently, rubbed salt in her fresh wounds.

Dennis had worn his best suit and tortured his hat in his concern about approaching her. At the moment, the contrast seemed significant to Carina, but she fought against resentment. She didn't think there was space in the room for both their ill tempers—and it was Jared's room, Jared's house.

She stopped just inside the door. "I hope your trip went well." Her voice sounded tinny and small to her ears.

The noise he made could have meant anything, but his expression was plain. It said, *A lot you care.*

Her appearance was beyond reproach. She knew because she had checked. Nevertheless, his stare made her hands itch to smooth her skirts and fuss with her hair. She willed them to be still. When he didn't speak she tried to leave. "You must be tired. . . ."

"What was Boynton doing here?"

"He came to visit." She wanted to stop there. His look forced her on. "He brought news of my family."

"What news?"

"That they are well."

He snorted rudely and threw himself into the chair standing before his meal. "You doubted it?"

She overlooked the fact that he didn't ask her to sit. "Of course I doubted it. My father has been ill. My brother was in jail."

"Conditions which would still prevail for all Boynton did about their problems," he pointed out acidly.

"Not everyone has your position or your connections."

"Now that you've had your use of both, you mean to

leave. Is that it?"

"No!"

"You mean he didn't ask?"

Sensing a trap, Carina hesitated to answer. She had never seen his mood so vile.

Giving her no time to think, he laughed unpleasantly. "Never mind dredging around for an answer. It's written all over your face."

"I didn't ask him here and I didn't welcome him," she said in her own defense.

That only added to his sour amusement. "I can see that welcome of any sort is in short supply here."

It was such a revealing remark that Carina couldn't quite believe her ears. She was tempted to give over her mood and cater to his, but the thought of turning herself inside out was repugnant. It smacked too much of her shameful role. For a wild second she even wondered if he was conducting an experiment with her emotions. It felt as though he was rubbing her nose in her dependency.

Pride came to her rescue. "I noticed the same lack," she said, staring back at him just as rudely. "Perhaps I should come back later."

He shot up from the chair, hands on hips, to tower over her. "I would hear the truth about your conversation with Dennis Boynton," he snarled. "All of it."

With her heart hammering as if a woodpecker were working on her breastbone, she held her ground before him. She'd had years of practice facing down intimidation, and the occasional blow that accompanied frustration when that failed. She didn't believe Jared would strike her; in fact, she knew he would not. But she feared displeasing him more than she had feared her father's anger.

She'd never been able to please her father. Never in recent memory anyway. But Jared had been tender and loving with her. All in the name of lust, of course, but she understood the limits of what she could expect. She didn't want to lose what she had gained, small though it was. To her, it was everything.

"I can't know his intentions, only what he said to me," she stated. It was important that he understand the bounds of her responsibility.

"I know what his intentions were. I want to know the rest."

"I asked about my family, particularly Papa's health, and Patrick's. He assured me that they are both recovered from their ordeals. He said Papa even benefited from the shutdown as it gave him rest."

It didn't seem to be the right time to chide Jared for withholding from her the news that he had secured his part of their bargain. She didn't feel like thanking him either. His impatience was thinly covered as it was.

"He said he considered that we were still promised in marriage. I disagreed, and he told me I should have come to him instead of you."

A muscle ticked along Jared's jaw as he laughed in derision. "What would he have done for you?"

"That's what I asked. He said he would have married me and that he still would. In truth, I don't think he had any stomach for it. I think he spoke out of obligation."

"How would marrying you have freed Patrick?"

"He didn't address that question."

"I'll bet he didn't."

She could see that he was pleased so far. But instead of feeling relief, she was growing more and more resentful of his smug satisfaction in bettering a man so much his inferior. It made her want to defend Dennis all over again. "He . . . offered to go with me to live somewhere else, where no one would know my story."

"Ah," he said, breathing deeply. "So noble of him. Were you touched?"

In that moment Carina truly hated him.

He didn't deserve an honest answer, but she gave it anyway. "I understood that making the offer represented a sacrifice to Dennis—"

"A sacrifice he knew you'd never require of him."

"Yes." She hated making the admission.

"And you refused him?"

"I did."

"Were you tempted?"

"Jared, I told you before that I don't crave to marry and certainly not under circumstances so ill favored as these. Dennis has little enough security in this world. If he gave up what he *does* have for me, I'd be taking on responsibility for every bad thing that happened to him for the rest of his life. I'm not an utter fool!"

He didn't look pleased. "No," he said thoughtfully. "No, you're not at all a fool." He put his hand under her chin, touching her for the first time. "Is that all of it?"

"Not quite. He told me that Papa tells everyone I'm dead." She hurried on, hoping to disguise the catch in her throat. "And I asked him to tell me if my brothers and sister should need me in the future." Glaring, she dared Jared to object.

He didn't. Instead, his eyes warmed with sympathy for her.

Now that he had his pound of her flesh, that is.

He coasted his hand along her cheek to her hairline while she held herself still and unresponsive. And even that, oddly enough, amused him. Whereas before, he stood ready to take offense at everything, now he was magnanimity itself.

The change ignited Carina's suppressed temper. She pulled her head back.

"There was one other matter," she said. "I wonder if you'd care to explain why you didn't tell me that first night that you'd already secured Patrick's release from jail?"

He gave her an infuriating smile. "Did I fail to mention that?"

"You know you did."

"And you think that oversight—"

"Oversight! You withheld the information deliberately!"

279

"And if I did?" He was all challenge again, his pretense of unconcern gone. "It wouldn't have made the slightest difference in the result between us."

"I could have left," she cried out.

"I offered you the chance."

"You said, 'I wish I could let you go,'" she argued, reliving the vivid past. Even though she knew she had given herself to him freely, she also knew that he *had* expected payment. What she wanted from him now was acknowledgment of that fact. It was important to her. "That's not the same," she insisted.

"Not strictly the same perhaps, but if you'd shown the smallest resistance I would have released you. You never did. Never."

"I felt the obligation," she stammered, ashamed because he was right. "You wouldn't let me work. . . ."

"You're lying to yourself, Carina," he said flatly, unforgivably.

Then he made it worse. He said, "You're the one who talks of bargains, not me. And you came to me."

Hurt beyond endurance, Carina grabbed with both hands the unlikely weapon he'd just given her. She drew herself up to her tallest and sneered. "That's what Enoch said, too!"

His reaction was instantaneous. He grabbed her by the shoulders and drew her toward him as if he would shake her—or kiss her. He did neither. He held her there while he ground out, "Don't . . . ever . . . compare . . . me . . . to . . . him," forcing the words through his teeth.

He dropped her abruptly and turned his back on her.

But not before she saw the hurt behind his anger.

She wanted to run from him, and she wanted to comfort him. When she didn't move, he said without looking around, "Get out of here, Carina. You came here spoiling for a fight, and you got it. I hope you're satisfied."

"Jared, I—"

"Don't! I don't want to hear it now. Leave me alone."

## Chapter Nineteen

Carina had the rest of the day to regret her exchange with Jared. At first she condemned herself out of hand for maligning his character, acknowledging that he was right about her intention. She had been spoiling for a fight.

Later, that didn't seem so true. She began to justify herself, if not her cutting remark. He had been ungentle toward her feelings, extremely so.

But after a great deal of back and forth, one thing was clear to Carina. Jared had anticipated a warm welcome from her and had been disappointed. Everything else followed from that fact.

The same was true for her. She had dressed becomingly for Jared, not for Dennis. His intrusion was just that—and bad luck besides.

Once she understood her feelings, she had to go to Jared. He hadn't wanted her apology earlier, and she didn't blame him. Now he'd had time to cool down, too. She would explain and apologize. He was a fair man. He would understand.

He wasn't in his room.

Puzzled, Carina stood at his door. With darkness coming earlier each day, the sun was well down. She had watched the changing light from her window and felt no need for a lamp. The hall was dusky but not dark, and

281

the house lay quiet around her. She picked up her skirts and found her way to the stairs.

He wasn't in his study either. Moving soundlessly, she walked the corridor to the kitchen without seeing him. He wasn't in the room where she had talked to Dennis, and she turned from there, feeling relieved. Then she saw the nearly closed door to the parlor. All was quiet from within, but when she eased the door ajar a faint line of light cut across the folds of her skirt.

Sure she had found Jared at last, Carina was suddenly uneasy about what she would say. Her nerves hummed with tension as she pushed the door back on its hinges. A lamp burned low on the small table next to the fireplace, lighting only the area nearby. Jared stood with his back to the room. He looked out a window in just the manner she had upstairs. She was touched by the notion that he was reacting the way she had.

He didn't greet her or move when she entered the room, but she knew he sensed her presence. Deciding not to see insult where none might be intended, she plunged into speech. "Jared?" When he didn't turn she made do, imagining that he waited for her to go on, his face intent with listening.

"When I was a little girl and I quarreled with Patrick, my mother told us we should never let the sun go down on our anger. I spoke harshly and thoughtlessly to you. At the moment, I felt wounded and I wanted to hurt you. I regretted it instantly and wanted to tell you so.

"You were right to refuse to listen then, though. That apology would have been sincere, but it wouldn't have covered everything I need to say.

"You must believe that I have no desire to marry Dennis. I didn't want to when I left home and I want to even less now. He's a good enough man, I suppose—probably better than I deserve—but he doesn't appeal to me.

"In all the years I've known him he never made the least attempt to get to know me. He sees Conn

O'Rourke's daughter when he looks at me. That's enough for him, but I'm more than that. In him, I see Conn O'Rourke's friend, and that's probably just as limiting. I can see no reason for us to marry and many reasons why such a marriage would be wrong."

It occurred to Carina that she was talking too much about Dennis. Jared gave no sign that he heard a word she was saying. She resolved to make him hear.

"I hope you know, Jared, that I never compare you to Enoch except in the most favorable way possible. To me, you are his opposite. You protected me from him and helped me when no one else would. If you'd done no more than that, I could never repay you. But you also gave me a place in your home and the gift of your warmth."

He stirred at that, looking as if he might turn to her after all. Suddenly, she didn't want to see his expression for fear she might be distracted from all she wanted to tell him. She stepped closer and urged, "Please, don't move. It's . . . easier this way." He did move, but only to rest his hand on the window frame.

Relieved, Carina sought the thread of her thoughts. "I didn't like having you point out the truth about the way I came to you. My father was a stern man who was quick to condemn anyone who was weak. Except for my mother, who stood far above me in virtue, he never approved of any woman. Those who were virtuous, he deemed shrews. If a woman smiled, he called her loose.

"I was his particular burden. He needed me to help with the children and to work for wages, but he never liked me. I always knew I would fail him by acting upon the sinfulness in me he sought to control. So I thought, well, as long as I'm going to fail him, I should try to exchange myself for someone he values. And I came to you with my bargain.

"But that's not why I stay, Jared. Truly it isn't. And it isn't because I promised not to leave. I . . . missed you while you were gone."

Apologizing was one thing, but this . . . confession was something else again. She looked down at her clasped hands. She was twisting her fingers together. The sight of her dress prodded her. "Since your message that you'd return soon," she went on, "I dressed up for you every day, hoping you would come."

Carina brushed the limp folds of her skirt. "This dress looked nice this morning—"

"It still looks lovely."

Carina looked up. She had missed his turning, but she couldn't miss the tenderness on his face. Surprised into naturalness, she rushed forward, closing the gap between them. She flung her arms about him. He met her with a bone-crushing hug that lifted her from her feet.

"Oh, Jared, I'm so sorry," she cried into his shoulder.

"Hush, love, hush." His hand smoothed the hair at the back of her head. In an oddly choked voice he asked, "This new way you have your hair, is that for me, too?"

She nodded, ashamed of how easily she had dissolved into tears.

"I like it," he murmured, trying to lift her face from his chest. "I was afraid you'd made yourself so beautiful for Boynton."

Carina laughed, recognizing that he teased her to get her to stop crying. She tried, but hiccuped instead. She was soaking the front of his shirt, which was now neatly buttoned and tucked. She wondered how she could have been foolish enough to resent his beautiful chest.

"I see what you've been doing all this time," he continued. "If I kiss you, I'll find that you've been into the sherry."

She shook her head, then raised it to look at him.

He grinned. "The port?"

She offered her lips, letting him kiss and taste her at will.

"Fermented molasses?"

She laughed, and he tried again.

"It's sweet, so sweet." Groaning softly, he deepened

his kiss until she had to push on his shoulders.

Freeing herself, Carina sniffed and said, "I need a hanky. And I've soaked *dozens* today!"

With a flourish, Jared produced an elegant linen square for her, smiling as she made inelegant use of it. To make a joke, she said, "You were well brought up. My mother only tried."

Her small quip backfired. Jared immediately lost his ease and amusement. He even backed away from her.

Confused, she stared at him, finally following the direction of his gaze. At first she didn't see what he looked at. Then she did.

It was a painting so perfectly suited to the space above the mantel she nearly overlooked the fact that it wasn't hung yet. It only leaned there in place. Which meant it was new. This was the parlor containing the two family heirlooms Trudy had pointed out with such pride.

Carina glanced from the painting to Jared. He looked stricken.

She touched his arm, making a connection he didn't seem to feel. "What is it?" It was the wrong thing to ask, but he didn't notice. She started toward the picture, then stopped and asked, "May I see?"

He led her to the fireplace. She saw now that the lamp was placed perfectly to illuminate the painting, bathing it in a soft, glowing light.

Carina's eye was drawn first to the woman at the center of the group. It was obvious to Carina that the artist had lavished attention on her, and for good reason. She was lovely. Her features, although pleasing enough, were not exceptional, but she had a loving, warm look that captured the viewer. As she was the focus of the picture, Carina was certain she was the heart of her family.

And the man standing just behind her was Jared.

As the artist had caught the woman's softness, so had he revealed the combination of masculine bravado and boyish pride that made Jared irresistible. One broad, strong hand rested protectively near the woman—Carina now called her Melissa—and the other stood guard over two handsome children, a lad older than Kevin and a girl four or five years old.

The children gave Carina pause. She looked at each again, sharply, then at Jared.

"That's . . . you."

"I was twelve years old."

"I thought . . . You look like your father."

"At the time, I thought I was nearly as big. I was running to catch up to him, always trying to be like him."

"It shows," she said, studying the boy he had been. "That aspiration and pride."

"A most undeserved pride," he pronounced harshly, drawing Carina's gaze to his face.

She was shocked by what she saw there—the rawness of his emotion. She put her hand on his arm in silent comfort. "I don't undertand, Jared."

He continued to gaze at the painting, his eyes blank and unseeing, turned inward upon some other scene. "You were told what happened to my family," he said.

She hated to say the word fire. It was surely the horror he was seeing now. "There was an accident—"

"No accident. It was murder."

"Oh, no, Jared. Surely not!"

"It's never been proved and probably never will be, but it happened. I was there and I heard—enough to satisfy me, at any rate. No one else has ever accepted the truth of what I heard. Silas Meade did once, but now he tells me he no longer believes it true."

Carina stood beside him, almost trembling with sympathy for him. She would believe him no matter what he said, but she wasn't certain she wanted to hear. The story would be painful and she didn't think she could bear it.

While she struggled to find a way to express her willingness to listen, Jared roused himself from his inner vision to look at the painting again. "It began with my mother," he said softly. "Felicity Cole."

"Such a beautiful name."

"It fit her. She had the softest way. Everyone loved her. You couldn't help yourself. And that was the problem. Uncle Nathan saw her first and loved her. I don't believe he ever stopped. He couldn't."

Carina wanted to turn away. She didn't want to believe that the woman in the painting with her sweetly serious smile had been unfaithful. Not to the man Jared resembled.

"Nathan brought her to visit in Boston where she met my father. They fell in love. Although she had no understanding with Nathan, it made things awkward in the family. Nathan was older, but Philip was the favored one. Of course, Felicity resisted making trouble. She went back to Philadelphia and tried to forget my father. He pursued and won her over.

"As a child I knew nothing about this history beyond a few hints of a connection between Mama and Uncle Nathan. She treated him with great kindness, but that was her way with everyone. She was even pleasant to Aunt Lucy, Nathan's wife, who was a shrew."

"But of course," Carina said. "He did marry someone else or there wouldn't be Enoch."

"Silas told me that story when I was grown. Nathan and my father were business partners with equal shares in the family enterprise. My grandfather, Graham Wentworth, built up a small empire in shipping and lumber. He put it all into the infant cotton textile industry just before he died. It was a smart move then, because shipping had been hit hard.

"Nathan met Lucy Farmington in the South where he went to buy raw cotton for the mills. Until she married him, she considered him quite a catch. Silas assumes that what went wrong between them in time was Nathan's continued devotion to Felicity. Enoch was born seven months after their wedding as well, so perhaps he felt trapped."

"Or she did," Carina added, surprising him. At his

expression, she laughed. "Why couldn't the feeling go that way?"

"I suppose it could," he said, frowning. Then he dismissed the notion. "Anyway, Nathan only had a short time to feel superior. My parents had been married nearly four years before I came along, the answer to their prayers for children. Enoch is almost two years older, but he resembles the Farmingtons, while I, as you can see, favor the Wentworths. It seems a silly point to me, but apparently it bothered Nathan."

"Were you and Enoch close as children?"

"My memories of him aren't pleasant. From his earliest days he was what he is now, a coward and a bully. Because he was family, he was always around. He picked on me relentlessly until I was four years old. Then I turned on him and bloodied his nose. It was a lucky blow because I was much smaller, but it did the trick. The sight of his own blood sent him screaming to his mother.

"Of course, she wanted me punished, and when my father promised that I'd get what I deserved, I figured I was in for it. After Aunt Lucy carried Enoch off to clean him up, Father asked for my story and then told me I'd done the right thing. He even said he was proud of me, not for hurting Enoch but for standing up to a bully. Mama made some token protest to his wording, but I knew she agreed.

"Enoch's problem was his mother," Jared went on. "Lucy filled him with notions of his own greatness. He could do no wrong. She encouraged his sneakiness and rewarded his lies. I suppose it was inevitable that she resented my mother, but she shouldn't have used a child to fight her battles. Nathan could have put a stop to it, but he didn't want to face the mess he'd made of his family.

"We lived in Cambridge on adjoining lots until Lucy persuaded Nathan to build in Boston on Mount Vernon Street. That was the rising neighborhood then. Once the Meades bought the Cambridge property from Nathan everything improved. That assocation was an altogether happy one. We each got a friend in the exchange. Mama got Indigo and my father got Silas."

*And Jared got Susan,* Carina added silently, hating her jealousy.

"Silas was—and is—in shipping, which was my father's real love. My mother wasn't a Quaker, but she absorbed many of their principles growing up in Pennsylvania. She disliked slavery intensely and wanted my father to break off from the textile industry. She saw it as exploitive of both Southern and Northern labor. Gentle as she was, she could be intractable when she felt strongly about an issue."

Carina could see the firmness behind Felicity Wentworth's smile. It reminded her of her own mother's strength of purpose. "What happened?" she asked.

"Nathan and Philip quarreled—constantly. Which certainly wasn't my mother's intention. It grieved her terribly and I suppose she felt responsible. More to blame, though, was the way my grandfather had set up the company. Both brothers loved the business and wanted to remain in it. Neither one wanted to sell out, but they couldn't agree on anything. Even with Nathan in Boston, the quarrel was tearing the business apart—not to mention what it was doing to the family."

"How terribly sad," Carina said. "In Lowell, we always assumed that the people who owned the mills lived like princes."

"They did. Like unhappy princes."

"But you were not always unhappy," she argued. "There is love in that picture."

"Yes." Jared fell silent a moment, contemplating the image before them. "Pippa was five years old and very shy."

"Pippa?"

"Philippa, for my father. But she was my mother all over again, except for the strength. She might have developed that, of course. We never got to see."

There was nothing Carina could say, so she waited to hear whatever Jared wanted her to know.

"We sat for the painting only a few times, just so the artist could see us as people, I guess. He worked mostly from a photograph and occasional sittings with each of us. Pippa and I weren't quarrelsome—she was so much younger than I—but we were restless. I hated standing there so much. I remember being flattered that he called me a fine little man. The little was insulting, though, and I had to work to overlook it. I wanted to be a man—just that, unadorned.

"Then, much too soon after the painting was done, I had to be a man and I failed."

"Oh, no, Jared. Don't say that."

"It's true. All my life I've relived that day, minute by minute, over and over. In dreams I've struggled to save them all, but I've never managed it. Not even in my dreams."

"Jared, look at yourself there. You were a child, a young lad! You can't be so hard on yourself. What could you have done?"

"First of all, I should have disobeyed my mother," he said, his tone certain. "I knew something was wrong, and I didn't want to do what she said. I argued, then gave in because she was so distraught. We heard my father and Nathan shouting at each other.

"I've tried to remember the words, but I don't. For years I was sure I could find evidence in those words that murder was done. Either I didn't hear them at the time or they meant very little to me. My mother's anxiety took precedence in my mind, blocking out everything else. I'd never before seen her afraid.

"She ordered me to take Pippa and leave. I was to go to the Meades' and find Silas. She told me to stay there until Silas said I could come home. It was a frightening command, especially as she was so agitated. She tried to make light of her concern, but I knew it was serious."

"Wasn't there someone near at hand to help?"

"There were women working in the summer kitchen, but the men, including Bagley, were away on a special project. She knew that, which was why she sent me to Silas. She kissed us both and hurried us away. She had to peel Pippa off her, and I remember being impatient with her."

Carina squeezed his arm.

His pain became more acute as he went on. "It was a long way for Pippa to go, and she was cumbered by her skirts and delicate shoes. She was frightened besides. I tried to urge her on because I was just as frightened. Between encouraging her and hectoring her, I made a bad business of it. Then she fell down and began to cry. I tried to comfort her and get her moving again, but she just kept crying.

"Finally, I decided she should stay where she was and I would go on. She liked the idea because she had a stitch in her side. I made her promise to wait for me, and promised in return to be right back for her. Thinking I'd made a brilliant decision, I ran on to get Silas. Only he wasn't there. His men were also away, off working a field somewhere, and it took me a long time to find anyone who would go with me to help my father.

"When I got to where Pippa was supposed to be, she wasn't there and we could already see smoke billowing up from the house. We ran back, two of the Meades' servants and me. The house was in flames."

"Oh, Jared."

"I never saw any of them again. I tried to go inside. I was crazed. I couldn't have done a thing for them, but I was determined. Bagley pulled me out. He has burn scars on his arms from rescuing me. It was a long time before I could thank him for doing it. I didn't want to live. I felt—I still feel—such guilt for my failure. I should have kept Pippa safe. I should have gone in and confronted Nathan during that quarrel. Perhaps I could have headed it off."

"More likely, you too would have died. What could you have done that your father failed to do?"

291

"I don't know. I'll never know because I didn't try."

Arguing with his conviction seemed pointless so Carina asked, "You hold your uncle responsible for their deaths?"

"I believe that he murdered them, yes. He doesn't deny the quarrel or being there as I say, but he calls it an accident that happened after he left. Although I have no timetable for any of it, he says he must have left shortly after I did. His driver tells of waiting outside to drive him to the Exchange in the State House on the corner of State Street and Washington Street. That's a meeting place for bankers and merchants in Boston, at the Topliff News Room. His cronies there backed up his statement, and I don't doubt that he *did* go there. I believe, however, that before he went, he bashed my parents over the head and set fire to the house."

"But that's so horrible!" Carina protested. "And you said he loved your mother."

Jared's look was hard and dark. "Love can turn to hate, they say."

She couldn't argue.

"Poor little Pippa probably came back after they had been felled. I'm sure she was trapped there, alive and conscious, after she came back, seeking her mother's security. She would be twenty-four now, Susan's age."

"Was she Susan's friend?"

"Not really; she was too timid. She was Mama's shadow. I knew that, so I should have known better than to leave her alone. Without me to buck her up, she would naturally run back home."

"You couldn't know, Jared."

"Perhaps not, but I've never been forgiving, not even of ignorance."

Tentatively, Carina tried to divert his mind. "The painting," she said, looking around in an effort to recall the oil being there when she'd seen the room with Trudy. "Is it new here? I don't remember seeing it before."

"I brought it back with me today," he answered, his

satisfaction evident. "As you can imagine, the fire destroyed the house and everything in it. If anything was saved, it was nothing I wanted, nor was any attempt made to recover things that I know of. I assumed, when I thought of the painting at all, that it was gone.

"Two years ago, Indigo told me she had heard that someone had seen the painting in an exhibit. She tried to trace the rumor and so did I. I tried again when I read that the artist had died. As nearly as I can determine, my mother had loaned the painting back to the artist for use in an exhibit. That's why it wasn't in the house.

"After the fire there was no one to claim the painting, so the artist kept it. He showed it occasionally and once or twice someone wanted to buy it from him. The deal never went through, for whatever reason, and I was able to make my claim on the estate."

"I'm so glad for you."

"When I built this house I had the mantel built to match the one I remembered from our house. I never found a painting to put here, and now I know why. I was saving the place for this portrait."

Turning to him, Carina offered the comfort of her arms. It was the only thing she could think of doing. And she needed to feel his closeness. She could not say she had grown accustomed to the feel of him against her, but having known his tenderness and warmth, and sensing his need for the same from her, how could she do anything else?

As his arms went around her, she saw the glitter of surprise in his dark eyes. He leaned down and kissed her, making the bottom fall out of Carina's stomach. Unable to control herself, she nestled close, her hands moving up and down at his shoulders and back.

Jared raised his head and let his gaze roam her face. Something dark and intense, having nothing to do with his family's tragedy, moved in his eyes. It was hunger, the hunger of a man for a woman. Like her desire for him, his feeling had nothing to do with comfort.

293

"Carina," he murmured against her brow. "I . . . need you."

Her heartbeat picked up speed, as Infidel did when roaring out of control.

Need.

It wasn't love, but wasn't it the next best thing? He had returned to her, anticipating a warm welcome. Instead, he'd found her with Dennis. Surely some of that pique he'd displayed . . . hadn't *some* of it been jealousy? In time, perhaps she could build upon that need of his . . . perhaps. . . .

Carina dared not complete the thought, but it rested next to her heart, a small seed of hope that, nourished, would grow and flower.

He kissed her again, this time bending her back over his arm with urgent possessiveness. His tongue parted her lips, seeking the tip of hers. Fire went streaking through her until she shivered and became pliant.

If she had not known him, the look he gave her when their lips parted would have frightened her. It was fierce. Under its influence, his features molded themselves into a mask very much resembling anger. He drew back and raised his hand to her cheek. His forefinger traced the curve to the tiny mark left by Enoch Wentworth's ring.

He took a deep breath, as if to steady himself. "I would not hurt you, Carina."

"No," she agreed readily.

He went on as though he hadn't heard. "I have no anger left in me."

She brought his hand to her lips and kissed each knuckle, giving him a radiant smile as his breath caught.

He turned his hand, offering it. "Come with me, my love. We'll make a new beginning."

The words sang in Carina's heart. My love.

She would be that. She would be everything.

Jared put out the light and led her to the stairs. Their passage was curiously like and unlike it had been on their first time together. He held her hand, drawing her along with him. There was no lamp burning in the stair niche, but Carina's sense of wonder at being there was undiminished. The wonder was different, containing more joy than fear, but fear was not entirely absent. This time it encompassed liberal dollops of dread, that heavy, heart-sinking emotion that was as much fascination as anything else.

He was so important to her—as himself, simply as Jared, not as the master of this household or as the man who held her fate in his hands. She drew him to her room with a subtle bit of guidance. She wanted to make him feel welcome. It gave her pleasure to lead him to her bed.

Her ways were not seductive, yet Jared found them more arousing than the deliberate arts of sophisticated women. Her art was no art at all, and from the beginning, her combination of courage and sweetness had enchanted him.

Now her charm was more potent than ever, for he sensed something new in her demeanor. He wasn't sure what it was until she moved away from him. He sought to keep her.

"Just a moment," she objected. "The lamp . . ."

Surprised, he sat back and watched her light the bedside lamp. When she turned back to him she wore a small pleased smile. His own smile grew to match and surpass hers. He wanted to hoot in triumph as he saw the way she looked at him. There was nothing of the vanquished maiden in her expression. So might a loving spouse look at her mate, he thought, pleased but also shaken by the idea.

He bent to remove his boots, buying time. When he straightened, she was there.

Confidence. That was what she displayed. And it delighted him.

The smile he gave her—its wicked gleam—made her feel daring. She put her hands to the smooth shirting over the broad expanse of his chest. Fine and light under her palms, it covered the sculpted surface beneath without disguising the corded muscles and the wedge of dark hair. He shifted restlessly as she opened the front and slid her fingers inside the cloth. Leaving the cuffs and waist to him, she nuzzled into his fuzzy warmth until he gave a growl of impatience.

"Carina," he warned, gripping her arms hard enough to force her back. She was so intent she felt deprived as she lifted questioning eyes to his. "Your dress," he said.

She turned to let him free the closings, lifting her hair from her neck. He kissed each bit of skin he uncovered, holding the cloth tightly to hide the fine trembling of his hands. Remembering her care of her clothes, he put the dress aside carefully before he put her down onto the bed.

No longer caring that his hand was unsteady, he skimmed her cheek tenderly.

Carina raised her eyes to his and asked anxiously, "Do you mind that so much?"

He pulled back. "What?"

"The scar," she said. "That's the second time you've touched it."

"Is it?" He was surprised. "I rarely think of it. It's tiny. Except for the harm it represents to you, it could be a beauty mark. It's perfectly placed to emphasize the delicacy of your cheekbones."

Her eyes closed in thankfulness. He made her feel beautiful—and light. Calling the emotion relief at pleasing him, she felt as if she could float above the bed, renouncing gravity for as long as he held her. And looked at her with eyes that burned with passionate need.

Smiling gently, he kissed the knick on her cheekbone. "I wouldn't call this a scar," he said, and turned over his arms to show her the undersides. "These are scars."

"Oh, Jared, I never . . ." Burn scars, she realized, giving him a look of sorrow and understanding.

"Not very pretty, to be sure."

"That must have been painful." She touched the slightly shiny skin gently. "It doesn't still—"

"Hurt? God, no." He chuckled. "It didn't at the time

either, that's what was remarkable. I was in shock, they tell me. Later it hurt, though."

Carina bent and put her lips there, skimming over the surfaces as if the touch of her mouth could erase them totally, healing the damage.

Jared felt something deep inside himself let go, releasing him. She hadn't pulled back from his ugliness. She hadn't been repulsed. Touched, he lifted her into his arms and held her tight.

She was a treasure, this Carina. He had treated her less well than any woman he'd known and she had given him the most. Pleasure? Yes, but more than that. Much more. She'd given him joy and tenderness as well.

He had never felt such complete welcome from any woman. Certainly not from Melissa. Carina gave with her whole heart, fitting her softness to him.

With subtle accommodation, she shifted her body, opening to him utterly. Everything she did gave him pleasure: her soft cries, the quick grasp of her hands at his shoulders, the irregular pace of her breathing. Even her scent—lavender overlaid with pure womanliness— went to his head.

He had never felt more manly—or more vulnerable. The mix of the two seemed insane, insupportable. It went beyond belief. He sucked at her breasts, hungry in a way he had never been before. Even as he entered her he knew having her now wasn't enough. It would never be enough. Each thrust into her softness elicited an answering response that drugged his emotions. He lifted her legs, wrapping them around him, locking him to her, pulling him ever deeper into her fiery core.

This was true heat. Carina was a fire that would burn him as no real fire ever could, he thought.

Breathlessly, Carina sought to follow Jared, yielding to him. In the yielding she lost him and lost herself, as her mind went whirling into the night sky. She might have been the star that bore her name for all she knew. His voice at her ear urged her on with words she couldn't comprehend. She felt their lure as they traveled her nerves, exploding like spent stars as they fell into the darkness of her soul.

Jared. Just Jared.

He filled her mind and captured her heart.

With her nerves coiled tight, ready to spring, Carina felt Jared gather himself. The relentless motion of his body halted. She opened her eyes, unaware that she'd held them shut, and gazed up into his face. He stared down, his gaze concentrated on her, completely still, completely fixed. Only on her. Time slipped away.

How long did they pause, filling their senses with each other? The moment stretched out to infinity, the fixed center of a spinning universe. It was timeless, both fleeting and everlasting.

"Carina!"

His cry and the soul-wrenching aftermath, like her long plunge into satiety, left Carina shaken. She didn't know she had shouted or that tears ran from her eyes. She only knew she wanted to hold him to her forever.

He didn't go far, only onto his side, taking her with him. Wrapped close in his arms, still joined and unwilling to part, Carina was helpless to control herself. She felt so stripped away from herself she didn't know how to go about putting herself back together.

If she was no longer Carina, who was she? Who would she see in the mirror now?

"So many tears tonight," he said. "I don't remember you crying before. I would have said you weren't the type."

Carina shook her head. "So would I." Then she saw the question in his eyes. He was unsure that he had pleased her. It rocked her that he didn't know, that he could be so powerful and still be, after all, just a man. Human. Unsure of himself as she was unsure of herself, especially at a time like this.

"I didn't know I was crying, Jared." She spoke carefully, glad that she wasn't sniffling. For all their flood, these tears were different. "I didn't know I could feel like that."

What did he make of her statement? She didn't know. He moved to his back and drew her head down to rest above his heart. The wild cadence of its beat was already slowing to a comfortable, reassuring thump.

She had given him what he needed. She had pleased him. She rubbed her cheek against his chest and gave a soundless sigh.

She should be happy.

She *was* happy, she argued, all the while knowing better.

And knowing why not.

For this time, along with pleasure and comfort, Carina had given Jared her heart.

She loved him.

And nothing in her life would ever be the same.

## Chapter Twenty

It was not the first time Rachel Farmington had wept upon leaving Tyler Meade's rooms, but this time her anguish was real and not a pretty show for his benefit. Her red-rimmed eyes told the story.

The spectacle saddened Tyler.

Apart from his looks, the principle reason for his success with women stemmed from the fact that he genuinely *liked* them. He liked nearly everything about them—their looks and softness, certainly, but also their occasional silliness. Men didn't have that.

He didn't underestimate them either, as many men did. He knew their strength and bravery at first hand. Wasn't he brother to Susan and son to Indigo? It was something women sensed in him, this liking for their sex, and it drew them like flies.

Rachel, however, was different, as was Tyler's whole relationship with her. Ordinarily, he would never involve himself with someone so young and innocent, no matter how lovely or forward she was. For the first time in his life, Tyler had deliberately seduced a girl. And he wasn't proud of himself or of his success.

He couldn't even say he'd done it for Jared, although that had been part of it, at least at first. She had attracted him powerfully in her own right, at first glance, so to speak. But if that had been the sum of Rachel, he'd have done no more than kiss her hand and smile at her. What set her up for his special attention was that she was a Farmington. Jared was not the only one who wanted to avenge Enoch Wentworth's sneaky attacks.

Then too, Tyler remembered all too well Lucy Farmington's constant and irritating whining about Felicity, the first woman Tyler had loved as a boy. He had immediately, at the age of eleven, taken on the role of her champion.

It hadn't mattered to him that Felicity didn't need or want his aid. After all, she had a husband, a son, a brother-in-law and probably others eager to take her part against Lucy. Nevertheless, Tyler was Felicity's slave. Later, he called it his first crush, but he never forgot that first, purest, and most sublime love of his life.

Nor had he forgotten how Lucy prided herself on being a Farmington, and not a Wentworth. And how she strove to make Enoch like herself. That she succeeded beyond her aspirations wasn't poor Rachel's fault, Tyler knew. And he also knew Rachel had nothing to do with the unspeakable tortures Enoch had performed as a child on Tyler's tabby cat.

But the look of her, and her voice—so like Lucy's— had sealed Rachel's fate, calling up demons of revenge Tyler hadn't known lived in him still. He hadn't been able to resist them.

"I'll *make* you marry me!" Rachel cried now from the doorway. "I'll tell Uncle Nathan how you lured me here and ruined me!"

Tyler shook his head with genuine regret. However he had started with Rachel, he no longer bore her any malice. "Ah, puss, I'm so sorry. The problem is, it doesn't work that way. Not with me. I wouldn't want to contradict your word, but if you do any such thing I'll have to defend myself. There are two gentlemen living downstairs who can honestly say that they've seen you coming here entirely on your own."

"Because you lured me here!"

"How? Did I promise you jewels? Riches? Everyone knows I haven't the money to pay my tailor."

"You promised to marry me."

Tyler raised his brows in feigned surprise. "Now you know that's not true."

"I know it, but Uncle Nathan doesn't. He won't believe I would compromise myself for any other reason. He'll believe me," she vowed.

"Perhaps, but you know his reputation isn't the best, sweetheart. Even if he does believe you, it won't do him any good. No one else will believe it. I'm too well known."

His logic and calm infuriated Rachel. She wanted passion from Tyler. She glared, knowing he had ony one kind of passion, and that was at the root of her problem. She was addicted to the way he made her feel. She loved him, damn his eyes!

"You're a well-known seducer," she flung at him.

He raised a cautioning hand as if he were a schoolmaster. "But *only* of women who know what they're about, sweetness. Everyone knows my scruples; I never play around with innocent maidens. If you accuse me, you label yourself before the world."

Rachel stamped her foot. "That's not true. You know I was a virgin!"

"Indeed, I do," he crooned, putting his arms around her in a tender gesture she hadn't the strength to shake off. It was typical of him to be comforting even when he was also being impossible. "But unless you remain one now, you can never prove that you were the exception in my life."

"If I were still untouched, I wouldn't need you to marry me now," she wailed, but softly, without force. Even hating him, she couldn't keep from nestling into his arms.

"But you don't need me. Unless you tell on yourself, my pet, no one—including your lucky husband-to-be—will ever know your plight."

Rachel knew there was a flaw in his reasoning, but she was too spent to seek it out. Instead, she tried to plead her case—again. "You can be that lucky man, Tyler."

He kissed her nose. Even reddened, it was a fetching part of her lovely face. He really did envy the man who would wed Rachel. Farmington she was, down to her pretty toes, but she was the best of the Farmingtons. In the hands of the right man, she would be a wife to be proud of.

"No, no, little pumpkin, you deserve far better from life. I have no prospects. Yours should be unlimited. Don't squander them in this silly way."

Tyler kissed the tear tracks that ran down over her cheeks, and she let him. He had a hundred sweet terms to use and a hundred ways to kiss. She'd heard those words murmured against every inch of her body. How could she live without that? How could *he?*

"You'll miss me," she whispered, hoping it was true.

He chuckled in that low, sweet way. "Now there you're absolutely right. No one will ever take your place in my heart."

"You don't have a heart," she complained.

"Minx." He sighed and tapped her nose reprovingly with his forefinger. "I suppose you're right again, but I'm sorry."

"Don't be Tyler. If we marry, your parents will see that you've changed and they'll take you back into the fold. Don't you see? You could have everything!"

He laughed harshly, all his tenderness draining away to reveal an implacable core Rachel hadn't seen before. For the first time, she realized that he was not entirely the wronged party in his difference with his family.

"You don't know the first thing about the situation, Rachel. My family has no affection for yours. An alliance with Nathan and Enoch and you would not endear me—or you."

"I have nothing to do with Enoch," she protested.

"But Nathan does, and my family only pretends to

303

believe in his innocence. No, Rachel, put any notion of reconciliation from your mind. I don't want it."

"How can you not? It's a fortune!"

"But it's not my fortune and it never will be."

"But, Tyler—"

"No more, Rachel." His tone was controlled, cold. "The very fact that you feel compelled to promote this proves to me that you and I have no future. You could never live as I do. You'd always be discontent, always at me to pursue my family's fortune so I could finance the frocks and frills you crave."

Sensing that backing down was expedient, Rachel did so. "I would be content with you. I promise I would."

He smiled in response, a patronizing expression, showing disbelief. "You think you would be, little monkey, but I know better. I'm glad I met you, and I'll never forget you. But now that we've had our fling, the best thing you can do is go back to your doting uncle and help him find you a rich husband. When he does, be a little nice to the fortunate man and then—perhaps— someday we'll meet again. You've learned a great deal already. We'll have no trouble getting along when we meet again."

Something deep inside Rachel shifted as she took in Tyler's cynical advice. Took it in but didn't accept it. She couldn't. She knew then that although she was younger and less experienced, she was the wiser of the two of them.

Or was she really the foolish one? After all, she had fallen in love, and with a man who didn't deserve to be loved selflessly. If that wasn't foolish, what was?

She pulled her cloak tight, rewrapping her tattered dignity about her. "That's not the way I'll live my life, Tyler. Not even for you. You're right, I've learned a lot. What you don't realize is that I've learned more than you have.

"I'm not going to sneak around anymore. Never. When we meet again—if we do—it won't be like this.

You'll never have this chance again. I was willing to give up everything for you. Now that I see what you really are, I'll pine no more for what can never be. You don't deserve the love you toss away so lightly."

As she shut the door behind her, Rachel engraved Tyler's image on her heart. He wasn't unmoved by her words, she could tell. He regretted her leaving, but he would never act upon that emotion.

She had won his affection weeks ago. Now, by being strong, she had won his respect. But love? She could see no love in his eyes.

"Mr. Enoch, sir," George announced ponderously from the door.

Nathan watched the opening over steepled forefingers as he leaned his elbows on the desk. It was all he could do not to put his head down on his arms and wail. He dreaded to see his son, and that fact depressed him.

They had not parted on good terms, and nothing had happened since to improve the situation between them. It seemed to Nathan that at this stage of his life he should not have to worry about Enoch anymore. His son was a grown man. Why could he not act his age? Why couldn't he be . . . responsible?

He had almost thought *like Jared*. That was a comparison he had resisted making since the day Jared was born. And yet, though he often made it, he had never spoken the comparison aloud—certainly not to Enoch. He had been scrupulous about not expressing his disappointment, but it was there. In every interview he'd ever had with his son, Nathan's disappointment had been a third party to their exchange.

This time would be no exception.

And, with the advent of Rachel into his life, Nathan had another person with whom to compare Enoch. But that was another worry, though different. Rachel was unlike anyone Nathan had ever known; part termagant, part child, and all of her more pleasing than he could imagine. Except for the Farmington in both of them, Enoch and Rachel couldn't be more different.

"Papa! How good to see you!"

Nathan unclasped his hands and put them flat before him as if he would rise.

"Don't get up," Enoch urged. "You look too comfortable."

That was as much a lie as his greeting, but Nathan went along with the pretense. "This cold weather is making me stiff, son. I'm getting to that age." He sat back and gestured Enoch to a chair. "It's good to see you, too."

"It is brisk out, and getting more so fast. We've been burning lamps at the mill now for over a month."

Nathan wasn't pleased to have the mill brought up so quickly. He had an ultimatum to deliver on that subject, but he wanted to ease into it gradually. "Well, yes. Winter is upon us," he said lamely.

"So, it is. Which is why I'm surprised to see you back here so soon. I thought you intended to launch Rachel into society?" Enoch accompanied this question with a raised eyebrow.

*So handsome and so empty,* Nathan thought, watching him.

"So did I," he responded with a sigh. "Evidently, that's harder to do than I realized. I thought she was having great success, but she wanted to come back here."

He didn't add that returning was his decision, for business reasons, and that Rachel had only asked to accompany him. At first he'd refused, believing she was being polite, but she had persisted, wearing him down with no trouble at all once he saw that her spirits were low.

He had yet to find the cause for that, but he suspected it had something to do with disappointment over a man. Another worry.

"I would have thought young Rachel would have her pick of suitors."

It sounded like criticism to Nathan, who rushed to defend his niece. "She does, although she seems little interested in the young puppies and the older ones are *too* old." He sighed heavily. "It's all beyond me. I'm completely out of my element as advisor to a young girl. All I can do for her is add up bank balances. She needs a woman to talk to."

"And Mother isn't here," Enoch said.

It was an entirely natural remark, yet it startled Nathan. Because he never thought of Lucy unless he could help it, he rarely considered that Enoch missed her. But of course Enoch did. Lucy had doted on him. Naturally he would miss that.

Nathan, on the other hand, continued to miss Felicity. He would think of her during his last conscious moment on earth. His hopeless inability to control his love for her was the major stumbling block that kept him from finding comfort in religious faith as well. He could not envision a heaven worth having that did not promise union with Felicity—and not merely *re*union, with its continuation of their earthly relationship. He'd had enough of that in this world.

Reason told him, however, that in the next world, as in this one, Felicity would continue to love her Philip to the exclusion of all others. Or it wouldn't be heaven to *her*. So he had concluded, with regret, that unless there were multitudes of privately designed heavens, each providing uniquely for individual needs and desires, he would find the hereafter just as lacking as life in the here and now.

The prospect shriveled his faith to nothing.

Sobered by Enoch's mention of Lucy, Nathan said, "She would be just the person to help Rachel, especially with her being a Farmington."

"I think," Enoch commented with a cynical smile, "that Rachel will manage somehow."

Nathan let the subject go. Fond as he'd become of the girl, he couldn't argue the point. He shifted, making his chair squeak and drawing Enoch's eye. Try as he would to

307

find love in his son's look, or even respect, he couldn't. He'd never been overly endowed with courage, and he badly needed some now.

"But you didn't call me here to discuss my cousin, did you, Papa?"

"No."

When Nathan didn't go on, Enoch laughed. "Did you think I wouldn't hear? I have my sources, too, old man."

"Sources of information," his father countered, "but not sources of money. For that you need me."

"I don't need you for anything. I never have and I never will."

The hatred threading Enoch's voice shocked Nathan. He supposed he should feel relieved that it was out in the open, but he wasn't. Not at all. It hurt—and damnably. Lucy had fed Enoch lies and distortions, but she had been dead for nearly ten years. Wasn't that time enough for Enoch to see him as he was?

"Without me," he said evenly, "you'd never be agent for the Shattuck Mill."

"No, of course not," Enoch shot back. "Without you, I'd be *owner* of the Shattuck!"

"Only if I will it to you—which I haven't chosen to do."

"*What!*" Enoch erupted from the chair to lean menacingly over the desk, his face inches from Nathan's.

Nathan held his ground—barely. Refusing to shrink back from his son, he said, "Sit back down, Enoch. Another childish display of temper won't help your cause."

"I won't sit down!"

*Crazy*, a voice inside Nathan warned. *Your son isn't just stupid and immature. He's crazy.*

"The mill is a business, not a toy you can have on demand. You still haven't proved to anyone that you know anything about running a business."

Enoch lunged at him and this time Nathan ducked back, deftly. Pleased that he'd proven himself agile under

308

attack, he felt his spirit soar. He was aging and not in the best of health, but he could still hold his own when it counted.

"What do you mean by saying you're not willing me the Shattuck?" Enoch demanded. "I'm your heir! You have no one else!"

"You're my son, but I can will my property to anyone I choose," Nathan said in a voice he held steady by great effort. Although he was maintaining his outward composure, his heart raced and his blood seemed to boil through his veins. "You've been on probation as agent at the mill. You knew that."

"I was being groomed!"

Nathan snorted. "Grooming is for horses and dogs. You were given a chance to prove that you aren't the fool you've always acted!"

Harsh words, but sadly true ones to Nathan. He saw their effect on Enoch and plunged on. "If it weren't for the organization Thompson instituted at the mill, the Shattuck would be drowning in red ink and everyone knows it. You strut the perimeters and chase after the unfortunate women who come there to work, but you do not *manage* the Shattuck except in name!"

"But I'm your heir, old man! Nothing else matters!"

"You will inherit this house and property," Nathan said. "In that sense, yes, you are my heir."

"And who inherits the Shattuck when you turn up your toes?"

Nathan made himself laugh. "To think people say you have no charm," he taunted.

Enoch stalked around the desk. "Answer the question."

"It's in a trust you'll share with Jared."

"Jared! What trust? What are you saying?"

"I believe the words are clear," Nathan said icily.

Enoch glared down at him. "Let me get this straight. If you die right now, the Shattuck goes into a *trust* that Jared has as much right to as I do?"

"The business was his father's as well as mine."

"You'd do that to me?" Enoch looked ready to choke.

"It's been that way since the start. I just never told you."

"I could kill you," Enoch said in a low, deadly voice.

"If you do, you'll never have the chance to prove yourself."

"Prove myself? Prove myself! What have I been doing for three years in that hellish place?"

Nathan told him. "You've been proving that you have no head for business, that you have no interest in learning and no idea of responsibility. That's what you've been doing."

"So tonight you called me here to do what? Issue a warning? Is that it?"

"More or less. I *want* you to succeed, Enoch. Don't you see that? You're my son," Nathan pleaded. "We need investors, but they won't put forth a penny as long as they think you'll throw it away."

"Use the rest of the Wentworth money," Enoch proposed with typical lack of concern. "We both know there's more."

"No, Enoch. I put that money aside for Jared. I vowed on his parents' grave that he would not lose from—"

"His parents' grave?" Enoch asked incredulously. "Are you crazy? He accuses you of murder and you put money aside for him?"

"That was what Philip and I agreed to do—"

"When?" Enoch interrupted. "You didn't sound like you were agreeing when you were going at it hammer and tongs that day—"

Enoch broke off at the very second Nathan comprehended the import of his son's words. His quarrel with Philip, that one so bitter it had frightened Felicity into sending her children from the house, had been about the business and how they should secure its future.

But Enoch had not been with him that day.

Then how . . . ?

"You?" Nathan felt his throat close over the word, making it a croak of disbelief.

There was no other way Enoch could know about that quarrel. Nathan had told no one what he and Philip had fought about. He'd been ashamed.

Philip had been insistent that they sign an agreement stating that neither of their sons, neither Enoch nor Jared, would inherit the business at the death of either of them, the principals.

As the light of full knowledge dawned in Nathan's eyes, Enoch began to laugh. The sound chilled Nathan's pounding blood.

"So now you know," Enoch said, giving a strange shrug.

Nathan shook his head, trying to clear away the fog there. He felt so strange.

This wasn't real. It couldn't be. "Enoch, no." He was almost pleading—no, he *was* pleading. "You can't mean . . ."

"Why not? You don't believe I could do it?"

"You wouldn't."

"That's where you're wrong, old man," Enoch said. His tone was proud, boastful. "The only thing hard about it was letting you take the credit all these years."

"Credit!" Nathan gasped.

"Yes, credit. I hated them both. You didn't care about Mama or me. No one mattered except Felicity and Philip!" His lips curled as he spoke the names, venom dripping from them.

"That's not true."

Enoch wasn't listening. "You didn't care where I was or what I was doing—ever. I used to follow you and you never knew I was there. Enoch the Invisible, that was me." He laughed again, horribly. "I heard every word you and Philip said—"

"Then you heard me argue against his plan," Nathan said in defense of Enoch's accusation that he hadn't cared about him. "You heard me defend you."

"Not very hard and not very well," Enoch said dismissively. "Mama was right. You didn't care about me. You would have folded. You always did. Whatever Philip wanted, you gave him."

Nathan protested, but weakly. "No, Enoch, no."

Inside, Nathan acknowledged the hit. He *would* have folded, but only because Philip would have been right, as always. Philip had proposed the agreement to keep the business out of the hands of their sons because he recognized what Nathan now saw just as clearly. That Enoch was unsuited to manage or participate in the running of an enterprise such as theirs.

Philip had sacrificed Jared's interest in the process, although both of them knew Jared would be good for the business. It had been that gesture of Philip's that had convinced Nathan he should go along with his brother on the issue. It hurt him to realize that it was necessary, but the truth was the truth. Like Philip, Nathan also distrusted his son.

And for good reason, as was now horribly apparent.

Nathan struggled to take it all in—all the ramifications of this disclosure. His son had *killed* . . .

Or had he?

"Son, what happened there . . . it was an accident, I know. A horrible accident."

"It was not!" Enoch shrieked. "I hit him with the poker—twice! He wouldn't stay down. I had to hit him again. Then *she* came in, screaming, and I had to chase her."

Sickened, Nathan saw Enoch's distorted face—double. Then the twin images slid together slowly, finally merging into one as he blinked. But when he opened his eyes again there they were, two Enochs, floating away from each other as though each were repulsed by the other.

Nathan put out his hand, trying to get up, to get away. "The fire," he whispered. "That was an accident . . ."

"That was *work*," Enoch complained. "I had to find

312

papers to kindle the embers in the fireplace. I even had to pull down the draperies to keep it going. Then I remembered the lamps. When I poured the oil around, *then* it started and I could leave.''

As Enoch laughed maniacally, Nathan heaved himself from the chair and fell face down onto the carpet behind the desk.

For a moment Enoch didn't notice that he had lost his audience. He was back in the past, reliving the sight of those dancing flames as they spread across Philip's room.

Poof, and a curtain was gone. God, it was a glorious sight! He'd hated to leave, and only when he'd seen the fire eating its way across the carpet to the door had he realized he had to go or be caught.

He never knew how that brat Pippa found her way inside. At the time he'd regretted that Jared hadn't been with her. But when Jared had told his story, heaping the blame on Nathan, Enoch had understood why Jared had been spared.

His father's suffering made it all perfect. Nathan had lost his precious Felicity and the scheming Philip, the people he loved most; *and* he'd got the blame.

Enoch walked around the desk and looked disinterestedly down at Nathan. Was he dead?

If he was, he'd never be able to undo the trust he'd told Enoch about. But did that matter? Jared could be killed.

Enoch bent over his father, peering intently at what he could see of his face. Nathan looked dead, but what if he wasn't? He knew about the fire.

Sitting back on his haunches, Enoch looked around the room. It was easy to imagine flames here. He savored the picture, then rejected it. A second fire would make people suspicious. It would be too much of a coincidence, and besides it wasn't necessary.

He rolled Nathan over and gingerly probed his neck, feeling for a pulse. It was so slight he could barely feel it. He considered pinching his father's nose shut, but the idea was distasteful. He didn't want to have to touch him anymore.

Then he noticed something that made him smile. Nathan's mouth dragged down on the left side.

Another picture flashed through his mind. Graham Wentworth had looked just like this before he'd died of a stroke. Enoch remembered being dragged to the old man's bedside. He'd hated it and all of them for making him go into that dim, smelly room. Now he was glad he'd gone. Because he knew. Nathan would die just as his revered father had died. Enoch wouldn't have to do a thing.

He stood up and stepped over the body to straighten the chair and put out the lamp. At the door he paused to check on what George would see if he came back that night.

Satisfied that the man would spot nothing out of place until morning and better light, Enoch shut the door behind him.

# *Chapter Twenty-One*

Rachel drifted down the shadowed hallway toward the anteroom where she had met Jared Wentworth. She looked and felt as insubstantial as one of the shadows she wafted in and out of along the way. She had been mooning about in her room ever since she'd returned to Lowell, and tonight she was restless. Too restless to stay cooped up anymore.

About to step into the foyer, she paused, halted by the sound of rapid footsteps approaching from the opposite direction. She thought immediately of George, but then decided to wait and see, warned by some difference in the pace.

When she saw Enoch she was glad she had not shown herself. She hadn't seen him often since coming North, but she recognized furtiveness when she saw it. She stood still as a statue, taking in every detail of his approach. His erratic haste. His pause at the door to glance in every direction before he left.

Rachel waited until the door clicked shut behind him; then she ran to the nearest window to watch him leave. He stood on the broad steps. Catching his breath? She willed him to leave so she could find out what had happened. He'd been to see Uncle Nathan, obviously. Had they quarreled?

Enoch might only have been savoring the cold night

air or checking the clouds to be sure there was sufficient moonlight for his ride back to Lowell. Might, Rachel thought cynically, but she knew better. She had been a sneak for too long not to recognize another. He didn't look back, but if he had he would never have spotted Rachel. She knew how to conceal herself until he was gone.

Uncle Nathan's study was dark and deserted. Rachel stood at the threshold indecisively. Could he have gone to bed already? Or had Enoch been alone in the room?

The second explanation made the most sense to Rachel. She would not have missed seeing Uncle Nathan retire. He always used the main stairs at the center hallway. No, Enoch being alone in the room would explain his stealthy exit.

But what had he done here? Had he stolen something?

Rachel slipped inside. The faint, singed scent of the lampwick told her she was right. Enoch had been here. She relit the lamp, her brow puckered in thought.

As the light flared up, she gasped and nearly dropped the glass chimney.

"Uncle Nathan!"

She ran around the desk and knelt at his head. He was dead, she knew it. He looked dead.

"Oh, my God. Uncle Nathan!"

She had seen her mother laid out in her coffin, but that was after she had been all fixed up. Uncle Nathan was pale and ugly. His mouth hung open, all droopy and horrible.

Of their own accord, her hands fluttered out to touch him. She tried to draw them back but they wouldn't mind her. And so she discovered that Nathan's body was still warm.

Then he made a sound. She drew back and screamed.

She was still screaming when George rushed in.

Hours later she was still in her robe and slippers when the doctor George had summoned came to talk to her. She heard what he said, that it was a stroke, that Uncle

Nathan was not dead and perhaps would not die—yet.

"What caused it?" she asked when he was silent at last.

"We don't know. It just happens to some people."

"Was he hurt? Hit on the head?"

"It doesn't happen from the outside, my dear."

"But he was on the floor. He could have . . . fallen." Could have been pushed, was what she thought, knocked down. She tried to fit Enoch into what Dr. Browning said.

"Well, he did fall, at least from the chair. But the fall wasn't what hurt him, and anyway, he landed on carpeting."

Rachel wasn't convinced. Enoch had been in the room. He had left his father without helping him. At the very least he was guilty of neglect, but she knew it was more than that. And so did he.


Summoned to his father's bedside early that morning, Enoch found Rachel sitting on guard at Nathan's side. She made no attempt to hide her hostility although she would never let him know she'd seen him leave the house.

"George tells me you found him," Enoch said, looking down from his lofty height. There was no chair at hand, save the one she occupied. He didn't seem to require one. "I guess it doesn't make much difference to him now. His father died of the same thing."

"Did he?" she responded coldly. "But as you can see, he's not dead yet."

"No, he's not." Enoch stared at Nathan awhile, then gave her a smile. "Perhaps you'll be able to nurse him back to his senses." He sneered. "And perhaps not."

"How concerned you are."

He laughed harshly. "Oh, my dear little cousin, you'll find that I'm very concerned. Very concerned indeed."

Without another word or glance at her, Enoch turned and left.

Rachel found she'd been holding her breath. She let it go slowly in an effort to relax. Moving her chair closer to the bed, she said, "He's gone now, Uncle Nathan. You don't have to worry. I won't let him get to you again."

"Do ye want me to come up with ye, Miss Carina?"

Ned's question and his concerned tone recalled Carina to the present—jarred her back to it, in fact. She tore her eyes away from her perusal of the bleak setting and gave him a smile, picking up her skirts. "No, thank you, Ned. I'll be fine by myself." She let him assist her over a snowbank, then reached back to take the bag of gifts from him. Once it was held securely, her smile broadened as if she were determined to erase his look of unease.

She had timed her visit to Chapel Hill in order to encounter as few people as possible. She told herself her care was for Ned's sake. As a Yankee, he was at a disadvantage here in the Irish district. In fact, her concern was as much for herself as for Ned. This was her home—*had* been her home. Surely no one would be unkind, but still . . .

Now that she'd taken her first, appalled look around, Carina glanced neither right nor left as she made for the back stairway to the upper room where, God willing, the O'Rourkes still lived. She refused to consider that her family could have moved. Coming at all was hard enough.

But it was Christmastime and no matter what her father believed or told the children about her, she was not dead. She was an O'Rourke. They were her family. She would not ignore them. The gifts she brought were simple things of her own making. Without coin or access to stores it was the best she could do for them. And it was what she wanted to do, because these gifts were from her, not from Jared.

Since November, Jared had been much away from Lowell. To keep herself busy and content, Carina had occupied her time with teaching his servants to read and with learning from them the intricacies of managing his household. She had also made her Christmas gifts. The handwork helped her pass the long evenings in her room.

Carina paused on the landing at the second floor. She wasn't winded or tired, merely apprehensive. Her mind was full of "what ifs." What if the room was someone else's now? What if Papa was there? She looked down at Ned and the horses for reassurance—and saw Shep Sweeney dart behind the corner of the house.

Shep would tell his mother and she would come to investigate and . . . Oh Lord, then what? Next to Papa, Mary Sweeney was the person Carina most dreaded to face. She had half-known she wouldn't be able to avoid Mary. Mary was the watchdog of the neighborhood. She'd always been kind to Carina, but that was before. Who could guess what Conn, or Dennis, had told her?

Carina didn't have to wait long to find out. Mary was remarkably agile for such a large woman; Carina had seen her simply *fly* across the road in pursuit of a child up to no good. At any rate, she was at the door by the time Carina had let herself inside and taken that long, affirming look around the room. Yes, this was the place.

Funny, Carina thought distractedly, she couldn't seem to call it home anymore.

She had no time to reflect on the strangeness of such familiar surroundings. Mary was there, her presence all Carina could cope with at the moment.

"So 'tis you," Mary said in her blunt way. "I thought 'twould be. By the sleigh. Them horses have the look of good feeding."

Carina wasn't insulted. The woman was at least talking to her. "How are you, Mary?"

"Fine," she answered, the word almost coming out as "foin" because Mary was too busy to concentrate on speaking correctly. For all her usual brogue, Mary Sweeney was a proud American who struggled to improve

319

herself as well as to help her children along. She was looking Carina over with great care. Finally she nodded.

Carina moved forward on unsteady legs to put the bag on the scarred table top. "I brought things . . . for Christmas." She looked for a chair, needing to sit down. Once she knew she wouldn't disgrace herself by falling in a heap, she gestured to another chair, inviting Mary to join her. "Do you . . . ? Will Papa let them keep the things, do you think?"

Mary remained as she was, but she answered, and Carina found herself feeling grateful for that. "I don't know, girl. Conn's a fey man."

Fey. Carina's mouth twisted in an attempt at a smile. "How is he? Really."

"Better and no better," Mary pronounced. "He coughs again now 'tis cold, but he ain't dead. Sometimes I think he's too mean."

Carina took in the room. Every article was familiar to her. "Margaret does well," she said softly. Agnes would fault every grimy spot and each scuff mark, but Carina knew how difficult it was to clean old, marred surfaces and to use poor soaps.

"Did she have a choice?" Mary asked.

"No." *No more than I did*. But Carina didn't say that. She glanced back at her gifts and asked, "Should I leave them? Can I?"

"I could take them and save them for the day. More than that I don't know." The older woman rested her eyes on the packages, childlike herself. "What's in 'em?"

"I made a doll for Margaret. She's quite beautiful—at least her dress is. It's a lovely bright green, the color Margaret loves. The hair is yarn, rather like hers but not perfectly." Carina frowned, thinking again how impossible it had been to find just the right shade of brown. Margaret's hair was the light brown of Olivia's, pale and soft as silk. Yarn could never approximate hair like that.

"Ah," Mary sighed in appreciation. "I could hardly pretend such as that was from me, now could I? And for the lads?"

Carina wished she had thought to make a handkerchief for Mary. She'd done one for each of Jared's servants, embroidering each hand-rolled square with an initial. It would have been so easy to do one more, and Mary would have cherished it.

She pushed aside her regret to satisfy Mary's curiosity. "The boys were harder for me, because I wanted to make everything myself. There's a willow whistle for Kevin and a kite for Patrick."

Without Marcus's help she'd have had to be content to make them each a fine shirt. They'd have been appreciative but not delighted, and Carina wanted to give her brothers delight. After all, they were boys still, not men, for all that they worked harder than many grown men.

Mary gave a nod of approval. "They'll be liking that."

"I wish I could get them each a pocketknife," she said wistfully. She fingered the last package in the bag, drawing it out slowly.

"And for Conn?"

Carina's eyes skidded away from Mary's. Except for Margaret's doll, she was more pleased with this gift than the others and more certain that it would *be* pleasing. The question remained, however, as to whether or not her father would accept anything at all from her.

"I copied out poems I thought Papa would enjoy," she whispered. "To make a book." Marcus had helped bind the pages with narrow leather thongs he cut for her. She smoothed the wrapping nervously and looked up at Mary.

"A good choice," Mary said.

Carina noticed the sympathy in her eyes and was well aware that Mary made no prediction about the gift finding acceptance or approval. That was no surprise to Carina. Mary Sweeney knew Conn too well to presume anything.

As she put each gift back in the bag Carina tried to attain the emotional distance she needed, the indifference. It wasn't possible. She had put too much of her heart, too much of herself into the making of each article. Her hands trembled as she fussed with the bag. "Do you think I should leave them here? Or would you keep them?"

Mary deliberated, then asked, "And when your papa asks why you came? What should I say?"

"That I wanted to know how everyone is," Carina answered firmly. She had meant only to leave the bag and hope Margaret or Patrick would find it first. Now she knew it would break her heart to think her gifts had been destroyed by Papa out of some form of pique. If Mary secreted them they'd be safe until Christmas. Then— perhaps—his spirit would be softened by the season and he'd be willing to let his remaining children have the pleasure of her surprises. Carina knew it was unlikely, but stranger things had happened—hadn't they?

"What shall I tell them about you, girl?"

"That I'm well," she answered in measured tones. "Very well, in fact. I've a good life with kind people."

"And when will you be having the babe?"

Mary's soft question exploded in Carina's mind, setting off shocks throughout her system. "The babe?" she repeated blankly.

She had only suspected it herself for two weeks or so, with the missing of her normal flow. Even now, it seemed too early for certainty. She had no other symptoms, no sickness or fatigue.

"You've a look about your face," Mary said, sending Carina's hands to her cheeks. "'Tis not for everyone to see, lass, but I've seen it too often to be fooled. Does *he* know?"

"Papa?" Carina asked foolishly.

Mary laughed. "The babe's papa. He's the one you'll be needing to tell."

"It's early yet," Carina said, daunted by the thought of telling Jared. "I wasn't sure myself."

"You can be sure, but where'll you go if he won't be

keeping you with him anymore?"

Carina had no answer to that question, and she couldn't deny her worry. "I don't know, Mary," she said honestly. "Not here."

"No," Mary agreed. "You love him?"

"Yes, and he's a good, fair man." She said that as much for herself as for Mary. Her thoughts, such as they were so far, were most inconclusive. She didn't yet know how *she* felt about a child, much less how Jared would receive her news. He had lost a child once at birth, but that was Melissa's. His wife's child. He'd told her he wouldn't marry again. She accepted that for herself, but could she bear to have her child stained by illegitimacy?

She didn't know.

Mary turned away quickly. To show disapproval? Carina wondered.

"It's a hard road you're traveling, girl. I wish you well."

All the way back to Falls Village, Carina thought of Mary's words. A hard road. But then, when had she had an easy one? Not with Papa, not working the mill. Jared was not a cruel man. He would want his own child, and would provide well for it.

She smiled. Her baby was not an it. She put her hand against her narrow middle and decided she was carrying a son. Jared's son. The thought made her glow.

Still, Carina would not tell Jared yet. He was home so seldom now that she needed time simply to get to know him again. When he returned, in time for Christmas she hoped, no misunderstandings would mar his homecoming, no surprise visit from Dennis Boynton and, she fervently hoped, no Susan Meade either.

In spite of her thoughts, or perhaps *because* of them, Carina was surprised when she discovered that Jared had just then arrived home. Elated, she sprang from Ned's market sleigh as soon as she saw the carriage. Ned, who had started forward to help the stable lad take the still-steaming horses from the traces, gave her a look of

323

consternation and apology. Carina waved to him, sending him a smile, and ran toward the house.

In her haste she nearly collided with Jared. He stood in the doorway and frowned at her lighthearted exchange with Ned and her scamper along the snowy path. Here the snow was bright and clean even where it was hard packed. But Jared, who had longed for the fresh country look of his home after what had seemed to him ages in the unsightliness produced by Boston's bustle, had eyes only for Carina. Where had she been in the sleigh? And why was she with Ned?

He tried to catch her shoulders and hold her away to read her face, but she barreled into him, embracing him, laughing up at him in apparent delight.

"Jared! How lovely! Oh, I was hoping you'd come soon!"

He looked for guilt and hidden dismay on her open countenance. Finally, he found it. She drew back from his restrained embrace and her face clouded over. It was what he expected, and yet he was disappointed.

Carina swallowed back sudden hurt and anguish. Over Jared's broad shoulder she had seen Susan scurry off to her room, there to be cosseted by Agnes and Trudy. Did this visit mean Susan and Jared planned to marry? At Christmas? Her smile began to freeze into something brittle and sharp.

Jared felt the coldness without understanding the reason for it. How could she run to him with glad cries one minute, then turn on that icy dignity the next? "Where did you go with Ned?" he demanded.

If he'd questioned whether or not guilt was the precise emotion she'd first displayed, he had no doubt of it now. She actually stammered and refused to meet his gaze. "To . . . Lowell. I hadn't been back. . . ."

Dennis, he thought, turning way abruptly. She followed slowly—reluctantly, it seemed to Jared—and that annoyed him. "I brought a child with me," he said. "He's sick. Do you know anything about nursing?"

Carina swayed and put out her hand to keep from falling. A *child?* Her brain raced to make sense of what he said, to fill in the gaps. With her own condition so much on her mind, she immediately assumed that he'd had a child by another mistress, probably in Boston. A hundred questions arose, demanding answers. By the time Jared looked back for her response, she had herself under control.

"What's the illness, do you know?"

"It's his chest. He has a fever, I'm sure."

"Oh dear. Well, I've a bit of experience with that— unfortunately." She hurried to keep up with him. "How old a boy?" she asked. "And what's his name?"

"Willie. And he's seven."

While Carina was trying to figure out whether Willie's age meant that his mother had been Jared's mistress before his marriage or during it, they reached the stairs. She halted there suddenly to ask, "What about Susan? Shouldn't she—"

Jared pulled her along by the arm. "Yes, damn it, she should. If it weren't for her, the boy's mother would be fine." His mouth was so tight he could barely force the words through his lips. "Instead, she's dead and this tyke is lost in a strange place."

Shocked, Carina gasped, "Dead? Jared, I don't understand." She couldn't seem to keep him from yanking her along.

"I had him put in your room," he said in a tone that challenged her to object.

They reached the door, where Carina stopped to regain her composure. "I'll do everything I can, Jared, but perhaps you should get the doctor. Isn't there someone you trust out here? Or in Lowell?"

"I wish I could, but no, there's no one."

Once she saw the child, Carina understood. Not everything, but enough. At least she understood that Willie was not Jared's child and she knew why there was no doctor Jared could trust to care for him.

Trudy looked up from tucking the boy into the big bed and started to leave. Carina detained her to get her assessment and to order hot tea and a plaster for his chest.

"Nellie will make up one. She does it best," Trudy said.

When she had gone, Carina asked Jared, "What has Susan to do with this boy?"

"She was playing God," he snarled. Then, at her blank look, he huffed out a fierce sigh and explained. "She's writing a book about the experiences of slaves. She detained the boy's mother in order to get her story. It's probably unfair of me to blame her for the woman's death, but I hate the way she uses people. She was totally useless on the way here." He gestured to the bed, then raked his hand through his hair.

"Not everyone can care for the sick, Jared." Now that he was angry with Susan, Carina could afford to be charitable.

"They were sick, but did she care?"

"Of course she did." Carina put her hand on Willie's hot forehead. Later, when he was settled, she'd listen to his chest and back, but for now warming him was more important than diagnosis. "As long as it really is his chest and not something else causing the fever, he should be fine in a while. We'll get some liquids into him," she said with more optimism than she felt.

Jared's relief was her reward. "I knew you'd be able to help."

"When Marcus comes, please have him come here, will you?"

Jared beamed. "Of course. Marcus has a way with children. I remember. There was a little girl who came with him. We had to pry her away from him when it was time for her to go."

"Does Willie have a home waiting somewhere? A family?"

Jared's face turned bleak. "No one." He looked at the

small, pinched face in the bed. "Poor little tyke," he repeated.

Carina felt the same stirring of sympathy that moved through Jared, plus something else. On a personal level, she was reassured by Jared's tender concern for a strange child, someone not related to him in any way. If he could care so much about Willie, wouldn't he love his own child?

Then she was ashamed of herself for the direction her thoughts had so easily taken. Was she so selfish she could think only about herself?

She was scarcely more comfortable with her next thoughts. They were so inappropriate, given Willie's dire plight. Surely it was wrong for her to see Willie and his need as a chance to right a great wrong in Marcus's life. The two of them might not suit. Willie might be too different from the son Marcus had lost years ago.

Or worse, he might be too like that child, and just his presence might be painful for Marcus. Perhaps, for Marcus, having no child was better than having a child who wasn't his own Tad.

Carina would have to see how they hit it off together. And she would have to be as tactful and subtle as the most sensitive matchmaker. She could raise no hopes in either heart before she knew what was possible. Jared would have to agree and help.

First though, little Willie had to recover.

But as Carina put her ear to Willie's chest, listening to the faint stirrings within his lungs, she was hopeful. Conn's lungs always sounded worse. Willie could get better. He would. After all, he was young.

She applied Nellie's plaster and wrapped the boy with clothes before she tucked him back under the covers. When his eyes opened briefly she saw that they were beautiful, dark and fine as rich chocolate. Like Marcus's.

For both of them, Willie and Marcus, she prayed that they would take to each other. Marcus meant so much to her. Next to Nellie, he had been her best friend and helper. His strong sensitive hands had helped her make the Christmas gifts for the men in her family. Once he was well, Willie would need a man like Marcus to help him grow up smart and strong, able to take advantage of his hard-won freedom.

And Carina already knew how much Marcus needed Willie.

## Chapter Twenty=Two

Two days until Christmas—and Carina couldn't remember ever being happier. Jared hadn't returned to Boston, and wouldn't until after the holiday, but today Susan's father was coming to fetch her back home. Carina would be glad to see her go, although not for the usual reasons—jealousy and anxiety over losing Jared to her. Not entirely anyway.

She still feared Susan as a rival, just not in the usual way. Jared did not love Susan as he should love a wife. In his mind, she was his younger sister, loved out of exasperation with an affection that would never ripen into anything more potent; Carina believed that. Even their clashes during this visit—and there had been many—were simply the wranglings of two people determined to go their different ways. Carina had listened and watched carefully for undercurrents of frustrated attraction. She had found none, not even in Susan.

Still, she didn't feel entirely safe. Susan's parents could yet bring pressure to bear upon Jared. Such was his regard for Silas and Indigo Meade, that he would find it difficult to defy their expressed wish for such a marriage. What Carina didn't know was whether or not the Meades would press for the match.

Which was why she anticipated meeting Silas with

painfully mixed feelings. Silas was important to Jared. Naturally, Carina wanted him to like her, and, just as naturally, she expected him not to. Because he was Susan's father. Then too, he was a Yankee man of excellent family. How could he possibly approve of her?

But she wanted him to—badly.

She watched Jared ride ahead of her toward the river. This had become their habit, to indulge in an early morning ride each day. With Willie ensconced in her room to complete his now-certain recovery, Carina had moved, at Jared's insistence, into his room. Carina had made token objection to the move, more out of deference to Susan's feelings than anything else, but Jared had brushed her protestations aside as he did everything that didn't suit him.

Although Carina was a fearless rider, Merrylegs could never keep up with Infidel once the stallion got going. Each morning Carina took the lead at the start of their ride, and then Jared took it back from her, usually by the time they crested the last rise just before the falls. Today was no exception.

He made a handsome sight, Carina thought as she took in every detail of his appearance. As usual, he was all in black, from his hat to his boots that gleamed against the backdrop of white snow. As he topped the hill, Jared slowed his headlong pace to half turn in the saddle. She caught the flash of his teeth as a grin broke over his features, and then, suddenly, Infidel reared, pawing the air.

Carina cried out in fright and urged her mare forward as Jared fought to keep his seat. She called out, but all sound was swallowed up by the thunderous roar of the water plunging over the cataract before them. Plumes of frost rose from Jared's mouth and from Infidel, testifying to their effort, but Carina heard nothing until she came near. By then Jared had his mount under control.

"What happened?" she shouted.

He patted Infidel's neck, yelling back, "I don't know!"

"You lost your hat!"

He put a hand to his head, laughing in surprise as he encountered his bare head. "So I have!" Keeping the reins secure, he got down to look for it.

"There it is!"

The wind tried to blow the hat away, so Jared stepped on it, making her laugh. But when he clapped it onto his head, Carina's laugh became a cry of shock.

"Jared!" she yelled, pointing at the hat.

He took it off and looked at it. The entire crown was gone. Blown away. No. *Shot* away.

Jared remounted swiftly, his eyes sweeping in every direction from that lofty height. Carina looked as well, but there was nothing to see. He gave a shrug and indicated that they should continue their ride. Before he could set Infidel toward the river again, Carina grasped his arm.

"I don't want to go down there!" she shouted. The path they would travel suddenly seemed too open, too exposed to hidden dangers from the fields and woods around them. All her joy in the crashing sound of water was gone. Now their inability to hear anything else, even each other, felt sinister.

"Please," she mouthed, unable to control her fear.

Jared hesitated, looking around once again as if to offer her reassurance. But at her continued look of desperation, he swept her a gallant bow, indicating that she should precede him.

Although she knew he was making a concession to her fear, Carina hated to go first. She wasn't afraid for herself, only unwilling to let him out of her sight. She had not been shot at; Jared had.

She hurried Merrylegs down the slope, her every sense on alert for trouble at her back. Each time she glanced behind her Jared was right there, smiling at her. Carina didn't slow down until they were back on the road where Jared could ride beside her.

He leaned down to put one hand over hers on the reins.

"I'm perfectly fine, Carina. It was only an accident."

"An accident! Jared, someone shot at you!"

"By accident."

"I don't believe that and neither should you."

Jared gave up trying to reason with her and rode silently at her side the rest of the way home. At the house they saw that Silas had already arrived, and as Jared helped her from the saddle, he said, "You're not to mention this up at the house, Carina. I don't want Silas to hear. He'd only be worried."

"I'd be worried about what?"

Jared's hands tightened about Carina's waist, then he put her onto her feet and took the outstretched hand of the man who had just stepped from the shadowed stable doorway.

Carina watched the men embrace, moved by their obvious affection and by the honest expression of their mutual regard. Silas was a fair man whose hair had darkened to an ashy brown that was now well-silvered and thinning. He would never be bald, she noted, deciding that "distinguished" as the word that described him best.

Susan didn't so much resemble him physically as she resembled the type of young woman who would be his daughter. Seeing the man her father was, Carina felt that she understood Susan better—and liked her. Her qualities were all present in this man: the high-mindedness, the forthrightness, as well as the privilege.

When Jared presented Carina, Silas greeted her politely without being deflected from the answer to his question. Jared tried to brush it aside, so Silas fixed his eyes on Carina.

Looking first to Jared, she said, "I didn't promise." Then she told Silas, "Someone shot at Jared while we were out riding just now."

"Good heavens! Are you all right, son?"

"Perfectly. It was only an accident."

Carina snatched his hat from under his arm and

showed it to Silas. "Would you call that an accident?"

"Carina!"

"I'm sorry, Jared, but I think the only accident is that you're still alive." She turned back to Silas, whose eyes were wide. The color in his face came and went, producing an oddly mottled look. Concern for him made her apologetic, even as his reaction affirmed her own sense of outrage. And terror.

"We ride there every morning at about this time," she said. "We follow the same path and the same pattern. At the start of our ride I go first; then, once Infidel gets up to speed, Jared dashes off ahead of me. Just at that spot Jared is *always* first—and alone. I can't believe it's an accident that he was fired upon right there."

"You're making too much of this," Jared said in a low voice that warned of his anger. "I just got in the way of someone out trying to shoot his Christmas goose."

"There are no geese there."

"A pheasant then," Jared said lightly. "It's nothing, I tell you. An accident."

"They why didn't the hunter show himself? Why was there no sign of anyone around?"

"We didn't stay long, thanks to you. And besides, if you'd just fired off such a shot, would you come forward and apologize?" He laughed. "Whoever it was, the poor man is probably still shaking in his boots."

Silas gave Jared a hard stare. "Regardless of whether or not it was an accident, I trust that you'll give up taking this particular ride for a while."

"Of course," Jared said easily. "Now let's go inside and find Susan, shall we?" His look to Carina promised repercussions if she told the story again and alarmed Meade's daughter.

She would not, of course. Telling Silas had been a way of emphasizing the danger to Jared. His nonchalance might only be a pose for her benefit, but until she knew he was taking the threat to his life seriously—and as a

333

threat—she intended to be firm with him.

Susan watched them come inside, bringing cold air, snow, and excitement. The last puzzled her, but she ascribed it to the emotions that ran like heat lightning between Jared and Carina. She envied them, but she no longer pined for Jared to notice and love her. Now that she saw him clearly she realized he was much too common for her. In spite of his fine family, Jared was rather like his great beast of a horse.

And he was harsh and judgmental. He would never forgive her for what had happened to that slave woman, young Willie's mother. No matter that the wretch's demise was not her fault. No matter that Willie had since been taken up by the other released slave, Marcus. No matter anything!

Jared's perspective on abolition was *particular* in the extreme, she had discovered. He saw each fugitive as an individual to be rescued, and in doing so he lost sight of the larger, more important issue—the institution of slavery in general.

Susan had puzzled over his attitude for days, ever since they'd come here this time. Theoretically, their opposite approaches to the problem should fit together, complementing each other. In reality, it didn't work out that way.

She was disappointed in Jared, and that was plain fact.

She hurried forward to greet her father. At least his coming meant she could go home. She'd had enough of Lowell. It was typical of the way this visit had gone that even her father's hug was interrupted.

"Ah, Mr. Meade," Agnes said, bustling forward importantly. "You're just in time for breakfast. I hoped you would be."

"So did I, Agnes," Silas responded affably, turning from Susan to greet her.

Susan didn't complain, but she noted that Agnes no longer even pretended to defer to her. The housekeeper didn't *quite* invite Carina to play hostess—yet. Susan was certain that was the next step, however. In a way it was a relief to have that hopeful and impatient stage of her life over. She'd wasted too many years waiting for Jared to recover from Melissa and discover her devotion. She wanted to blame Jared, but she'd done it to herself.

She followed Agnes to the dining room, giving her attention to her father who came next. Jared seated her, while Silas saw to Carina. Susan noted, though Carina was too distracted to observe, that Agnes had tactfully chosen to put them at a round table. That way there would be no distinction attached to any particular seat. The ploy made Susan smile, but what really delighted her was Carina's calf-eyed infatuation with Jared.

It would do her no good, of course. Susan recognized futility when she saw it. Jared simply was not a marrying man. He would have his little alliances as the spirit, or more accurately, the *flesh* moved him. But that would be it. Since that was the case, perhaps it was doubly sad that Melissa had died. Apparently, Jared deserved a Melissa— or a Carina O'Rourke. *She*, obviously, did not require marriage.

"I have some good news for you, Suzie," Silas said, interrupting her dismal thoughts. He tipped his head in Jared's direction. "And for you."

"Oh?" Jared asked.

"Tyler will be with us for Christmas."

Before Susan could respond, Jared said, "That is good news! Indigo must be ecstatic."

Susan saw that her father's pleasure was just as deep. Well, well, she thought. So Tyler is mending his fences at last.

"That's wonderful, Daddy. I'm so glad." Out of the corner of her eye she saw Jared shoot a quelling look at Carina. But by the time Susan looked, she could see no glimmer of understanding on the girl's face. *More mystery.*

Did Tyler have some connection with Carina O'Rourke? He'd cut a broad swath through the women of

335

Boston. Perhaps he'd done the same in Lowell. If so, he'd probably been involved with Carina.

Susan shuddered with distaste.

"Were you able to complete your shopping in Lowell yesterday?"

Carina's polite question jolted Susan back to the present. "Oh, yes," she answered, fighting down a wild desire to laugh. She had not shopped at all. She'd gone in search of Dennis Boynton, not gifts.

"You should have asked me to take you," Jared said.

"I didn't want to bother you." In fact, Susan had been careful to pick a time when he was occupied elsewhere. Planning the escapade had been part of the fun.

In retrospect she had to admit that planning had ended up being the *only* fun of the day. She'd been clever but ultimately unsuccessful. She'd dressed plainly, thinking Dennis would prefer that. With his ideals, she was sure he would find her usual elegance offensive. Then too, in simple apparel she was able to blend in better with the mill girls who made up most of the shoppers in Lowell.

In that she'd been successful. She'd also managed to "lose" Trudy, her companion on this excursion. Ned drove them in and also helped Trudy search for Susan when she was "lost." Susan had been clever there, too. She'd known that Trudy and Ned were sweet on each other. Because of that, although both of them were conscientious servants, they didn't notice just how long Susan was alone, nor did they really care.

So Susan found the *Chronicle* office and Dennis. She had her diary and the outline of her tract to show him. Thinking of the way her meeting had gone, Susan frowned and shook her head, still unable to believe that he could mistake her so completely. She knew he was intelligent. Where had she gone wrong?

The interview had gone badly right from the ferocious frown he'd at first bestowed on her. She'd been confused initially because she had expected to see his name on the door, not that of R.R. Sherwood. Confronted with the fact that he did not own the *Chronicle* or serve as its publisher, Susan had suddenly doubted the wisdom of her mission. She hadn't doubted *him*, she'd only worried that she would cause trouble by appearing at his workplace with what amounted to a personal request.

Staring at Dennis's ink-begrimed clothing, she stood with one hand on the opened door. "Oh, I'm sorry, Mr. Boynton. I . . . perhaps you don't remember me, but—"

"I remember you."

She let go of the door, wanting to be pleased and finding it hard. "Oh? Well, Mr. Wentworth suggested that—"

"I'll have nothing to do with him."

"This has nothing to do with him," she said boldly, finding backbone somewhere in the midst of the mush he made of her. "If you'll only listen to—"

He put down a blackened rag and wiped his palms on the legs of his pants in a way that drew her fascinated eye. "If *you'll* only come in and shut the door," he said, looking down his beaky nose at her. "Or perhaps you're afraid you'll get dirty?"

She shut the door decisively. "I don't care about this old—"

"I thought you weren't rigged out quite so grandly as usual."

"Mr. Boynton," she said, "perhaps you could confine your attention to business?"

"I could if you'd leave," he answered with pointed rudeness.

"This is not a social call. I'm in need of the services of a printer. Is it your custom to turn away business?"

His hooded eyes studied her. "Sometimes it is."

Susan took a deep breath and tried again. "Mr. Boynton, it's well known that the *Chronicle* serves as the voice of social justice. I'm preparing a tract based upon notes taken over the past few years. I've collected writing from my diary—"

"We don't publish gushings from a lady's diary," he

said flatly.

"I do not gush! What I have here—"

"Doesn't interest me at all."

When he turned his back on her, Susan wanted to stamp her foot and scream. But she wouldn't give him that satisfaction. Instead, she controlled herself and said in the tone she usually reserved for a misbehaving pupil, "You will regret your rudeness, Mr. Boynton. I'm sorry we could not do business, but you'll be sorrier still."

With that she left. She didn't even slam the door behind her. But when she was well away from the building, she sought out the privacy of a little park next to a church. There she could cry. Because she had to go back and face Trudy and Ned, she didn't dare indulge herself as she wanted. It would be difficult to explain reddened eyes.

Now she was sorry she'd shed any tears. Just thinking of the incident made her so frustrated and angry that her expression was drawing her father's eye. She knew he would attribute her temper to Jared and Carina, but even that wasn't important any more.

In one way, Jared's sordid little association with Carina gave Susan hope. If he could disregard convention and cross the barriers of class and social order in the name of true love, why couldn't she do the same? Of course, he was a man, but what did that matter?

She had enough money to live on for the rest of her life, and it was securely in her own name. Regardless of what Tyler did, she was financially independent. Couldn't she win Dennis somehow?

She was sure that the key to doing that lay in finding a detour around his pride. But first she had to make him see that she was as serious about and as dedicated to social change as he was. She'd hoped he would help her organize the material in her diaries. Now she knew she had to do it by herself in order to prove herself worthy of Dennis.

"Are you feeling all right, my dear?" Silas asked.

338

"You're not coming down with a fever, are you?"

"Only a fever to be home again, Daddy. I've missed you all so much, and I can't wait for Christmas this year." She turned her smile on Jared and Carina. "Would you forgive us if we eat and run today? My bags are all packed and—"

Silas jumped to his feet. "Say no more!"

Grinning, the two men went off to prepare for their leave-taking. Susan started to feel insulted, then decided to laugh. She *had* always delayed departures before, so perhaps she couldn't blame them for their gleeful haste.

Left alone with Carina, she couldn't quite bring herself to apologize for her past behavior, but she was gracious, even profuse, in her thanks for Willie's care. Then, as she was about to leave, she thought of proud Dennis and unbent even more. After she kissed Jared she did the same to Carina.

Jared shut the carriage door behind Silas and stepped back, smiling broadly as he waved them off. "Well, well," he said, just loudly enough for Carina to hear. "I do believe my little sister is growing up. Will wonders never cease!"


George added his careful signature to the document and gave the pen back to Kenneth Gibson.

"Thank you, George," Nathan said. His mouth still dragged down on the left side when he smiled, but with every day he grew stronger and more sure of his recovery.

"I'm honored, sir."

Gibson gave them both a sour look as he inspected the signature.

"Come, come, Kenneth. He wrote his name for you. God knows, you know who he is. He's been with me for centuries. Must you make such heavy water of everything?"

"It's—"

339

"Irregular," Nathan snapped. "Yes, I know. You've said so a dozen times. But it's what I want, and as long as I'm paying the bills, you'll do as I want."

"You know why I'm concerned, Nathan. It's this . . . subterfuge. It's unlike you."

Nathan nodded with understanding and sympathy. Kenneth was one of his few true friends. A blunt, bluff man, he looked ten years older than his sixty-plus years, older even than the mirror showed him to be—and Kenneth wasn't the one recovering from a stroke.

"Shall I bring you some port now, sir?" George asked. It was his way of asking to leave.

Nathan looked to Kenneth, who shook his head. "Just one then, George. And thank you."

Coming close to death as he had, Nathan found himself changed, mostly for the better, although there were still things about himself he didn't like. There was his core of impatience, for example. That had become worse, because now he truly understood that a man's days on earth are finite.

He appreciated the good things in his life so much more: this fine old house, George's devoted service, friends like Kenneth, a good glass of port, and . . . well, he could go on and on. Sometimes he did that now, too. If he felt the possibilities of each day more now, and enjoyed small things more, he also came up hard against the same old sticking points. And now they hurt worse than ever.

He was working on them, though.

"Don't worry so, Kenneth. I know what I'm doing. I promise you."

"Enoch is your son, Nathan. Your own flesh and blood."

"Yes, and I'm not cutting him off entirely. You know that. Ah, George, this is just what I need. Thank you, my man." He turned his body in order to reach the glass. "An awkward business," he muttered to Kenneth as George helped him and then retired, accompanied by

340

more thanks. Nathan knew it was excessive, this need to thank people, but he couldn't stop himself.

Kenneth let him enjoy his drink without more scolding, then helped him slide back down into the bed before picking up the thread of his argument. "He'll maintain that you were rendered incompetent by illness and that this new will was written under duress, while you were dependent upon the care of your niece."

"I know all that, my friend. But you and George—and Rachel, perhaps—can tell my side of things."

"But why should we have to? That's what I don't understand. Can you tell me? Not as your lawyer, as your friend? The will isn't the issue with me. You can do whatever you want. You know that. But I care, Nathan, and I—"

Nathan held up his good hand to stem the flow of words. He was tired. All day he'd husbanded his energy, saving it up so he could accomplish this hard task. He'd done it and now he needed to rest. "I'm leaving another document. Not a will, an . . . explanation, if you will. It will make everything clear, though I mustn't now. Trust me, Kenneth, as you always have. Your loyalty has helped me through the years. Let me rely on it for these last days."

"Last days? You're getting better! *I* may not live to see this document," Kenneth sputtered. "That's why I want to—"

The door burst open upon Rachel, who entered in a blur of flying skirts, sleeves, and scarves. "Uncle Nathan!" she cried. "Enoch is here!"

Nathan gave Kenneth one beseeching look before he submitted to Rachel. "You have the new will," he said. "Keep it out of sight and only stay a few more minutes to talk to Rachel. Then leave, understand?"

Rachel saw immediately that the attorney was confused. "Just leave everything to me, Mr. Gibson. Follow my lead and everything will be fine."

She removed the pillows that propped her uncle into a

341

semisitting position, straightening the bed covers as she did so. Quickly pulling two chairs to the side of the bed, she directed the lawyer to sit in one and put her uncle's empty glass at his side.

After casting one last look about the room for any sign betraying the state of her uncle's health, Rachel plopped unceremoniously into the second chair. Within seconds, she had composed her face into an expression of mournful solemnity appropriate for a death-bed watch.

And just in time.

"Miss Rachel?" George spoke from the doorway. "Mr. Enoch to see you and Mr. Gibson."

Rachel looked up slowly, as if pulled from deep contemplation, to focus on George. He continued to detain Enoch, preventing him from entering. "Oh, yes, George. Thank you."

A glance at Uncle Nathan showed that he seemed to be sleeping. Mr. Gibson, on the other hand, looked as though he would jump out of his skin if anyone came near him. Instead of greeting Enoch directly, Rachel leaned over her uncle and said in the voice people usually reserve for addressing the deaf, "Uncle Nathan, Enoch is here to see you."

There was not the slightest indication from Nathan that he heard, but Mr. Gibson started to his feet. Rachel gave his arm a reassuring squeeze as Enoch came near. "You mustn't rush off, Mr. Gibson," she said heartily. "I'm sure Uncle Nathan is enjoying your conversation."

Enoch gave her a look of incredulity that simmered with malevolence. "Still busy pretending?" he asked.

Rachel ignored his sarcasm. "You remember Mr. Gibson, don't you, Enoch?"

He inclined his head in recognition, finally taking the hand Gibson extended in greeting. Although Rachel gestured her uncle's friend back to his chair, she was relieved to see that he wanted to leave. She couldn't help being amused that his obvious discomfort in the face of her charade with Uncle Nathan played perfectly into her hand. Enoch would interpret Gibson's unease as further proof that Nathan was still comatose and that Rachel had lost her grip on reality.

Mouthing pleasantries, she saw Mr. Gibson to the door before she turned back to confront Enoch.

"What was he doing here?" he demanded.

"Why, visiting Uncle Nathan, of course. Just as you are," she said sweetly, baiting him. "They're old friends."

"This is just the place to come for good conversation." He sneered. Imitating Rachel, he bent over his father and bellowed, "Isn't that right, Uncle Nathan?"

Rachel winced at the noise he made, wondering how her uncle could keep from flinching under the assault. Had he done so, she had an explanation prepared that was consistent with her pose. To Enoch, she pretended to believe that Nathan was getting better every day. Any sort of muscular twitch was just more ammunition. Unlike Enoch, Rachel was in the enviable position of being unable to lose.

She put herself in Enoch's way, sitting close to her uncle, and gestured his son to the second chair, asking with forced cordiality, "Did you have a good Christmas?"

"It was wonderful," he snapped. "My father is a vegetable and the price of finished cotton just fell again."

"Your father is getting better," she stated as if by rote, adding wearily, "and you know you shouldn't talk that way within his hearing. It's very discouraging to him, Dr. Browning says."

"Dr. Browning is an idiot. Look at him! He's no more than a turnip, just lying there!"

"Enoch!" She got to her feet indignantly. "I know it's hard for you to accept—"

"Oh, cut it out, little cousin. This act of yours doesn't fool me for an instant. All you want from the old man is a chunk of his fortune. Well, there isn't all that much, and what there is, belongs to me. So why don't you scurry back to Boston and wiggle your bustle at the eligible fools there. You'll do a lot more for yourself that way than you will sitting here waiting for him to rise up and walk."

"If you're going to talk like that I must ask you to leave." Rachel's indignation was not all feigned. That a man's son would talk so callously within his hearing made her sick.

Enoch only laughed at her. "Don't worry, I have no intention of staying. I just came to see if he'd died yet. Let me know when it happens," he said. "And then pack up your bags and head South again, because there's no way *I'm* going to support you when he's gone!"

Rachel was genuinely shaken by the blast of hatred Enoch directed toward her. She struck the chair with a thump as soon as the door slammed behind him.

"Are you all right?" Nathan asked quietly.

"Yes." She looked at him, unsurprised to find that his skin was pallid again. He hadn't moved. "Oh, Uncle Nathan, I'm sorry."

"Ah, but you didn't spawn him, my dear. That honor is mine alone—though I did have help," he added in afterthought. Lucy. She had helped make Enoch what he was. But much as Nathan wanted to, he couldn't blame her completely.

The first feeling he'd become aware of on the way to recovery was a cross between fear and dread. At first he'd thought the emotion was caused by his physical condition. It seemed so like the heaviness in his limbs and his weary inability to move. And he couldn't remember anything.

Then, slowly, he'd begun to piece together bits of himself and to relate those bits to what happened around him. The dread eased, lightening especially in Rachel's presence. Then he heard her talking to George, telling about Enoch.

His dread now had a name. Long before he could speak and make himself clear, he knew Enoch was his enemy. Rachel knew it also and tried to protect him with her mediating presence whenever Enoch came. But one evening Enoch arrived as he had today, unexpectedly, and found his way past Nathan's guards to catch him alone. Enoch didn't stay long, just long enough to make it clear why Nathan had been afraid of his son.

*I should have killed you when I had the chance.* The soft voice had brought Nathan awake so sharply he'd had to work to maintain his passive expression. *I thought you'd die without my help or I would have.*

Suddenly Nathan remembered the horror he'd been trying to escape just before his collapse. Enoch. His own son had murdered Jared's family, and now he wanted his own father dead.

"Don't make me wait too long, old man," Enoch had said. "Or I'll be back."

No, Nathan thought, Enoch's latest outburst didn't surprise him. He'd passed being surprised long ago. Since then he'd agonized over and over, wondering if he'd caused Enoch's evil by distrusting his son so early and for so long. But for all his consideration, Nathan still had no answers. He felt responsible for Enoch—and hated the feeling.

He looked at Rachel's bowed head, and his guilt doubled. "I know you worry about Enoch, my dear, but there's something else troubling you as well, isn't there?"

She gave him a quick look, her soft brown eyes wide and startled.

"Enoch's right about one thing," he said, watching for her reaction. "You should be in Boston, not here at my bedside. We were going to launch you into society, like one of those lovely clipper ships the Wentworth Company used to set upon the seas. You're missing the height of the season, the holiday balls."

"I've no interest in those."

Nathan could see that it was true. "What happened, my dear?" When she remained silent he said, "Tell me. You know the worst about me. It can be no worse than

345

that. And perhaps I can help mend things. If I can, I will. You must know, Rachel, that you've become my only joy." He fought the way his voice thickened with emotion. It happened all the time now and he hated the old womanishness of it.

"Your heart is broken," he said, making a stab in the dark. With a girl her age, what else could it be? He wasn't entirely amazed when she began to sob.

"Oh, Uncle Nathan, I was so foolish. I'm ruined, and he didn't even care!"

Nathan took full responsibility for Rachel's plight. In toying with this girl's heart, Jared had been seeking revenge on Nathan. There was nothing he could do to alter that, but he *could* bring them together now. Obviously, Rachel cared for him and she'd make an admirable wife. Her constancy to him in illness proved that she was not the shallow child she'd once seemed. And by marrying her to Jared, Nathan could protect her once and for all from Enoch.

"Ruined?" he asked. "How do you mean ruined, child?"

To his dismay, her sobs increased.

"Is there a child?"

That stopped her. "No!"

Nathan wanted to smile at her indignation. "Never mind," he soothed. "We'll say there is anyway."

Then he did smile.

# Chapter Twenty-Three

"Miss Carina, did you see the news?"

Carina looked up from her sewing. Jared had liked the shirt she'd made as his Christmas gift, so she had started another. "No, Gwen, I haven't."

She felt vaguely ashamed of her lack of interest in the outside world. Since becoming aware of her pregnancy, she felt herself increasingly turned inward, cherishing private dreams rather than studying the larger world. Seeing Gwen's concern, she realized that it more than made up for her own lack of interest.

"It says here that the senator from Illinois, Stephen A. Douglas, has proposed a new bill that would allow the territories of Kansas and Nebraska to enter the union as either free or slave states."

Carina sought to grasp the implications. "Do you mean the people living there are to vote their preference for allowing slaves within their borders?"

Gwen rattled the paper indignantly. "That's what the paper says."

"Is that the *Chronicle*?" Carina asked, ever suspicious that Dennis's paper did not always give the facts without sensationalizing them.

"What difference does that make?" Gwen demanded. "The words are right here, plain to see."

"May I read it?"

Carina realized belatedly that she had offended Gwen, who was still sensitive about her newfound reading ability. Even taking the words with a liberal dose of salt, Carina could see the reason for Gwen's alarm. She withheld her lecture about taking biased accounts at face value. This was serious indeed. Protest meeting were planned in Boston and Lowell, with petitions already circulating for signature.

"Perhaps it won't pass."

"Of course it will," Gwen said. "All the Southerners will support it."

"But not Northerners."

"Mr. Douglas is a Northerner."

The fact was irrefutable, and the questions it raised were unanswerable. The issue forced Carina back into the real world.

If the institution of slavery expanded from the South into the West and the Territories between, what would happen to people like Marcus and Willie? And to people like Jared who fostered their freedom? Enoch had sent the law after him once. Would he try again? And be successful next time?

Carina worried and waited for Jared to return from Boston again. He would know what was really happening there. More importantly, he would be able to interpret the news for them—and perhaps offer reassurance.

But when he came he didn't bring good news. He was so upset and concerned about the direction the government was taking that Carina postponed yet again telling him about the baby she carried. He might be pleased, but what if he was not? She knew the time would come when her condition would become obvious, but until it did she decided to wait for the moment when everything between them was . . . well, perfect.

And when a letter came, summoning Jared to his uncle's bedside, Carina was glad she had not spoken up. Jared had very mixed feelings about his uncle's illness, and hers were no clearer. Because he blamed Nathan for his family's murder, she shared Jared's antipathy for his uncle. But at the same time she was grateful to Nathan for intervening between Enoch and her family. And because of what had happened to Patrick, Carina understood that any person, even Nathan Wentworth, could be accused of a crime he did not commit.

Jared resented everything about his visit to Belvidere. When he had been told weeks ago that his uncle was near death, he'd felt cheated because Nathan might die with their quarrel unresolved. Now that he'd seen his uncle's handwriting he felt something else. He called it grudging admiration, but that didn't begin to describe the range of his emotions.

Clearly, Nathan wasn't near death at all. The black scrawl of letters on heavy paper was much too vigorous for that. And too much like Jared's father's imperious hand. As a child, he'd tried to imitate his father's penmanship. It had looked so much more adult than the style taught in school. Uncle Nathan's writing was as much like it now as Jared's own grown-up hand. If handwriting revealed character as some believed, did that mean that Nathan was as honest as Philip had been? Or as honest as Jared was?

Jared didn't want to think about that possibility.

Nathan's man ushered him into his uncle's room, leaving as soon as he'd provided them with glasses of port. The drink was welcome.

"You're looking well," Jared said over the rim of the glass, drawing a chuckle from Nathan.

"Better every day, although that fact is something of a secret."

"Oh?"

Nathan didn't explain, merely eyed him in a way that would have been disconcerting had Jared been younger and less self-assured. Finally Nathan said, "Won't you sit down?"

After a moment's hesitation, Jared did. He didn't want to exhibit his curiosity, but it was growing by the minute.

He raised his glass to savor the wine. "Madeira," he said almost reluctantly. It was his father's drink.

Nathan's eyes suddenly—surprisingly—filled with tears. He blinked furiously and looked away. When he had himself under control again, he said in a voice still thick with emotion, "I think of him with every glass. Sometimes I think I drink it for him."

Jared didn't know how to respond, and his confusion was as daunting as Nathan's tears.

To cover the awkward moment, Nathan slugged down a too-large swallow and nearly choked. He settled down finally by laughing. "I knew this would be impossible," he muttered. "I need Rachel here."

"Ah," Jared murmured for want of something to say. "Your lovely niece. How is her search for a husband going?"

Instead of answering, Nathan nodded. "She is lovely, isn't she?"

Having already said so, Jared contented himself with waiting and cataloging the effects of illness on his uncle. In spite of his vigorous handwriting Nathan looked old and worn. Dressed and propped upon pillows, he now failed to fill up his clothes. Unwittingly, Jared was reminded of Grandpapa Wentworth during his last illness. Was a predisposition to strokes something he had handed down along with his money and the Wentworth mole?

It wasn't really a mole, Jared had since learned, but that was what it was called by the family. It was more a gathering of pigmentation, like a cluster of freckles. Jared's was on his chest, hidden now by hair. In friendlier days of childhood, he and Enoch had compared notes. Enoch's was quite near his navel, probably similarly hidden now.

Even Pippa had been blessed, though hers had been appropriately dainty and well placed. He had once teased her, saying that as she grew older it would migrate from her arm to her face, where it would be a blight on her beauty and on her expectations of a good marriage. He'd expected to be scolded for that, but Mama had only laughed.

Nathan brought him back to the present. "It's interesting that you should bring up the subject of Rachel's marriage."

"Is it?" Jared laughed. "I can't think why. With a girl of that age there's nothing else to talk about. All they are is walking marriage traps."

"She'll make a fine wife. She has great loyalty, I've discovered. And she will be my heir."

"Sweetening the pot?" Jared asked, not bothering to hide his amusement. "Well, I've no doubt it will work."

Nathan seemed pleased. "Good. I'm glad you approve."

Jared could have asked how Enoch was taking the prospect of losing his inheritance to Rachel, but he was out of patience. He'd had a long, cold ride to get here and faced its equal in order to get home again. And Carina was waiting for him. Even the excellent Madeira wasn't compensation enough for all that. After another sip, he put the glass down. "You didn't ask me here to discuss young Rachel's marriage prospects, Nathan, why don't—"

"But I did."

Jared stared, open-mouthed. Then he collected himself to . . . what? Protest?

Nathan was satisfied with his reaction. "I want you to do the right thing by Rachel, Jared." He waved his good hand dismissively. "Oh, I know you have O'Rourke's daughter for a mistress, and I hear she's lovely; but it's Rachel you must marry."

Jared found voice enough to say, "You're insane!"

"I know better than most men that marriages of this kind can bring a great deal of unhappiness, but you should have thought of that when you were taking her innocence."

"Taking . . . ?" Jared finally heard what Nathan was

351

saying. "You think that I—?"

"I know you did, and man to man I'll admit that Rachel is a walking provocation; but that doesn't excuse you any more than it did me. I faced up to my responsibility and damned if you won't, too! I'll see to it!"

Jared shook his head as if to clear it. "Let me get this straight. Rachel says that I took her virginity?"

"And left a child."

There was no disguising the triumph Jared saw on Nathan's face. "Now wait just a minute," he began.

"Don't bother to deny it, son. Rachel said you would. She said you even *told* her you would. I can tell you right now, that turned my stomach. You've sowed some oats— I know all about your carousing out on the Tyngsborough Road—but . . ."

Jared wanted to howl. His "carousing" was only a rumor, carefully planted and nurtured to cover his absences from home when he carried fugitives from one place to another. That it should be used against him in this way was unbelievable.

"She's lying. I don't know why, but—"

Nathan's face grew dangerously red. "She's not! I tell you, she's not like that. You've broken her heart, abandoning her this way. She wasn't going to tell me at all, but she's been so low in spirits that, even sick, I couldn't help but see. I had to drag it out of her. You've some kind of hold over her, and I tell you I don't like it one bit. If I could think of anything else on earth to do but this, I'd do it."

"Of course you would, you ruthless old dog." Jared suddenly began to laugh. "This is your revenge, isn't it? You've finally found a way to make me pay for accusing you of murder."

He saw his remark hit home even as Nathan denied it. "That's another issue entirely."

And I'm Father Christmas, Jared thought. But he said, "Who can you produce who ever saw me with Rachel?"

352

"I have her word," Nathan said stiffly. "I don't need corroboration."

"But I do." Jared thought of the oldest male trick used in this circumstance, getting a friend to claim he'd also been intimate with the woman—and that brought Tyler to his mind.

Tyler!

Of course. Tyler was the one who'd seduced Rachel, or who'd been seduced by her into breaking his own cherished code.

"Tell me how I spent my time with Rachel?" he asked. "I never took her anywhere, as you surely know. Where did we meet?"

"She came to your rooms."

"At the Meades'?"

Nathan frowned, indicating that he knew he was on shaky ground here. "No. You took rooms somewhere else, for privacy."

"Ah, of course." He was almost beginning to enjoy this. "But Rachel couldn't be persuaded to disclose the location. Is that it?"

"I didn't ask," Nathan snapped. "I don't want to know the sordid details."

"No, of course not." Jared finished his port and got to his feet. "It's been an interesting evening, Nathan, I'll grant you that. You've managed to surprise me."

"I'll have more than that from you. I'll have your word that you'll make things right for Rachel."

Jared looked down at his uncle, trying to see into his mind. He was innocent, but that wouldn't be enough. He did have one other weapon in his arsenal, one that would unquestionably outstrip any accusation of Rachel's, but he wouldn't use it. He couldn't. It was his secret and his shame. To employ such a weapon against his uncle would mean handing over a far greater victory to Nathan than marriage to Rachel.

No. He wouldn't do that; neither would he marry

the girl.

But he would do something about Rachel's plight. Yes, indeed.

"This . . . ah . . . birth," he said, smiling. "Is it imminent?"

Nathan plainly mistrusted Jared's humor. "I don't believe so," he said stiffly.

"Good. Then I have . . . uh, time to arrange things?"

Mistrust grew to alarm on Nathan's face. He wanted to think he'd won, but his nephew looked too complacent. Warily, he answered, trying to believe in his victory. "Of course, you have some time. But no tricks now, do you hear? I won't have Rachel treated badly."

"I hear you, dear uncle, and you may be sure I'll see that Rachel gets what she deserves."

Jared turned on his heel and left. The last thing he heard as he shut the door solidly behind him was the clamor of the bell at Nathan's bedside, summoning George.


Riding home that evening, Jared was more amused than apprehensive about Nathan's demand. His uncle was in no position to bring pressure to bear against Jared and they both knew it. To do so would only damage Rachel. The interesting question was why Jared had been designated the groom-to-be, especially when Nathan knew about Carina. Jared decided he had been chosen by his uncle, with or without Rachel's knowledge, as a stand-in for Tyler.

Jared, of course, was responsible for throwing her at Tyler, but he had not expected the attraction to stick. Why had it? *If* it had.

There was the possibility that everything was a lie, but that was easy to check. A discreet word with Tyler and he'd know where they stood.

But, no woman was going to drag him to the altar this way, certainly not Rachel Farmington. He'd rather resurrect Melissa than yoke himself—in Carina's apt phrase—to Rachel!

But Tyler was another story. He and Rachel?

Jared had to give that some thought.

But not that night or for several days. At home he found Carina tending Willie, who was again in her room, this time with a racking cough. She did not have to nurse him alone because he was a great favorite with everyone. Agnes, Trudy, and even Gwen, took shifts sitting with him.

Carina had devised a way to ease his suffering by propping him up with pillows and tenting his bed, which she had moved next to the fireplace, with blankets to keep the air he breathed moist. She swore by the method, and it seemed to help, although tending the steam kettles was a chore.

By the time Jared urged her to go to bed, Carina was asleep on her feet, her face flushed and ruddy with heat. He tried to hold her, but she pushed him away and flung off the covers. Long before morning, he knew she was sick when she burrowed into his side, seeking his warmth to offset her teeth-chattering chill.

"Carina," he murmured, wrapping her in his arms. "My God, sweetheart, you're burning up!"

"Cold, Jared," she complained. "I'm so cold."

As soon as he had her warmed enough to leave her tightly wrapped in blankets, he ran across the hall for help. He found Trudy dozing in the chair next to Willie. As soon as he touched her arm, she came awake. "Oh, Mr. Jared! I'm sorry." Her eyes flew to Willie, now sleeping comfortably. Even she could see that his crisis had passed.

"It's Carina," he said. "She's got a fever. Would you mind sending Ned to get the doctor?"

"She's not coughing?"

"It's different than this. I . . . don't want to take a chance."

"No. No, of course not." Trudy smoothed her rumpled

355

clothes. "I'll wake Ned and send Mum up to help." A final look at her charge and she said, "He's all right now. It was one of those children's things, I guess."

Jared didn't need to be told that Carina wasn't a child. He'd never helped nurse anyone in his life, but under Agnes's guidance he did what he could. Although she barely seemed conscious and her eyes were wild and unfocused, she responded to him, trying—sometimes with heartbreaking effort—to follow his instructions, to sit up or to swallow the drink he held to her parched lips.

Dr. Browning came and went, his brow furrowed, promising nothing. When pressed, he would say only that she was young and healthy, that her lungs "weren't too bad" because she'd only worked a few years in the mills.

Jared was not reassured.

He remembered another time when the house had been alternately hushed or filled with hurrying footsteps, when muted conversations broke off as soon as he appeared. He knew those pitying smiles. And he was afraid.

He sat with Carina as often as he could bear to. Frequently the women would not let him near. Then he paced and worried. He didn't go to Boston or seek out Tyler or think of Rachel. The one woman whose presence was tauntingly near—or perhaps hauntingly—was Melissa.

His luck with women was so bad. The ones he loved left him. They died. Perhaps he deserved no better than Rachel.

"Perhaps you should go to Lowell, sir," Bagley suggested as he brought coffee after Dr. Browning left one morning.

When Jared didn't answer, Bagley went on. "Marcus says Mr. Nichols is asking for you, and I think the ride would do you good."

Lowell seemed so far away, and he was tired. "I don't know, Bagley."

"Agnes said she's getting better, you know."

"She is?"

"I think so. No one wants to offer false encouragement, but she slept all night."

"She did?" Jared brightened at the thought of such improvement. Already he was wondering what Billy Nichols's problem might be.

It wasn't anything Billy couldn't have handled by himself, as it turned out; but getting away from the house and his worry was just what Jared needed. On the way back from Lowell, he chuckled to think how adept Bagley was at managing him. His mood was now light and optimistic.

He gave Infidel a good run, then let the animal settle into a smooth ground-eating lope. It was a pace that let Jared relax and enjoy the rush of snow-crusted trees. Each frosted branch, it seemed, held the last rays of the setting sun for his inspection.

The overturned sleigh that lay across the road as he neared Falls Village raised no alarm in Jared, just impatience. Anxious to get home, he cursed under his breath as he checked Infidel. He could not bypass a recent accident here where so few people came. It might be hours before another rider passed this way.

"Can I help you?" he called from his circling, sidestepping mount.

A weasel-faced man stood ineffectually by the still-attached horse. He gave Jared a glowering look, tossing his head toward the sleigh. "Overturned," was all he said.

Jared beat back his annoyance at having to deal with the sleigh *and* a blockhead. He swung down from the saddle to take charge. "If we both put our backs to it, we can get this—"

Suddenly another man popped up from behind the sleigh. He had a gun.

Jared groaned inwardly at his stupidity. Of course this was a robbery.

Stopping, he spread his hands and said, "You've picked the wrong man to rob, my good fellow. I haven't a thing that would interest you."

The weasel-faced man edged closer to Jared, waved there by the gunman. Both were nervous, Jared noticed, but the unarmed man was especially so. Then he realized why. The man was afraid of Infidel. To reach Jared as he was being instructed, he had to keep his back to Jared's horse. He was, in fact, badly positioned, stuck between the two horses. It made him of little use to the man with the gun.

Certain the gunman would not shoot his accomplice, Jared whistled sharply between his teeth, knowing that would set off Infidel. Obligingly, the stallion reared. The frightened thief either lost his footing in the packed snow or threw himself to the ground, distracting his partner.

The one moment of confusion was all Jared needed to launch himself at the portly gunman, whose reaction wasn't swift enough for him to manage to fire the pistol more than once. That shot went wild, but it served to agitate the horse harnessed to the overturned sleigh, trapping the second man.

Jared struggled briefly with other one, kicking the gun into the deep snow as soon as he forced it from the man's grasp. "Grimes!" the man yelled in outrage just before Jared knocked him down.

Before his crony could recover, Jared bounded to Infidel and mounted up. He wheeled the stallion around and galloped away. Over his shoulder he saw the two men crawling in the snow, their heads bobbing up and down. The one he'd hit now hit the other, in payment for his failure; then they both tried to recover the gun.

For the distance of perhaps half a mile, Jared enjoyed the fact that he'd outwitted and escaped them, fools though they were; but then he grew sober. Although the ambush had certainly been an attempt at robbery, something about it didn't ring true.

Why had they been waiting there? The setting was so

isolated. He was the only traveler likely to be seen along that stretch of road, especially at this time of day. Could it have been a trap set just for him?

That didn't make sense, and yet the thought had great staying power. Then Jared remembered another incident, that morning when his hat had been shot through. He'd dismissed that as an accident, but what if it wasn't? What if this inept "robbery" was another attempt on his life? Jared tried to shrug off the notion.

It wouldn't leave.

As soon as he reached home he sent Ned and three others, all armed, back to investigate the scene. He didn't expect them to find anything, but he gave them orders to search the ground for the gun. Possibly the thwarted robbers hadn't found it before they had to leave the scene. Jared couldn't imagine them feeling comfortable enough to make a protracted search.

Without the gun, he would have only the name Grimes and his clear images of two unsavory faces to guide him in his search for the men. It would have to be enough, because he didn't intend to forget the incident—or to forgive whoever was behind it.

That decided, Jared strode to the house, eager for news of Carina. He waved Trudy away from the room and took the chair. She said the same thing her mother had told Bagley, that Carina was better. Jared wanted to see for himself. She woke up once and stared at him.

He bolted up from the chair. "Carina?" he cried out, but she slipped back before he could be sure she had recognized him. When Agnes came with his supper, she told him Dr. Browning had given Carina a mild sleeping powder.

"He expects her to be much better by morning," she said, shooing him away.

"I want to talk to him then," Jared told Agnes. "I'm tired of getting secondhand notice."

By morning he had Ned's report that they had found nothing at the scene of the overturned sleigh, just disturbed snow. He took Infidel for a ride back to the spot to double-check his premise that the ambush was meant for him alone and not just any unlucky traveler.

He found no evidence either. Hyperalert to everything around him, he found the ride uncomfortable. No one shot at him, but he knew it would be a long time before he would ride out again without that edgy awareness of his own mortality going with him. He didn't like the feeling, but he accepted the need for it.

On his return to the house, Jared found Dr. Browning waiting in his study. "I hope you have good news," he said dauntingly.

"I do. Our patient is going to recover very nicely, I'm happy to say."

The tightness in Jared's chest finally eased, and he tried to smile.

Browning succeeded where Jared couldn't. His smile was full of understanding. "Now you won't have to shoot me," he joked.

"I'm sorry. It's just—"

"I understand, believe me." After he paused, allowing Jared to collect himself, he added in a soft voice. "Do you intend to marry the girl?"

Jared's head jerked around in surprise. "Marry?"

"You care for her, that's obvious," Browning said. "I thought—"

"That's not your job."

"I see."

The statement was loaded with implication. "That's not your job either," Jared snapped.

"Then you don't know," the doctor said softly. "I wondered."

"Don't know what?"

"The girl is about three months along, Jared. Knowing your experience, I thought perhaps some of your concern was for the child. But they're going to be fine, both of them."

Jared's mouth opened and closed, soundlessly as a fish's.

Browning gave him a wide smile. "Ah, well. So she's kept her counsel, has she? Women do that sometimes. She probably didn't want you to worry. In her case you really shouldn't, you know. She should deliver well, and this little upset hasn't done either of them any harm. Once she's on her feet again, in a week or so, everything will be fine."

That wasn't the way Jared saw it. Not at all.

# *Chapter Twenty-Four*

Jared never went to Tyler's rooms, but he was about to break that rule. It was a day for exceptions. Well into the month of March, Boston was being teased by the promise of spring. False spring, Jared called it.

He strode up Beacon Hill, his long legs stretching out to level what was in fact a modest slope. Tyler's place was even more modest. Not all of Beacon Hill was fashionable, and Tyler had found a section that was just faded enough to be romantic without slipping past some indefinable standard into seediness. As Jared surveyed the puddling piles of slush at Tyler's doorway, he conceded that his friend had managed to find a perch precisely on the cutting edge of distinction.

Typical Tyler, he decided, banging heavily on the door. The man who answered looked worse than the neighborhood. His hair stood on end, and his eyes narrowed to slits against the bright sunshine pooling around Jared. "Mr. Meade is not receiving callers this morning."

Jared pushed on the door, catching him off guard. "He'll receive me."

An overturned chair in the parlor gave the cramped room a dissolute look. Stepping around it, Jared opened the door beyond, sending it crashing back against the wall.

Tyler sat up, cursing, then fell back to hold his head and demonstrate his fluency within a narrow range of expression.

Jared folded his arms over his chest and leaned against the door frame, his head cocked in an attitude of interest. Before Tyler finished, he took two steps to right another upset chair at the foot of the bed.

"Have a care, will you?" Tyler groaned. "The poor fellows downstairs are even worse off. They don't want elephants tromping over their heads at this hour."

Jared looked at the bare floor. "Downstairs? There are people under you?"

"The house is built on a hill, Jared. Must you be dense?"

Jared was looking the room over. "So this is where my future wife lost her virginity," he said in a wondering tone.

"What . . . ?"

"I *said*—"

Tyler sat up slowly. "I heard, I heard. But it doesn't make sense."

"Nor to me," Jared answered. "Especially now that I see the place. It lacks . . . well, almost everything, wouldn't you say?"

Tyler twisted uncomfortably, as though he searched for his misplaced dignity in the welter of the bed. "Where's Edward?"

"The man who answered the door? I don't think he's in any better shape than you are. Do you always carouse with your manservant?"

"He wasn't here," Tyler snapped. "He has other fish to fry."

"I see." After a few more seconds of watching Tyler as if he were a captive creature on display, Jared asked, "Would you like me to help you or should I leave?"

"Guess."

"I'll be back in"—Jared consulted his watch—"twenty minutes." Snapping the cover back, he pocketed his watch and left, warning, "I will be back, don't doubt it."

The air outside seemed doubly fresh now, and Jared used the time to check the number of buildings in the area that boasted entrances to below-ground rooms. Always interested in finding out new things, he was in a better frame of mind almost immediately. But, when he returned, Tyler wasn't interested in hearing his figures. They merely earned Jared another grim glare.

"What's this nonsense about Carina?" Tyler asked. Dressed now, he had wet hair, plastered to his head. The improvement in his appearance was minimal.

"Carina was here, too?"

"Miss O'Rourke has never been here. You said something about your future wife—"

"And you assumed I meant Carina."

"Jared, if you came here to kill me, just get it over with. Don't torture me."

"Why would I want to kill you?"

"Perhaps because you're talking marriage. In that case, the person to kill is yourself, not me."

"Why not the woman?"

"Kill both of you, I don't care." Tyler turned away indifferently.

"Not even if the woman in question is Rachel Farmington?"

His head snapped around. "Rachel? What has Rachel to do with you?"

"That's what I asked my uncle."

"Nathan?" Tyler started up from his chair, then thought better of the effort. "I don't follow this. Start at the beginning."

"I wasn't there at the beginning," Jared said. "Or perhaps I was. I did introduce you to my lovely cousin, maliciously, I admit, hoping that you'd distract her from me. Now, months later, Uncle Nathan is looking for someone to marry the girl, and whom does he suggest? Not you, her constant attendant, but me."

"Well, I'm not the marrying kind. That's well known." Tyler's smile was smug.

"That's true. You're a well-known waste. I guess I can't blame Rachel for seeking better for her child."

"Her *what!*"

"You've heard of children. They come as either male or female, in small squalling bundles. The consequences, sometimes, of the act of—"

"Jared!"

He fell silent and simply looked at Tyler, who stared back.

Finally Tyler said, "She didn't tell me. I mean, she cried and carried on . . . but she didn't say . . . *that.*"

"Perhaps she was ashamed. She *is* young. She might not have known then, or been sure." The subject was so painful to Jared he couldn't speak normally. He'd wanted to taunt Tyler. Instead, he was twisting the knife lodged in his own gut.

*Who had fathered Carina's child?* That was what he wanted to know.

No. He didn't.

But, God help him, he had to know.

Tyler said Carina hadn't been here. He knew that. She'd barely left Falls Village. But Tyler had been there once when Jared was gone.

And there was Dennis Boynton. He could have come at night. . . .

God, but he was sick of his thoughts on that score.

"Why did she name you?" Tyler asked.

For a moment Jared couldn't make sense of the question. Then he recalled his reason for being here. Rachel. No, not Rachel. He didn't give a damn about Rachel. She was an excuse for this confrontation.

"Didn't you just tell me you turned her down?" he asked Tyler. "Perhaps she took you at your word. Besides, it may just be Nathan's way of getting even with me."

Silence stretched between them. Outside, a wagon

stopped at the next house and two men began a loud discussion of how best to unload a large crate.

Remembering his purpose in coming, Jared said, "It won't be so bad, perhaps. Rachel's a lively sort, and Nathan did say he's making her his heir. If the child has your looks, no one will notice because Rachel is fair. Unless the child has your eyes. Hers are sort of brown, aren't they?"

Tyler heaved himself from the chair, not even bothering to groan over his head. The news had sobered him. "You're going to marry Rachel?"

"Why shouldn't I?"

"What about Carina?"

"What about her?"

"Well, don't you owe her some"—after a search, Tyler settled on a word—"consideration?"

No, Jared thought bleakly. Not after what she's done.

"Marrying Rachel changes nothing," he said. "All I'm doing is giving my name to her child. I can still have Carina."

Tyler paced to the narrow window and gazed out sightlessly. "Rachel won't like that."

"No, she probably won't," Jared said evenly. "Little better than I like marrying her."

"You don't have to do it."

"No."

"Then why?"

"It comes back to another question, one of indifference. Why not?" Jared waited for a reaction, and when there was none, he added, "Besides, I've always wanted a child."

Tyler sent him a look of disbelief. "Another man's child?"

The pain inside Jared shifted, pieces of it rubbing together the way sections of rock grate against each other just before an earthquake. "Why not?" he repeated. "It wouldn't be the child's fault."

366

"Then why not marry Carina and have your own children?"

Jared made sure his smile was nonchalant. "Marriage doesn't guarantee paternity, Tyler. Surely you know that."

Evidently, he didn't have the tone right, because Tyler wasn't fooled. "You doubt Carina." It wasn't a question.

"Would you vouch for her?"

Tyler simply stared at him.

"There? You see? You're not sure of her, so why should I be?" His triumph tasted bitter as gall.

"You're wrong," Tyler said flatly. "If ever a woman wore her heart on her sleeve, it's Carina O'Rourke. She's plain as window glass."

*Plain? Carina?* Jared smirked. Even as a virtual prisoner in his household, surrounded by his people, she'd found a way to betray him. "Perhaps she's loyal to you, then," he said, watching Tyler carefully. "You were there when I was not."

"You think I . . . ?" From incredulity, Tyler went to grim amusement. "Even if I'd wanted to, it wouldn't have been possible, Jared. The woman is besotted with you."

Because Jared wanted to believe, he refused to do so. He told himself he was being strong, being a man, taking his nasty medicine instead of accepting his friend's word. Tyler wanted him to feel good. For that reason, his words were suspect.

"Jared, I went there expressly to test your little bluebird, I admit that. She seemed too good to be true. I wondered if Dennis Boynton sent her there as a trap of some kind. He's devious enough for it. But I never got the slightest response from her."

"She's clever, Tyler. Smart. She knew what you were doing."

"Yes, she did. But I swear she cares for you. No one could be that good an actress."

"She is. I've seen her play all sorts of roles. It's a gift she has."

"Tell me why you suspect her? What has she done?"

"I . . . can't. Really. But it's major."

"Jared, this is me. Tyler." He put himself in Jared's way. "Did you find her in bed with—"

"No!" Just the thought hurt him.

"What then?" He followed Jared, dogging his steps in the small room. "I'm not going to give up."

Jared couldn't stop himself. The words exploded from his mouth. "She's pregnant!"

Tyler waited. There had to be more. "And?"

"She didn't tell me."

He studied his friend, thinking back to the trim-waisted woman he'd visited. Not a child conceived before she went to Jared, obviously. Then what? Something about the telling. "How far along is she? And if she didn't tell you, who did?"

Even when Tyler had heard Jared's confused out-pouring, he couldn't find Carina's offense. But when he said so, he alienated Jared. He didn't give up, however. "There's something you're not telling me. Something that makes sense of all this. What is it?"

"I can't tell you."

"Won't, you mean," Tyler guessed. "But don't worry. You've intrigued me. I'll figure it out."

Jared wasn't pleased to hear that. He'd never meant to reveal his own hurt, only to make Tyler face up to his responsibility to Rachel. Had he really been blind enough to think he could—or should—arrange Tyler's life for him? Especially now that his rift with his parents seemed on the mend. Word of his marriage to a Farmington would not please the Meade family.

Tyler blocked the door. "What does Carina say about this baby?"

"I've not talked to her . . . since . . . She was ill, as I told you." His voice was thin, strained. "I left."

"Good God, man! While she was sick?"

"She recovered. I told you."

"And you haven't been back?"

"No." Jared bit off the word, then went on, "You don't understand, Tyler."

Tyler beamed. "Not yet. But I will. I love a puzzle." He paced from the door, too busy with his thoughts to notice that he was leaving the exit unguarded. "You weren't practicing some form of birth prevention I don't know about, were you, old man? No, no." He laughed, holding up his hand. "Don't tell me. It's all too dreary."

Jared had reached the door and was about to make his getaway when Tyler made the connection and stopped him.

"Of course! You . . . Jared, your child, the boy who died at birth—"

"Was not my child." Jared supplied the information in a strangled voice. "So now you know. I'm infertile." Shoulders slumping, he could barely keep himself upright.

"By whose word?" Tyler asked.

"What?"

"Who said the child wasn't yours? How do you know?"

"Why . . . Melissa told me. Her exact words—do you want those?" Jared asked bitterly.

Tyler watched him with intense eyes. "I'd like to be merciful and say no, but I think I need to hear them. And, more importantly, I think you need to say them to someone else." After the pause lengthened, he asked, "You never have told a soul this, have you?"

"Would you?"

"I don't know," Tyler answered truthfully. "I'm not as tough as you are." But tough or not, Jared looked as though he would fall down at any minute. "Here, sit down." Tyler pushed Jared into the single chair and took a seat on the bed facing his friend. "Now, tell me," he ordered.

"Lord, I loved Melissa, you know that, but . . ."

369

"But she was a bitch." Tyler finished what Jared couldn't.

His friend grimaced. "Once I would have knocked you cold for saying that."

"I wouldn't have said it then, but it was the truth before you acknowledged it."

Jared sighed heavily. "I guess so. She had me fooled, though. For so long. I've been thinking about all that." His eyes met Tyler's briefly, then slid away. "That's why this whole business has me in an uproar. Carina, well, she seemed so different, and then to have this—"

He broke off again and Tyler waited for him to find his own way.

"Melissa didn't tell me either, not until I noticed . . . I mean, I *saw* how . . . Well, anyway, she wasn't happy about it, but I was." Jared looked sheepish. "The truth is, I made a fool of myself over it."

Tyler felt driven to say, "That's the way it's supposed to be. The whole thing is such a goddam miracle, when you think about it."

Some of the pinched whiteness left Jared's mouth. "Melissa wanted to go to Boston long before it was time. She didn't like Dr. Browning, she said. We had heavy storms that time of year, you may remember, and we didn't get away in time. When her labor began, early I thought, I sent for Browning and the women helped her—primarily Nellie, but Agnes, too. They did their best, and I sat with her to hold her hand and wipe her face."

At Tyler's look of surprise, he said, "I know it isn't done, but, damn it, I wanted to help and it was my child." A flare of pain went through him, stopping his words. "That's what I thought anyway."

"When did she tell you?"

"Dr. Browning came. He said the baby was large, and Melissa was small. He took me away to warn me. I argued that she was delivering early, but he remained firm about that and he wouldn't let me go back to her. I would have insisted except that Melissa didn't want me there either. It seemed a kindness to respect her wishes.

"It went on forever, but finally the baby was delivered. I never saw him—never wanted to."

"Why not?"

"By the time I could have, I'd learned that he wasn't my child," Jared said in a voice he willed to steadiness. "Melissa was in trouble, bleeding terribly. Dr. Browning had her packed in snow—it seemed a horrible thing to do, and Melissa certainly thought so. She demanded to see me, as I was demanding to see her. Dr. Browning took everyone away so we could be alone."

"He knew she wouldn't make it?"

"I think so. He probably thought we'd exchange loving vows." Jared gave a bitter laugh. "That's what I intended, but Melissa had other plans. I can see her now, her eyes glittering. I've thought perhaps she was insane with pain and fear. Maybe that's why she wanted to hurt me. Maybe she blamed me for the fact that she was dying. I don't know.

"All I know is that she grabbed my hand and said, 'Don't congratulate yourself for this baby and for getting rid of me.' Can you imagine? I was stunned. I tried to soothe her. I said she wasn't herself, that she'd get better. She cut me off. 'It's not your child,' she said. I've never seen such hate in anyone's eyes, Tyler, and it was all for me. She kept saying the baby wasn't mine.

"Finally, I demanded to know who the real father was. She laughed. Laughed! She said I'd never know. That it was a friend, a *good* friend of mine. She said he was a real man and I wasn't. That she'd never have had a child by me, that I wasn't man enough to give her or any woman a child."

Tyler tried out in his own mind different ways to reassure Jared. They all sounded empty, *felt* empty. And anyway, Jared was still lost in the past.

After a long silence he said, "So you see how it was."

"You believed her?"

"Wouldn't you?"

"Not necessarily. Even if that child wasn't yours, it doesn't mean you're incapable of fathering a child. And I wouldn't take Melissa's word for anything."

"You think she'd lie about something like that? On her death bed?"

Tyler nodded.

"Why?"

"To hurt you. Tell me, did she know the child had died?"

"No. He outlived her, and anyway, no one would have told her. To have her go through what she did and have the baby die, too? It would have been cruel."

"Cruel," Tyler repeated. "After what she told you?"

"No one knew that. I . . . left her and went off, crashing around the woods. I was probably certifiably insane just then."

"Did you think I'd been involved with her?" Tyler asked after a pause.

"At first, yes. You were—and are—my closest friend. But you didn't like her. I knew that."

"Do you know why?"

"I can guess."

Tyler saw that he had figured out some of Melissa's meanness. "She wasn't worth your little finger, Jared. I could never figure it out. You treated her so well."

"I was a blind fool," Jared said. "I'm afraid I still am."

"I was afraid of that," Tyler told him. "That's why I wanted to see Carina for myself, to see if she was like Melissa. I have good instincts about people. But she's the real article. You can trust her."

"No. My mind is made up." While Tyler watched, Jared pulled himself together, bit by bit. "I came to tell you about Rachel. I wanted to be sure of how you felt about her before I tell Nathan I'll marry her."

Tyler exploded. "That's the craziest thing I've ever heard of!" He'd nearly forgotten about Rachel in light of Jared's revelations. "Why should you marry Rachel?"

"I told you—"

"I know you did, but think, man! Just listen to yourself. The woman you love is pregnant, but you won't marry her. Instead you'll marry someone you barely like, someone who's carrying my child!"

Jared didn't argue. He listened and waited, as if he wondered when Tyler would get to the point of his diatribe. "Yes," he said finally.

"Why not marry Carina instead? Obviously, you don't mind that Rachel's child isn't yours. Why not have the woman you love? The one who loves you!"

"I'll keep her with me and take care of the child. Don't worry, I won't be cruel to her. I just won't marry her. I don't care what Rachel does, or did. I don't care what she does in the future, either. Don't you see? But I won't—I *can't*—trust Carina."

"You can, Jared. I tell you, you can. What's more, you have to."

"No."

"Otherwise, you let Melissa win. She poisoned your mind, and if you let her have the last word, you give over your whole life and happiness to her. Then you have nothing to give Carina or any woman. Even Rachel."

Jared sat like a stone.

"You think you're being noble, don't you?" Tyler demanded.

"No. I'm being realistic."

"You're being a fool. And if you marry Rachel thinking she'll let you tuck her away somewhere while you keep Carina and a child right in your household— think again. That's not the way Rachel works. That's one very strong-minded young woman."

Jared gave Tyler a superior smile. "Then maybe you should marry her."

"No!"

Jared got to his feet slowly. He put out his hand to Tyler, who, puzzled and wary, took it. "It looks like a standoff to me, but then, why not? Advice is cheap, they say."

The man Jared left behind was frustrated and irritable. He kicked at the chair and sent it toppling over. One of the men downstairs banged on the wall in protest. Tyler stomped on the floor, then gave up and fell back on the bed.

He knew what Jared was up to, and he wasn't going to fall for it. Jared had no intention of marrying Rachel. He was trying to force Tyler's hand, make him jealous. But it wasn't going to work.

No one—not even boneheaded Jared—was stupid enough to marry someone he didn't love when the woman he *did* love carried his child. Carina and Jared would work things out, he was sure. And Rachel would never allow herself to be used that way. She'd show herself as she was, and Jared would go running back to Carina.

But he couldn't get Rachel out of his mind. He kept seeing her as she'd looked when she'd left him. Her dignity. Her strength of mind. She had such fire, and she had his baby growing inside her. . . .

If Jared did marry her, he'd never love Rachel's child as he would Carina's. And whoever heard of such a situation? It was absurd. Rachel deserved better and so did Carina.

But, oh God, he didn't want to get married. He'd have to give up being Tyler Maxwell, and he wasn't ready for domestication.

He put the whole situation out of his mind—or tried to. He thought he was doing rather well at it, too, until he looked across a crowded salon three nights later and saw Rachel on Jared's arm. She was watching him talk to Natalie Brisby, looking at him as if his every word came edged in gold.

The next thing Tyler knew he was across the floor, hauling Rachel from the room. He went to three doors before he found privacy, in the process passing his sister without a sign of recognition. Susan turned to stare after him, then blinked and shrugged, turning away.

The place Tyler settled on was not even a room. It was a storage area off the music room where chamber musicians sat about tuning their instruments for a concert later. Tyler heard none of their scrapings and pluckings. He didn't even notice Rachel's struggle to free her arm as he spun her about, demanding, "How could you do such a thing!"

"And what is it that I've done?" she asked, kneading her upper arm to restore her impaired circulation.

"Trapping Jared into a marriage he doesn't want."

"That's not the impression he gives me." Rachel smiled with infuriating composure. "He's very . . . gallant, I would say."

"You know he has a mistress. And he's not going to give her up."

Rachel's smile widened. "I know his intentions along that line, but I have great faith that once we're married he'll change his mind. I can be quite . . . persuasive."

"His first wife played him false, Rachel, so have a care how you proceed with him," Tyler warned. "You'll not find him overtrusting."

"I never wanted a fool for a husband," she retorted. As Tyler had known she would, Rachel gave as she got. "He's been honest with me and I'm honest with him. I think we'll deal together well."

"Deal together! Just listen to yourself! Is that the way to go into marriage?"

"You think I should simper about *love*." She sneered. "I've learned about that, Mr. Meade. From a master. Now I want a life that makes sense. You taught me well, so you can hardly blame me for growing up at last."

"Growing harsh, you mean. You sound like a desperate spinster, too long on the vine."

"Your names don't disturb me, Tyler. I know myself, and I know what I want."

"You want a man who doesn't want you."

"And you do?" she challenged. "How strange that I

didn't notice when I offered myself amid tears of anguish."

Tyler plowed his fingers through his golden hair as though he would uproot every strand. Instead, the sculpted waves fell back into place the instant he removed his hand. Rachel watched in such fascination she had to ask him to repeat his question to her.

"What are you doing here anyway?"

"Here?" She puzzled. "Why I'm going to hear the chamber music and talk to—"

"You were in Lowell."

"Oh, that. Jared brought Uncle Nathan and me here for safekeeping. Now that I'm Uncle Nathan's heir, he worries that Enoch will do us harm."

Tyler ground his teeth. "Enoch! The man's a menace."

"Which is another reason I need a strong, smart husband," Rachel said.

"I should be that man!"

"Is that a proposal?"

She was laughing at him!

"Yes, damn it all, it is! That's my child you're carrying, and I can take care of my own responsibilities."

Rachel merely patted his arm consolingly, provoking him to absolute fury. "Don't worry, Tyler. You can go right on living your free and unfettered life. I make no claims on you. Jared will take care of everything."

Before he could stop her, she opened the door and stepped out into the now-quiet music room. The moment she appeared, the men bent over their instruments and resumed tuning.

# Chapter Twenty-Five

"Jared? May I talk with you?"

The look he gave her wasn't promising, but Carina forced herself to wait at the door without flinching. She'd come to his room out of desperation. Jared was seldom at Falls Village anymore, and when he was, he avoided her. It was almost May. Everyone in the household knew about her baby except the father. It was time to correct that oversight.

"Can it wait for another time, Carina? I'm really very busy."

She wanted to laugh out loud. He stood at the clothes press with his back to her, for no other discernible reason than that his shirt was untucked. She permitted herself a wry smile and said dryly, "Yes, I can see that. But I won't take much of your time."

He didn't turn until he had set his clothes right. And then his expression was both impatient and disdainful.

It wrung a cry from her. "Oh, Jared, what's wrong between us? Why do you look at me like that?"

That wasn't what she'd meant to say.

"I don't know what you mean." His voice was so cold she felt her skin crawl.

"I mean you look at me with indifference, or perhaps it's loathing. You have ever since I was sick. Did you want me to die?"

"Don't be dramatic. It's not your style."

Carina's knees went weak. She put one hand on the door frame to steady herself. The other hand went, unconsciously, as it did so often now, to her thickened abdomen. Her dress was designed to disguise her changing shape, but the protective gesture undid all of that, drawing Jared's eye.

He moved forward quickly and led her to a chair. In her travail, Carina missed seeing his concern for her. Instead, she was further undone by the touch of his hand, the first touch she'd received from him in weeks.

"It's late. You should be in bed." His voice was gruff but soft. It gave her hope.

"I'm not sick anymore, Jared. Is that what you think? Is that why you keep your distance now?"

"Of course not."

"I didn't mean to get sick and be a burden. Everyone told me how kind you were, how upset." She smiled as winningly as she could. "You stayed with me until I was out of danger; then you left." She hoped he would hear the question in that statement. The one she didn't dare ask.

If he heard it, he didn't acknowledge the fact. "I did nothing," he said, as curt now as before.

Carina swallowed back the hurt that rose like bile in the back of her throat. How had she gotten off on this tangent? She took a deep breath and tried to regain her dignity. "You were very kind and I want to thank you."

He made an impatient move, and she hastened to say, "But that's not why I came to talk to you." Going on was harder. "I have something to tell you."

A look of near panic came over Jared's face, and somehow that helped settle Carina. It occurred to her that here was the explanation for Jared's behavior of late. He already knew about the baby, and it frightened him! After all, he had lost a wife and child in childbirth. Naturally, he would worry about the danger her condition presented.

All at once everything made sense. He was no fool. He must have noticed the physical change in her, perhaps in the intimacy of the sickroom, and, out of misplaced concern for her, had decided to keep his distance.

It was exactly the explanation Carina had sought since her recovery. Along with her sudden, intuitive understanding came a surge of joy such as she had not known before. Jared hadn't rejected her after all. A confused mixture of tenderness and exasperation bubbled up inside Carina.

She had been so worried!

Laughing, almost crying with relief, she got to her feet and faced him. "You know what I'm going to say, don't you? *That's* why you've stayed away!"

He backed off, alarmed by her altered mood. "Carina . . ."

"But it's all right, Jared. It's a perfectly natural state, I promise you. I'm well now and nothing will happen to me. Oh, Jared—"

He sidestepped to avoid her touch. He didn't exactly lunge, but the degree of his avoidance was deflating. "Please. Sit down," he said urgently. "You must."

All Carina's fears came back as she obliged him, sitting down hard. "I'm sorry. I must sound like a madwoman."

"Carina . . ."

Wary now, she asked, "You do understand what I'm talking about, don't you? I'm going to have a baby."

"Yes, I do know that."

"And you're not pleased."

He laughed harshly. "Is that what you expected? That I'd be pleased?"

"I hoped you might be," she said in a voice barely above a whisper. "You're so . . . kind to children."

His expression didn't soften. "Children are innocent."

Carina wasn't sure what to make of that statement. "I know of nothing I could have done to prevent this child, if that's what you mean."

"Don't you?"

"I don't understand what you're saying."

Instead of explaining, Jared paced to the window. His heels hit the uncarpeted floorboards like blows.

All Carina's optimism had flown, leaving formless doubts and fears that were not relieved by the uncompromising set of Jared's back and shoulders. She tried to think of something to say to him, of some way to reach him across the widening gulf that yawned between them.

"Perhaps I should leave."

As she started to rise, Jared spun around. "That's always your solution, isn't it? Running away!"

Her strength deserted her and she subsided. Waving a hand toward the door, she said weakly, "I meant, go to my room."

He wasn't listening. "You're not going to go anywhere. You're going to stay right here. You'll live here and bring up your child here."

Hearing her intention put like that, as an ultimatum delivered in a near shout, took away any sense of reassurance the words might have carried. Her mind became swamped with confusion.

Jared slowly stalked back to her. "Did you think to trick me into marriage?"

Carina sought and found her temper. "I told you I don't want marriage."

"No, of course not." His smile was sarcastic. "Neither did I—for all the good that does me."

"I won't marry you, Jared. I won't be forced."

Her grand declaration fell flat.

"I'm not asking you." He put a slight emphasis on the last word.

Carina could only stare at him.

Before she could gather her wits, he went on. "You always said I should marry a lady, someone who could stand at my side in society. So that's what I'm going to do."

Her head swam. Denials rose and she bit them back.

She wet her dry lips, feeling that speaking would make them crack and bleed. They barely formed the name—Susan.

"Not Susan," Jared said, reading her lips easily. Her dismay was evident, and he took an almost unholy pleasure in the fact that his announcement—one he'd had no intention of making at this time—was bringing her pain. "Her name is Rachel Farmington. She's Enoch's cousin and Nathan's heir. She's young, just eighteen or nineteen at most, and very beautiful."

Carina's face grew pale. For a moment Jared was afraid that she'd faint, but then she fought back. He almost laughed. How could he have worried? Carina O'Rourke was made of sterner stuff. Susan would be unconscious on the floor by now. Rachel would have heaved the washbowl—or the chamber pot—at his head.

Not Carina. She had her dignity. Always.

"I see," she said.

"I very much doubt that you do. I barely do myself," he said, turning away from the sight of her. Somehow he didn't enjoy watching her control her feelings. She was disappointed, not mortally wounded, and he wanted so much more.

She didn't bleed; he did. He had trusted her, believed in her honesty—and been wrong.

"It seems that Rachel, too, is with child," he said without looking at Carina. He heard, or felt, some disturbance from her, but when he turned back she was as composed as before. He kept his eyes full on her face, unwilling to miss her reaction to the rest of his statement.

"Like your child," he said deliberately, "Rachel's child is not mine. Nevertheless, I will marry her."

He saw the precise moment his meaning penetrated, saw Carina's surprise—shock, really—and the way she gathered herself to protest her innocence. Before she could add to her sins by lying to him, he raised his hand. "Don't! I don't want your lies. It's bad enough that you've abused my trust as you have."

She came to her feet, her natural coloring restored now. "You think this child isn't yours?"

"I know it's not."

Her lips formed a gentle, chiding smile. "Jared—"

"Don't say it. I know all that."

"Tell me what you 'know,'" she challenged.

"I know that *in spite of* what we have done together many times, the child you say is mine, cannot be."

"Jared, I have known no other man. Only you."

He smiled—hideously, he was sure. "Naturally, you would say that."

"It's the truth."

"No, Carina. I wish it were. God knows, I wish it more than you can imagine, but it's impossible. I cannot give you or any woman a child."

Carina stared at him as a slow-burning color rose from her neck. "You mean to say you . . . you're *barren?*"

Jared tried to find amusement in her terminology. "Infertile is the word you seek. Barren is the term for a woman." He sounded stuffy and punctilious, but whether it was his tone or his words that set Carina off, he didn't know.

She burst into incredulous laughter. "Oh, my dear Jared. You're so wrong! How can you think such a thing. Here I am! Living proof that you are fertile indeed."

"You prove only your own fertility, Carina."

"And who else could have fathered this child?" she demanded, still not really serious.

"Only you can be sure, of course, but I strongly suspect Dennis Boynton."

"Dennis! How? When?"

"Again, that's for you to say."

"Evidently not," Carina retorted. "Everything *I* say, you disbelieve!"

"All right," he responded, goaded. "My best guess is that you spent time with Boynton when you went to Lowell."

"Before Christmas? Jared, I took gifts to my family. Things I made for them as I made your shirt. I went to my father's house. That's all. As a matter of fact," she said, "I was already pregnant then. Mary Sweeney, the only person I saw that day, guessed my condition as soon as she saw me. She was concerned for me."

"Then you saw him some other time," Jared snapped.

"I don't know."

"No, you don't, do you?" She gave him a sad look.

"I don't want to know."

"Why do you doubt me? What have I done? I'm always here, surrounded by your household." Then Carina thought of something else—as he'd known she would, given time. "Your wife had a—"

"That child was not mine either," he said, cutting her off.

"Not yours? Jared, this is insane! You disbelieve your wife, me, and—" She stopped herself at that point, as if she were unwilling to speak of Rachel.

"You're wrong there. I didn't disbelieve my wife."

"What?"

"I loved my wife. I trusted her and welcomed the thought of our child. She herself disabused me of my foolishness just before she died. I argued with her, but she was adamant. The child was not mine."

"Oh, Jared. How . . . terrible."

"She hated me. It was obvious then as never before. I . . ." He faltered, then forced himself to go on. "I never knew why."

"I'm so sorry. She must have been—I don't know—perhaps out of her head, Jared. Sometimes laundanum does that, I understand. She probably had no idea what she was saying. You mustn't credit—"

He drew himself back from her sympathy. "You don't know anything about it."

Chastened, she said quietly, "Perhaps not. But I do know that what you're doing, condemning me because of someone in your past, is as wrong as what she did.

Humanly, I can understand somewhat, but I won't suffer for another's wrongdoing. Being here with you as I am is my own fault, I know. And perhaps I have to suffer for that. My father would certainly say so. I never thought that you would, though."

"Don't try to put me in the wrong over this, Carina. I've done you no harm."

"Nor I you, Jared. I swear it."

He dipped his head, acknowledging their impasse.

Carina looked at the door, uncertain whether or not she'd be able to walk back to her room under her own power. If only she hadn't come tonight. If only she'd kept quiet. Then she could go on pretending that Jared wanted her child. His child.

But she'd spoken as impulsively as she did everything else, and now she had to go on. The baby fluttered within her, reminding her that it was there and had to be considered.

As if she could forget.

Before she could leave she had to ask another question. "Your . . . marriage," she asked in a voice that quavered, "will be . . . when?"

"That's up to Rachel. She hasn't set the date."

"You know her well?" The awkward question slipped out. "I mean, I've never heard her name before."

"I barely know her and I don't particularly care for what I do know of her."

"Then why would you marry her?"

*And not me?*

"It's a business arrangement. Much like ours in some ways."

"Ours?"

"Our famous bargain," he reminded her. "You can't have forgotten so soon."

"That's in the past, Jared," Carina said, striving for dignity. "We no longer have classes, and you must agree that I've outstayed my welcome."

"I don't agree. I meant exactly what I said earlier. You

384

will stay here and bring up your child here."

"Why? You don't believe me. You don't trust me. You don't"—this last, it nearly killed her to say out loud—"even desire me anymore."

"I desire that you remain. That's all that matters."

"That's not true. My feelings and desires count as well. I have more to consider than you."

"I won't let you go to Boynton."

"I make no promises, Jared."

On that note, Carina tried to leave. She was seconds away from disgracing herself by letting fall a torrent of tears. She got to the door by concentrating on each step. There she attached one hand to the frame, her other arm braced across her abdomen as if the precious life she carried there would fall out otherwise.

"I make a promise to you, Carina, and you'd be a fool to ignore it. If you try to leave, I'll spare no expense, no trouble, no *anything* to bring you back. And I'll make your life a living hell once you're here!"


Jared shouldn't have told Carina he intended to marry Rachel. He knew it before she left his room, and the days that followed underscored that fact. His servants were like servants everywhere. They gossiped freely, and nothing set their tongues wagging faster than a hint of scandal. Carina's arrival had first roused their endless appetites, her pregnancy had fed them, and now that he had announced his intention to marry someone else, they were doubtless outraged.

He didn't know who had been Carina's confidante, most likely Trudy, or perhaps Agnes. She had told someone, he could tell. Although she herself was conspicuously absent—holed up in her room, he presumed—the servants watched him with disapproving eyes. He had not felt such censure since the first days Carina had been in his home.

At times the leaden atmosphere of the household

amused him. More often he was irritated. He could have gone to Boston, but that would have been running away. That was Carina's way, not his. His way was to face them down and say: I am master here. This is my home. It will be run to suit me.

He didn't actually do this, of course. One reason he didn't harked back to an adage of his grandfather's: If a man must announce that he is a gentleman; he is not. The same rule certainly applied to mastering one's household.

The second reason Jared held his tongue was less noble. His too-frequent absences made him feel that he no longer *was* master here. Somehow, in some way, Carina had become mistress in his stead, changing his house from a fortress where the lord of the manor ruled to a home where people lived. Except for what that signaled to Jared about his loss of authority, he liked the changes.

There had been a time when the furnishings in any given room were never moved. Then a man could walk anywhere in the dead of night with need of nothing more than a good memory. Now, each time he returned home he found that things had wandered away from their assigned positions.

His study was a case in point. His desk had always stood against the wall, facing blank space. Similarly, his lamp had been placed in the same spot for so long the wall above it bore the smoky residue of years of midnight oil. Sometime after Christmas, he'd discovered that the desk had been moved to, of all places, the middle of the room and set there at a strange angle. He'd been about to protest when he'd noticed something else. From just that place and no other, the person seated at the desk could rest his eyes and refresh his vision by gazing out upon a remarkable stand of birch trees.

It had become his favorite view. Birches were magical trees. Their parchment-clad limbs caught the first rays of the morning sun and reflected the amber and lavender tints of sunset. At night they plucked moonglow from the darkness to announce, radiantly, that they were still standing sentinel. In all lights and all seasons, the birches would remind Jared of Carina's thoughtfulness. In placing his desk just this way, she had tried to please him—and had succeeded.

Her success in that, as in so many things, only emphasized the incongruity of her larger failing. But he didn't want to think about that anymore. Since Dr. Browning's announcement, Jared had thought of little else. He was tired of it.

A familiar step at the door distracted him from the view. His gaze went to the books spread across the desk. Marcus had brought them from Billy Nichols and would return them in the morning—that is, he would if Jared did more that night than push them around and sigh. The prospect was unlikely.

The steps didn't go by, and Jared bent over a page, trying to look busy.

"Jared, I'd like to talk to you."

Frowning, Jared wondered when Bagley had stopped calling him *Mr.* Jared. Probably at about the same time he had switched his allegiance to Carina. All in all, Jared decided, he preferred the deferential way Carina approached him to Bagley's parental tone.

"I don't suppose you'd go away if I said I was busy, would you?"

"You're not busy. You're hiding," Bagley said.

"Not well enough, evidently."

Refusing to be goaded, Bagley shut the door and came to stand before the desk. He wore a serious expression that completely lacked deference, and, in spite of himself, Jared felt a great rush of affection for this intrepid little man well up inside him. He didn't want the lecture Bagley was about to give, but he would take it anyway.

Bagley cleared his throat noisily. "I never had a son, Jared, so I don't know much about being a parent. In spite of that, I've tried to stand in for your father—bless his soul—on those few occasions when it was necessary."

Jared sighed to himself. This was the full treatment. The big guns.

"When you brought Miss Carina here—"

"For the record, Bagley, Miss Carina brought herself here."

"That's not the point."

"No, you're right. It's not the point. And I did bring her back when she tried to leave." That still rankled. "I'm responsible for Carina. I recognize that."

Bagley looked slightly relieved, but only for a second. He was not a man to take the easy way. He would do his unpleasant duty. "I'm glad to hear that. Now, if you'll tell me one more thing, I'll go away and leave you to your work."

"And what might that be?"

"I want to hear that you intend to marry Miss Carina and—"

"Make an honest woman of her?"

"She's already that," Bagley said. As he was about to do when he was standing on his dignity, Bagley spoke stiffly and peered down the length of his bulbous nose at Jared. "And a devoted one. She would make you a fine wife."

"I won't debate Carina's merits with you, old friend, and I'd like to send you away happy; but I can't. Although I'm not ready to make a general announcement at this time, it's obvious that Carina has told someone my intention."

"Your intention?" Bagley's face brightened with hope.

That irked Jared. The lecture he would bear, but not the pretense of innocence. "As you well know, Bagley. It's what set you off, isn't it? Carina's crying in her room, and you can't stand it. Good God, man, she's got you wrapped around her finger. Did she send you to plead her case?"

"Certainly not. She is upset, but—"

"But nothing! I've told her, and I won't change my mind. I've told Rachel Farmington I'll marry her—"

"What! A *Farmington!*"

Jared smiled unpleasantly. "It has a certain neatness to it, doesn't it?"

"You've lost your mind!"

"Perhaps," he said equably, beginning to enjoy himself at last. "If that's so, then Carina can't blame you for your failure."

"Miss Carina did *not* send me here!"

"No, of course not. You heard from Agnes, who heard from Trudy. I know how these things go."

"It does explain Miss Carina's sorrow. We *have* been speculating on the cause for it," Bagley admitted thoughtfully, "but I never dreamed . . ."

"Now you know," Jared snapped. He wanted the interview over, especially now that he suspected that once again *he* had been the one to be speaking out of turn. It bothered him more than he wanted to admit that Carina had confided in no one. He put it down as another black mark against her character—unfairly, he knew.

"You do know about the baby she carries?" Bagley asked.

"I've known for a long time." For some reason, Jared didn't want to appear ignorant to Bagley. He should have known better. When Bagley disapproved, he *disapproved*.

"I thought as much." Bagley sniffed.

Jared had had enough. He got to his feet, squaring off against the man to whom he owed his life. "Since the child she carries is not mine, I suggest you take your lecture to Miss Carina, my friend. She's the one who needs it!"

Deeply shocked, rebuffed and affronted, Bagley opened his mouth, then shut it without another word.

When he was gone Jared sank back into his chair, trying to tell himself that shocking Bagley was victory enough to offset the hurt he'd put on the old man's face.

From the sidelong questions put to her by Trudy, Agnes, and even Nellie, Carina realized that her secret shame was no longer a secret. The whole household knew that Jared intended to marry Rachel Farmington. And worse—far worse in her mind—they also knew that he refused to accept her child as his. That each and every member of the staff believed in her truthfulness was no comfort to Carina. She felt shamed and exposed.

And trapped. Trapped in Jared's household and trapped in her room. She'd felt that way once before and had overcome those circumstances. She would do it again.

She forced herself to go on walks, alone and at odd times of the day in order to avoid Jared as well as those who were more sympathetic. These outings were, again, first steps she had to take. They were painful and slow but necessary.

As she returned from the grove at twilight three days later, she heard masculine voices in the quadrangle. Her first thought was to go back and wait awhile before going to her room. But she was tired and wanted to go inside. Indecision held her fast, and anger—Jared's anger— guaranteed she heard every word he yelled.

"Where is that boy? I swear there isn't a person in this place doing his job anymore! I'm surrounded by incompetents! *Sullen* incompetents!"

At first Carina wasn't sure who answered him, Marcus or Ned. Fearing that the boy who had annoyed Jared was Willie, she rushed forward, forgetting her need to avoid Jared.

"What's wrong?" she demanded.

The one with him was Ned, who, relieved to be rescued from Jared, greeted her with undisguised joy as he apologized for the fuss.

Which set Jared into another rage.

Ned shifted from foot to foot, embarrassed and uncertain. Seeing his dilemma, Carina gestured for him to leave, indicating that she would handle the problem. He walked away quickly, not even pausing when Jared redoubled his verbal abuse.

"Were you leaving or arriving, Jared?"

He turned away from Ned's hasty retreat to glare at Carina. "What difference does it make?"

She took in his belligerent stance, his surly expression, and said crisply, "Come with me, please." She didn't need to look back to know he was behind her. She could hear the ring of his heels against the paving stones.

Fuming, Jared followed, feeling like a child summoned from the playground by the teacher. He went only because he intended to nip this reverse in their relationship in the bud. Her exchange with Ned, her *daring* to give the man permission to leave before Jared himself chose to do so, proved that Carina had overreached herself. She had no authority at all in his household, nor would she ever, he told himself furiously.

Because his temper was roused, Jared didn't hurry as Carina did. When she reached the door ahead of him, she compounded her offense by opening the door herself instead of waiting for him to perform the service for her as a true lady would. Indeed, she didn't stop until she reached his study, sailing into that room, he noted, as if she had as much right to enter it as he did!

As Jared tallied his list of grudges he was secretly delighted that there were so many. He shut the door behind him, hoping she would sit in the desk chair. He gestured to it. The chair was wide, masculine looking, and his to offer, "Perhaps you'd like to sit down?"

His sarcasm was lost on Carina. "No, thank you. I will not be staying."

"How unfortunate," he sneered.

"Jared, I don't understand you. Your behavior is upsetting everyone."

"And that's why you see fit to dismiss a servant from

under my nose while I'm still talking to him?"

She didn't pretend not to understand. "You weren't talking, you were ranting."

He drew breath in order to start in on her, but before he could she held up one hand in warning. "Jared, please," she said in her softest voice. "I know you're angry at me. I don't really know why you—"

"Don't you?"

"I know your claim, but the point is, you mustn't take your anger out on everyone else. It's not fair to these good people that you should berate them in my stead."

"How noble you are! That must be the reason why everyone here takes your part against me."

"There is no 'my part,' Jared. I don't know what you mean."

"Of course you do. Your part is the story of how innocent and faithful you are as opposed to my part, which doesn't believe a word of it."

"Believe me, I've never discussed our differences with a living soul. If 'everyone' here believes anything about the issue, it's because you yourself told them about it. And for that, I most assuredly do not thank you!"

"No. You'll just creep around the house, being the injured party and making me the brunt of everyone's anger."

"You ask the impossible of me. I *am* the injured party, and I can't change that just to make you feel justified in your tyranny, Jared. I have done nothing at all against you—ever. And if I interfered between you and Ned just now, it was only to keep you from alienating a good and loyal servant. I may be able to forgive you for misjudging me—someday, perhaps—but not everyone will, you know!"

"I don't need or want forgiveness!" Jared snarled. He was ready to explode.

Carina shook her head sadly. "This is impossible, don't you see? Do you hear yourself? You're going to marry another woman, yet you insist that I remain here. It's crazy. You can't have two families. If you don't believe in me, you have to let me go—for your sake as well as mine. This situation is spoiling your life, too."

"I'll be the judge of that," he said stiffly. "And you will not leave."

"I haven't decided about that yet. I have to think what's best for my baby. The way you're acting now makes me believe you would not treat the child fairly. If you mistreat your servants because you're angry at me, might you not be unkind to him?"

Jared's face grew warm as he was beset by a curious combination of anger and embarrassment. "I wouldn't."

Carina tipped her head to the side, studying him. "I wish I knew why you're so insistent."

He said the only thing he could. "You are my responsibility."

"No, Jared. I'm responsible for myself. I came here of my own will. In spite of everything that's wrong between us now because of this child, I want and love it already. Perhaps I'll decide to stay—perhaps not. But whatever I do, I'll do it because it's best for the baby. Either way, I won't let you vilify me."

Still wrapped in her damnable dignity, Carina left him repeating over and over to himself that he insisted on her staying out of responsibility, not love. He didn't love her. He didn't believe her.

But he wanted to.

And it was tearing him apart.

## Chapter Twenty-Six

Carina looked up from her sewing as Willie stumbled over a word in the story he was reading to her. After a glance her way, he bent over the book and tried again.

"Cover the end of the word with your thumb and sound it out," she directed softly.

"But-ter-cup," he said, then flashed her a gap-toothed grin. "Buttercup! That's a good name for the yellow kitten." Ned had told Willie he could name the marmalade cat's new litter. "Now I just got the black one to go."

"Have you thought of any names yet?"

"Two. That's the trouble. I like Midnight *and* Inky both, so's I can't choose."

Carina knew the feeling. She was trying out names in her own mind. A girl would be Olivia for her mother, but finding a name for Jared's son wasn't easy. She had dreamed of having him choose, or at least of discussing names with him.

It was not to be. Two days after their confrontation in the study, Jared went back to Boston. It was not usual for him to go there so late in the spring, according to Bagley, so Carina could only assume that he was avoiding her or dancing attendance upon Rachel Farmington.

His dire threats aside, Carina believed she should move

from his household. Her love for Jared was what kept her tied in place, it and her hope that—somehow—Jared would come to believe her. Bagley and Agnes vied with each other to support her, encouraging her to be patient with Jared.

Bagley in particular swore that Jared would never marry Rachel, that he would die before allying himself with Nathan Wentworth's niece. Servants from both households often met on neutral ground in Lowell, where they exchanged gossip. Word from Nathan's servants was that Rachel, although inclined to put on airs, had proven herself staunch in support of her uncle during his illness.

Until Carina could decide about leaving, she kept busy making baby clothes and teaching Willie to read. He was bright and eager to learn—usually. Today his mind was not on reading. As she heard him mangle words he usually pronounced perfectly, she marveled at his beautiful soft voice, so different from the horrible Southern accent she had affected to fool Constable Meggers.

"You're gonna have a baby, too, ain't you?"

"Why, yes, I am, Willie. That's why I'm making such little clothes." She held up the gown she was hemming. "Can you believe you were ever so small?"

Instead of giggling or scoffing at the thought, Willie ignored the garment entirely. "My mama had a baby when she died," he said, then asked baldly, "Are you gonna die, too?"

Carina's sympathy was immediately aroused by his mention of his mother. "Oh, Willie, I'm sorry to hear that. I didn't know. It does happen sometimes, but not very often. You must miss her terribly still."

He looked away from her as though he was afraid to have her see his sadness. "'Twas a long time ago."

"Not so very long," she said, trying to let him know it was all right to mourn his loss. "My mother died years ago, and I still miss her. I'm sure I always will."

"You thinkin' of Jassie," he said.

"Jassie?"

"She wasn't my real mama. She just said I could call her that. My real mama died down South."

"Was that a real long time ago, Willie?"

"I was little, but I'member."

Like Marcus, Willie didn't know his age or his birth date. He seemed to be about eight or nine years old, as best Carina and Marcus could figure from their experience of children. Given the choice, Willie had decided to be eight so that more of his life could be spent with Marcus. Together they had decided to celebrate his birthday on the Fourth of July, a day Willie could be sure no one would overlook.

"Of course you remember," Carina murmured, shaken by this new information about Willie. "Did Jassie become your mother right then?"

He shook his head vigorously. "Didn't have no mamma for a long time. I followed Jassie 'cuz I didn't want to feed the master's dogs. They was *scary!* And when I kept goin' after Jassie, she said I might as well be her chil'."

"I'm glad she helped you, Willie. You've been a brave boy all this time."

But Carina's sympathy had not answered Willie's most pressing question. He asked again, "How you know you ain't gonna die havin' your baby?"

Carina let her needle fall still, and she looked at Willie. He was worried about her, afraid that he would—again— lose someone he'd come to rely on. She had to find a way to reassure him without lying. "I can't know I won't die, of course," she told him, "but I know the doctor says I'm fine and healthy. And my mother had four babies without dying."

"But you said she's dead."

"Yes, but not because of childbirth. She got a fever. It had nothing to do with having babies. I can't promise you that I'll be here forever Willie, but I promise I'll *try* to be. I don't want to miss seeing you grow up to be taller than Marcus."

That was Willie's professed ambition. Reminded of that, he smiled happily. "I'm gonna be this much taller!" He raised his hand as high above his head as it would reach.

Over the boy's head Carina saw Bagley, his face contorted with emotion, come to the door. A stab of alarm went through her. She put her needle into its case for safekeeping and nodded to Willie as Bagley told him he was to go help Ned. He didn't argue about the early end to his lesson with Carina. He liked Ned, and it was almost time for Marcus to return from Lowell.

"What's wrong, Bagley?" She got to her feet, clumsy after sitting for so long. "Is it Jared? He's not hurt?"

Bagley shook his head, trying to look reassuring and sympathetic all in one. His attempt doubled her misgivings. "I'm so sorry, Miss Carina. A messenger came with news . . . oh, I'm so sorry."

"Please tell me, Bagley. You're frightening me."

The little man wrung his hands and tears stood in his eyes. "There's been an accident. A boy came—"

"Not Marcus!"

He shook his head. "You should sit down, Miss Carina. The baby."

"What accident, Bagley!"

"At the mill. At the Shattuck." His eyes begged her to understand. Finally, he got out the words, "The picking room . . ."

Then Carina knew. "Oh, no! Papa! No! Not a fire . . ." She never really said the word, just formed it with her dry lips. "Are you sure?" she asked on a whisper of air, sinking down again into the chair. "Who . . . ?"

"A lad came, said his mother sent him. A neighbor."

"Sweeney."

"I believe that was the name."

"Where is he?" She tried to rise, but Bagley was there

397

to urge her to stay down.

"Cook gave him a bite to eat and something to drink, miss." He took her hand between his and patted it energetically, first with one hand, then the other. "He said to tell you your brothers and sister are with his ma— his mother." He quickly corrected the direct quote.

"Then Patrick wasn't there, too. Oh, Bagley, I can't believe . . ."

Carina began to cry as sorrow overcame her. Bagley stood by her side, giving her the comfort of his sympathy and presence. Questions surfaced in her mind, but at first she was unable to express them. The horror of death by fire, by explosion, consumed her.

Finally, she used the handkerchief Bagley pressed on her and pulled herself together. She had things to do.

"I must see Mary's boy, Bagley."

He steadied her as she rose, helping her until she could walk by herself. Going before him, she didn't see how closely he followed and how prepared he was to assist her if she faltered.

Sean Sweeney, not Shep, sat at the kitchen table, his eyes wide as he took in everything around him. At another time Carina would have enjoyed the way his wonder echoed hers on her first exposure to Jared's household. Today she saw only a familiar face from her past, someone who knew her father and the others who had died, someone who knew the mills. He was younger than Patrick, probably fifteen now, but well on his way to manhood.

He suffered her embrace with composure, aware that all eyes were on him as the bearer of bad news. In answer to her questions he revealed that no one inside the picking room had survived. The loss of life was said to be less than it might have been, because the explosion happened during a shift change when fewer workers were inside. For the same reason, the men involved were not all from one shift. Some, like Conn, had tarried to finish a task, and others had just begun to work.

Carina took in the information soberly, thinking of luck, of how her father's luck had run out. As if he read her mind, Sean said, "'Twas your Da's bad luck to be there at all, Rina. He's been in the yard so long now, but he was fillin' in for Tim Sullivan. He hurt his back, you know. I 'spect Sully's feelin' pretty strange. Lucky and guilty both, seein's it could'a been him gone now."

Carina's head reeled. She had forgotten. Part of her bargain with Jared had freed her father from the dangerous work in the picking room. Here was more irony, more coincidence, more evidence that her bargain had been made in vain. She squeezed Sean's hand in answer, unable to speak.

Releasing his hand after the painful moment passed, Carina got to her feet carefully. "If you'll wait a few minutes before you leave, Sean, I'll go with you."

Agnes came forward then. "Miss Carina, you mustn't. You have to think of—"

"My family, Agnes. My sister and brothers need me now." She summoned a smile for Agnes and for Bagley, who also stepped forward. "I'll pack a few things to take with me," she said, decisive now. "If I could have the use of the wagon, I'm sure Sean can drive me."

"Ned will take you in the carriage," Bagley said.

Trudy and Agnes helped pack her belongings, with Agnes displaying a pronounced reluctance that Carina was unsure how to interpret. She herself was so aware that she had arrived with nothing that she wondered if Agnes objected to her taking the clothes she had accumulated. She selected only those she could wear now that she bloomed with her child, and only the most practical and simple of those.

When Carina turned her attention to the baby garments she'd made, Agnes could not hold her tongue. "You don't need to take those, Miss Carina. You're coming right back!"

Carina knew better. Sad as the loss of her father was, it removed the single stumbling block in the path of her return home. She could go back to her family now, knowing that they needed her and that they would not judge her.

But she would not say that to Agnes.

"I know it's silly, Agnes, but I like to have them with me. And I use the ones I've made as patterns for more. I may not have time to make others, but I might; I don't know how long I will be needed."

Although Agnes couldn't refute Carina's reasoning, she made her displeasure plain. "I wish Mr. Jared was here. He'd have something to say about all this!"

Carina didn't doubt that, and part of her ached to lean against Jared's strength. But he wasn't there, and she had no assurance that he would ever comfort her again. Like her father, Jared had taken her measure and pronounced her lacking.

It seemed to be her fate to be turned away from love. Crying over it didn't help. She knew from experience. It would help no more now than it had years ago when she had pleaded with Papa for understanding. Now Papa was beyond her reach, just as Jared was. She couldn't change that, but she could help Margaret, Patrick, and Kevin, and she could do her best for Jared's unacknowledged child.

Bagley brought Sean with him to help carry parcels. Carina knew from his expression that everyone in Chapel Hill would soon know about the splendor of her recent surroundings. The lad's stories would not help her reenter her old life, but there was nothing she could do about that. She would be envied by some and reviled by more. But her family needed her, and that would have to suffice. She could change nothing, not her past and certainly not human nature.

The need to pretend that she was not leaving for good, only visiting her family, prevented Carina from saying good-bye as she wished. She would never forget Jared's people or the way they had opened their hearts to her, and it grieved her not to be able to express her gratitude.

She missed Gwen, who was off for the day, but got warm hugs from everyone except Agnes. Carina understood that the older woman wasn't demonstrative. Agnes showed her concern by fretting and disapproving. Cook, on the other hand, gave Carina boxes of food, some still warm from the oven.

But it was Willie's stricken face that drew Carina down again from the carriage. He hung back by the stable door, a shadow in the shadows. Appalled that she had overlooked him, Carina went to enfold him in her arms.

He didn't draw back, but he didn't respond either. "You promised you wouldn't go!"

"Oh, love, I know I did. I promised to *try*. But something happened, Willie. My papa died, and my brothers and sister have no one to care for them. I won't be far away, just in Lowell, and I'll come back to see you."

Hope and doubt stood as plainly in his eyes as the tears he tried not to let fall.

"I will see you again, Willie, I promise. I'll miss you so much . . . and Marcus." She fought her own tears, drawing him back into her embrace. "Be a good boy, sweetheart, and help Ned and mind Marcus. Perhaps he can bring you to my house. You're just about Kevin's age, you know. He's my brother, and I know you'd have a good time together."

Gradually, as Carina spoke, something of her conviction got through to Willie. His arms went around her, tight and hard. Over his shoulder, she could see the back of the waiting carriage still circled by Jared's servants.

"Give me a kiss, Willie love, and remember to do your reading every day now."

"I will," he promised gravely.

It was asking too much to hope for a smile. Instead, she kissed him back and walked quickly away. As soon as she was inside the carriage, fortunately alone, since Sean chose to sit up front with Ned, Carina burst into tears. She didn't look back to see if anyone waved good-bye.

She wouldn't have been able to see them, and she especially didn't want to watch Jared's house grow small behind her.

A steady stream of people passed through the O'Rourkes' door in the next day and a half. Conn had been well known in Chapel Hill, and Carina was now, she suspected, notorious. By offering condolences and delivering a dish of food, the curious and the censorious could come and stare at the neighborhood's newest fallen woman.

Carina greeted each visitor with courtesy, and she thanked them all for their kindness. Many were, indeed, kind. Many gave food they could ill afford to part with and pressed Carina's hand in sympathy, murmuring about Masses to be said and prayers already prayed. Carina focused on them, overlooking the envious glances that added up the cost of fabric in her dress and the spiteful looks that measured her thickened waist.

Conn's presence so permeated the room that Carina expected to hear his heavy tread upon the stairs at any minute. She half believed, she'd look up, and there Papa would be. He'd make one of his extravagant gestures, like the one in the picture of Christ cleansing the temple in Mama's Bible. "Get those sanctimonious old biddies out of here!" he'd roar, and the ladies would run.

The picture became so real, it overwhelmed Carina. She tried to laugh at herself. How could she miss such an irascible old scoundrel?

But she did.

At length she found herself alone, almost as if Papa had magically scattered everyone from her path. Solitude was a well from which few Chapel Hill people drank. At Jared's house, she realized, she'd come to appreciate privacy and separation. Now, suddenly, she had been granted time alone, and she wasn't taking advantage of it.

She urged herself up. She had to find suitable clothes for each of the children to wear to the funeral. Patrick was the best off, which was fortunate indeed. He seemed to have grown almost a foot above what she remembered.

He'd also steadied since his ordeal with Enoch Wentworth, becoming a man. Her return would affect him the least and Margaret the most. Carina hoped, with little expectation of fulfillment, that her reputation would not rub off on Margaret and make her young sister's life difficult. Margaret had already borne more than her share.

Carina sorted through the children's meager apparel, holding up first one garment and then another to the light. As she shook out what was obviously Kevin's best shirt, something fell to the floor. She bent to pick it up and discovered the willow whistle Marcus had helped her make.

Holding it to her breast, she let the tears roll down her face. "Oh, Papa," she said aloud to the room, addressing his spirit, which felt so close to her just then, "you did let them have their gifts. Thank you, thank you."

That was the way Jared found her, lost between joy and grief.

Carina didn't notice the draught of fresh air that came inside with him. But she smelled it on his clothes as he took her in his arms. It was exactly what she needed. His comfort. His nearness. His strength. With Jared she didn't have to be strong. She could cry and cry. And she did.

When she was finished he mopped her face and held his handkerchief for her as if she were two instead of twenty-two. Then it was time to face him.

"You came."

"As soon as I heard. I'm sorry, Carina."

"It's so horrible to think of—but you know that." She had been aware of the parallel between her father's death and his parents' murder from the start, but standing with him like this brought the pain closer. It also made it curiously easier to bear, because he understood.

"Yes."

"He . . . didn't need to be there, Jared. I keep thinking of that. You got him out, and then he went back as a favor to someone else. That wasn't really like him. I mean, he didn't generally do for other people that way. It makes me think it was his *fate*, almost."

Jared continued to stand close to her, supporting her with one arm about her back. She was afraid to think about his nearness, afraid he'd notice and move back. His response was a sympathetic murmur that encouraged her to go on. Later she would wonder at her lack of self-control and feel ashamed, but for now she had to talk or burst—and Jared was the only person with whom she could be totally honest.

"The worst thing for me is that he's gone now and I can never know if he forgave me for leaving."

"You did nothing wrong, Carina."

She understood that he spoke only of her leaving home, but she didn't dwell on that. "Now I can never make things right between us. It's over, and I always thought someday I'd come back and he'd be glad to see me. That he'd *love* me . . ."

"I'm sure he did love you. You're a daughter to be proud of."

Carina took his words for what they were, the comforting sounds one makes over someone who is suffering. She didn't take them to heart. She didn't dare.

Because she still clutched Kevin's whistle, she told him about the gifts and of her worry that Conn wouldn't let the children receive them. "Now I know he did," she said with a radiant smile.

"That's a good sign then, isn't it?"

It was exactly the right thing to say. Throughout the day he continued doing and saying the things she needed. He helped her prepare for the funeral, physically and mentally. And when they left for the church he was at her

404

side, with Margaret on his left. Patrick took her other arm, while Kevin clutched Margaret's hand like a lifeline.

The children took to Jared immediately, and Carina had never doubted that he would like her brothers and sister. Together, they made a formidable line, whether walking to the church or stretched out across half of one pew. They were conspicuous, of course, but allied with Jared, Carina felt the stares they got designated them as special, not as an oddity. They sat in the last of the rows reserved for the families of the dead, an altogether appropriate place, Carina thought.

After the Mass, each of the nine coffins was placed in a wagon for the drive to the cemetery. The solemn parade stretched out in both directions from Jared's carriage, with hearses and primary mourners in front of them and people on foot trailing behind the last vehicle to form an endless black river in the street.

What had begun as a fine May morning had changed during the lengthy service, so that the mourners emerged from St. Peter's under gathering clouds, and it was under a darkening sky that Carina walked with Patrick from the carriage to the burial site, following just behind him along the narrow path. When Patrick stopped abruptly she bumped him. Looking up, she saw why her brother had stopped.

Dennis bowed to her and stared at Patrick, who decided to go on and give Dennis time alone with Carina. Boynton had come to see them once just after she'd arrived home, but they had not spoken in privacy. Without thinking of how it appeared to Dennis, Carina glanced around to locate Jared, who had been detained.

"You give him every consideration, don't you, Carina?" Dennis commented acidly. "But does he do the same for you?"

"He is here."

"Does he give you his name? Does he give your *child* his name?"

"I am satisfied with my life, Dennis. You needn't concern yourself on my behalf." A strong gust of wind blew against her gown, molding it to her burgeoning shape. As Carina looked away from Dennis, she caught two matrons eyeing her, their mouths pulled down in distaste.

Then Jared was with her, taking her arm, facing down Dennis. He didn't speak to either of them, just placed himself beside her.

"He dishonors you," Dennis said, speaking over her head, addressing Jared in spite of his wording. "*I* would not do such a thing. *I* would marry you." His ringing tones made Carina cringe even before he added, "Even now!"

"She doesn't need you, Boynton," Jared said through bared, clenched teeth.

Before Carina could do more than catch her breath, Jared marched her past Dennis, into the line of mourners at the graves. Although the exchange between the men had set Carina's teeth on edge, nothing could take away the impact of so many graves, so many gaping holes in the ground, so many bereaved families.

Her annoyance with Dennis did serve her well in one way. It kept her rooted in the real world, aware that Jared's support was no more than a temporary crutch, on loan to her, so to speak, from Rachel Farmington. It reminded her that after this service Jared would go back to Falls Village or to Boston, and she alone would remain behind in Chapel Hill.

The thought was as sobering as the sight of all those yawning graves.

The wind picked up strength as the coffins were lowered into place. Around them, people turned away from the sight, sobbing. Margaret turned to Carina and buried her face on her sister's shoulder. Kevin clutched Carina's skirt, burrowing into her side.

Seeing the boy's distress, Jared picked him up and held him so that he didn't have to watch. At the very moment when they could leave, he led them all away, still carrying Kevin. Patrick brought up the rear, after Carina and Margaret.

Their small procession paused often as people spoke consolingly to Carina or Patrick, and soon Jared was effectively cut off from them, separated from them by the clumps of people who stood about under the increasingly threatening skies. From somewhere before them, Enoch Wentworth appeared, blocking their path. Carina halted, tightening her protective hold on Margaret and placing herself in front of Patrick.

Enoch bowed to them, saying with stiff courtesy, "My condolences on your loss, Miss O'Rourke."

She should not have been shocked to see him. The accident had occurred at the Shattuck, the mill he managed. Naturally, he would have to be here. But Carina had not seen him since the night he'd tried to drag her inside his house. His presence seemed a desecration of everything they'd just witnessed.

Her only proper response was a regal nod of her head, dismissing him to go and mouth his empty words to the next group he met. But Carina couldn't move. Couldn't form a word. She saw his outstretched hand and the gleam of gold from his ring. The one that had marred her cheek. She couldn't make herself reach out to take his hand.

Because she didn't, Enoch turned his spurned social gesture into something he undoubtedly intended to be avuncular and patronizing. He reached out to Margaret.

Carina moved then, instinctively. Fast as a striking snake, she slapped his hand away from Margaret. "Don't you dare touch my sister!" she warned in seething tones.

She had acted with characteristic impulsiveness, delivering a stunning insult, but she had spoken in low tones that didn't travel beyond their small knot of people. No one except Margaret and Enoch saw her strike Enoch's hand. Even Patrick, who was closer than any other person, missed the exchange. Had Enoch continued past them or withdrawn from the path before them, no one would have known about her offense.

Enoch did neither. Incensed, he reared back to bray down at Carina, "You dare to slap me? You little bitch!"

"I protect my family, Enoch Wentworth!" Carina threw the words at him, her voice still low but intense.

To Jared, who turned along with everyone else upon hearing Enoch's shout, Carina looked like a great cat, hissing at an enemy. He had never seen her look more beautiful or more female. She was the essence of motherhood, protective, warm, and strong.

In that moment, the scales fell from Jared's eyes, enabling him to see Carina as she was. She was wholly and completely a woman, a woman of honesty and integrity. Those qualities surrounded her like an aura he had been too blind to see. He knew then and there that she could never have betrayed him with another man. The child she carried was his.

His.

The knowledge rose in him, filling him with its sweetness.

The child was his and so was Carina.

Even as he hurried back to stand at her side, he knew she didn't need his intervention. Not this time. Perhaps she never had.

He went anyway.

By the time he reached Carina, Enoch had fallen back—in disgrace, if Jared was any judge of the disgusted looks cast his way. By opposing Enoch, Carina had spoken for everyone there. Her daring and courage, her willingness to defend her loved ones had instantly won over public sentiment, making her place secure again in the community she had left.

In the moments before the blindness of rage drained away from Carina, she sensed that Jared had come back. Knowing he was near to catch her if she fell meant that her legs didn't give way as the realization of what she'd done swept through her.

But her trials were not over yet. After a few steps her path was again blocked, this time by an elderly gentleman with a young lady on his arm. They were roughly the same height, the man leaning on the lady and supporting himself with a cane as well. He was well dressed, in sober clothes a little too big for him. A close look at his face revealed signs of illness, particularly the downturn of the left side of his mouth.

Before Carina could make the identification, he said, "Miss O'Rourke, I'm Nathan Wentworth. And this is my niece, Rachel Farmington."

After all she'd been through that day, it was torment for Carina to meet the woman Jared would marry. She inclined her head in greeting, too distraught to do more than stare witlessly at the two before her. Jared's uncle didn't look like a murderer, but his niece was as lovely as Jared had said.

What is she thinking? Carina wondered wildly. Does she know I am—have been—Jared's mistress? Does she care?

"Please accept my apologies for my son's insulting behavior toward you," Jared's uncle said. "I sincerely regret that his disgraceful conduct has added to your sorrow today."

His graceful apology was such a surprise to Carina that she found herself smiling. Her thoughts were too scattered for expression, but she loosened her hold on Margaret to let her sister stand alone.

"Your family has suffered a great loss, for which I'm terribly sorry," Nathan continued. "We value all our employees, and we've been proud to number the O'Rourke family among them. I hope you will call upon me if there's any way I can help you." With that, he balanced himself on his cane and reached out to shake Patrick's hand.

Extending himself further, he took Jared's hand, too. "It's good to see you, Jared." Nodding toward Carina's family, he said, "You take good care of these folks. I

409

meant what I said." Turning back to Rachel, he managed a tottering about-face with her help. "We'd better be getting back, my dear. Those clouds look serious."

Indeed, all around them people scurried to reach shelter from the coming rain. Carina moved along with everyone else, but her eyes were fixed on Rachel. She had given Jared a nod of greeting, totally unaccompanied by special warmth.

What did it mean? Jared called their relationship a business arrangement. But were they strangers to each other? Carina was too tired to sort it all out. Too much had happened.

She gave up the struggle to understand and let Jared and Patrick propel her along as if she were a leaf blown by the scudding wind. They made it to the carriage just before the storm broke. As soon as Jared had them all bundled inside, he signaled to the driver, but they could not go far because of the crush of people and vehicles.

The first drops that fell were huge, and soon the wind drove lashings of rain against the windows. Seeing it, Carina became agitated.

"They're getting wet, Jared!" she cried.

"I know, but there are too many people for us to help, and they're already wet now. It can't be helped. They'll be home soon."

"No, no." Carina wasn't thinking of the people outside. Another concern, another picture filled her mind with unbearable sorrow. She couldn't stand to think of all those bare graves, those raw open wounds on the ground, getting soaked. She resisted when Jared drew her into his arms, soothing her—or trying to.

"Not them, Jared," she said on a broken sob. "The others . . . Papa. Oh, Jared! It's *Papa* back there!"

## Chapter Twenty-Seven

They walked across the mill yard in V formation, like Canada geese flying south for the winter. Enoch Wentworth cut the morning air just ahead of the two bulky guards at his flanks, setting a brisk pace.

Inside the mill, the men paused while Wentworth surveyed the stilled machinery. The air was dense and unpleasant, filled with moisture and fiber. The eerie quiet hummed with something unheard, something that wasn't there, the din of the machinery that would soon throb and pound again.

With the two guards stationed by the door, Enoch paced the narrow lane between the rows of looms. "Look at this!" As always when he was excited, his voice rose to a shriek that sounded strange from so large a man. "A whole day's work lost ! I have quotas to meet. Don't they know that? Do they care?"

Neither of his men answered. They knew better.

"We lost a day's work yesterday to bury those men, and for what? Nobody cares that the fire burned up a lot of good cotton along with those people!"

Strother shifted uncomfortably. They'd listened to a whole night of this. No one would call Strother softhearted, but the idea of dying in the inferno of the picking room tore at his gut. It was a hell of a lot more than an inconvenience and a setback to the mill's

411

schedule. Hearing the poor bastards and their hellish deaths dismissed that way made his skin crawl.

"One of you go up and check my office," Enoch said.

Strother moved toward the stairs. They took turns following orders. It was their method of coping with the job of protecting and serving E.W., as they called him. No matter what he wanted done, one of them did it. From the trivial to the illegal, they took each order as it came, alternating responsibility for it. That way, over time, everything between them evened out.

The office was a small cubicle overlooking the main operations area of the mill. As he or Grimes did each morning, Strother checked for the explosives E.W. feared might be placed in the room overnight. Although the mill was guarded around the clock, the boss didn't trust his precious skin to the keeping of those guards. Knowing how hated the man was, Strother didn't blame him for his caution.

Back downstairs, he heard E.W. send an order to the gatekeeper. It denied entrance to the mill to any member of the O'Rourke family. "I won't have any of them working here any longer. They're a menace to the mill. Let them go without work!" Enoch shouted, still marching up and down the aisle like a general before his troop of looms. "See how they like starving!"

Grimes went to carry the message to the man at the gate.

Strother wished he'd seen Enoch's confrontation with Carina O'Rourke at the graveyard. He'd heard the story over and over since. How she screamed at Wentworth before the world. How she'd slapped him and *dared* to insult him.

Carina O'Rourke was a looker. He'd have enjoyed watching her. He remembered the night she came to the agent's house and E.W. sent them away. Strother had his own ideas about what had happened that night, and they didn't agree with what the boss had told them.

Gossip said old man O'Rourke's daughter had run

away that night, *to* Jared Wentworth, who still kept her as his mistress. Which told Strother that E.W. lost out. He and Grimes had a bet that their "master," as they'd called him when they were new to the job, never got her inside the door of his house, much less got anything else of her.

He'd bragged to them that the Irish whore had given him a rowdy night before he'd sent her away. But his jaw was discolored and swollen the next day, and Strother, for one, never bought the story of a sore tooth. They'd seen Jared Wentworth on the street that night. It didn't take a genius to know he'd won the fight and the girl, too.

That was probably why E.W. wanted to get rid of his cousin. J.W. was as much trouble to them as E.W. More, really. They'd twice failed to kill him because of his damned horse, once by spooking it, once because the horse was trained better than a dancing dear.

"Strother! I'm talking to you!"

Pulled back to the present, the bodyguard focused on E.W.'s face and saw that it was red. His boss had been drinking through the night. But that much?

The truth was, E.W. was acting strangely now. The shock of seeing his father walking around the cemetery seemed to have unhinged him. But then, why wouldn't it? After weeks of thinking the old man was only a breath or two from being planted in the graveyard himself, it must have been upsetting to find him at the funeral, greeting the workers' families just as though he'd never been sick.

That would be a shock to anyone.

"Go down to the gate and tell them I want Margaret O'Rourke brought to me just as soon as she gets here."

"I thought you wanted them turned away."

"I've changed my mind, you idiot. I've thought of something better. That bitch told me to keep away from her sister, so I'll take the girl up to the office and have some fun with her. *That* should fix the little whore!"

"And the rest of the family?" Strother asked. "Do you want them turned away still?"

"No, of course not. She only has brothers left—young brothers. I want them to know I've got their sister."

Of course, Strother thought, turning away with a shrug. Meeting Grimes, who was just coming back, he said in passing, "New plans."

The gatekeeper didn't take the news placidly. "What's wrong with him?" he demanded of Strother. "Has he gone crazy?"

"Probably, but that's what he wants."

"He messes with that girl and he'll have the Paddies in more of an uproar than they are now," the man warned angrily.

"Maybe that's what he wants."

"The man wants shootin', that's what he wants."

Strother heard the frustration and ignored the threat. Old Joe wasn't going to do anyone harm. "Just do it," he ordered.

It wasn't long before the workers filed in. Up in the office, E.W.'s head frequently appeared at the window as he paced about the small room.

The noise was already deafening. Neither of the bodyguards knew the workers names, although each had a favorite girl he liked to watch, but at this hour of the day, and after a sleepless night, not even their favorites had much appeal. Most workers were yawning and as bleary-eyed as the guards.

Strother clapped his partner's shoulder and said, "This turn's yours."

Grimes returned from the gate, alone and distressed. Strother followed him outside for an explanation. "They didn't come to work. None of them," he said.

"How many are there?"

"Three. The girl and two brothers, Patrick and a little one." He held a hand about waist high.

"Maybe they're just late."

"They're never late, Joe says. He can barely contain himself, he's so happy they're not here."

Strother didn't care about Joe. He smirked at Grimes.

414

"Good luck tellin' this to himself."

"He'll blame me," Grimes whined.

Strother grinned. "Of course."

"He's been drinking. Maybe he'll fall from his perch up there."

"Be a man, not a mouse," Strother goaded. Because of Grimes ratlike, pointed face, that remark always fired him up. Today was no exception.

Strother watched him climb the narrow stairs to the office. The amusement he derived from the dejected droop of his partner's shoulders was offset by the realization that the next job would fall to him—and it wouldn't be pleasant.

He was right. Enoch Wentworth came down the stairs ahead of Grimes. His face was redder still, making his pale hair seem almost white. He looked like one of those preachers who set up a meeting place just outside of town, then rant and rave at the church folk about sin. Crazy was another word for him.

Wentworth signaled that Strother should follow him, and again they fell into their V formation to stride across the mill yard.

Enoch stopped outside the gate. "Find out where the O'Rourkes went, Strother. I want that girl. I don't care what you have to do to get her."

"Which girl is that?"

"The young one!" Enoch forced himself to make allowances for the stupidity of his men. They were loyal, but so far they'd done nothing right. He was giving them one last chance to do what he needed. Another failure and he'd turn them over to Meggers for prosecution.

He knew who to blame for everything that had gone wrong recently. His father. Nathan was supposed to die. He should have. It was Rachel's fault that he hadn't. Enoch knew that from the look on her face at the cemetery. She'd smirked at him like the cat she was. But it would do her no good. He'd see to that. His father would suffer a terrible relapse. It happened all the time after strokes.

Enoch decided he wouldn't be able to deal with Rachel as she deserved, because to do so would call too much attention to his father's sad death and to Jared's unfortunate accident. But she wasn't important. What was important was keeping his perspective—and winning.

But first Enoch had to call on his dear father. He would rejoice in Nathan's miraculous recovery. He would be solicitous and loving. He'd spend as much time at his father's side as Rachel did.

And he'd wait for the chance to make his move.


In the aftermath of Conn O'Rourke's funeral, Jared used Carina's fear of Enoch to persuade her to return to Falls Village with her family. Although part of him knew he could help them all, another part—his honesty—acknowledged that he needed Carina more than she needed him. Vaguely aware that he was preying upon her fears for Margaret that were perhaps groundless, Jared was nowhere near ashamed enough of what he was doing to let Carina stay on alone in Lowell.

Once he had her home, he meant to spend time with her, settling in her family and winning her trust. Instead, he was called to Boston almost immediately, where the unspeakable had happened—again.

Another fugitive slave, one Anthony Burns, had been arrested from his job in a clothing store on Brattle Street. A United States Deputy Marshal and six assistants had taken him into custody on the pretext that he was wanted for robbery. A burly man, Burns did not resist arrest because he was innocent of any such crime. He knew they had arrested the wrong man.

But they had not. Once Burns was in custody and charge of robbery was dropped. Burns was immediately confronted by his former master—Colonel Charles Suttle of Alexandria, Virginia—and accused as a runaway under the Fugitive Slave Law.

Everything about the arrest, its secrecy and deceit, its timing and allocation of forces, contained a message. The government of the United States was using Anthony Burns as a test case in the hope of crushing the resistance of abolitionists in Boston.

Knowing that Silas Meade, and perhaps Susan, would be in the thick of the attempt to free Burns, Jared had to leave Carina. He did so with vast reluctance, his mind eased slightly because she had her family with her again. Being with her brothers and her sister, he believed, was the best medicine for her just now.

Carina's breakdown in the carriage as they were leaving the cemetery worried him, as did her pregnancy. Reason told him that her emotional collapse was temporary, brought on by grief and loss as well as the confrontations of that day. Reason also said her pregnancy had not weakened her mind or her overall health.

Unfortunately, he remembered that Melissa had died in childbirth. Now that he knew he loved Carina, he was terrified that he would lose her the same way. Given what she had been through, however, Jared believed the best thing he could do for her now was to protect her from further harm and let her get reacquainted with her family. Once they all knew each other again, Jared intended that they would come to know him, too.

He arrived in Boston too late for the protest at Faneuil Hall. Which meant he also missed the attempt by protesters, armed with revolvers and butcher's cleavers, to free Burns from his courthouse confinement. The attack, although a surprise to the United States Marshals guarding Burns, failed in its purpose, hindered as much by the number who turned out to help as by the opposition.

"It was a disaster," Silas told Jared. "Disorganized and

ineffective. I wouldn't be surprised to find that we did poor Burns more harm than good."

"You expect him to be convicted?"

"The president sent two thousand troops to patrol the city," Silas said. "Higginson heard that he's vowed to incur any expense in the name of providing an object lesson to Boston. That doesn't sound promising."

"And to think Franklin Pierce is a New Englander. He's a national disgrace!" Jared's disgust showed in the curl of his lips. "Has Higginson recovered from his injury? I heard he was hurt in the charge on the courthouse." Thomas Wentworth Higginson, the Unitarian minister who was one of the leaders of the Boston Vigilance Committee, was distantly related to Jared.

"His chin was cut by a saber. Fortunately, it missed doing greater damage," Silas replied with a shake of his head. "He and Dana have their heads together, trying to find a way to defend Burns, but it's hard when the deck is stacked against them. Dana had to talk fast to persuade Burns to accept any counsel. The poor man was convinced that it would go worse for him back in Virginia if he fought being returned to slavery."

"He may be right," Jared said.

"Well, if anyone can help him," Silas said bracingly, "it's Dana." Author of the extraordinary book, *Two Years Before the Mast*, Richard Henry Dana, Jr., was also a distinguished lawyer who donated his services without charge to escaped slaves.

"I heard that Colonel Suttle fled the city. Is that true?"

"I believe so," Silas answered. "Of course there are rumors everywhere. And hotheads. I hope he *has* gone, if only to keep him from becoming a martyr to his cause. We don't need the situation made worse than it is."

By the next day, Jared learned that the United States District Attorney had refused to allow Suttle to sell Burns. Twelve hundred dollars had been raised to meet Suttle's asking price, a move not all abolitionists approved. Some, like Susan, said they wanted a legal settlement, a judgment that denied the right of one man to own another. Jared suspected that many of those who refused to help the individual slave, standing on principle, really wanted a martyr for their cause.

Either way, the drive came to nothing.

With the beginning of the trial, Burns's supporters stepped up their petitions and demonstrations outside the courtroom. All to no avail. The wheels of injustice ground on, smoothly, implacably.

Against his will, Jared was drawn back to the scene again and again. No sooner did he turn away in disgust than some rumor of salvation sent him back, forcing him to be a reluctant witness to what he saw as the nation's shame.

Each day all the Meades except Tyler, who had left the city, went with Jared to stand watch over the proceedings. After four days it was obvious from the reports coming from inside the courtroom that Dana had built an excellent case for dismissal of the charges against Burns. It was equally obvious to Jared from the build-up of militia in the streets that nothing less than dismissal would save Burns.


Jared was not the only man who had come to Boston from Lowell for the trial. Dennis Boynton was also there, sent by the *Chronicle* to report on the story. Dennis had not fared well so far. He had a printed card identifying him as a newspaper reporter, but the guards around the courtroom refused to honor his right to enter. No matter how early he arrived, he was pushed away rudely.

By Friday, his fifth day in Boston, Dennis was nearly resigned to the fact that being on hand for the trial was not the breakthrough assignment he'd hoped it would be. Each time he inched forward, he was rebuffed. It was hard to argue with the men bearing fixed bayonets and holding back the crowd. Slowly, inexorably, the solid phalanx of soldiers forced everyone away from the courthouse.

"What's happening?" Dennis asked anyone who would answer. Tall though he was, he could not see anything except the empty street before the courthouse.

"He's been convicted," someone shouted over the babble of voices. "He's being shipped South today!"

The crowd jeered and pressed forward, only to be forced back once again. The struggles for position and information went on and on as Dennis tried to surge to the fore.

"They're bringing him out!"

The crowd swept ahead, carrying Dennis along, now pushing him back against a building, then up against a lamp post. Finding himself stuck there, Boynton decided to climb up for a better view. Shinning the post like a boy, he soon had an unparalleled look at everything. Soldiers marched down the courthouse steps, forming a solid wall around the single manacled figure at the center—Anthony Burns.

From his vantage point atop the lamp, Dennis watched as people below and around him crowded forward, challenging the troops with raised fists and cries of "Shame!"

Burns and his guard passed quickly and without incident. But then, suddenly, Dennis saw the file of militia across the street break from their closed ranks.

People poured into the breach and flowed like water into the roadway. The soldiers flanking the opposite side of the street stood firm at first, but then they, too, moved into the road. If their intent was to round up the spectators who filled the street, chasing after the prisoner and his guard, they had no hope of success.

The crowd had become a mob.

For at least a minute Dennis watched, noting everything he saw. Here was his story, the one that would win him notice when he wrote it up for the *Chronicle*. But then he saw something else in the crowd below him, a woman getting pushed by soldiers. He started down the lamp post even before her hat came off and he recognized her.

Susan Meade. She had drawn the ire of a red-faced soldier at the head of a bayonet-brandishing wedge of men.

Susan stood her ground, facing the charge of soldiers as long as she dared. Two men and a boy in front of her broke before she did. When one of the men fell and still the soldiers charged, Susan whirled around to flee. She had lost her father and Jared long ago in the crush of people. Her mother, thankfully, had not come.

Seconds before, Susan had watched Anthony Burns's martyred march, her heart full to overflowing. She'd even felt envious of his opportunity. He would suffer, yes. But, oh, what glory was his! She'd wished she could do something as meaningful.

In that spirit, she'd gone with the crowd, surging forward into the streets. Her father and Jared would have held her back if they'd been able to, but it had happened so quickly, so fortuitously, they hadn't been able to do anything.

The flash of sunlight on sharpened steel changed her mind about the joys of martyrdom. Those guns fixed with slashing knives were real. She could die!

In a jumble of terror, Susan saw the booted soldiers barely break stride to avoid the man on the ground. In trying to run, she slammed straight into a wall of a man behind her. Before she could react, he caught her up and carried her off.

One minute she was facing a military charge, the next she was safely wedged between the comforting bulk of a man's solid frame and the rough shelter of a brick wall. The man held her in a fierce and most improper embrace. She covered her face with her hands, too excited to cry. She heard the mob distantly now, its roar merely the background for the closer sound of a runaway heartbeat at her ear.

Her savior didn't let her go, and she was strangely glad as well as grateful. She took a great gulp of air into her mouth and took down her hands to look at the man who held her.

Her eyes grew round. Dennis Boynton!

"You idiot!" he said through harshly clenched teeth.

Still excited and much too happy to cry. Susan did the only thing she could in the face of his masculine mix of fury and relief.

She fainted.


Now that Enoch had come to live at his father's house, Rachel found herself largely displaced from Nathan's side. But it wasn't her lack of usefulness that bothered her. The house had become an armed camp. At Nathan's request, George had hired men to guard her uncle's life, and since two nasty-faced men followed Enoch everywhere, Rachel was quite uncomfortable.

Since her frustrating conversation with Tyler, she'd had no contact with him and entertained no expectation for more. Nevertheless, she hoped—and longed for him—so excessively that she was afraid she was losing her mind. He haunted her dreams so, she was afraid to go to sleep. Each morning she reminded herself that he was in Boston, far away. with Nathan and Enoch locked in their strange dance of conflict, she knew she would not get back to Boston soon.

The day promised to be warm. June. Almost summer. A year since she'd come North, and what had she to show for that time? She lifted the curtain to look down on the gardens. The roses were budding, ready to bloom. As she started to turn away, a man got up to carry away some weeds. She watched him sharply, then began to laugh. It was the young Irishman. Last year she'd been chasing him. At least she was over *that*.

Seeing him at work made Rachel realize she'd progressed in other ways, not only in improving her taste in adventure and men. Last year her careless accusation against the man had cost him his job. Remembering that injustice, she'd gone to Harold early this spring to set the record straight and urge him to rehire the man and raise his pay. Perhaps the year has not been wasted after all, she thought as she went downstairs.

George approached her as she lingered over her breakfast tea and toast. Although his face remained impassive, something in the way he held himself alarmed her. "What is it, George? Is my uncle worse?"

"I don't know, miss."

She cocked her head, regarding him soberly. "Did he leave with Enoch?"

"Yes, mum."

His slip—calling her mum—rang another alarm. "Please tell me what's on your mind, George."

He looked pained. "I don't know if I should."

Rachel put down her cup and waited, but not patiently.

Standing stiffly, George fixed his eyes on a wall sconce. "It's Mr. Nathan, miss. I don't know what to make of it." His glance skated over her and went back to the safety of the light fixture. "He came to my room last night. Late."

Rachel straightened. Uncle Nathan was a formal man. If asked, Rachel would have guessed he didn't know his way to George's room. "What did he say?"

"He brought me something. He said I was to keep it safe until after he died. Then I was to see that it got to Mr. Gibson." After faltering his way through that rather set speech, George cried out, all in a rush, "But, oh miss, I don't like it. He looked so strange and sad!"

"What did he give you?"

"I don't know. It's in a box."

Rachel stood up. "Show me."

George looked relieved, though nervous. "I put it under my bed, but after that I didn't sleep a wink."

"I'm sure you didn't." Stepping around him, Rachel started for George's room, with him at her heels. He didn't object, but his reluctance was as palpable as a third person being dragged along.

George brought out the wooden box, handling it reverently. It was beautifully made, with an oriental scene inlaid on the cover, a relic of the China trade. Rachel had seen it on her uncle's desk. "It's not locked, miss. And he said I should keep the box . . . after . . ."

Without asking permission, Rachel sat on the carefully made bed. "You were right to tell me about this. I know you were," she said. "He wouldn't have come to you unless he needed help. This was an unspoken request. There is no violation of trust in what we're doing. We both know he's not safe with Enoch."

"Yes, mum." But still George clasped both hands together in a knot of indecision.

"If it's nothing of import," Rachel went on reassuringly, "we'll put it back and say nothing about this. You have my word on that."

She lifted the cover and peered inside. There was a folded paper bearing Nathan's seal in wax. Without a moment's hesitation, she broke the seal and opened the paper. She read the words with rising alarm.

They were a straightforward documentation of Enoch's crimes against humanity, ending with Nathan's sworn statement that Enoch was reponsible for the deaths of his uncle, aunt, and cousin—Jared's immediate family—all those years ago. Enoch had made the admission with pride, Nathan recounted, and he had also threatened Nathan's life on numerous occasions.

"I write this in the sure knowledge that my son will soon seek to carry out his threats against my life. For that reason, I have made my niece, Rachel Farmington, my sole heir in the event of my unnatural death and I offer this witness to my son's intent against my life."

Pale and visibly shaken, Rachel looked up at George. "You witnessed this," she said, pointing to his signature.

"Yes, ma'am, but I don't know what it says. Mr. Nathan said that didn't matter. All I had to do was sign."

"Yes." She refolded the paper. "All you do is attest

that he wrote these words."

"Is it bad?"

"Very. It says that Enoch killed Jared Wentworth's family and threatens Uncle Nathan." She got up, putting the box aside. "Return this to its place. I'm taking this letter to Jared. He'll be able to help us—and Uncle Nathan."

"Will he believe Mr. Nathan?" George asked. "There's bad blood between them. Always has been."

Rachel considered a moment, during which time she alternately longed for Tyler and cursed his absence. Then she said, "We'll just have to find out, George. It's our only chance. More than that, it's Uncle Nathan's only chance."

# Chapter Twenty-Eight

Seeing Dennis with Susan made Jared's teeth ache. It also made him realize his own hunger for Carina. Without being the least bit subtle, he left for home, intending to make amends to her. Although he knew Carina was not without pride, he was certain he could win her eventual forgiveness.

The closer he got to Lowell, however, the more doubtful he became. With every mile his offense against Carina grew, until it loomed on the horizon, a huge obstacle to his happiness. The more he put himself into her shoes, the more he knew she would not forgive his lack of trust. How could she? No matter how he sought to express his anguish, he couldn't find acceptable words.

By the time he reached the outskirts of Lowell, the pendulum of his remorse began to swing away from abject apology and headed toward resentment of his need for forgiveness. In his own mind, he had already groveled. Now he was as angry with himself for that as he'd have been if he'd actually crawled on his knees before Carina.

Justification had set in, perhaps inevitably, for Jared hated to be wrong. If Carina had pride, so did he. Too much.

But it wasn't his pride that turned him away from Falls Village, sending him to Lowell instead. The nearer he came to the city the more obvious it was that something was seriously wrong. The air was sharp with the smell of smoke.

Pounding along on Infidel, he yelled to the firt person he saw, "Where's the fire?"

"Down in the Acre! Started in a stable and it's goin' every direction!"

He took Infidel to the machine shop. It was too close to the fire to suit him, but it appeared to be safe for the horse—for now. He first joined a bucket brigade from the nearest canal. As others joined, he gave over his position and gradually took on a more responsible role.

The Acre was home to hundreds of families. He plucked four likely looking men from the crowd of fire fighters and, with them, began going from house to house, searching for people who might still be inside the threatened buildings.

They found a bedridden old lady, a baby, and a small boy who was looking for his cat. Sweeping them along, they carried others to safety. Everywhere he looked, Jared saw evidence that this could be where Carina and her family lived. Each girl was Margaret, each boy little Kevin. Like one possessed, he led his little band of refugees back from the devastation that had been their homes.

"Take 'em to the Shattuck!" a man called out to them. "They've made a shelter there!"


Carina descended the stairs slowly, her eyes fastened warily on the self-possessed young woman standing at the bottom. It was early for callers, especially for this one.

"I'm sorry to bother you, Miss O'Rourke. My uncle needs help or I would not be here."

"How can I help your uncle?"

Rachel turned back to Bagley as if for guidance, then said, "I seek Jared. Do you expect him soon?"

"He doesn't consult with me, Miss Farmington. You

may know more of his plans than I." Carina spoke with a certain bitterness that was not lost on Bagley. She was surprised that he had called her down to confront the woman Jared was bent on marrying. Bagley wasn't a cruel man; so why had he done it? To show Rachel that Carina was mistress here?

"I very much doubt that," Rachel said. Again, her lack of rancor was obvious. What did it mean?

Carina left that subject. "Why seek Jared's help when you must know he bears his uncle no favor?"

"I have no other to help me."

A familiar story to Carina. "He has a son," she said.

"Enoch threatens his father. He's the one I fear."

"Surely not," Carina said, making the conventional protest. Personally, she could believe anything of Enoch.

Rachel looked away from both Carina and Bagley. "I don't know what to do," she said to herself.

Something of her urgency spoke to Carina, making it evident that Rachel's coming was motivated by genuine concern for Nathan Wentworth. Try as she would to dislike Rachel, she couldn't. There was nothing of Susan's superiority and hostility in her. Perhaps Carina could like Rachel because Jared professed not to. She didn't know the reason; she only knew she trusted this young woman. If Rachel was afraid, she had cause.

"Jared has been in Boston for the trial of the fugitive slave Anthony Burns," she said, telling Rachel what she herself had learned only the day before. Gwen had told her about the trial and showed her the papers. Carina looked to Bagley for confirmation. "We expect him to return when that is over."

"It ended yesterday, Miss Carina," he told her.

She looked back to Rachel. "Then perhaps today . . ."

"I can't be away from the house overnight," Rachel said. "I'm afraid for Uncle Nathan. He had bodyguards now, but so does Enoch. They all went to the mill today. . . ." Her voice petered off irresolutely.

"Would you like Bagley to go with you to Lowell? Or

would you prefer to take others with you?"

"I don't know." Rachel lifted her face, showing golden brown eyes full of agony and indecision. Her lips stretched into a humorless smile. "I don't even know what I want to ask of Jared." She shrugged. "What can he do?"

"Probably many things," Carina answered soothingly. The question in her mind concerned Jared's willingness to help, not his ability. She left that unspoken, instead urging Rachel to make herself at home while they waited, then providing comfort, food, and an opportunity to rest for Rachel, as well as her own easy companionship.

Nevertheless, both women felt the strain. Rachel was ever mindful of the cause for alarm, and Carina constantly consulted her mind for ways to help. Margaret and Kevin provided welcome distractions, but ultimately they were reduced to sitting in tense and expectant silence while waiting for someone neither could be sure would come.

A flurry of activity outside brought all of them to their feet. Carina ran from the parlor first, grateful for a chance to move. Her own inactivity always seemed to spur the baby to exercise, and today was no different.

But it was not Jared who'd arrived. A stranger on a well-lathered horse spoke urgently to Ned, who tried to keep the man from answering Carina's questions.

"Ned, please," she insisted. "I must know."

"There's a fire in Lowell, ma'am."

Not another picking room, Carina prayed wildly. She had heard that Enoch had put up a temporary structure already. "Where?"

"In the Acre. Started at Dempsey's stable and spread to the barn next door."

"Dear Lord! That's terrible!" Instinctively, Carina folded her arms over her middle as if assuring herself that her child was still there. "That's worse." She felt faint for a moment as the realization of what that meant coursed through her.

"Ned, you must gather up everything you can find that

will help. Buckets, clothes, men—everything! All of you men go quickly. Leave one wagon for me. I'll get clothes and food together and follow." Her mind was awhirl with plans. "We'll need sheets for bandages. Medicine."

"You can't drive the wagon," someone at her back said.

"No, but I can," Rachel called out. "Don't worry. We'll be fine."

Carina had forgotten Rachel. She stopped to protest, but Rachel pulled her along.

"I can help, Miss O'Rourke," she insisted. "The Shattuck is the nearest mill to the Acre. I have to be there. But you should not. Help me gather the things you mentioned, and let me take them."

"Not without me. I know those people. I lived and worked with them."

"But you have a baby to consider."

"So do you, and your time is more delicate than mine."

Rachel put her hand on Carina's arm. "May I call you Carina? I feel I should now." Barely waiting for Carina's permission, she went on. "There is no child for me, Carina. That was my uncle's invention. He was trying to help me, but it didn't work out. He went after the wrong man, and for a while I let him because Jared was also trying to help me.

"Jared and Nathan are more alike than they realize. You've been too kind for me not to tell you the truth. Jared and I won't marry. We would never suit. You've been victimized in almost the same way I have, and somehow we'll just have to make them pay for that. But not today. First we have work to do."

Carina gave Rachel a blinding smile. "Good. And I must do my share."

She did more than her share, but she didn't drive the wagon. Nor did Rachel, although Carina never doubted that she could. As they rode together in the loaded cart, they tore up sheets to make bandages and put together parcels of medicine and food. Rachel, like Carina, was not experienced, but she was practical, intelligent, and determined.

Long before they reached the city they smelled the smoke and saw some of the effects of the fire. Close to the center, they were mired by traffic, some escaping the area, others like themselves trying to get near.

Rachel squeezed Carina's hand encouragingly. "It could be worse. It could be night, with people abed." To Ned, she urged, "Get as close as you can to the Shattuck." When they were blocked, she climbed down and went to stand at the head of the horse. Holding the harness in one hand, she made room for them by yelling out, "Let us through! Supplies and food for the fire victims!"

Slowly, she brought them to the gate of the Shattuck where pandemonium was in full sway. Carina saw people she recognized and more she did not, but before she got down, Rachel had worked the wagon to the place she preferred. Carina saw that it was ideal, set aside for safety and to be out of the way, yet close to the entrance where they could help sort out the arrivals. She saw that immediately as the greatest need. There were so many people, some hurt, but most merely confused and frightened.

They went to work quickly, enlisting help from the unharmed who were calm enough to follow directions. Mothers with young children took on others who were lost and terrified. They washed faces, gave out water and bread, and found safe places for the old and sick to rest.

Seeing that no one among the mill workers or the women displaced by the fire showed any concern for how hard Carina was working, Rachel gradually realized that among ordinary people pregnancy was not seen as something that reduced a woman's effectiveness. Wherever possible, she acted as Carina's legs, sparing her if she could, and she decided, with a satisfied grin that was inappropriate to the misery around them, that they

431

made a formidable team.

Only one thing, her worry about her uncle, kept her from glorying in her newfound capabilities.

Riding to Lowell that morning with Enoch and his guards, Nathan had successfully fought down his rising sense of panic. Now it was back again. He had put himself in Enoch's way, forcing the deadly issue between them in a most uncharacteristic way. He'd been up most of the night—unwisely but unavoidably—and he feared being overtaken by weariness.

Mostly, though, he just plain feared.

He stood at the gate to greet the workers as they arrived. Most did not know him or care who saw them stumble to their posts, tired before their work began. The older ones, those who recognized him, became apprehensive upon seeing him. Impulse told him to smile reassuringly, but he knew it wouldn't comfort them. His being there at all was out of the ordinary. It was a bad omen, one that would unsettle them all day. He was sorry to upset them, but he was driven to do this by a deep inner need he didn't understand.

When one of the yardmen came inside, gesticulating excitedly, Nathan began to feel calmer. He looked down upon the workers, his back to Enoch. Before the manager, Mr. Thompson, reached the stairs, Nathan had gone halfway down to meet him. He bent his ear to Thompson and heard the word "fire."

Others gathered in an anxious knot at the foot of the stairs, muttering. Nathan walked them to the door where it was easier to hear. Church bells tolled. The fire was not here. The men shouted and pointed.

"We must stop work and release everyone."

"No!"

Enoch. He stood in the doorway with his arms spread. There was no overlooking the maniacal gleam in his eyes.

"Mr. Thompson." Nathan raised his voice to override

the noise. "Don't let everyone go in a rampage. It must be done in an orderly fashion. The men will be needed to fight the fire. Organize them into crews, but keep the women and children here. They could get hurt."

"Do no such thing, Mr. Thompson!" Enoch shouted. "We're falling behind our schedule!"

"Enoch, please come with me."

"No! This is my mill! You've had your day, old man. This is my—"

At a signal from Nathan to two men who had appeared at the side of the crowd, Enoch was set aside. His men tried to interfere, but others, yardmen and workers, stepped forward to aid Nathan. In their eyes, Enoch's authority was only derived; and besides, they hated Enoch and his men.

With an angry cry, Enoch broke away from Nathan's bodyguards and ran back inside the rapidly emptying mill. Before he followed his son inside, Nathan leaned on his cane and pointed to Grimes and Strother. "Take these two men away from Lowell right now," he ordered, adding a warning for good measure. "If either of you show your face here again, I'll have you arrested."

Chance—and one small boy—took Jared to the mill yard and Carina. He'd meant to hand his charge on to another in order to continue the house-to-house search for other threatened people, but as soon as he'd tried, the boy's arms had tightened around his neck. Although he could easily have broken the grip, Jared had found he didn't want to. He liked knowing this tyke wanted him. Going on seemed a small thing to do for someone so young.

"Easy now, little fellow, I won't let you go until you're safe," he declared, but even then the little boy refused to be parted from his rescuer. He set up a howl that made the woman who was trying to pry him free back off.

Distracted by the boy, Jared didn't see the second

woman who came to help him.

Nor did Carina recognize Jared. He was just a soot-covered man being strangled by a frightened child. "There, there," she said to the boy, "come with me now, lad, so this good man can go help others. You're safe now." Without conscious effort, she had slipped into a soft brogue that was reassuringly familiar to the child.

It was familiar to Jared as well. As the boy let go of him to reach for Carina, Jared recognized her. Instead of leaving, he planted himself in her path to demand angrily, "What are you doing here?"

She stepped around him and carried the boy to another woman who bribed him away with bread. Jared was not so easily deflected. He caught her to him and took her out of the maelstrom of activity.

"I'm helping," she said, calmly answering his question.

"You shouldn't be here! The baby—"

"Will be fine. I'm very well, Jared. Please be careful yourself. It's terrible out there." She had to work to keep her hands from reaching out to touch him. She longed to wash away the smoke and kiss him.

"Carina, great God, I mean it! Won't you go back home?"

"This is also my home. I worked here. I have to help."

"Carina, I was wrong to doubt you. I know that. That's my child you carry. I . . ."

Carina could only stare at him, as addled as if he'd suddenly begun to spout Gaelic.

"Jared!"

Unaware that she was interrupting something important, Rachel threw herself at Jared. She was too agitated to notice that Carina and Jared stared at each other while she pleaded with him. She had just seen Uncle Nathan's men going off to help fight the fire when they were supposed to be guarding him. She was frantic.

"You must help Uncle Nathan, Jared. He's in grave danger. Enoch means to kill him, I know. Uncle Nathan hired men to guard him, but they've left him alone with Enoch."

Most of what she said failed to capture Jared's attention. He was still caught up in his effort to make amends to Carina. He did hear Rachel's last words, about the hired men. Since the attempted robbery, Jared had been aware that Enoch had set his two men against him. He'd learned their names long ago. But what had those men to do with his uncle? Or with Rachel?

For that matter, what was Rachel doing here?

As he asked himself that, Rachel saw that he wasn't listening. She didn't know what to do. Perhaps she would go inside herself. With that in mind, she started to leave Jared to Carina.

But the moment between them was gone. As one, they turned to look at Rachel, roused from their absorption in each other. Carina said, "I'm sorry," then, "Jared, you must believe her. It wasn't Nathan who destroyed your family. It was Enoch. Rachel has proof."

Jared stared at them uncomprehendingly. When had Carina taken on Rachel's cause? "I don't understand."

Moments before, they had all been battling in their separate ways against the fire raging through the Acre; now they stood apart from the furor, locked in consideration of an event from the distant past, while others took over their jobs.

Rachel tried one last time to make Jared feel her urgency. "Uncle Nathan is inside the mill—alone with Enoch. He has no protection and he can't even walk well. Enoch is crazy, Jared. He hates his father!"

Jared began to see. He could easily accept that Enoch was dangerous. Hadn't he been behind the attempt on his own life? And Nathan was half-crippled still. Suddenly he had a new focus for his hatred of his family's murderer.

Enoch.

Jared had been too late to save his mother and father and sister. His family. But Nathan was also his family. Nathan was threatened now, and this time Jared would not be too late.

Just before he entered the mill, Jared checked the gun he had carried since the day he'd been beset on the road by Grimes and Strother. He had no idea what to expect inside. He'd been in other mills, but not the Shattuck. Although it was free of smoke, the air within was oppressive in a heavy, damp way. One breath of it and Jared remembered how Carina had spoken of the pleasure of fresh air after a day of work.

He expected dimness and silence within, but the huge windows set high into the walls clearly outlined the rows and banks of looms. There was also noise; not the full-bodied thunder of normal production but a clacking and thumping that grew louder as Jared listened.

It was another sound that raised the fine hairs at the back of Jared's neck, however. A howling that rose and fell, like someone chanting. As he put his hand under his coat, reaching for the gun butt that was his security, someone touched his other arm. He jumped and nearly shot himself in surprise.

"It's Enoch," Nathan said in low tones that carried only to Jared. "Either the workers went away before they could turn off all the machines or he's starting them up."

"What's he saying?"

"I don't think it's anything sensible."

Because of the large room full of obstructions and because of the noise, it was hard to determine where Enoch was. Jared didn't care. He had come for Nathan. Having found him so easily, he intended to take him out. Let Enoch try to run the whole place by himself, Jared didn't care. "Come out with me, Nathan. Rachel is worried about you."

Nathan's face softened into a smile. "Ah, Rachel. She's a wonderful girl. She's made my last days of life bearable. Be good to her."

"*You* be good to her. Come with me. Your life isn't over yet, and Rachel still needs you." He tried to steer him toward the door.

"I failed with Enoch, but perhaps Rachel will make up the balance. I went to Charleston and brought her back. I didn't have to do that, you know."

"No, of course not," Jared said, humoring him. But no matter how he urged and herded, Nathan didn't budge.

"I didn't kill your father, Jared."

"I know you didn't. I'm sorry it took me so long to understand. I've been a blind fool about so many things."

"I don't blame you, son. I didn't see it myself. I didn't want to. Enoch had to tell me. He bragged about it—and he was only a boy then." He clutched Jared's arm the way a desperate man does in his fever to convince another.

"I'm sorry, Uncle Nathan. Come with me and we'll get to know each other now the way we should have years ago."

But Nathan didn't move. "I failed him. I can't fail him again." The way he looked down the aisle between the machines Jared knew he meant Enoch, not his brother.

The weird, wailing sounds were increasingly drowned out by the rising cadence of the machinery, making the snatches they could hear more unearthly. "Nathan, forget him now. He's gone over the edge. You know that. There's nothing you can do to help him."

For a moment Jared though he'd won. Nathan started to respond when he tugged at his sleeve. But then another sound rang out, the crash of metal on metal, and Nathan lunged away, revitalized enough to take advantage of Jared's hesitation as he tried to place the sound.

It was destruction; Nathan knew it at once. "Enoch!" he bellowed, stumping rapidly down the aisle. "Stop that at once!"

Jared ran after him. But Nathan turned on him and raised his cane, brandishing it to keep Jared at bay.

"Nathan, don't!"

Distracted by each other, neither of them saw Enoch as he popped from behind the bulk of a loom, wielding a sledge. As the movement caught Jared's eye, he fended off the cane and brought out his revolver. At the same

437

time, Nathan saw the sledge begin to fall, aimed for Jared.

Using his last ounce of strength and agility, Nathan threw himself into the path of that unwieldy weapon and took the fatal blow on the back of his head. Jared's shot went wild as Nathan fell on top of him, pinning him to the floor.

"Both of them!" Enoch shouted in exultation. No longer in need of the sledge, he left it where it fell, intent on celebrating his victory.

He would burn the mill. There was a fire outside, but that didn't count. He wanted his own. He ran down the aisle, deciding how he would get the blaze going. There was plenty of material; the cotton he hated was all around him. He'd burn it all up, everything at once—his father, the mill, and Jared.

As soon as Enoch was gone, Jared rolled out from under Nathan's dead weight. A touch to his uncle's neck confirmed what he already knew. Moving silently, Jared arranged Nathan in a dignified position, placing his hands over his chest with his cane at his side. "God bless you and keep you," he whispered.

He found his gun and was starting to rise when he heard a shout. Running forward at a crouch that kept him low against the machines on either side of him, Jared stopped to peer around. The voice didn't sound like Enoch's, but who else could be here? Jared was afraid he knew.

Enoch's men had come to his aid.

But as he got nearer the front of the building, away from the clanging machines, he realized who it was.

Enoch was almost at the top of the narrow, steep stairs to his office at the top of the mill. The man was going up after him.

Jared stood up and yelled. "Tyler, no!" He braced his feet, steadying himself to get off a shot at Enoch. He fired, not sure the gun had range enough to go that far.

At his yell, Enoch looked away from Tyler. His body jerked and his lost his footing. Seeing Enoch tumbling toward him, Tyler jumped sideways from the stairs. He crashed to the floor in a heap.

Jared ran to stand over Enoch at the bottom of the stairs, his gun pointed at him. "Tyler! Are you all right?"

Tyler groaned.

"Answer me, damn it!"

"My leg . . . oh, God!"

Enoch didn't move, and finally Jared was able to see why. His neck was broken. Using his foot, he nudged Enoch's body. It flopped down the last step, limp and lifeless. Bending over stiffly, Jared checked to be sure there was no pulse; then he went to help Tyler.

Tyler hadn't fallen as far, but it was obvious that his leg was broken. "I'll have to get help for you. Dr. Browning will be nearby." Jared eased Tyler into a more comfortable position. "How did you happen to be here?"

"Rachel," Tyler got out through clenched teeth.

"Well, she'll nurse you back to health, I'm sure."

"Is he dead?"

"A broken neck, I think. There's some blood on his sleeve. Either I grazed him with a bullet or it's from Nathan. He's dead, too. He took a sledgehammer over the head in my place."

"No! Nathan? My God. Rachel will be lost. She's . . . she never believed he could kill anyone."

"She was right. It was always Enoch." Jared took off his coat, folded it, and put it at Tyler's back. "Are you in shape for me to leave?"

Tyler must have help, but aside from that, Jared's need to be away from the mill was overwhelming. He wanted Carina. He wanted to grab her up and carry her far away from this horrible air, far away from the machines and the noise and the dirt.

And the fire.

God. The fire. He had forgotten.

"I'll bring help," he said, giving Tyler a pat on the shoulder. "And Rachel. I'll get Rachel, too," he promised.

But it was Carina he ran to, for himself.

It would always be.

439

# Chapter Twenty-Nine

Carina stepped back to survey Rachel from head to toe. "You look magnificent. You must be the most beautiful bride ever to be married."

"Only because you choose to scorn the wedded state," Rachel said, lifting a sweep of draped skirt with evident satisfaction. Heavy faille silk, the color of rich cream, fell in elegant folds from her wasp waist to the floor, making the dress the image of the one Rachel had said her mother had worn.

Noting the gesture, Carina overlooked Rachel's remark in order to reassure her. "It looks just like the drawing you made, Rachel. And the bodice fits like a second skin."

"Oh, it's tighter than that." She laughed. "I can sit down in my skin."

Carina joined her in laughter. She loved Rachel's outrageousness. Like most disguises, it revealed as well as concealed. Jared, who would give Rachel in marriage, had also come to appreciate her—although not *too* much, Carina was relieved to see. For all she admired Rachel, she recognized a sharpness in her she would not wish for Jared.

On the other hand, Tyler Meade—the man Carina had met and feared as Tyler Maxwell—could profit from liberal applications of Rachel's acerbity, even while confined to crutches. Now that Carina knew he was a Meade, she wondered that she had not seen his resemblance to Susan. Carina believed, along with Jared, that marriage to Rachel would be the making of Tyler. Along with her, came responsibility for running the Shattuck Mill. For that, he would need good fortune, as well as good sense, particularly because he wanted to run it along less exploitive lines. Only time would tell if that was possible.

Rachel put out her hand. "Thank you for everything you've done for me, Carina. I've never had a good friend before, so these past weeks mean more to me than you can imagine."

Since the fire, Rachel had lived at Falls Village instead of returning to Belvidere wthout Nathan. Overcome, Carina could only squeeze her hand in return.

"The only thing that could add to my happiness today—other than having Uncle Nathan here—would be to share the ceremony with you and Jared."

Reminding herself that Rachel's ability to get under one's skin was part of what made her Rachel, Carina tried to draw back her hand. It didn't come free.

"You know Jared loves you," Rachel went on. "Don't you think you've punished him long enough?"

"I'm not punishing him!" Carina wrenched her hand loose.

"Aren't you?"

"No." It wasn't like that. *She* wasn't like that. The issue of marriage was more complicated than that. She wasn't punishing anyone—except, perhaps, herself. "This is your day, Rachel. Yours and Tyler's. That's the way it should be."

"You mean that's the way you insist it *will* be." Unyielding as Rachel was inclined to be, she nevertheless relented now, for Carina's sake. She made a wry face and sighed. "Never mind me. I'm just practicing to be a properly shrewish wife. Forgive me and go let Trudy put the finishing touches to your hair. I won't be selfish and insist on having everything I want in one day. I can wait for you to come to your senses."

Smiling, Carina edged to the door. "If you're sure you're ready . . ."

"I'm as ready to be wed as you are to give birth," Rachel teased.

"Oh, dear. Well, in that case, I'll hurry."

Although Carina laughed, there was an edge to her humor. The day was already difficult, and promised to get worse. If she could have her way, she would hide away in her room so as not to mar her friend's day with her embarrassing condition. It was one of the reasons she resisted Jared's stated desire to marry. She loved him, but *his* reason for marriage was obvious. Now that he believed her, he wanted his child.

Perhaps after the baby was born, she told herself, hurrying along the hallway.

Trudy was waiting for her. "Oh, Miss Carina, you look wonderful," she gushed. "That color makes your eyes look like stars."

"It is lovely, isn't it?" Jared had chosen the material and brought in special dressmakers to outfit her as well as Rachel and Margaret. She sat down so Trudy could do her best, feeling—in spite of what she heard—like a large blue mountain. Seeing her reflection, she worried that the sparkle in her eyes would soon run down her cheeks. And that made her angry.

When Jared appeared in the mirror behind Trudy, Carina nearly came undone. Of all the principals, including Rachel, he was, to her eyes, the most beautiful. He wore new clothes, an inky black coat with snowy white linen, that made him utterly handsome.

"You've done beautifully, Trudy," he said as she stopped fussing and slipped away. He took Carina's hand and turned her. "My lovely lady." He lifted her hand to his lips.

Carina tried to smile with trembling lips. "You mustn't, Jared," she said. "I'll cry."

He held out a package for her to take, and finally she did. Inside the velvet-lined box lay a length of perfectly matched pearls, centered by a star sapphire. "Oh, Jared," she breathed.

"They're not as lovely as your eyes and skin, my dear. Perhaps they'll gain beauty from you." He took the necklace from her to put it around her neck. "It belonged to my mother's family."

Carina put up her hands to entangle with his. "Jared, you shouldn't—"

"I must. I love you, Carina. You are my life."

She closed her eyes and clung to his hands.

"I have to ask you one more time. Please, Carina, marry me now." When she tried to loosen his grasp—for now he held her—he didn't let go. "Hear me out, please. From the beginning I've treated you selfishly—"

She had to object. "Jared, no! You were kind and generous."

"I took your innocence without consideration for your future."

"I had no future. I *gave* myself to you, the man who saved me from Enoch. You were the first and only man to step between me and my disastrous fate. Jared, I came to you, knowing—"

He bent quickly, stopping her with his lips. Lifting his head, he smiled. "I never asked, but now I have to. Do you love me at all?"

"Oh, Jared, yes. Of course I do."

"There's no of course about it. You've been captive of my will, and for too long I was ashamed that I couldn't let you go. Even now as I ask, I'm aware that I have ever conspired to take your choices from you. In truth, I'm still trying to do that."

She placed her fingers over his mouth. "You're too harsh."

"That's true. It's one more reason why I need you. Help me, Carina," he said, kissing her fingertips. "You have my heart and my child, won't you take my name as

443

well? Marry me today."

"But this is Rachel's day," she protested. "It's—"

"We have all our friends assembled," he reminded her. "Would you make them all return on another day? And Rachel wishes it. You know you can't hide behind her."

"I can't hide behind anything!"

It was a wail from her heart, full of purely feminine pique that made Jared smile—and hope. "That's it, isn't it? You don't want to marry so close to birth."

"It seems so—"

"Right," Jared supplied firmly. "There can be no shame between us and no shame for our child." Seeing the cloud of doubt lingering in Carina's eyes, he ran through all the arguments he had assembled to use. What had he forgotten? The issue of legitimacy. Would that do it?

Then he had a flash of intuition.

"Carina, bear with me. Imagine for a moment that we're down in the parlor—not as it is now with flowers and people awaiting a wedding ceremony. Remember the evening I brought the portrait home. You came to me there at dusk. Imagine yourself as you were then. There was no child yet, was there? There was just the two of us. I loved you then. Did you love me?"

Carina smiled, the memory strong within her. Of talking to Jared's back, of pouring out her heart to him. "Yes." She said it again, firmly. "Yes, Jared, I loved you then."

"Then marry me. I was blind then. Let's be those people again. Give yourself to me—let me give myself to you. Not because of any child, Carina, but because I love you."

Tears ran down Carina's face. She didn't feel them; she only saw Jared's wavering shape. And his smile, so tender. "Oh yes, Jared. Yes!"

\*     \*     \*

444

The wedding was more than doubly happy, but it was not perfectly smooth. There were too many people for that, several doing double duty. Jared gave Rachel in marriage, then became a groom. Margaret attended both brides and Kevin carried both rings. Patrick, standing tall and proud, delivered Carina to Jared with a kiss.

All the Meades were there, with Dennis, whose star was rising, next to Susan. His report of the federal troops' attack upon the crowd during Anthony Burns's removal from Boston had recently won him a better position with the *Chronicle*. And along with that, he was collaborating with Susan on her tract.

As Carina put her hand in Jared's to repeat the solemn vows of marriage, she knew herself to be the luckiest, happiest woman on earth. Feeling herself surrounded on all sides by love, she let her left hand rest, as it did in moments of extreme emotion, on the mound her unborn baby made under her dress. Noting the gesture, Jared turned and, with perfect naturalness, placed his free hand atop hers, making a closed circle of them.

Like everything that happened in that room, Jared's gesture was noticed. By Indigo Meade, who smiled through her tears; by Bagley, who beamed proudly; by Agnes, who nodded with approval; by Marcus, who hugged Willie tighter in his arms.

After the ceremonies, Carina and Rachel sat at the center of a long dining table during the wedding feast, their husbands flanking them, their families and friends seated beyond. As Carina looked over the smaller tables set for their other guests, she turned to Jared and said, "You fox! You knew I would consent to this marriage today."

His smile grew wider. "Of course. You've always found me irresistible."

Pretending irritation, Carina said, "Now you show your true colors! What happened to the man who pleaded with me so desperately but an hour ago?"

"He became a husband."

His reply was so quick and serious that Carina gave up and laughed. "I should have suspected your plot when you hired extra servants for the occasion," she said. "I did wonder at it, knowing how capable yours are, but I put it down to our kindness and generosity."

"And now you've decided that I'm cruel and sparing?"

Carina tore her eyes from Jared's teasing dark ones to look over the room. "Oh no, my love. You are all that I believed and more."

Who else but Jared would seat every member of his household in the same room with his most distinguished guests? There they were—not just Bagley and Agnes, but Ned and the lowliest stable lad—all dressed in their best, all dining from the same elegant china as the Meades.

"This pleases me," she said. "Seeing everyone together like this. It's a wonderful gift to me."

"And to me," Jared said with simple honesty. "Until you, they have been my family."

The very next day Carina went into labor. At first she tried to hide the fact from Jared, but he wasn't fooled. He sent for Dr. Browning and took charge.

To Agnes, his presence was a jinx, but in this case she had no authority. She was reduced to muttering fiercely to Nellie, "Birthing is no place for a man!"

Carina disagreed and so did Nellie, who was tactful enough to keep quiet. Carina knew Jared had to be there. And not just for himself. She needed him. He gave her a strong hand to grip and tenderly wiped her brow. She felt the force of his will joined to hers, helping to bring their child into the world.

They were almost at the end when Dr. Browning arrived, joking. "I knew I should have stayed here last night. I could have saved myself a lot of trouble."

Under their combined care and guidance, Carina labored against and with the pain until she was barely conscious of anything else. Finally, from far, far away

446

she heard excited voices coming to her in waves of sound. Then another voice threaded the maze, a high thin cry that grew louder until it was a lusty protest.

"A son for you, my dear girl," came Dr. Browning's friendly boom.

"A son." Magical words. "He is well?"

"Beautiful," Jared told her. "Perfect."

Laughing and crying at the same time, Carina sought Jared's hands. Instead, someone put the baby into her arms. She had never felt anything like it, that tiny, moist, warm bundle of life. "Oh, Jared," she cried out, "his forehead wrinkles as your does when you're cross."

"Another Wentworth, I'd say," Browning proclaimed. "Even to the mark on his rump!"

"Mark? Don't tell me my baby is marked!" Carina protested.

"Why not? Jared has one. It's subtle, but even his sister had it," the doctor explained. "It's just a bit of handed-down pigmentation every Wentworth seems to get. And it could be worse. This fellow has it in a better place than the other little lad. His was on his forehead."

Carina looked up to see that Jared, who had been stalwart throughout the birth, was pale. Dr. Browning's "other lad" was surely Melissa's child, the one she had claimed was not Jared's.

But he had been.

Unaware that he had caused hurt, Browning reclaimed the baby and took him away to be washed and wrapped. Agnes and Nellie took their cue from him and also withdrew, leaving Carina and Jared alone.

"You mustn't blame yourself, Jared," she said, taking his hand. "You could not have known."

"No, but I didn't mourn him as I should have."

"Ah, but you did, my love. I know you. You have mourned his loss since that day." She took his face between her hands, drawing him down to her gentle kiss. "I'm sorry. We will never forget that little one."

"No." Jared was quiet; then he sighed, releasing a

world of agony and regret. "But now we have a fine healthy boy, as healthy and beautiful as his mother. What shall we call him?"

"I had only a girl's name chosen. I wanted you to name your son."

"I never dared name him in my mind, but I think I'd like to call him Philip Nathan. Does that please you?"

Carina smiled. "It's wonderful and strong. And I think he'll need a strong name, don't you?" They could hear his continued cries from the next room.

"Did you want a girl so much?"

Her smile softened, becoming secret. "I knew I carried a boy, just as I know our next will be a girl."

She was teasing, but suddenly she saw them all in her mind—her family in a portrait as real as the one in the parlor, though different. She was seated, with Jared standing at her side. Before him stood Philip, uncannily like Jared. Brown-haired Olivia leaned against Carina to play with the girl in her lap, Felicity, a baby just old enough to sit erect. Next to them all, on the floor with a toy dog, sat Silas, just old enough to wear his first suit.

Four children.

As quickly as the vision came to her, it was gone.

Jared grinned at her. "You're already talking about another? So soon? Don't you think you'd better rest first?"

Carina closed her eyes and brought his hand to her cheek. Thinking of what she had seen, she looked up at him with a tender smile. "Yes, I do. As a matter of fact, I think I'd better rest as much as possible—while I can."